Jungle Planet

MĀNOA 16:2

UNIVERSITY
OF HAWAI'I
PRESS

HONOLULU

Jungle Planet

and Other New Stories

from the Pacific, Asia, and the Americas

Frank Stewart

GENERAL EDITOR

Bruce Fulton

Eric Gamalinda

Leigh Saffold

Arthur Sze

John Whalen-Bridge

GUEST EDITORS

John Valadez. *Getting Them Out of the Car*. Detail. Pastel on paper.

Editor Frank Stewart

Managing Editor Pat Matsueda

Associate Editor Brent Fujinaka

Designer and Art Editor Barbara Pope

Fiction Editor Ian MacMillan

Poetry and Nonfiction Editor Frank Stewart

Reviews Editor Leza Lowitz

Assistant Editors Susan Bates (fiction), Lisa Ottiger (poetry),
Michelle Pond (editorial)

Abernethy Fellow Meredith Desha

Staff Natalie Champa, Tim Denevi, Kathleen Matsueda,
Gabriel Prince, Lance Uyeda, Phyllis Young

Corresponding Editors for North America
Fred Chappell, T. R. Hummer, Charles Johnson, Maxine Hong Kingston,
Michael Ondaatje, Alberto Ríos, Arthur Sze, Tobias Wolff

Corresponding Editors for Asia and the Pacific
CHINA Howard Goldblatt, Ding Zuxin
HONG KONG Shirley Geok-lin Lim
INDONESIA John H. McGlynn
JAPAN Masao Miyoshi, Leza Lowitz
KOREA Kim Uchang, Bruce Fulton
NEW ZEALAND AND SOUTH PACIFIC Vilsoni Hereniko
PACIFIC LATIN AMERICA H. E. Francis, James Hoggard
PHILIPPINES Alfred A. Yuson
WESTERN CANADA Charlene Gilmore

Advisory Group Esther K. Arinaga, William H. Hamilton, Joseph O'Mealy,
Franklin S. Odo, Robert Shapard, Marjorie Sinclair

Founded in 1988 by Robert Shapard and Frank Stewart.

All images are from the collection of Cheech Marin, except as indicated, and were printed in
Chicano Visions: American Painters on the Verge, the catalog of the touring exhibition of the
same name. Reprinted by permission.

Mānoa is published twice a year. Subscriptions: U.S.A. and Canada—individuals $22 one year,
$40 two years; institutions $40 one year, $72 two years. Subscriptions: other countries—individu-
als $25 one year, $45 two years; institutions $40 one year, $72 two years; air mail, add $24 a year.
Single copies: U.S.A. and Canada—$20; other countries—$20. Call toll free 1-888-UHPRESS. We
accept checks, money orders, Visa, or MasterCard, payable to University of Hawai'i Press, 2840
Kolowalu Street, Honolulu, HI 96822, U.S.A. Claims for issues not received will be honored until
180 days past the date of publication; thereafter, the single-copy rate will be charged.

Manuscripts may be sent to *Mānoa,* English Department, University of Hawai'i, Honolulu, HI
96822. Please include a self-addressed, stamped envelope for return of manuscript or for reply.

http://manoajournal.hawaii.edu/
http://www.uhpress.hawaii.edu/journals/manoa/

CONTENTS

꒰ **New Stories from the Pacific, Asia, and the Americas**

Editor's Note

Jungle Planet and Other New Stories is the latest in the *Mānoa* series of new writing from Asia, the Pacific, and the Americas.

Readers familiar with the series know that, since 1989, *Mānoa* has published established contemporary writers as well as emerging authors from the Pacific region—often in translations that make their work accessible to English-speaking readers for the first time. *Mānoa*'s writers live in far-flung places, with widely differing cultural and linguistic backgrounds; but their stories have in common the power to draw us immediately and vividly into their characters' fortunes and fates, immersing us in the lives of others as if they were our own.

It has been said that with the increasing use of the Internet and high-speed travel, no place on Earth is remote anymore; however, remoteness is not merely a question of geographical proximity. We are still blind to everything we choose not to see, deaf to voices we refuse to hear, and uncomprehending of cultures we are incapable of embracing with our imaginations—no matter how nearby or far away they may be.

Three years after September 11, 2001, the Congressional Commission appointed to investigate that day's catastrophic events concluded that the principal cause of America's vulnerability to surprise attack was not a shortage of spy satellites or secret agents, but a failure of imagination. Properly understood, this finding is one of the report's sanest moments. Failure of imagination doesn't mean an inability to forsee horrible events; instead, imagination's singular strength is that it enables us to see the world through the eyes of others and, with new insight, to look back at ourselves. It's the failure of this kind of imagining that leads to misunderstandings, intolerance, and tragedy.

The 9/11 Commission's closing section, "Agenda of Opportunity," recommends that the United States should

> support the basics, such as textbooks that translate more of the world's knowledge into local languages and libraries to house such materials [because] education about the outside world, or other cultures, is weak.

John Valadez. *Getting Them Out of the Car.*
1984. Pastel on paper.
Photograph by John White.

Unfortunately, the recommendation does not reflect on our own imaginative weaknesses, but instead focuses on the presumed shortcomings of other nations, concluding that foreigners will give up terrorism when they at last have access to translations of Western books. There is no paragraph in the commission report recommending translation in the other direction—although one of the most insulated and provincial nations on the planet is, without doubt, our own.

When Americans are thoughtfully exposed to international perspectives—particularly through art and literature, which have the power to place us vividly in the lives of individuals with other histories and alternative futures—we can perhaps become truly compassionate citizens of the world.

The works in *Jungle Planet* are each distinct in expressive techniques, voices, and styles, and this variety is one of the volume's delights. But it's worth noting how often the characters in the stories are challenged with understanding the emotions and reasoning of someone else—a brother, a lover, another tribe, another culture, another generation, an adversary, a spouse—and their success or failure at understanding themselves.

The title of the volume is taken from a story by Filipina writer Lakambini A. Sitoy. The little girl who is the main character lives in a world of seemingly irreconcilable forces. She is not allowed to go to school because it is too dangerous. She spends her long afternoons at home watching nature programs on television, absorbed by the beauty of graceful, endangered creatures in a green landscape that's fundamentally different from her surroundings. She gazes into the television screen at the image of a forest leaf "so clear and perfect that she could see the network of tiny veins along its spine," the leaf holding a drop of rain as exquisite as a pearl. Meanwhile, the rain outside her door is "saturated with filth," and her mother warns her that if she stands in it, she will "sizzle and dissolve into a lump of viscera." Yet, when the young girl crouches in her concrete-enclosed yard, peering into the cracks, she notices laces of moss that look like a miniature savannah, that are "so beautiful that her heart [stops] for a second." In her world, beauty is in very small details. Larger things, such as the mountain looming over her village, threaten to entomb her.

Many other pieces in *Jungle Planet* can be seen as meditations on the power of imagination and the role it plays in enabling characters to cope with and interpret a life of suffering and joy, compassion and cruelty, beauty and despair. In Wayne Karlin's "Coming Home," for example, the story of a child's loss of her parents and her adoption of a shell-shocked North Vietnamese soldier becomes interwoven with an American's remembrance of the country he tried as a young man to help defeat. In Manjushree Thapa's "Friends," two young men form a friendship in the tourist district of Kathmandu, "this patched, foggy mirror image of Western dreams: a mirror quicksilvered with incredible mountain stories, some fantastic tales." In Bay Anapol's "A Stone House," a mother emotionally withdraws from her daughter, reminding her "that loving anyone is like invading a country: no matter how far you get across the borders, you remain a foreigner." The metaphor dominates the mother's life and injures the daughter, until the young woman "snaps awake one morning with one clear and final memory." In Andrew Lam's "The Palmist," an older Vietnamese man encounters a teenager on a San Francisco bus and sees in his palm the potential for a startling and extraordinary future.

The visual art reproduced in *Jungle Planet* is selected from nearly fifty works by about thirty artists brought together in the 2001 traveling exhibition *Chicano Visions: American Painters on the Verge*. In 2002, the paintings in the exhibition were reproduced in a book of the same title. Almost all of the work is from the collection of Cheech Marin.

In his introduction to *Chicano Visions,* Marin identifies Los Angeles and San Antonio as the birthplaces of the thirty-year-old Chicano art movement; many of the painters in *Jungle Planet* were founders or early associates of several important groups, such as Con Safo, Royal Chicano Air Force, Los Four, Los Streetscapers, and Asco. Diverse in outlook, training, and styles, the artists who have been seminal figures in the movement are bound by what Marin calls "the DNA of common experience." Essential to their common identity, he adds, is their response to and representation of America's bicultural society:

> Chicanos "code switch" amongst themselves all the time: they go back and forth almost at random between languages and cultures both spoken and visual. Code switching allows for total immersion, the creation of a whole greater than the sum of its parts.

At their best, the painters in *Chicano Visions* are dazzling synthesizers of many cultures, languages, and art movements. Gloriously juxtaposing and hybridizing high and low iconography, heritages, and traditions, they are street smart, artistically sophisticated, and bold. Many began as muralists in the poor barrios of Los Angeles, inspired by the robust work of Diego Rivera, David Alfaro Siqueiros, and José Clemente Orozco. To this list of predecessors and influences, essayist and poet Max Benavidez adds "Frida Kahlo, the assertively nonconformist *pachuco* street style of the early 1940s, and the visual bravura of L.A.'s ubiquitous Mexican-American gang graffiti." Benavidez points to the combination of exuberance and lamentation that permeates Chicano painting—and, we might add, many of the literary works in *Jungle Planet.* The late Carlos Almaraz referred to this quality as "something both horrifying and absolutely magical." He wrote:

This lament, like the elegies of the vanquished Aztecs shortly after the Conquest, has been transformed into art by generations of Chicano artists. The healing of wounds, ancient and new, and of the basic suffering of life will continue as long as artists create a visual salve for the hurt.

According to Chicano mythology, wholeness will come again when Chicanos inherit Aztlán, their promised land, the place where they will find cultural and psychic unity. Until that day comes, Chicano artists will continue to create an Aztlán of the imagination, a memorable counterpoint to the mass hypnosis of our age.

Unfortunately, we were unable to reproduce here the dramatic and often explosive use of color in Chicano art. However, we hope these images will lead our readers to exhibits of the original works, to the artists' web sites, and to such books as *Chicano Visions*, published in 2002 by Bulfinch Press, an imprint of Little, Brown & Company.

We wish to thank the many people who made this issue possible, especially Cheech Marin, Clear Channel Entertainment, the individual artists and authors for generously allowing us to publish their work, and our guest editors: Bruce Fulton, Eric Gamalinda, Leigh Saffold, Arthur Sze, and John Whalen-Bridge.

Margaret García. *Eziquiel's Party*.
2000. Oil on canvas.
Photograph by John White.

The Brothers

My brother went on national TV to prove he was a woman. I don't know which talk show it was, but these words kept flashing at the bottom of the television screen: IS SHE A HE? IS HE A SHE? YOU DECIDE! The show went like this: a guest would come out onstage, and the audience would vote on whether or not she was the real thing.

They came out one at a time, these big-haired and bright-lipped women, most of them taller than most men. They worked the stage like strippers, bumping and grinding to the techno beat of the studio music. The audience rose to its feet, whistling and hooting, cheering them on.

Then came Eric.

My brother was different from the others. He was shorter, the only Filipino among them. He wore a denim skirt and a T-shirt, a pair of Doc Martens. His hair, a few strands streaked blonde, fell to his bony shoulders. He was slow across the stage, wooing the audience with a shy girl's face, flirtatious, sweet. But he wasn't woman enough for them: they booed my brother, gave him the thumbs down. So Eric fought back. He stood at the edge of the stage, pounded his chest like he was challenging them to a talk-show brawl. "Dare me?" he said, and I saw his hands move down to the bottom of his T-shirt. "You dare me?"

They did, and up it went. The audience went wild.

He put his shirt down, lifted his arms in triumph, blew kisses to the audience, and then took a chair with the other guests. He told the audience that his name was Erica.

I glanced at Ma. She looked as if someone had hit her in the face.

Eric had left a message the night before, telling me to watch Channel 4 at 7 P.M. He said it would be important, that Ma should see it, too. When I told Ma, she looked hopeful. "Maybe he's singing," she said. "Playing the piano?" She was thinking of the Eric of long ago, when he took music lessons and sang in the high-school choir.

I reached for the remote, thinking, *That bastard set us up.* I turned the TV off.

That was the last time I saw him. Now he's lying on a table, a sheet pulled to his shoulders, dead. The coroner doesn't hurry me, but I answer him fast. "Yes," I say. "That's him. My brother."

Eric's life was no secret, though we often wished it was: we knew about the boyfriends, the makeup and dresses. He told me about his job at HoozHoo, a bar in downtown San Francisco where the waitresses were drag queens or transsexuals. But a year and a half ago, when Eric announced on Thanksgiving night that he was going to proceed with a sex change ("Starting here," he said, patting his chest with his right hand), Ma left the table and told him that he was dead to her.

It's 6:22 P.M. He's been dead for six hours.

"We need to call people," I tell Ma. But she sits there at the kitchen table, still in her waitress uniform, whispering things to herself, rubbing her thumb along the curve of Eric's baby spoon. Next week she turns sixty-one. For the first time, she looks older than she is. "We have to tell people what's happened."

She puts down the spoon, finally looks at me. "What will I say? How can I explain it?"

"Tell them what the coroner told me. That's all." He had an asthma attack, rare and fatal. He was sitting on a bench in Golden Gate Park when his airways swelled so quickly, so completely, that no air could get in or out. When he was a kid, Eric's asthma was a problem; I can still hear the squeal of his panic. *Can't breathe, can't breathe,* he'd say, and I'd rub his back and chest like I was giving him life. But when he became an adult, the attacks were less frequent, easier to manage, and he called his inhaler a thing of the past. "The severity of this attack was unusual," the coroner explained. "There was no way he could have prepared for it." He was dead by the time a pair of ten-year-olds on Rollerblades found him.

The look on Ma's face makes me feel like a liar. "He couldn't breathe," I say. "It's the truth." I go through cupboards, open drawers, not sure what I'm looking for, so I settle for a mug and fill it with water, and though I'm not thirsty, I drink it all down. "He couldn't breathe. And then he died. When people ask, that's what you say."

Ma picks up the spoon again, and now I understand. "Ang bunso ko," she's been saying. *My baby boy,* over and over, as if Eric died as a child and she realized it only now.

The morning after the show, my brother called me at work. When I picked up the phone, he said, "Well…?" as if we were already in the middle of a conversation, though we hadn't spoken in months, maybe half a year.

"You grew your hair out," I said. "It's blonde now."

"Extensions," he said.

"They look real."

"They're not." He took a deep breath. "But the rest of me is."

It was a little after seven. I was the only one in the office. Not even the tech guys were in yet. I turned and looked out the window, watched an old, bent man unlock the door to his newspaper kiosk, get ready to set up shop.

"Come on, Edmond," my brother said, "say something."

I didn't, so he did. He went on about being on TV, about flashing the audience and everyone at home. He said he was sorry if it hurt Ma and me, but this was a once-in-a-lifetime opportunity. "I showed the world what I'm made of," he said slowly, as if it was a line he'd been rehearsing for months. "What do you think of that?"

"I saw nothing," I said.

"What?"

"I saw nothing." It was the truth. When Eric lifted his shirt, they didn't use a black rectangle the way they sometimes do on TV to protect a person's identity. They didn't cut to a commercial or pan shocked faces in the audience. Instead, they blurred him out: just below his shoulders was a strip of scrambled air. It looked like he was disintegrating, molecule by molecule. "They blurred you out," I said.

I could hear him pace his apartment. I never went there, but I knew he was living in the Tenderloin in downtown San Francisco. The few times he called, things were always happening on his end: cars honking, sirens, people laughing or screaming each other's name. But that morning, there was just the sound of us breathing, first one and then the other, as if we were taking turns. I imagined a pair of divers at the bottom of the ocean, sharing the same supply of air.

"You there?" I thought we'd been disconnected. "Eric, are you there?"

"No." Then he hung up.

And that was it for Eric and me.

I go to my apartment to get clothes, and I stay the night at Ma's. My old bed is still in my old room upstairs, but I take the living-room couch. I don't sleep, not for a minute. Before light comes, I call Delia in Chicago; her fiancé picks up. I ask for my wife, which irritates him. Technically, I'm right: the divorce isn't final, not yet. I'm still a husband, and I won't let that go, not until I have to.

He says she's not there.

"No message," I tell him, then hang up.

I'm still wide awake in the morning. Driving to the funeral home in North Oakland, I don't even yawn.

Loomis, the man who handled Dad's funeral eleven years ago, waits for us in a small square of shade outside the main office. He's heavier now, his hair thinner, all white. Back then he walked with a limp; today he uses a cane.

"Do you remember me?" It's the first thing Ma says to him. "And my husband?" She pulls a picture from her wallet, an old black-and-white of Dad in his navy days. He's wearing fatigues, looking cocky. His arms hang at his sides, but his fists are clenched as if he's ready for a fight. "Dominguez. First name Teodoro."

Loomis takes the photo, holds it at eye level, squints. "I do remember him," he says, though he only saw my father as a dead man. "And I remember you, too." He looks at me, shakes my hand. "The boy who never left his mother's side."

That was Eric. Ma knows it, too. We don't correct him.

The funeral doesn't take long to plan: Ma makes it the same as Dad's, ordering the same floral arrangements, the same prayer cards, the same music. Only the casket is different. Dad's was bronze, which best preserves the body. Eric's will be mahogany, a more economical choice. "It's all we can afford," Ma says.

Later, Loomis drives us through the cemetery to find a plot for Eric. We head to the west end, stop at the bottom of a small hill. "There," Ma says, walking uphill toward a small eucalyptus. She puts her hand on a low, thin branch, rubs a budding leaf between her fingers. "It's growing." She quickly surveys the area, decides this is the place.

"But your knee." I point out the steepness of the hill, warn her that years from now, when she's older, getting to Eric will be difficult.

"Then you help me," Ma says, starting toward the car. "You help me get to him."

Back home, Ma calls the people we couldn't reach the night before, and each conversation is the same: she greets the person warmly and pauses, but can't catch herself before she gives in to tears. Meanwhile, I get the house ready, vacuuming upstairs and down, wiping dirty window screens with wet rags, rearranging furniture to accommodate all the guests who will pray for my brother's soul. We'll have nine nights of this.

"I hate the way Filipinos die," Eric once said. It was the week of Dad's funeral. "Nine nights of praying on our knees, lousy Chinese food, and hundred-year-old women asking me where my girlfriend is." The businessmen were worse. On the last night of Dad's novena, one guy—he said he was related to us but couldn't explain how—tried selling life insurance to Eric and me. He quoted figures on what we could get for injury, dismemberment, and death, and even took out a pocket calculator to prove how valuable our lives were. "Promise me, Edmond," Eric had said, "when I die, take one night to remember me. That's all. No kung pao chicken. No old people. No assholes telling you how much you'll get for my severed leg." He came close to crying, but then he managed a smile. "And make sure Village People is playing in the background."

"'YMCA'?"

"'Macho Man,'" he said. "Play it twice."

He started laughing. I started laughing. The house was full of mourners, but we kept to ourselves in one corner of the room, wearing matching two-piece suits from Sears and joking around like the closest of brothers. But now I know that we were wrong to talk as though I would outlive him. I was five years older than Eric, and he was only twenty-six when he died.

Brothers are supposed to die in the correct order. I keep thinking, *Tonight should be for me.*

By six, the house fills with visitors. A dozen or so at first. Soon it's fifty. I stop counting at seventy-five.

Strangers tell me they're family. They try to simplify the intricate ways we're related: suddenly they're cousins, aunts and uncles, the godchildren of my grandparents. Not one of these people has seen my brother in years, has any idea of the ways he's changed. All they know about him is that he's dead.

Twice, an elderly woman calls me Eric by mistake.

When an old neighbor asks, "Where's Delia?" Ma answers before I can. She's embarrassed by the idea of divorce, so she says that Delia is on the East Coast for business, but will be here as soon as possible. I wish it was true: I keep checking the door, thinking that Delia might walk in any moment, that somehow she found out what happened and took the next flight out to be with me. Eric's death could have been our breakthrough, the turn she said our life needed. I try not to think of tonight as a lost opportunity for Delia and me.

At seven, we get to our knees, pray before the religious shrine Ma's set up on top of the TV—a few porcelain figurines of Jesus Christ and the Virgin Mary, laminated prayer cards in wood frames, plastic rosaries. In front of the TV screen, an arm's reach from me, stands an infant-sized ceramic statuette of Santo Niño, the baby Jesus Christ. All good Filipino Catholic families have one, but I haven't seen ours in years. He still looks weird to me, with his red velvet cape trimmed with gold thread and a crown to match, silver robes, brown corn-silk hair falling past his shoulders, the plastic flower in his hand.

When Eric was small, he thought Santo Niño was a girl: I caught him in his bedroom, kneeling on the floor, and Santo Niño was naked, his cape, robes, and crown in a small, neat pile by Eric's foot. For the first time, I saw how he was made: only the hands and face had been painted to look like skin; everyplace else was unglazed and white, chipped in spots. "See," Eric said, his finger in the empty space between Santo Niño's legs, "he's a girl." I called him an idiot, tried to get it through his head that he was just a statue, a ceramic body that meant nothing. "Santo Niño is a boy," I said, "say it." He wouldn't, so I took Santo Niño from Eric, held him above my head. Eric jumped, reaching to get him back, then knocked him out of my hands.

Ma heard the crash, ran upstairs, and found pieces of Santo Niño scattered at our feet. Before she could speak, I pointed at the pile of clothes on the floor and told her what Eric had done and said.

I tried putting Santo Niño back together in my room as I listened to Eric getting hit.

But my brother had a point. At eye level and an arm's reach away, this second Santo Niño—the one Ma bought to replace the one we broke—does look like a girl: glass-blue eyes, long black lashes, a red-lipped smile, a rose in one hand. While everyone's eyes are shut tight in prayer, I reach out and try to take the flower. It's glued to his fist.

What started as prayer is now a dinner party, and Ma is on top of everything. She makes sure the egg rolls stay warm, that there's enough soy sauce in the chow mein. I hear her gossip with neighbors who moved away long ago, watch her hold the babies of women who grew up on our street. In the Philippines, my parents threw three to four parties a year, and Ma boasted how her wedding was the grandest her province had ever seen. She promised equally grand weddings for us. But I was twenty-one when Delia and I eloped, and she gave up on Eric long ago. Funerals and novenas, I think, are all Ma has left.

People keep coming. I try to stay close to familiar faces: I comfort Mrs. Gonzalez, Eric's second-grade teacher, who's brought the crayon portraits he drew on paper sacks. I talk with Isaac Chavez, Eric's best friend from grade school and the first boy, Eric confessed to me later, he ever loved. He never told Isaac. Maybe I should. But when Isaac introduces me to his new wife, I know it's best not to complicate the night.

When the Agbayani brothers walk in, I stay away. At a Fourth-of-July picnic long ago, they found Eric under a slide, making daisy chains and singing love songs at the top of his lungs. I watched as they called him a girl, a sissy, a faggot. "That's what you get for playing with flowers," I told him later.

Ma catches me in the kitchen. "We're out of ice," she says. Beside her is a Filipino woman rattling ice cubes in her plastic cup. She looks like she came to dance instead of pray: her black hair falls in waves past her shoulders, and her tight, black dress ends above the knee. In her high-heeled boots, she's as tall as I am.

"No problem." I lift the cooler, step outside. The freezer is in the backyard, and its low hum is the only sign of life out there. The lawn is nothing but weeds. Ma's roses are gone. And the four stalks of sugar cane Dad planted when he bought the house—one for each of us—have been dried sticks for years.

I take out a blue bag of ice from the freezer, then pound it against the concrete, breaking it up. Behind me the glass door slides open: it's the woman who wanted ice. "This OK?" she asks, indicating the cigarette between her fingers.

I slide the door shut. "It is now."

"I'm Raquel."

"Edmond." We shake hands.

"The brother." She lets go. "Cold."

Icy flakes stick to my fingers. I wipe them on my pants. "You're friends with Eric?"

"Sisters. That's what we call ourselves, anyway." She lights the cigarette, takes a drag, then lets out a long breath of smoke. "I have no family here. They're all back in Manila, pissed at me for leaving. So she became my sister. Sweet, huh?"

Sisters. She. It's like this woman is testing me to see what I know and don't know about my brother.

"Eric always wanted a sister," I say.

"Well, if we're sisters, then that makes you my Kuya Edmond, right?"

"Kuya?" My Tagalog is more rusty than I thought.

"Big brother." She unfolds a lawn chair and sits down. She crosses her legs, rests an elbow on her knee, places her chin on her hand, and looks at me closely. "How are you?"

Not even the coroner asked me that when I saw the body. "Fine." I squat down, smash more ice. "Holding up."

"Not me. Last night, when you left that message at the bar, I wanted to erase it. I was thinking, 'I don't know anyone named Eric, and I don't know an "Eric's brother."' But I knew who you meant."

She describes the rest of the night: how they closed the HoozHoo early, gathered the waitresses and the regulars together, drank and wept and sang songs until morning. Before everyone went home, they stood in a circle on the dance floor, held hands, and said a prayer. The music was off, but the lights were on, a disco ball spinning above them. "It looked like heaven," she says. "All the girls wanted to come tonight, but I told them no. It should just be me. Out of respect for your mother."

It's like the start of a joke: *A dozen drag queens walk in on eighty Filipinos on their knees praying*...I can picture the rest of it: six-foot-tall women in six-inch heels, glittering in a crowd of people dressed in black. I can see the stares, hear the whispers, Ma in the middle of it all, wishing them away. But maybe everyone would have been fooled, taken them as the very girlfriends that old ladies pestered Eric about. I knew from the start what Raquel was, but so much of her looks real, like she was born into the body she made.

"You're staring at my tits, hon."

The ice slips from my hand, slides across the cement and onto the dirt.

She manages a smile, shrugs her shoulders. "People look all the time." She looks at them herself. "Four years ago, when I came to the States"— she puts her hand over her heart—"there's nothing here. Empty. So now, if people want to look, I let them. They're mine, right?" She puts out her cigarette, lights another. "It's the same thing with Erica. Hers turned out really nice, really—"

"More ice?" I point to the freezer. "There's ice."

She reaches out, puts her hand on my shoulder. "I've embarrassed you. Sorry. That wasn't Coke in my cup." Raquel pulls a silver flask from her purse, unscrews the top, and turns it upside down. "All gone," she sighs. "I should be gone, too." She gets up, but she's off balance. I catch her in time. "Walk me to the door?" Her hands are tight on my wrist. I don't know that I have a choice.

We step inside, work our way through the crowds in the kitchen, the living room. People look but don't stare, and I think we can slip out quietly. But when Raquel remembers her coat and walks to the closet by the stairs, I think of leaving her to rejoin the crowd. The Agbayani brothers are on the couch, eyeing Raquel and smirking at one another. My guess is that they've gone from being childhood bullies to the kind of men who would follow a girl to her car with whistles and catcalls.

I help Raquel with her coat. "Let me walk you to your car."

She smiles as if it's the nicest thing anyone has said to her all day. "I'm at the end of the street." We step outside, walk down the driveway. Beyond tipsy, Raquel takes my arm again.

"Maybe you should've had Coke after all," I say.

"No," she says, "I need to be this way tonight."

We get to her car, a Honda covered with scratches and dents. Where a back window should be are plastic and duct tape. "Time for you to go back home," she says to me while leaning against the door. She searches her purse for her keys, not realizing she's holding them in her left hand.

Then she says, "Oh, shit."

On the corner, seven tall women empty out of a minivan and head toward Ma's house, their heels clicking loudly against the sidewalk. They look like a kind of sorority, all of them made up the same way to let the world know who they are. "I told them they shouldn't," Raquel says. "I told them." She rubs her forehead, starts toward them, but I don't let her go. "Let them pay their respects," I say. "It's fine." I take her arm, slip the keys from between her fingers, and walk her to the passenger's door. Then I help her in and return to the driver's side.

"What about your guests?" Raquel asks.

"I don't have any." I start the car, watch the women enter Ma's house one by one. "Where to?"

"San Francisco."

I drive down Telegraph Avenue, head for the bridge.

"You're a nice man, Kuya Edmond." Raquel reclines her seat, turns to the window as if she's watching the moon. "Can I call you that? *Kuya?*"

"Why not." No one else will, and Eric never did.

It's less than ten minutes from Ma's house to the bridge, and yet I never cross it. Yesterday, when I drove to ID the body, it was the first time in nine years that I'd been to San Francisco.

The time before that was when Ma kicked Eric out. He was seventeen. She found him in his bedroom, made up as a girl and in bed with a guy. She told them to leave and warned Eric not to come back. "For good this time," he said on the phone. "But there's nowhere for me to go." He was breathing fast and heavy, fighting tears.

"Find a place," I said, "and I'll drive you there."

When I got to the house, he was sitting on the curb, a duffel bag and a yellow beanbag at his feet. He looked up at me, and what I thought were bruises was just smeared makeup. "She tried wiping it off with a dishrag," he said. "Couldn't she have just slapped me instead?"

"Get in the car." I went inside to check on Ma. She was sitting at the top of the stairs, still in her Denny's uniform, Dad's terry-cloth robe draped over her lap. She had just gotten home from a late shift when she found Eric. "I brought home a sandwich for him," she said. "He doesn't want to take it. If you're hungry…"

"I'm not," I said.

She nodded, went to her room. I heard her lock the door.

I went back outside, got in the car. Eric was in the passenger's seat, putting on lipstick. I grabbed his wrist, squeezing so hard that he dropped it. "Didn't I tell you," I was shouting now, "you don't do this here! You want to play dress-up, that's fine. But not in Ma's house. You keep it to yourself."

"I'm not playing dress-up."

I started driving. "Just tell me where to go."

He gave directions, and before I realized it, I was on the Bay Bridge, bound for the city. He had a friend with a spare couch who lived in the Mission District. I headed down South Van Ness, turned in to a dark street that got darker the further down we went. "Stop here," he said, and I pulled up in front of an old peeling Victorian.

"Take this," I said, and I put four twenty-dollar bills in his hand. He looked at the money like it was more than a person deserved, then took one bill and gave the rest back. "Mother's Day is coming up," he reminded me. He asked if I could buy Ma flowers, if they could be from the both of us. I nodded.

He got out of the car, but before he closed the door, he leaned in and said, "It was the first perfect night I ever had. Know what I mean?"

I didn't. "Call me in a few days," I said.

Eric walked toward the front door, dragging his things behind him. At the top of the driveway, he turned around. We looked at each other as though neither of us knew who should be the first to go.

What I wished then I'm wishing now: that I'd reached over and opened the passenger door. Maybe then we could have made our way back home, or someplace else. An all-night diner. A road that dead-ended with a view of the city. If we'd had more time, maybe things could have stayed the same.

It took me hours to find my way back to Oakland.

Ma spoke to Eric again a year later, just in time for his high-school graduation. But she never asked him back, and he never asked to come back. Eric's room is storage space now, but mine is as I left it: my childhood bed against the window, my blue, square desk beside it, Dad's wood-and-wicker rocking chair in the corner. It's like she knew that Eric was never coming back and that I always would.

I tap Raquel on her shoulder. "Wake up," I say. "We're here. Tell me where to go."

For now, Raquel is homeless; a pipe burst in her apartment building three weeks before, flooding every unit. She'd been staying with Eric ever since. Had she said this before I got in her car, I'm not sure what I would have done.

It takes over thirty minutes to find parking, and when we do, it's blocks away. Walking, we pass drunken college boys flirting with prostitutes, homeless kids sharing a bottle, cops who seem oblivious to everything around them. "I get scared at night," Raquel says. I let her hold my arm.

Eric's building is on Polk Street. Two teenaged girls sit on the front steps, smoking cigarettes. "New boyfriend, Miss Raquel?" one says.

"Ask me again in the morning and I'll tell you." Raquel laughs, high-fives both girls.

We take the stairs to the third floor, head down a narrow hallway lit by fading fluorescent lights. Eric's apartment number is 310. The door is white, like all the rest. "I'd meant to visit," I say. Raquel says nothing.

She takes the keys, opens the door. "After you, Kuya." I don't know how I'm getting home.

Those times I spoke to Eric on the phone, I imagined him sitting on his windowsill and pictured what his apartment might look like: wigs and dresses piled on a red leather couch and scattered on the floor, Christmas lights framing every window and wall or hanging from the ceiling. It was a place where I would stand in the middle with my arms folded against my chest, careful not to touch anything; I'd keep an eye on the door, ready to escape at any moment. But when I step inside the apartment, everything is muted: metal desk, cream-colored futon, cinderblock shelf with a stack of books. On the windowsill are two framed pictures: one of Ma and Dad in Long Beach, when they first came to the States; and the other of me, from a time I don't remember. I'm just a kid, four or five, looking unbelievably happy. I don't know why or how. It seems impossible that anyone could be that pleased with life.

Raquel offers tissue. I tell her I'm fine.

She opens the tiny refrigerator beneath the desk, takes out a Mountain Dew and a small bottle of vodka. She mixes them in a paper cup, stirs it with her finger.

Then she takes out a bottle of pills from her purse.

"Headache?" I ask.

"Nothing's wrong with my head." She pops a pill in her mouth, sips her drink, makes a face when she swallows, as if it hurts. "Hormones," she says. "No pain, no gain." She takes another sip.

"There's pain?"

"Figure of speech, Kuya. It goes down easy."

"There must be pain. There has to be." I think of Eric on a table, surgeons cutting into his body, needles vanishing into his skin. I think of that studio audience, giving him the thumbs down, like a jury deciding his life. I think of Ma telling Eric he's dead. "The things you do. To prove yourself. We loved him as he was. That should have been enough."

Raquel walks over, stands in front of me, eye to eye. "You think that's why we do this? To prove a point to you? Listen, Kuya Edmond. All of this"—she unfolds her arms, takes my hand by the wrist, and puts it on the center of her chest—"I did for me." She presses my hand into herself as if she wants me to feel her heartbeat, then lets me go before I can feel anything.

I tug at my watch. "I should go home."

"I'll walk you out."

As we go down the stairs, I make a tentative plan to stop by the following week and pick up some of Eric's things, though I'm not sure what I can rightfully claim. Raquel says yes, of course, anytime, like she doesn't believe that I will ever come this way again.

Outside we stand on the corner. Raquel flags down a cab for me. Before I get in, she hands me forty dollars for the ride back to Oakland and refuses when I tell her to take it back. "You brought me home," she says. "If you didn't, I could be dead, too." She starts crying, then puts her hand on my face. I don't come closer, but I don't pull away either. "She loves you," she whispers, "believe me." Then she holds me, her body pressing against mine. I wonder if this is how Eric felt after he changed, if the new flesh made him feel closer to the person he held. I won't ever know, but I wish I could stay this way a little longer and listen to Raquel whisper about Eric the way she just did, in the present tense, like he's still going on.

The next morning, Ma is sitting at the bottom of the stairs, a vinyl garment bag over her lap. Eric's body is being prepared for the viewing, and we need to deliver his clothes. She says nothing about the girls from HoozHoo, doesn't ask me where I was the night before. But on the way to the funeral home, I can feel her staring at me, like she's waiting for me to confess something.

Loomis is waiting in the lobby. "We've set up a room, Mrs. Dominguez," he says. We follow him through the lobby, pass his office, and continue down the hallway. "There's a phone right by the door, if you need anything." We stop in front of a metal door. He looks serious, like he's worried for us. "It's not too late to change your mind."

Ma shakes her head.

Loomis takes a breath, nods. "All right then." He turns to me. "It's good that you're here," he says, then leaves.

Ma opens the door. I close it behind us. Eric lies on a metal table with wheels, a gray sheet covering him from the neck down. Hanging over the edge is a single strand of hair, the darkest thing in this white room. I can see the incision on his neck, the thread keeping his lips shut.

Ma takes the garment bag from my hands. She goes to Eric. I stay by the door. "They have staff who can do this," I tell her.

She hangs the bag on a hook on the wall, unzips it. It's a suit. One of Dad's. "We have to change him." The sheet between them, Ma puts her hand on Eric's right arm and rubs it up and down. She bends over, whispers, "Ang bunso ko," between kisses to his cheek, his forehead, his cheek again, weeping. For a moment I mistake this for tenderness, her gesture of amends, a last chance to dress him the way she did when he was a boy.

Then she wipes her eyes, stands up straight, takes a long, deep breath, and pulls several rolls of Ace bandages out of her purse. Now I understand.

She lifts the sheet, folds it neatly down to his abdomen. For the first time, we see them, his breasts. They look cold and hard and dead as the rest of him, like they have always been part of his body. If this was how he wanted to live, then this was how he wanted to die.

"Lift his arms," Ma says.

I don't move.

"This will work. I saw it on TV. Women who try to look like men. This is what they do."

"You can't."

"Everyone will see him tonight," Ma says. She unrolls the bandage, fingers trembling.

I tell her to forget tradition and custom, to keep the casket closed, locked up for good. "You picked out a nice casket for him. Beautiful flowers." I keep my voice calm and move toward her slowly, as if I'm trying to stop her from jumping off the ledge of a skyscraper. "Just let him be this way. They won't see," I say, "they won't know."

"I will," she says.

I reach for her arm, but she pulls back. She steps around, stands behind Eric's head, slips her hands beneath his shoulders, and manages to raise him a few inches off the table, but he slips from her hands. She tries again, her arms shaking from the weight of him. "Please," she says, looking at me. One way or another, she means to do this, and I know she'll hurt herself if I don't help.

I walk over to the body. The light in here is different from that in the morgue. Yesterday, the room seemed filled with a gray haze, and it took me only a second to identify my brother. Today, the light makes shadows on his face, and I notice the sharpness of his cheekbones, the thin arch of his eyebrows. His lips are fuller than I remember, his neck more narrow. "It's still him," I say, but Ma ignores me.

His body hard from the embalming fluid inside him, he is heavier than I expect. To lift him up, I have to slip my arms beneath his, fold them across his chest. I hold him and I don't care how we look: we are together and we should stay this way, for all the moments we can. We have been apart for so long; soon he'll be gone for good. "Leave him alone," I say, but Ma doesn't listen. Her hands separate me from my brother as she works the bandage round and round his breasts. I kiss the back of his neck once, in love and in apology.

Ma continues, bandage after bandage, rolling so tightly the breasts vanish back into him like they never existed. If my brother was alive, he wouldn't be able to breathe.

I say nothing to Ma on the way back to her house. When I let her off at the bottom of the driveway, I don't wait until she makes it to the door. I just drive away, refrain from looking in the rearview mirror, in case she's still there.

Before I know it, I'm on Telegraph Avenue, heading for the bridge. Once I'm past the tollgate, I have to force myself not to speed. I take slow, deep breaths as I get closer to the city.

I make my way to the Tenderloin and, as if I was meant to, find a parking spot right in front of Eric's building. I hurry inside, pass the two girls on the doorstep who were there last night, run up the three flights of stairs and down the hall to the end. I knock on the door, hunched over, out of breath.

"Who is it?" Raquel says.

"Edmond," I say. "The brother."

And she opens to me.

A Stone House

for J.M.A.

Now that her mother is dying—will, in fact, die very soon—Kit manages most of the time to forget her. She types her dissertation. She weeds the garden. But her mother creeps in anyway: unannounced, unwanted. Kit imagines 1938, the year her mother's parents rented a stone beach house on the unfashionable edge of Cannes. They took their daughters out of the heat of Paris as if they were any other middle-class French family. Kit imagines the stone house as small, gray, and perfectly square, the kitchen stocked with ingredients for Croque Monsieur, buttered croissants, chocolate pieces tucked in baguettes. Kit's mother, Solange, is perfectly calm, like all French schoolchildren, the part in her hair not the slightest bit crooked. She strokes each stone of the house with her little hands. She is smiling. She does not know what Kit knows: that in less than a year, the war will take over her life, and she will lose her father, her sister, everything. But now—in this last wonderful summer—Solange sheds her clothes, her city skin, and runs down to the water slapping the white sand cold and pure, far from the smelly streets of Paris. It is only 1938. She dips a clean toe into the sea.

This may or may not be the real story, but Kit adds details to the one she tells Jon. She adds a German boy swimming with a blonde girl very close to the stone beach house, so close her mother's heartbeat stops and starts again at the words: *Werner, nein. Nein.* Kit adds a broken-down train on the way back to Paris, her grandfather searched and taken to Auschwitz, never to return. In the true story, Solange returned to Paris and to school, and the terror, the important things happened later. But Kit cannot help twisting her mother's fate for effect. She's been with Jon for more than a hundred nights, but every night, she spins a tale to capture his attention once again. Her ordinariness is like a birthmark—how can Jon not see it? There is no other dramatic incident to share with him, so she makes the most of what she has.

    Kit continues to curl up in the bed, under her mother's old silver comforter. It's true that the stories she tells Jon come from her grandmother, second-hand. Her mother said almost nothing of her life before the war, before she left France, before she married a dull American who called her So. There are many stories Kit doesn't know about her mother: her first kiss, her first love, what it was like sailing into Ellis Island. *I don't remember,* her mother says, brushing aside all her questions. *It isn't important.* Her mother was strong. She had willed her past to evaporate as completely as clear water in a jar.

"That was the last time she felt safe" is the way Kit ends the story of the stone house. Jon is not listening. He comes into her bedroom with carefully washed strawberries and whipped cream in a small blue bowl. It's like a movie scene, Kit thinks, a perfect movie scene of passion. In a movie, however, the stems from the strawberries and the red stains on the sheets would magically disappear.

Jon smiles, but his smile is far away. "Organic berries are the best." Kit understands this is not the first time he has eaten strawberries in a woman's bed. She feels for her heart's relentless pound, buried under clothing and skin, refusing to halt.

There is another story she could tell him, but what would it help? In this story, it is Kit who is nine and at a beach house with her parents. The beach house is in America, not France; it is made of pink stucco instead of stone. Florida, where the sun shrieks all day and the cars are white and turquoise, the color of wind-up toys. Her mother is standing by the doorway, calling for her, unsmiling, impatient. Kit is always late. For the beach? What does it matter? Her mother's graying hair is pulled back with an old barrette. The other mothers have bright-colored hair, magically afloat above well-fed faces. Solange doesn't dye her hair blonde or puff it up with hair spray. She doesn't shellac it to her shoulders.

The beach is crowded with other mothers, the kind Kit yearns for: younger mothers in tight bathing suits cutting red marks in their jowly thighs, mothers playing mahjong with bits of damp tile, mothers lighting cigarettes and smoothing chalky cream on peeling red noses. Kit's mother would never play mahjong on the beach or talk to the others in their coarse, singsong New York accents. The other mothers are thick branches, bending to everyone's demands. Their children eat hot dogs and swim without waiting an hour. It's vacation, the mothers say to each other. Who has the energy to fight?

And Kit is afraid of all that sand, the drying starfish, the water retreating and invading in sudden bursts at her feet. She turns around to run back to her mother. Here the memory stops. Where is her mother?

Kit slides out of bed and dumps the remaining sticky berries in the disposal. She enjoys the grinding noise of their disappearance. She almost wants to make Jon disappear as easily. Jon, who has lived in dirty rooms in Afghanistan and Lisbon, furnished but without running water, without a current passport, or a ticket home. He walked through Spain with only a tiny backpack and five dollars in American money. He stayed six months, then ten. His sandy-haired girlfriend back home waited while a dark-eyed

Spanish woman took him in and fed him rich, strange stews the color of blood. She loved him, but he left for Pamplona.

The day Kit told Jon about her mother's illness, he held her face and traced her wet eyes with his fingers. Now Kit cannot possibly tell him the truth: that she is not crying for her mother. She is crying because he is a man who has lived in too many places, and none of them was home. Her mother is dying and all she feels is relief. She has wanted her mother to disappear since she was a child; she has willed this final illness. Now she crawls back into bed. She places Jon's hands on her, on the narrow curves between her hips and breasts. His hands are astonishingly warm.

"I like the way you use the word *just*," Jon says suddenly. "Most women use it to slice down their demands: like *I* just *want you to tell me about your day; I* just *want you to love me as much as I love you.* You don't demand like that."

"I don't need anything," Kit says.

"It's a wonderful thing about you. I love that about you."

Oh, the great lie of this. It is Jon who needs nothing, who wants nothing. He is an air fern. But Kit is aware of how very much she wants. She wants a stone house and a cocker spaniel and a child. She wants to look at Jon each and every morning of her life. She wants to immerse herself in the odd junctions of his face, the tiny quirks of expression, the way his nose bends slightly to the left, the high lift of his cheekbones. She wants to press him to her, to crawl between his arms, to be as necessary to him as water. She can mete out these desires carefully, but in the end he will realize that they add up to the same catalogue of wants, the same amount of yearning. For now, she can hide in the crevices of his body, in his hard skin. She can cover him like a secret. She can wrap her ankles around his, which always seem to be moving, to be running from her, running, even in sleep.

It is frozen in her memory: the day she was alone without warning on a crowded, noisy beach. How could this be? Her mother was always there, picking her up from school when other little girls rode the bus or waiting for her after her ballet class, watching through the big glass window as Kit practiced third position and later calling her "my little elephant." She says this as if Kit is yet another burden put on her life, a child so bulky, so lacking in grace that even a leotard and pink stockings will not lift her from her American shortcomings. French children are not fat she tells Kit, saying it with so much authority that the summer they visit Paris, Kit looks everywhere for excess weight. But the French children are wispy. They fly through the winding streets and down the subway halls, leaving Kit with nothing to do but count the endless Dubonnet advertisements as they speed through the metro tunnel.

On the day Kit can't forget, she is looking frantically for the beach chair and her mother standing in front of it, dressed in a plain white top, dark-blue slacks. Solange is French, but she is not glamorous. She wears no makeup, not even lipstick. Kit has done something bad to make her leave. *Kitty, when I count to ten, you better be in this house.* Solange likes to use American expressions. When Kit loses toys by not picking them up, she says, *The way you make your bed is the way you'll sleep in it.* When Kit makes fun of an ugly red burn down a little boy's back, her mother snaps, *People who live in glass houses shouldn't throw stones.*

When her mother is angry, there are tight lines around her eyes. Kit squints until she imagines her mother is with her, then far away, a tiny speck of white and blue. She puts a shell to her ear, a shell she has saved from the tide, but it is her mother's voice that she hears. *Come back here.*

Why won't she remember being found?

Kit keeps the shells of that summer. She layers them in tissue and buries them carefully in a tiny cedar crate. Jon loves this about her: her passion for keepsakes. He loves the photo albums with their dateless, disordered progressions. He loves her overflowing jewelry boxes, the tangles of silver charms and gold chains, the tiny suitcases filled with French coins and old receipts.

He tells her that he saw her standing in front of a clothing store she had always admired but never shopped in and that he watched as she began to laugh, laughing at the unbelievable expense of hoping for nice things—the way it spoils you for what is possible—and decided then to approach her. He touched her arm gently so as not to scare her and said, *I just wanted to tell you how happy you look. I've never seen anyone look so happy.* What Kit hides is how very unhappy she is; she is broke, her mother says she will amount to nothing, and Kit sees quite clearly even then the terrible price of wanting anything as beautiful as Jon. But when he touches her arm, Kit is suddenly, magically happy, and later too, when they wait for the store to open and she tries on all the expensive clothes, the linens forming to her skin, the silk folding and unfolding above her head, parachutes of silver and gold. She buys nothing, she can buy nothing, but she is speechless at how soft the fabrics feel when she dares to touch them. And later, when she moans, he slides against her body like an expensive dress. It is not until much later that she wonders how often he has touched down like this into other women's lives, how often he has opened them and sprung away without leaving a trace.

"How old are you here?" Jon asks, flipping through the photo album she has pulled out and dusted off. He points to a photograph of a small girl standing barefoot, hidden by trees. He is waiting for a phone call from a "friend." He will claim it is a magazine sending him on a travel assignment. The girl's stare in the photo is solemn.

"That isn't me," Kit says. "It's my mother."

"It can't be, it's in color."

Kit looks again. The photo is of her, Kit, with her mother's pointy fox expression. She has so much from her mother after all. The lessons in the value of expensive silk scarves with tiny names scripted onto the corners.

How to layer her perfume in stages so it lasts: first the soap, then the powder, then the touch at the wrist, the temples. Now her mother's hair is gone from the chemotherapy, and large Xs are marked on the sides of her bald head where the radiation strikes. I love you, Kit said to her in the beginning, six months ago, sweetly, falsely, I've always loved you.

You never said that before, her mother answered, raspy voiced, chicken headed, unforgiving to the last. You never said that when I was *alive.* She pulled away from Kit's hand with her last ounce of strength. She would remind her that loving anyone is like invading a country: no matter how far you get across the borders, you remain a foreigner.

"Where was it taken?" Jon asks idly. The photograph. He is holding the phone now, tapping it against his thigh. Perhaps he is having an affair with a famous actress, someone who changes her name and number every week, who registers at a fancy hotel under the name Dorothy Parker. Or, more likely, Wilma Flintstone.

"Pennsylvania," Kit says. It was in a park in Amish country. She was ashamed to be a tourist in a place where people wore serious black clothes in the summer heat and traveled in buggies instead of cars. Jon thinks there are things she won't share, he thinks her charming in her inaccessibility. But this is a lie. There are simply things not in her interest to share, which is entirely different.

In 1942, when Solange was thirteen, she stood in front of a German, an SS soldier. It was only her and her mother then; her father was already gone to the camps, her sister lost in the stream of lost children. They did not wear the yellow stars on their arms. The stars, the ones that say *Jude,* are at the bottom of a brown leather bag. They run from Paris and hide with a Christian family not too far from the stone house, an hour or two north. Solange averts her eyes as they pass near the turnoff; she is too old for games and beaches. They have a car, a miracle, and Solange wills herself to drive, although she is not quite sure how to. She knows, however, that when the car sputters to a stop, the problem is gas. Gas is not easy to come by. The two women wait in silence for an hour, then two. Finally, a jeep with German soldiers. It is Solange who waves them down. *Vas nicht?* they ask. *Vas nicht?* Solange is very pretty when she smiles, and she smiles at the soldiers. She looks into their faces without fear. *We need gas,* she responds in perfect German.

When Kit tells Jon this story, she fills in the details, what cannot be explained. For example: how did her mother know German? And more disturbing: why do the soldiers give them the precious gas? Why do they leave Solange and her mother alone?

Back in bed, the silver comforter is like a frame for Jon's golden skin. He flickers next to her in the dimming light. His ear is cocked towards the phone. Kit is only the background. She will always be the background. She imagines Solange dead and calling to her from the grave: *Why did you dress me in the blue for the funeral? I wanted the red. I told you the red. Kit, you never concentrate.*

Kit is out of stories. Jon knows everything of any interest. Even the true thing: that her mother will die. He thinks Kit will be brave about it, but she won't be brave. He will be gone. She will want him so badly she'll weep.

But she knows he will soon fade away like Solange, who was practiced at ghostly silence. She could punish Kit with it. Silence even as the other children on the beach make sand castles to show their mothers and scatter potato chips in all directions. Her mother leaves the beach, leaves her alone, the sand forming scary shapes in the late-afternoon sun, the sky darkening. *I survived,* the silence says clearly to Kit, *and now I have an American child who demands Barbie dolls and rubber rafting toys.* Does she wish for her mother to go away, to have never arrived, to have remained in Paris, where she belonged? The soldiers taking her. The white shutters of her grandmother's empty apartment swinging like ghosts or angel wings, high above the noisy Rue du Chemin Rouge.

"I'll probably be sent to Barcelona again," Jon says, as if it is a fate worse than death to spend time in that beautiful Spanish city. Kit realizes she has never actually seen any of the travel articles Jon has written.

"You might as well go," Kit says dryly. They stare at each other for a moment. Then he shuts his eyes and dreams, she thinks, of galloping horses. She wants to laugh at him, she knows she should laugh at his horses and bowls of red soup, but she can't. She never will.

When the phone call comes, Jon packs up. She is not home. The magazine has given him an assignment, he writes on a tiny note stuck to the refrigerator. He wants to spare her, or himself, a scene. He does not add where he is going. She finds an old shirt on the bedpost, but no explanation. It is possible that there is no explanation. People leave because they simply want to leave. His memory fades slowly, like old clothing too often laundered. He becomes as much a ghost as Solange.

So it is amazing, truly amazing, when Jon is long gone and her mother, of course, is dead, that Kit snaps awake one morning with one clear and final memory.

Her mother did not leave her. Her mother is there on the beach, and she is not angry. She went to get lunch, and she is hurrying back, laughing, carrying cool red slivers of watermelon, curled slices of cheese on bright-yellow plates. And Kit is frantic because she loves her mother so much that she cannot bear for her to be out of sight, not even for a moment. The beach shines like polished ivory under Kit's little feet, and she picks up a starfish and is not afraid. And when Solange comes close, she smells wonderfully of Arpège and strokes Kit's hair and calls her *monkey, my little monkey.* Oh, she is hers, she is hers after all. *Watch me,* Kit cries to her mother, *watch me,* and she cartwheels until her mother reaches out and brings her close, so close Kit is sure in that moment she could dive right into her skin and swim that warm red stream directly to her heart.

Patssi Valdez. *The Dream.* 2000.
Acrylic on canvas. Collection of the artist.
Photograph by Peggy Tennison.

Marriage Among the Believers: A Love Story

Here's a riddle for you: how does a Christian fall in love?

The answer is this: Christians don't fall in love because a fall is an occasion for sin, and as we all know, true love, *agape* love, is the opposite of sin. Love that people fall into is of a different sort altogether.

It's not much of a joke, I agree, and it begs the question of how a single Christian living in a backward, out-of-the-way commune in 1978 ever managed to find a wife.

So here's the answer to that riddle as well.

Tammy and I met during one of those freakish early-spring storms that happen about once a decade. Snow was falling, coating the ground and piling up in the trees. Flakes landed on my neck and trickled down my back like the chill of death. Our septic tank was malfunctioning yet again—my memory of our barn is of one such problem after another; anything with a pipe either leaked or became clogged—and manure was bubbling to the surface in the meadow beside the barn. I was digging a hole where we could empty our slops until such time as we could get the septic tank pumped and repaired. And then I heard someone sneeze.

"*Gesundheit,*" I said, "and God bless you, especially if you don't know enough to stay out of the cold."

"Thank you," said a thin, high, shaky voice exposed too long to the chill.

"Oh," I said, peering through the white branches. "Hide-and-seek. Is that it?" I shook the bough nearest me and watched the powder swirl and fall.

"Look," I said, "no more foolishness. I'm not really interested in Twenty Questions. It's about twenty-five degrees right now, and after I finish digging this hole, I'm going inside, where it's a toasty forty-six, and thaw out." Along with our sewage system, we never did get the insulation up to snuff. We may have loved Jesus the carpenter, but we never did learn the first thing about the construction trade. We couldn't even make fire hot, if you know what I mean.

I watched the branches move and a young girl step into view. "Only a complete moron would play games in this kind of weather," I said.

"So what does that make you?"

"An oxymoron," I said, "since I'm digging a hole to fill it in. Just remember: as quick as you are, you're shivering and I'm not."

Her teeth were chattering, and her cheeks were blue. A bit of bone, a hank of hair: there wasn't much more to her than that. She would have been cold in a desert at noon. She was wearing a denim jacket without a liner, a flannel shirt, and a pair of jeans, warm enough for our customary drizzle and mist; but in this bone-chilling weather, she might as well have stripped and rolled in the snow.

"Don't tell them where I am," she whispered. "Please? Even if they're looking?" And at that point she promptly fainted into a slushy drift, which meant that there was nothing else to do but pick her up in a fireman's carry and haul her wet, quickly freezing self into the barn. She moaned as though her dreams had taken a terrible turn.

When I opened the door, Rachel Sidwell, the wife of our leader and the woman I had once thought to be my girlfriend, was there to meet me. "Now you're bringing them in from the highway?" she said. "Are you so selective that you have to import them? Besides, I thought clubbing a woman on the head had gone out of fashion."

"Look here," I said, "this is serious."

I lowered the girl from my shoulders and rested her on one of the common tables, just cleared of the dinner dishes. And that's when Rachel saw the color of her face.

"She's freezing."

"That's what I've been saying."

"She must have been out there for hours."

It turned out that Tammy'd been in hiding for a day and a half. She'd slept under the trees and the stars the first night and thought herself lucky for escaping, but when the cold front blew through, she realized that she could not survive another night in the open. That's when she caught sight of me digging my hole. Rachel and three other women carried her into the kitchen, where they heated water and helped her wash and bring back the color to her skin. They gave her a nightgown to wear and put her to bed, and she did not awaken until three o'clock the next afternoon. By my watch, she had been asleep some twenty hours. I didn't recognize her until dinner that night. She sat over her plate of spaghetti with her blonde hair hiding her face, and I said, "You're one of the Gaston kids, aren't you? Your brother is in my fifth-period class."

"Stepbrother," she said. "I'm a Ueland."

There were Gastons and Uelands everywhere—eighteen that I knew of. In three years, seven of them had come through my classroom. Somehow I had missed Tammy. Her mother had divorced her father for being shiftless; her stepfather had divorced his wife for being fat. They married each other in Reno and threw their two noisy families together as if they were the Brady Bunch, minus shoes and middle-class aspirations, of course. They were loud, coarse, uneducated people who believed in love among the beer cans; they produced children faster than rabbits, and as a result they were working on a whole new brood. During the week, Gaston worked the big saw at Avison's, slicing whole trees into planks, and on the weekends he drank at the Dew Drop Inn. Stories went around the school that he wasn't particular whose door he opened at night, there being so many available to him, and his wife was more than willing to turn a blind eye. Two of the older girls, as well as their mother, were pregnant.

"So, you're running away from that house. The only surprise is that you're the first one to do it."

"Shelly took off last spring," she said, "but the police brought her back."

Shelly was seventeen. She made it as far as Portland before she came home in a marked car with roof lights. Now she had a baby due in April.

"You're safe here for the time being," I said. "But you can't hide forever. There's school and the police and missing persons. You don't think your mother will miss you?"

"My mother," she said, "can't keep track of herself."

She stayed longer than I expected, and she was right: no one looked for her, not a policeman or parent or truant officer. We never heard a word about a missing girl in that pre–milk-carton era. Evidently, Shelly's mistake had been her choice of destination. The Salvation Army reported runaways, and the police were obligated to respond, whereas Tammy found a spot in our barn with the other unmarried women and was soon pitching in at mealtimes and on washdays. She put on a little weight and lost her American Gothic look. She attended every study session, and I once heard her talking to Rachel about the doctrine of predestination. But it would be a mistake to think that I saw her very often or in anything like an intimate environment. After all, I was at school during the day, tormenting twelve-year-olds with the value of x, and if there was a meeting or Bible study in the evening, I might see her, but only in the company of thirty other people. Still, that Christmas after Tammy's arrival, Bonner Sidwell asked me to go for a walk along the creek bed, which was the closest thing he had to an office. The water and the trees. The open air. We were bundled up in parkas and scarves, and our watch caps were as frosty as our beards.

"That's quite a girl you brought us," he said.

"Who? Tammy? She was half-dead with the cold when I found her, but she seems to have revived."

"It's been nearly a year, and she has no intention of going home or moving on. You may have some responsibility for her."

"What are you saying? It wasn't my doing that she's been here this long."

"No. I mean it seems clear to me that Jesus has intended the two of you to be together."

"Now, you're joking. She's sixteen, and I'm a teacher. She should be in school, playing softball and passing notes. I don't need to tell you what would happen if I got fired over this. We would be out of luck all the way around. And I don't mean just the loss of income."

"That's nothing we can worry about." He looked at me from under his icy brows. "Are we to dictate the will of the Lord?"

Now, I should mention that Bonner had that habit of speech in which each sentence was a sermon and a reproof. We had known each other for four years at the time, but he still spoke to me as though I were a devoted disciple waiting at the bottom of the hill. Then again, I probably asked for it. After all, it's not such a bad thing having a guru of one's own, someone to give direction, and I'd been glad to be on the receiving end. So, he was given to making pronouncements of various kinds, and he knew how to use that breathy, quiet voice of his, making each one of them sound as though it was a revelation from God Himself.

But no matter how high-minded he tried to sound, we could ill afford bad relations with our neighbors; they already had their doubts about Christians living together in a structure made to accommodate animals. If they knew that our barn also sheltered runaway girls, there would be no end to their complaints. And having a little money wouldn't have been such a bad thing either. I couldn't understand how he could be so cavalier about our economic prospects, since in order to buy the property and barn we lived in, he had to use up most of the inheritance Rachel had gotten from a distant cousin. After that, there wasn't much left, and each month was hand-to-mouth. There were only a few of us who had paying jobs, not because the others had no skills, but because such a high priority was placed on study and meditation. A little money came in from the arts-and-crafts crowd for our tacky attempts at beadwork and pottery, but being thinkers more than doers and believing our souls more important than our stomachs, our general inclination was toward the cloister and the abbey. And yet periodically, those of us who were gainfully employed would have to deal with our resentments whenever dinner was marked with the block letters of government surplus.

"I'm not dictating anything," I said. "I know better than that. Still, I don't think you can ask a sixteen-year-old girl to get excited about some-one ten years older just because he carried her home in the snow."

"Why would she need to be excited? After all, if it's His desire, who is she to say no? Who are we to say no?"

"Oh, sure. Bring out the artillery, why don't you?" Bonner had stopped walking and was squatting near a spot in the creek that was covered with ice, scratching away at it with a stick. "You're going to tell me that that is what my heart is like, aren't you? Frozen over. Too cold to understand what the will of the Lord is. Well, let me tell you something. I know almost nothing about that girl, except that her family is a horror show and she deserves to be spared. But I don't know that I'm the one to do it."

He stood up and placed his hands on my shoulders—a gesture that I'm a patsy for, I admit. "You're the perfect person," he said, "and together you'll be a perfect fit. You just don't know it yet. What she lacks, you'll provide, and where you have doubts, she'll be the answer. For in His image, He created them, the male and female, that His portrait might be complete. Besides," he said, "you think you're being so quiet and no one knows, but we can all hear you at night, and I'll tell you this: it's no way to live, Brother. At your age and not getting a day younger. No way at all."

I should probably tell you what Bonner's thesis was, and now is as good a time as any. Bonner believed in several things, but foremost among them was the principle of confession. He didn't think of it as a sacrament, like the mainline denominations did, but he had latched on to a verse from the Epistle of James and rode that idea for all it was worth. That verse said that if anyone was sick, he or she should call for an elder, be anointed with oil, and confess his or her sins in as public a manner as possible. Bonner took this to mean that any affliction—physically or emotionally felt—could be cured by the understanding that sin was the root cause of all illness. Those of us at New Aurora were thus big believers in salad oil and the spiritual badgering of anyone with a fever. Anytime someone had a cold, that brother or sister was suspected of harboring something undesirable, and *Praise Jesus!* it became time to find it out. Of course, confession was likewise viewed as preventative medicine, so there we were on many an evening, toting up our sins of commission and omission, as the Catholics like to say, lest the hand of God descend and ungently nudge us toward a more amenable state of mind.

That I hadn't contracted some sort of repulsive physical ailment—a puss-filled skin condition, say, or an infected, swollen eye, not to mention hairy palms—for jacking off in my bed at night was something of an affront to the principle that Bonner held so dear. To my mind it seemed too embarrassing in comparison with spiritual pride or envy, and I couldn't imagine standing up and describing the details of my sin; nor did I want to imagine the reaction of my fellow barn residents.

The corollary to confession was restitution, and Bonner set great store by this as well. It wasn't enough to confess to the family at large; the confession needed to lead to some sort of concrete undoing of the sin. So we were married, Tammy and I, for the sake of my restitution—never mind that my confession was not verbalized—and this is how it came about. Bonner and Rachel called Tammy and me into their room in the barn.

Since there were no chairs, we took off our shoes and sat on the bed Indian style, as though we were having a coed slumber party. While Bonner announced what he had in mind, Rachel, who was round and puffy and in the eighth month of pregnancy, nodded and nodded. Tammy and I were to marry, the ceremony taking place directly after dinner. There would be no marriage license—at least not for a couple years—since Tammy was underage and we had no desire to risk her parents' or the authorities' attention, but in every other way, we should understand the marriage to be as ironclad as any in God's sight. I expected her to run screaming from the barn and throw herself into the creek so that my embarrassment would be complete, but when Bonner was through, Tammy started nodding and nodding, just as Rachel had been doing, as though the message had come from on high.

"How do you feel about it?" she said to me.

"Well, it all seems a little sudden and rushed, and I'm a pretty old guy by comparison with you. It'll be like dating a former student, except that we won't be dating—we'll be way past that—and I never had you in class."

"Maybe this is too drastic," Rachel said, "no matter how good an idea."

"If you need a little time to get used to the idea," Tammy said. "If that's what it would take."

"Well," I said, "I'm not sure." I was looking into Tammy's eyes. They were not remarkable for their color or depth; they were merely blue—nothing eccentric regarding their shape or size, no flecks or strange glints. They were what they were without messages or portents, and I wondered again if such an irrevocable act could transpire on such short notice.

"No," Bonner said, "this is the perfect idea and the perfect time. You will know love through the passage of years, and we would be remiss to let the specter of doubt intrude. This is a case of cold feet, but that's all too common, even after months of preparation."

So it was settled, and after our dinner of Spam and powdered eggs, Bonner brought the membership of the Colony together to celebrate.

"As Paul tells us, it is better for a man and woman to marry than to be alone and give occasion for sin. So, to have this brother and sister united in the Lord, this is the will of God." A scattering of *Amen*s and *Praise-the-Lord*s followed. "What can you promise to each other?"

Tammy made a beautiful speech about her model of marriage being everything that her mother's wasn't. She promised to be truthful and supportive and trusting. She promised to be faithful, sober, and kind. She left out obedient, she said, because that was an old way of thinking about the sexes. If both partners were obedient to the Lord, then nobody needed to be top dog. In less than a year's time, she said, she had learned any number of things, not the least of which was the nature of true love, for which the ideal was Jesus and His sacrifice on the cross, and she promised to sacrifice for me. Sacrifice and sacrifice, and then sacrifice some more, as much as she was able to. When she was through, there was an upwelling of applause and even a few tears, and I thought I would be hard pressed to come anywhere near her in feeling. This little slip of a teenaged girl had stolen all the good lines, and the only thing left was honesty.

"So," I said. "So this is what we've come to. I'm a little flustered, I don't mind telling you that. When I woke up this morning, I never thought I'd be a married man by nightfall, so let this be a lesson to us all. Our destinies can change at a moment's notice, at the whim of the Lord. And here I am whimming along. But I've gotten off track. I'm supposed to be promising myself to my bride, which is my intention, believe me: promising myself to her since it seems like the right thing to do. Tammy, do you hear that? I'm yours. We don't know a thing about each other, except that we met in the cold. You might say we're mysteries of the moment, but I suppose we'll learn about each other soon enough. In a year's time, we'll no doubt be like all the other marrieds, wondering how to keep the spark alive. At least we're starting fresh."

When I was through, there were a few confused murmurs and one or two folks clapped a bit before there was silence. I had been something of a letdown, but I couldn't think of any way around it. Afterward, a blanket was placed over our heads, as was our custom, and Bonner led the Colony in prayer while Tammy and I breathed on each other in the dark. First one person and then another asked God to bless us, and we were blessed at length. Jesus give them this, Jesus give them that. I'm sure He thought we were terrible beggars, and I guess we were. Underneath our blanket, I could tell that Tammy was weeping. "This is the happiest I've ever been," she snuffled, which did not seem to be the best of signs: not if the pinnacle of happiness were to be found under a wool blanket still redolent of mothballs.

When the praying was done, Bonner and Rachel and the rest of the Colony led Tammy and me outside the barn, which was another one of our customs.

"Now, you know what comes next, don't you?" I asked Tammy.

"Not in so many words," she said. "But you're probably thinking what I think you're thinking. I can guess, you bet. Hoo, boy," she said, "boy, oh boy."

"Well, we have a bit of a hike," I said, "and unless we have a little help, we'll have a few things to carry."

On the hill above our creek, there was an eight-by-eight shed with a pallet bed and a foam pad. In the winter, we used it to store extra perishables, and in the summer the marrieds might spend a night or two there for a little privacy. The night we were married, a fine rain continued to fall and the threat of a full-blown ice storm seemed real enough, so we were hauling blankets and sleeping bags. The thermal underwear beneath our clothes would be our pajamas for this little honeymoon getaway. Holding a pair of sleeping bags and a pair of flashlights, Bonner was leading the way.

"I should probably warn you," Tammy said. "I'll probably be a disappointment."

"I wouldn't be too sure," I said to her. "It's not like I've taken a lot of test drives."

"Well," she said, "even so."

Bonner opened the door, and we cleared a space on the pallet, setting on the floor the cartons of powdered milk and the unmarked bricks of cheese.

"OK, kids," he said, "get to know one another, and we'll see you in a week, give or take a day or two. Someone will leave your meals outside."

And then he was gone, taking one of the flashlights back down the path. We watched the beam of light parry with the trees before it suddenly disappeared. The kerosene lantern in the shed cast its harsh light on every corner, every one-gallon can of pork and beans, every three-pound box of Bisquick on the shelves. We were alone. Tammy sat down on the pallet and drew one of the sleeping bags around her shoulders and over her head. It was really quite cold. "I don't know what I was thinking," she said, beginning to sniffle. "Men are men, even if they are Christians, so I guess I've got what's coming to me. It's the price of a marriage. Men being men and women being women."

"Look," I said, "I'm not a bad guy, and I hate to hear you talk like this. This has all been a whirl." I started to restack the cheese on the pallet. "I don't know what we were thinking. It's just a case of Bonner's persuasiveness. He could convince the Pope to be Jewish, but let's face it: you're too young to be married, and I'm too old to be married to you. Like I said in the barn, we don't know a thing about each other. Maybe that's the way it's done in other places, but it's hardly the American way. It's silliness. Silliness to think otherwise."

With that thought, she began to sniffle again, but harder this time. Her body began to shake, and the sleeping bag over her head was bucking up and down like one of those bobble-head dolls in the backs of people's cars.

"But you can't cry," I said. "Oh, come on now. There, there. You may be a girl, but you're practically grown up all the way. You can't fall apart for every little thing—not even a marriage that hasn't really happened."

"You don't understand," she said.

And I didn't. She wasn't upset about the marriage, and she wasn't upset about the sex, at least not in the sense that I had first imagined. The act itself was something she was already quite familiar with, given the presence of her stepfather. The old bastard had started in on the girls the moment they suffered their first periods, and he was working his way down the line as though they were a set of stairs, as though he had to step on each tread or suffer bad luck. In Tammy's case, she had been stepped on more than once.

Her door opened and she pretended to be asleep, but that never stopped him. The last time he opened her door, she had had enough. She hit him over the head with an aluminum softball bat, threw on her clothes, and climbed out her window. Then she walked around in the woods until the snow started to fall, which was when she found me. That's why she was concerned about people looking for her: she assumed that she was wanted for murder. Evidently, though, she had pulled her punch or hadn't hit him square because a week later, Bonner saw him driving his pickup toward the mill, his head encased in a gauze bandage that made him look like the world's fattest Q-Tip. Bonner had made a joke about it at dinner, and the color had drained from Tammy's face. At the time, I hadn't known why.

"If I never see a man's dick again, I won't be unhappy," she said. "Or his balls. All that floppy stuff you guys drag around with you like an extra leg. Who needs it?"

"We're not that bad."

"You'd push it in a knothole if you thought it would make you happy."

"Now you're exaggerating," I said, but then I wondered. I was twenty-six years old, living in a religious commune and wondering where my life was going, a guy with a slide rule and the daily company of junior-high-school students with their hormones on display for the whole world to see. On the other hand, I had no romantic life except the one conducted in my own head and hands, and the fact that it was common knowledge was more than faintly embarrassing. "So you're saying that if it weren't for all the in-and-out, this marriage thing wouldn't be so upsetting?"

"Would you want to be buried alive—in your own bed, no less?"

"When you put it that way, no."

"You're quick, I'll give you that."

"Do I deserve that?" I asked. "I could do without the sarcasm, especially since I think a compromise is in order." So much for sacrifice, I thought.

This is what I proposed: there would be no sex, and we would manage separate beds somehow in the cramped spaces allotted to us, but maybe we could figure out a way to be friends and intimate on other levels. It would be a marriage of minds and hearts, altogether pure. We would know one another without the confusions of physical intimacy—she'd grow more comfortable with me, and I'd grow less needy as well—and maybe one day…

"Why would you want to do that?" she asked. A very good question indeed.

"I'm no prize," I said. "And I'm beginning to see Bonner's point: you have your problems and so do I, but together we'll supply what we lack separately. I won't touch you."

"We don't have to be quite that drastic," she said. "I wouldn't mind a little cuddle every now and then, and having someone to sleep next to doesn't sound like such a horrible thing either."

"No," I said, "it doesn't. But I snore, and I can't guarantee to be perfect in the face of temptation."

"I'll buy earplugs," she said. "As for the other: one slip-up and I buy a bat."

So we zipped our sleeping bags together and took off our boots. We fumbled with our first kiss but did better with the second. By the third, we were feeling chummy.

"See," she yawned, "you're not so bad." And five minutes later, she was asleep. Rolled over on her side, breathing like a machine while I stared at the ceiling, wondering how I had gotten here: married after all this time to an adolescent runaway so traumatized by sex that I would have felt guilty putting my hand on her waist.

Look, I'm no different from any other male of the species, Christian or no. I had my fantasies—most of which folded open and were stapled in the middle—whereas Tammy had no breasts to speak of and her hips were just a nod to the feminine. Although she'd put on some weight over the past year, her arms and legs were as thin as sticks, her cheeks and jaw as sharp as blades. But when we had kissed, her lips were soft, and I could tell that she was smiling.

Would it surprise you if I said my Christianity had once been on the shaky side? Before coming to New Aurora, I attended a church housed in a building that resembled a concert hall. The choir wore shiny fire-retardant robes, and the minister's hair was so perfect, it looked like a toupee. Maybe it was. There's no need to name names or cast aspersions. Suffice it to say that it was one of the lowest of the low Baptist branches. But the women were beautiful, with the sharp, practical understanding that beauty and a summer dress demand. They left their late-model cars and flounced through the rare Portland sunshine as though they were the answer to a question I hadn't known to ask. This was where I first met Rachel Sidwell. She hadn't met Bonner yet, and her name was Walters then. We became close friends during a college-group potluck in which the minister talked frankly about sex before marriage. Don't do it, he cautioned us. The physical relations of a man and a woman are sacred and one of the Lord's great mysteries. "It's a mystery to Mr. Plastic Man," she whispered to me. "What would he know about it?" The minister's three children were Korean and adopted and the subject of a sermon about once every three months, during which they sat silently and without expression, like the good props they were. The minister's wife, on the other hand, always smiled, even during funerals, and there was some talk that twice a week she saw a psychiatrist in Vancouver, then hit the card rooms.

Rachel's father owned a car dealership in Beaverton, and she had grown up in that church. She wore her sunglasses on top of her blonde head, drove her father's black Mercedes coupé, and drank like a sailor. When the meeting was over, she tugged my sleeve and said, "I'm thinking it's time for the sacred and mysterious. How about you?"

"Sure," I said. "When you think about it, the sacred and mysterious are walking on two legs all around us. Let him who has the eyes to see, see. We're all naked underneath our clothes anyway. That's Toastmaster philosophy in a nutshell."

When we were through, she pulled the sheet up to her neck. "Thank God for the sacraments," she said. Our clothes made a collage on the floor of her room, which was on the third story of her parents' enormous and tasteless house. Her mother was at a spa in central Oregon, and her father was on a golf vacation in Hawai'i. From her bedroom window, we could see the Willamette River and the log barges floating south. Mount Hood was to the east, and Mount Saint Helen's to the north.

"This is OK," I said. "I could learn to live this way."

"Don't be ridiculous. Living here is like believing in advertising."

"I could do that."

"You'd hate it. I hate it, and I'm superficial in all the worst ways."

"No, I just don't understand rich people who complain all the time about how meaningless their lives are," I said to her. "I've never been rich, so I don't have a lot of sympathy. All I have is envy for the view from this window."

Rachel rose from her bed naked and went to the adjoining bathroom. She spoke to me over her shoulder. "You're welcome to it, Buster. It's never done me a damn bit of good."

A week later she met Bonner Sidwell, who was preaching on a street corner in front of the courthouse in downtown Portland. He promised her poverty and rustic living conditions, and she became an instant convert, much to her parents' mortification.

"We're buying a farm," she told me. "It's a ground-floor opportunity with Jesus—like nothing I've ever seen. Bonner knows what he's talking about."

She had turned demure overnight, and I was curious, yes I was. So I came out to the barn at New Aurora. About twelve people were living there. I was done with school, I had a teaching position in the nearby boonies, and I couldn't think of anywhere I'd rather live. Besides, Rachel was there, even if she had become a different person and was already committed to Bonner. So, I guess you could say that I went to church in the hope of meeting women, and I came to New Aurora for the sake of one in particular, and then when it came time, I married a teenaged runaway because none of my original plans worked out. Pretty pathetic, really. But in my years with Bonner and Rachel, I'd latched on to a whole catalogue of principles, and I lived and died by them even if I didn't always believe.

Besides, Tammy and I were not unhappy, not by any stretch. We spent seven days and nights in the shed on the hill above the barn, walking in the woods and talking. For a sixteen-year-old girl, she had seen her share. She told me stories about her mother's habit of singing college fight songs while drunk and her stepfather's way of lighting a fire in the fireplace with a blowtorch. He kept it on the hearth for that purpose, and when he was drunk or angry, which was often, it was a threat to everyone's safety. She cried about her stepfather's sarcasm and those nights when her door opened and her mother's unwillingness to see what was happening or even to care. We covered everything, and I spent one entire afternoon holding her and telling her that I didn't think a thing less of her as a person, that she wasn't the one to blame. If I weren't restricted by our faith, I told her, I'd feel compelled to kill her stepfather, gut-shoot him and slice off his balls.

"Now you're being stupid," she said, wiping her eyes with the back of one hand. "But thanks, it means a lot."

"He's sick and should be put out of his misery."

"OK," she said, "enough's enough."

One day we walked to the top of the small hill we called Mount Carmel. A light rain was falling, and we came back drenched and shivering to find that someone, maybe Rachel, had left a package on our doorstep: a thermos of hot chocolate, two mugs, and a can of whipped cream. We spent another day reading the Gospel of John and praying together because Tammy thought a marriage should begin with good habits. I grew more and more nauseated with our earnestness, but when I opened my eyes and found her staring at me, she patted my hand and said we didn't need to continue. At that moment, she didn't seem as young as I had first imagined. That night, we crawled into our double-wide sleeping bag and snuggled against each other. Although there were moments when we began to warm to each other and might have let our impulses take over, the nights were cold and we didn't do anything more than stick our tongues into each other's mouth or sleep like spoons stacked in a drawer. When we came back down the hill, the teasing we received our first night back was fierce. There's nothing like your virtuous Christian for making innuendo—it's all so lusciously dirty and forbidden, like apples in the garden—and I felt a bit unmanned that none of it was true. Which was the beginning of our first argument.

"You promised," she said.

"It's a matter of principle," I said. "Aren't we lying? Think about it. We're letting them think something that's not so."

I was taking advantage of her character. She was really a very honest person in those days—maybe the most honest I've ever known.

"What do we care?" she said with little conviction.

"They're family," I said, "in the better sense of the word."

"So we tell them everything?"

"We could," I said, "but I have to confess I'm a little embarrassed. What would I say?"

"Well, that's your problem, isn't it?"

"Tammy," I said, "you're right. It's my problem, and I made you all kinds of promises that night, but it wasn't exactly a normal courtship. You have to admit that."

"Fine," she said. She was gritting her teeth, and her jaw muscles were so tightly clenched that I'm surprised she didn't crack a molar. "I admit it. Happy?"

"Don't take it that way," I said.

"All right," she said, "I can see there won't be any peace until we get this over with."

We had been washing the dishes after dinner, our assigned chore: washing and drying and arguing. Tammy untied her apron and pulled the loop over her head.

"Come on," she said.

"You're joking. We have the baking dishes and the soup pot yet, and you know how tough they can be. I'll probably be scraping them with a knife. If we only had the money to join the twentieth century and get a dishwasher."

"Right now, and I'm not kidding."

She grabbed my hand and dragged me back to our cubicle of a room, newly hammered together. Our plywood walls still smelled like fresh cuts and sap. There was sawdust on the floor and indentations around the nail heads.

"Tammy," I said, "we don't have to do this. You're making me feel horrible."

"This offer," she said, "will not be repeated." She pulled the curtain across our doorframe, then unbuttoned her shirt, untied her boots, and dropped her jeans while I stood watching. "Well? Come on. Time's a-wasting."

"But everyone's awake," I said. "We'll have no privacy whatsoever. I saw Brenda Caldwell reading three rooms ago. You can hear Arnold Stone scraping away on his violin. Bonner and Rachel are probably doing their devotions. You know how they are after dinner. They pray for an hour or more with their lips moving."

"Fine," she said. "Do what you want, but I'm warning you: it's now or never."

What was I to do? I took off my clothes, and there we were: exposed to each other and the air.

"Well," she said, biting her lower lip. "OK. Here we go."

She hardly looked bigger or more developed than the girls from the elementary school who took accelerated course work at the junior high. One arm went across her chest and grabbed the elbow of her other arm, which hung down, her hand shielding the sparse pubic hair at her crotch. Her breasts were really no more than mere suggestions. I could count each rib. Her belly was a cave, and though her knees were together, I could easily see between the parentheses of her thighs. And after a year of eating our government-surplus food! The boards creaked as she tugged off the army blankets and lay back on our newly built bed.

"Tammy," I said, "we can't do this."

"I knew you were going to say that," she said and covered her face with her hands. I touched her shoulder, but she pulled away. "Who would want me? After what I've been through. I can't say I blame you."

"I want you," I said, "of course I do." And the moment I said it, I knew that it was true. "I love you," I said.

"*Hah!*"

I knelt between her legs and kissed her hands, which still covered her eyes, while I fit myself into her.

"Stop that," she cried, frantic, trying to buck me off with her hips, but I was too heavy for her.

"What?" I said. "This? Or this? When I move a little here, is that what's bothering you?"

"All of it," she whimpered. "All of the above."

"I'm your husband," I said, "and you know that such things are allowed. That's why people get married in the first place."

Her fists were balled up, and she was hitting my shoulders. Not very hard really, just spastic little punches that a toddler might have laughed at, thinking them playful. But she was crying and kicking me with her heels and craning her head back and forth. Holding her was like holding a pile of mismatched sticks in a strong wind: I was waiting for her to fly into pieces.

"Get off," she sputtered. Her voice rose in pitch and volume. "You're too heavy. I can't breathe. You're hurting me."

"Now, now," I said, "I think you're telling me a story. You don't want me to touch you, but you don't want me *not* to touch you. You say you can't breathe, but you're screaming at me."

"Oh, Jesus," she said, "he's killing me."

"I'm not your stepfather. I'm your husband, and you know Saint Paul and the Book of Ephesians: husbands and wives together are the image of Christ and His Church."

"If that's what it takes, then let me die!"

"There is some debate about authorship, I agree, but that's no reason to doubt everything. You can't throw the baby out with the bath water. It's a good book, all in all. In any case," I said, "we won't be this way much longer."

When I rolled over to my side of the bed, her face was wet and shiny with tears, and she was sobbing so hard that she had begun to hiccup.

There was a knock on our doorframe and a tentative voice on the other side of our curtain.

"Yes," I said, huffing and puffing a little. "What is it?"

It was Rachel's voice: "Everything all right in there?"

"Just fine," I said. "Just a newlywed tiff is all. And then making up. We're still adjusting to one another."

"Tammy," she called, "tell me the truth. Is he being awful?"

"No," she hiccupped. "He's no worse than any other man."

"That's not saying much," Rachel replied, but we heard her walk away nonetheless.

"So much for coming to my defense," I said. "Thanks for sticking up for me."

"You're a prick, and I hate you."

"Please don't say that. I love you. We'll get better in time. 'Let me not to the marriage of true minds admit impediment,'" I said. "That's Shakespeare and the Anglican prayer book, and we're true minds if there ever were such a pair."

What I meant to say was that, all things being equal, we were cripples of a kind, not perfect beauties or perfect souls, and we would just have to learn how to get along day by day. I probably hated myself for the way I had acted even more than Tammy did, but we had moved toward each other and that moment one step at a time, and when decisions had to be made, they were inevitable and impossible to undo. If there's any one thing I wish I could do, it would be to apologize to everyone I've ever met for being who I am. And I suppose I would have to start and end with my wife.

There's nothing so bad that it can't get worse. Then again, it can always get better, and if Christianity is built on anything, it's built on grace and the notion that things can get better even if there doesn't seem to be a reason why they should. Tammy hated me for a time, and then she didn't. *Praise God,* and I mean that sincerely.

There came a night some days later when she asked if I was ready to go to bed, and I knew what she meant. After the dishwashing-interruptus evening, I hadn't touched her. We had gone to bed each night much as we did on our honeymoon—minus the cuddling, of course. I pressed my face against our room's plywood wall and gave her as much space as I could. Tammy wore her thermals to bed and a flannel nightgown on top of them. So, I wasn't prepared when she put on her happy face. It was Wednesday night and our designated time for REC—which stood for Reproof, Exhortation, and Confession—when she leaned over to me and put her lips to my ear.

"I have a confession to make," she whispered near the beginning of the meeting. "The other night. I didn't have a horrible time. I mean, it wasn't completely awful. There were parts that I almost enjoyed."

"That's good to know," I whispered back.

"And you're not a prick. He was a prick," she said, "but you're not. At least I don't think you are. It was a little hard to tell at the time."

"That's also good to know," I said.

"I still have a problem, I'm not going to lie to you," she said, "but I'm willing to get over it. I'm willing to try."

Bonner was scolding Rachel for being too concerned with her looks, but we all knew that he liked them just fine—who wouldn't?—and if anyone was too concerned with them, it was Bonner himself. I saw him looking at her as though he were gauging where his wife ended and his baby began. His criticism was just for show anyway—priming the pump, so to speak, for others to follow.

"So, I'm feeling a little sleepy," she said. "How about you?"

"Now? It's only seven thirty, and Bonner's just getting warmed up."

"No one will miss us."

But when we stood up to go back to our room, Bonner stopped speaking midsentence. "Ah, the newlyweds," he said, "leaving so soon?" *Wink, wink, wink*—as racy as our faith would allow.

"Something in your eye?" I said. "That's too bad, but we have one or two things of our own to take care of."

"I'm sure you do," Bonner said. A waggle of his eyebrows, and there was a wave of laughter from those sitting around the common tables. They were waiting to confess their flaws and deficiencies, so any little relief was welcome.

"We have something to…we're going to—," I began.

"I'm ovulating," Tammy said.

Applause and laughter followed, and we were waved out of the meeting area and pointed toward our room by the good will and blessings of our family.

"You're what?" I said.

"You were on the hot seat, and I thought I could help you out. Besides," she said, "I don't think I'd mind having a baby. One of these days. Not now, but soon. I see Rachel and the others. They look happy."

What she wouldn't do was have more than one. After seeing all those brats issuing from her mother and sisters, she had no desire to become one more breeder of neglect. No, what she had in mind was one cherished child, two at the absolute most, cared for by their parents and the larger community of belief, trained and disciplined and sent out into the world with the best that loving humans could offer. She would get the job done right the first time, and she would make up for the sins of her mother and her mother's generation in the process.

"If that's what you want, then we should start practicing," I said.

"I think so."

I can't say we were terribly athletic or proficient, but we managed to feel good about things, and we didn't care who heard us in the commons or the next cubicle. They were listening anyway, those devout voyeurs. And four hours later, when the barn was pitch dark, we tried again, just to make sure we remembered everything we'd learned earlier.

"Thank you," she said.

"My pleasure," I said. And it was, it was.

If I remember anything at all about those weeks and months before the deputies paid us their pre-dawn visit and drove us from our ramshackle Eden, it would be the pleasure of our practice, learning how one body fit with another, how love could grow and flourish no matter how rocky its start. How we would continue to pray and hope for the perfect, redemptive child, even after we were told that Tammy was not ever likely to have a baby. How we would continue to pray even when we had begun to doubt whether Jesus was likely to care.

Carlos Almaraz. *Southwest Song.*
1988. Serigraph.
Photograph by John White.

Galveston Bay, 1826

On their second day, Old Bull's party began to see many wolves and coyotes in the distance, slung low to the ground, throwing backward glances. The animals appeared in the midafternoon as mirages through a heat-wave gauze that rose off the plain and made things shimmer and seem not as they were. One stopped and sat on his haunches and looked behind him. He licked his chops, then looked right at Old Bull before slinking away. Something extraordinary was happening, plainly, but Old Bull was unconcerned. There were many days to cover before reaching this Great Lake he had heard so much of. They were Old Bull, Red Moon, Sandman, and Whiteshield. Other than strips of dried meat wrapped in skins and an extra horse each on a side rope, they carried no excess baggage. Their horses were lean and muscled and born to run. But this wasn't a war party or a scouting trip. This was plain-and-simple joyriding, an adventure, and who wants to be bogged down on an adventure? Privately, Old Bull thought the stories were exaggerated: days and days of water in either direction? The absolute end of the Earth? If this was true, this would surely be the very origin of their existence, he thought.

The water was very low in the Red River, and they let the horses drink after they crossed. Toward evening the antelope came—sand brown like the terrain and splotched with white—first one, then in twos and threes. Soon, Old Bull's party was surrounded front and back by the usually very skittish animal. They stopped their horses and looked in all directions. Old Bull liked the way the antelope sprang in long, graceful arcs, one after the other, like they were playing children's games. But Sandman drew and shot an arrow into one's neck right at the top of its jump. It fell on its two front legs and lay quivering in the grass. He got down and pulled out his arrow, then slit its neck with a quick jerk. He did all this calmly. Old Bull shook his head. Red Moon laughed. That damned Sandman.

Later on, Whiteshield was almost thrown from his horse when it nearly stepped on a rattlesnake. The horse dipped suddenly and reared up, but Whiteshield brought him down and calmed him, scratching the side of his neck. Old Bull told him he better watch where he was going next time.

They splashed through a small creek, and on the top of the next rise a grasshopper flew into Old Bull's face. He felt its scratchy little legs on his cheek and tried to flick it off, but it leapt away. Sandman pointed. Old Bull looked and saw waves of insects flying toward them, heard their wings fluttering. There were locusts, grasshoppers, crickets. The riders hid their faces against the sides of their horses and galloped through the cloud of bugs. Once past, they slowed to a lope. The horses smelled smoke, raising their heads and flaring their nostrils. Old Bull's horse sneezed sharply. Then Old Bull himself smelled it. At the top of the hill, where they could see for miles all around, they saw a fire to the west. It rose up like the bluffs of a red canyon, its flame lapping and advancing. Animals fled as it progressed— more animals than Old Bull had ever seen at one time. That night, they dozed on their pallets in a cottonwood grove, the remnants of antelope fat spitting and sizzling on embers. A strand of Red Moon's hair was caught in his lips. It went in and out as he snored. Breezes came and went, rustling leaves and making music.

The fire now behind them, they left at sunup. Sometimes they rode in a lazy zigzag, taking it easy, or abreast in an easy lope. Sandman's horse would always begin to gallop when it smelled water, and Sandman had to check him. After two days they came to hilly, elevated country, and had to dismount and lead their horses around granite boulders and rocks and under clumps of juniper and pine. This landscape came upon them unexpectedly, protruding from the wildflower- and grass-whipped prairie like a miniature mountain range. They made camp near the top, which had a wide-open view of the plains to the south. Taking a leak, Red Moon saw a line of three or four schooner wagons, crawling insectlike into the sunset. He joked with Old Bull that they better not tell Sandman. No telling what he'd do.

Two days later, their horses began to smell water, raising and dipping their heads, wild eyed, snorting, difficult to control. They were on marshy lowland, and saltgrass and wispy cane had taken the place of wild cotton and tumbleweeds. A sudden gale slung Old Bull's hair forward, and he traced the wind ahead of him, its current visible as it curled through stands of Johnson grass and willow. Soon there was water everywhere: low-lying lakes, bayous, and swamps. The men stopped and surveyed. Nearby, geese and cranes covered a shallow pond, and more were dropping down, falling with outstretched wings and extended feet, settling with soft splashes. The birds bobbed upon the water, their mild puttering and clucking reminding Old Bull of a flock of wild turkeys he once spied up north. He was mildly disappointed, though. There was a lot of water, but this couldn't be the Great Lake. There were many lakes like this up north. Whiteshield said that they would probably have to cross here to make it farther south be-cause soon the water would be too deep. With a yell, Sandman whipped his horse suddenly into the backwater, and his piercing scream, the splashing and frantic hollering of the geese, began to fill the universe. One by one, the entire raft of wildfowl rose up and blotted out the sky, and Old Bull felt the wind from their wings on his skin.

They started out before sunrise, and as they rode, the stars paled and the sky turned deep, clear blue. Red Moon halted and pointed out the Indian. A figure, apparently smeared in clay, knelt at the edge of a lagoon with a dark surface clear as a mirror. The men stroked and whispered to their horses, keeping them silent. The Indian rose and carried water up and over a hill, out of sight. They untied their spare horses, then secured them and quietly followed him, steam trailing from the horses' nostrils. When they topped the hill, about a dozen Indians faced them with bows drawn. Sand-man reached for his bow, but Old Bull grabbed his arm and with his other arm waved back and forth in a friendly way. He told the others to do the same. They did, but an arrow flew by Whiteshield's ear and slammed into the riverbank, buried to the feather. They whirled around and galloped down to where their spare horses were waiting behind a cottonwood stand. Old Bull tried it again when the Indians appeared on the rise. Waving, ges-turing. *No weapons. Friendly.* Red Moon and Whiteshield had their bows out but were hidden behind the trees. Sandman rubbed his knife, making sure it was there. Old Bull walked out farther into the open, arms up. He tried to signal that they had come from *the north,* were trying to go *that way,* to the *big water,* they meant *no harm.* His arms were wide open. They could have shot him through the heart. Then Sandman came out on his horse, followed by Red Moon and Whiteshield. They flanked Old Bull, showed *no weapons. Came in peace.* The Indians lowered their bows and began to approach. Old Bull said, Come on, meet them halfway. These Indians were odd, very odd, Old Bull thought, unlike any other he had seen. They were smeared in some sort of grease, half their faces clay red and half black, their nipples pierced with slivers of cane. The bows they held were as tall as they were. Red Moon untied his spare horse, the pal-omino, and went up to the man Old Bull was trying to talk to. He assumed this was the headman and offered him the horse. That seemed to ease ten-sions. The group began to yell and chant and retreat. The headman sig-naled to *come.* As they were untying their spare horses, Old Bull said that this Great Lake had better be worth it.

All night until dawn, the Indians gave a big dance for them, the craziest dance Old Bull had ever seen. The women shook rattles made of snapping-turtle shells tied on sticks with leather straps, and some of the men played little flutes made of reeds. The birdlike sounds made Red Moon smile. There were drummers and chanters, some of whom blew low, mournful sounds from pinkish-colored shells. Of course, none of it made sense to the Cheyennes, but it seemed to make their hosts happy. The dancers contorted around a big fire, bending backwards or spinning sideways, seemingly without design or purpose, sometimes leaping through the flames. Some of them wore the strangest rainbow-colored feathers and necklaces of teeth. A spark flew into a dancer's hair, and he jumped and yelped and slapped himself on the head as he continued around the fire. The Cheyennes assumed it was part of the dance. Platters of roasted scallops, shrimp, and oysters were passed to the guests. The headman showed them how to shuck out the meat with a wooden, spoonlike device and dab it on sea salt that had crystallized in a depression in a stone slab. Sandman believed he had never tasted anything as fine and ate so much that his stomach protruded. The Indian they had seen getting water that morning came up to Sandman and signaled that it was *him* getting *a drink,* and that he *saw them* in the *reflection of the water.* Sandman told the others, and they had a big laugh while the dancing and music played on.

The next day, the headman and three others dragged out four canoes and they all set off: Old Bull and the headman in one canoe; Sandman, Red Moon, and Whiteshield and their guides in the other three. They traveled down a canal to a narrow stretch, then into a broad bay, which they crossed. Once on the opposite shore, each pair swung their canoes over their heads and followed a well-worn path through palmetto and sawgrass. When they came upon a wide tributary, they got in the canoes once more. While Old Bull paddled, the headman untangled a limber net constructed of vine and let it unfurl in the water. When they reached the opposite shore and hauled it out, the net held three big fish and dozens of fat, long-whiskered shrimp. They pulled the boats inland and flipped them upside down. While their hosts set about making a fire and gutting the fish, the Cheyennes hacked through sugar cane into a clearing, and there spread before them was a startling expanse of blue and white, roar of surf, glimmer of sand. Old Bull showed no expression, but his heart leaped. They walked together along the beach, saw gulls whirl and dip. Sandman picked up a shell and blew through it loudly. Almost immediately, one of the Indians came trotting out of the thicket to investigate, then retreated. Old Bull walked to the edge of the water. He liked the way the little stick-legged shorebirds followed the water as it flowed back out to sea, then tiptoed madly back as the surf came in again. That's how you run, he joked to Whiteshield. Sandman threw down the shell, stripped off his leggings, and sprinted into the ocean, screaming and scattering birds. He ran until he was up to his chest, then dove into the next incoming wave. He surfaced, swinging the hair from his face, and spat out a mouthful of water. Salty, he yelled. They all laughed. It was true, Old Bull thought, water as far as you could see. Absolute end of the Earth. The sun was sinking, a fat globe that laid down an orange stairway on the waves. The Johnson grass and saw-grass cuts stung when Old Bull entered the water, but he figured it was good for them. He tasted the water first on his palm, then took a small drink. A little salt is good for you, he thought. The water was warm near shore but cooled farther out and was shockingly cold when he dove and touched the sandy bottom. Surfacing, he saw Sandman showing Red Moon and Whiteshield a trick. When a wave curled in, creamy and white, Sandman would float on his back and let the wave carry him close to shore. They were all yelling and having a good time. Old Bull bobbed in the water, wondering from what direction the white men had come and how many more would follow. How big were their countries, and how far away? On what type of boats would they sail? How many days did it take? He care-fully scanned the horizon for boats but saw none, blinded momentarily by a crescent of sun.

They ate boiled shrimp and roasted snapper around a fire on the sand and slept on grass mats their hosts set out. Sandman braided his hair, looking into his little mirror occasionally. The Indians were fascinated by it, taking turns looking at themselves, but Sandman wasn't about to give it up. In the morning, the sky was mottled purple and strong winds had turned the surf rough. They all took wake-up dips, then set off.

Back at the camp, a crowd had gathered around two boys who had shot a big fish. Old Bull had never seen anything like the creature. With slick-looking leathery skin instead of scales, the fish was taller than either of the boys. An arrow protruded through the fish's back and out the stomach. Its eyes were wide open, and one of the boys knelt down and pulled its jaws apart. It's got teeth like a bear! Red Moon shouted. Old Bull thought that it looked fierce with its slanted eyes and rows of curving teeth. One of the boys signaled that the fish normally lives in the *big water,* but came up through *the canal* and got *trapped.* They could see its *fin poking above* the shallow water, so they *shot it.*

Old Bull told the headman that *he and his friends* would be *leaving today,* that their journey would take *seven days,* that they *appreciated* everything and would be *their brothers.* Old Bull went to his horse and got a heavy knife with a sparkling beaded handle and gave it to the headman, and the headman took off the tooth necklace he was wearing and gave it to Old Bull. The headman pointed at his mouth, then at the fish the boys were dragging off to the canal to clean. Soon, the dancing and singing began again, and the children rode the palomino around the perimeter of the camp. If we don't leave now, Old Bull said to Red Moon, we'll never get out of here. They'll dance all night. The Indians were dancing and singing even as the party rode off, four abreast, their spare horses trailing. The headman and a few others stood on the top of a small hill and watched them, their hands raised in farewell.

After a while, the sound of the Indians' drums faded and blended with far-off thunder. Southerly winds picked up and brought gentle rain that dissipated the pressing humidity and ushered in cool air. Fat drops peppered Old Bull's back. Flocks of honking geese flew north in staggered V-formations. Looking behind them, Red Moon said it looked like storms, but that they'd probably blow over in an hour. The men found shelter in a thick cypress grove. Whiteshield passed around dried buffalo, delicious after their recent diet of seafood. After an hour, though, the rain intensified and the treetops were bending north from a steady gale. The men were getting soaked, but there was nothing to do but wait. When it grew dark, they drew their horses in a circle and huddled inside them. Blue lightning illuminated the horses briefly; their heads were lowered and eyes shut, as if to sleep through it all. The horizontal rain, the spooky howl of the wind reminded Old Bull of a tornado he had experienced as a young man, but at that time, the wind and rain had passed quickly, albeit ferociously. This storm had more stamina. He heard leaves being stripped from their branches, then a big limb snapped with a wicked *crack!* As if on cue, the rain slowed to a trickle and the trees returned to their original shape. The clouds broke to reveal a pure-blue circle in which gulls and terns swirled. After the din of the storm, their cries came to Old Bull slowly, then with startling clarity. Rain dripped steadily from overhead branches. They untied their horses and remounted, anxious to make up for lost time and find high ground.

Pools of water lay all around, mirrorlike in the bright light. It seemed to Old Bull that the sun shattered off every drop of splashes Red Moon's galloping horse made. To their backs, spinning clouds and sheets of rain were swallowing the blue sky. The party rode all-out for the cover of an adobe structure rising forlornly near the edge of a bayou. It reminded Old Bull of some houses he had seen out west, on the other side of the mountains, while on a trading trip several autumns ago. White men in robes had lived in them. The party squeezed into an archway, and Old Bull was amazed to see that there was no roof. Fat mottled clouds raced overhead in the purplish twilight, so close Old Bull wished they could rope one and fly home. The adobe walls had already crumbled to the ground. All that remained was the façade, but it shielded them from the wind and rain, which were on them again. Gusts gathered into steady gales, the rain tilted sideways, darkness descended. For hours the rain and wind assaulted the mud bricks. Slowly, they began to melt from the top, red streams flowing down the sides and collecting in gullies around their feet. A chunk of mud and straw fell on Whiteshield's horse, causing it to bellow and rise. It kicked hard with its hind legs, slamming the building solidly, and the entire east side caved in. Bewildered, the horse turned in nervous circles, this way and that, until Whiteshield spoke to it and rubbed its neck, calming it. The Cheyennes huddled with their backs against the west wall, their horses turned away from the rain and their heads lowered. Then the winds lessened, and the rain suddenly quit. The men looked south. The sky was an electric pink. A blast of cold air delivered a hard spray of sleet, and, glancing at the white pellets, Old Bull saw they were up to their ankles in water from the overflowing lagoon. Lightning popped over their heads, and the horses jumped. Sandman's pinto pony, ears twitching, heard the whistle first, distant but growing louder. Again, lightning cracked the air above them. Again, the horses jumped. The whistle turned into a roar. They looked all around, up at the low ceiling of sky, out over the lagoon. They all pointed at once. Skinny dancing ropes, three of them, had dropped from the bruised clouds hovering over a big tree. The tree began to lean backwards slowly, bending as if pulled magnetically. When its tops began to brush the ground, the trunk exploded and stark-white chunks as big as clubs splintered free, whirled, and speared the mud wall. Ride! Red Moon yelled.

They jumped the south wall. Behind them the three ropes had meshed into a fat snout, which whined and skipped along the ground. They were showered with mud and rocks. Old Bull kicked and whipped his horse to catch up with the others; a tree limb sailed overhead. Red Moon, Whiteshield, and Sandman plunged into the bay, intent on crossing at a narrow inlet. It was too deep, and the horses lost footing, listed sideways, and tried to swim. Instantly it grew dark again, a shadow enveloped the earth. Old Bull yelled, but the wind snatched away his voice. He felt himself being lifted from his horse, rather had the sensation he *and* his horse were rising. Then suddenly, his horse wasn't there and Sandman was twirling above him, mouth open in a silent scream, his face a dazed mask. They reached for each other but were repelled. Three arrows pointing upward floated past Old Bull at eye level, followed by a limp swamp rat and Red Moon's appaloosa, upside down. Old Bull felt himself turn a flip, one slow revolution as he pawed at the air, and then he was dunked underwater. He opened his eyes briefly, saw midnight. Deeper and deeper he sank until hitting his back against the muddy bottom. He paused a moment, stunned, before realizing he was out of breath. In a sudden panic he sprung off the bayou floor and shot up, kicking his legs and fanning his arms. He rose and rose, and just when he thought he couldn't hold his breath any longer, he broke through, gasping and spewing water, arms flailing. The sky was dark, but from nightfall. He grabbed a tree trunk bobbing past him in the roiling current. At first he floated swiftly between what appeared to be bluffs; then the water lessened, then stopped, and he was beached on the floor of a small canyon. He stumbled to his feet, slipping in mud. It was still and quiet. A silver spray of stars pulsed in the bleached sky. He began to walk, northward he hoped. He yelled once, Anybody out there? But his words only echoed back to him: out there, out there, out there...

He never saw Sandman, Red Moon, or Whiteshield again but dreamt of them often, even as an old man. It took him ten days to reach home, riding the final two nights on a horse coaxed from the fringe of a camp in the black of night. When he was certain he was in his own territory, he relaxed, nearly hallucinating, and drifted in and out of sleep. That was how his people found him when he arrived: riding but slouched over, his face buried in the horse's mane. He was shirtless and shoeless and wore a strange necklace of teeth that clicked softly when they pulled him off the horse. Eventually, he recuperated on corn soup and antelope meat. He didn't speak of the trip for some time, but eventually told his wife and fellow chiefs all that had happened. There were dances for Sandman, Red Moon, and Whiteshield late every fall. Gradually the trip assumed a dreamlike quality in his mind, and children and grandchildren loved to hear the stories of turquoise-colored fish, screaming pigs with tusks, birds that talked and had yellow and blue feathers, and orange beaks. He embellished things when talking to the children, who were awestruck to hear of white men from different worlds who rode on big ships with billowing masts and wore brown robes and lived in mud houses, of giant fish with big, sharp teeth like a bear's. He would hold up his necklace as evidence.

Old Bull dreamed of these things—not entirely unconvinced himself.

Occupation

A play commissioned for the 2002 Singapore Arts Festival, *Occupation* was first presented by Straits Theatre Company at the DBS Arts Centre, Singapore, on 4 June 2002. It was performed by Claire Wong, and directed by Huzir Sulaiman and Claire Wong. The play was published in Huzir Sulaiman's collection, *Eight Plays* (Kuala Lumpur: Silverfish Books, 2002). The interviews with Haji Mohamed Siraj quoted in the play are excerpted from recordings held by the National Archives of Singapore.

Cast of Characters

Played by one actress:

Sarah, *Chinese Singaporean, early thirties*
Mrs. Siraj, *Malay-speaking Indian Muslim Singaporean, seventies*
Last Girl, *Chinese Singaporean, twenties*
Tony, *Chinese Singaporean, early thirties*
Ogawa, *Japanese, early thirties*

IN MEMORY OF MY GRANDFATHER, HAJI MOHAMED SIRAJ (1914–1999)

1

Mrs. Siraj So when he was coming back from work he used to come. He was friendly with my brother, but he was more friendly with my brother-in-law. So he will come, knock the door. Why? Give *paan*…the betel. So whoever knocks the door he will give. And always, it was wartime, we cannot have bright lights, so we used to have dim, we put the cloth around. Then one day, I went to open the door—you see how God, God's this-thing—I opened the door, took the *paan*. My hand touched his hand, just like that, and then he went off. And it was from that, donno how, it's God's this-thing.

David Botello. *Alone and Together
Under the Freeway.* 1992. Acrylic on canvas.
Photograph by Peggy Tennison.

2

Sarah Times and places. They're all alike. They're never the same. Marine Parade. Marine! Parade!

With a pleasing circularity, here is where our story starts, and likewise here it'll end, in ninety minutes, with a wiggle six decades back, then a wriggle back again to now. We start right here, in blocks of flats, upgraded by a grateful People's Action Party, with views of ships from every room, a harbour's worth of blue beneath the steely hulks, great grey-hulled tankers from God-knows-where bleached by tricks of heat and light to match the whitened beach. And from this thirteenth floor it settles, framed by green, the slivered coastal park a border to the scene, a fragile membrane taut between the town and sea. Perhaps that's all a lie. Words come easy to me.

Occupation. My occupation: Oral Historian. Yes. Assigned to sift and dig through people's tangled mess of words, to interview, collect, refine, collate, and package everything politely for the State. Though let's get this straight: it is appreciated by the State. Thank you, they say, imperceptibly.

Bing-bong, madam, *bing-booooooooong.*

I'm here to conclude the interviews we've done with Khatija Dawood—or Mrs. Mohamed Siraj, as she is known—pioneering feminist and champion of Muslim women's welfare, et cetera, et cetera. My chosen image today is the Caring Bureaucrat. I look out at the morning sea, shimmering, flat.

3

Sarah Mrs. Siraj, hello.

Mrs. Siraj You're Sarah, is it?

Sarah We spoke on the phone. How do you do?

Mrs. Siraj Come in, come in. So you're taking over from the last girl—what was her name? Jacqui? She said she had a better offer, she's got to take it up. And so she took it up. Come in and sit down. You've got a tape recorder for recording? You're going to record?

Sarah Yes, I'll set it up. What a lovely flat you have, Mrs. Siraj.

Mrs. Siraj Well, thirty years already we've been here.

Sarah You and your husband?

Mrs. Siraj Yes, he passed away two years ago. Around this time, actually. You're not married?

Sarah Uh…no, no. Not married.

Mrs. Siraj Would you like some tea? Always, four o'clock like that I have some tea. After all, we are British-era people. We must take tea!

4

Sarah I reviewed the tapes last night, tapes from the last interview sessions conducted by my former colleagues—Jacqui, Agnes, and Haslinda—all consecutively and inexplicably departed for the private sector, or for academia, which is the same thing in many ways.

Last Girl [*voiceover*] So, Mrs. Siraj, pre-war days.

Mrs. Siraj [*voiceover*] I was still quite young.

Last Girl [*voiceover*] Were you aware of your family's wealth when you were a small girl?

Mrs. Siraj [*voiceover*] You see, how can we not be aware, we're living in such a big, huge house? Up and down, seventeen windows in front, all along the front, seventeen windows.

Last Girl [*voiceover*] Did anything in particular make you feel privileged?

Mrs. Siraj [*voiceover*] My mother only did shopping in Robinson's and Whiteways. Specially they would open for her only. Whiteways, now it's the China Bank in town. Battery Road. Lovely, big, huge. My mother was in *purdah,* so when she's going, eight o'clock, they would only open for her. She comes in the *purdah* car, and we all get down with her, the whole shop's open! Robinson's…Battery Road.

Sarah To recapitulate her background for a bit: Mrs. Siraj was born in 1925, the fifth of six children of Mr. T.K.S. Dawood, the wealthy founder of Dawood & Co., whose goods supplied the ships of P&O and Dollar lines. Ship chandlering and stevedoring was a fine profession in the early days of Singapore, and when he died in '35, he left them more than half a million dollars, property, and gems. Before the war, the Dawoods' life was good to them. Serangoon Road was where they lived a disciplined existence under Mak's watchful eye, a house with wings for servants and for children. English blouses, silk saris. The Johor Sultan came for tea. On Stevens Road, an orchard. Beach house by the sea.

5

Mrs. Siraj Robinson's, Whiteways, Gian Singh. So they open at night for her, and we would all troop in with her. All open. How privileged we were. My mother would go and pick out everything, what, what, everything and all this and that. Such beautiful things, I tell you. Lovely. All British-made goods. After all, we are British people, I always say.

   Really lovely things. Sometimes she will ask us what we want, and still we dare not say, because she ask, and you cannot say you want this or that. Everything just sign, the next day the Robinson's van will deliver.

And then the material. She fancies the material, she buys. The best part is we had special tailors who come to the house. *Darzi,* they're called. They come with the bag. And all the fashions, my mother would get all the fashion books. Now my mother is unique. She won't allow us to choose what we like. She will look. "Oh this is very nice, this is nice, call the *darzi.* Tailor, *tengok ini,* ah: the body of this dress, the skirt of this dress, the sleeve of that dress."

I tell you, we all used to get so angry even though we were young. Because we were young, we couldn't say anything, because everything was her way. And we three of us older ones would look like that. Can you imagine that: the body of one pattern, the skirt of another pattern, the sleeve of another pattern? My mother was like that. A unique person. She can never take one straight pattern. And somehow or other they turned out all right, because the tailor is good. Bengalis, first class. And the tailor will look at us. He knows, you know, and he will tell us, "Missy, Missy"—after my mother had ordered, he would quietly say—"Missy, Missy, *jangan takut,* we know what to do." And somehow, because they're really good tailors, it turns out very beautiful.

Last Girl [*voiceover*] So you weren't allowed to choose for yourself?

Mrs. Siraj Of course not! My mother was very strict.

Last Girl [*voiceover*] Was there anywhere you were allowed to choose anything yourself?

Mrs. Siraj The ten cents stores.

Last Girl [*voiceover*] The ten cents stores?

Mrs. Siraj The ten cents stores. Because it was ten cents. Everything cost ten cents. Mostly it was toys, Japanese, they were all run by Japanese, all along Middle Road. And the most loveliest thing was the paper balls, from so big, they fold it, and the size, size, size until so small. And there's a hole that you blow and you play, so nice. As big as your thumb until so big.

6

Sarah Ah, the Japanese. I was wondering where they would come in. [*pause*] My boyfriend Tony hates the Japanese. He loves them too. He says the combination makes the love more true and lets the hatred slowly set like wet cement until the yield has bled from it, an unrelenting smoulder fanned to flame by mentioning the war. His occupation: hurt. The fall of Singapore he took a little personally. He's thirty-one, but carries scars six decades old from Syonan. I interview my pensioners and think of him, fast-forwarded, rewound, old anger in his limbs.

7

Sarah [*voiceover*] Session number 8230. Mrs. Mohamed Siraj. Reel 16.

Sarah Mrs. Siraj, I wanted to ask you about your views of Japanese people before the war. Did you know any Japanese?

Mrs. Siraj One chap in particular. This chap has a plating shop, silverplating, his speciality is that he cleans up the silver and then some of them he plate them back again.

He's a very nice chap, but of course Japanese. Being Japanese, he's really short. Later on, he had glasses. But in the beginning, no glasses. And you know, he's such a friendly fella, as all the Japanese are, pre-war days. They bow and bow and bow to you. Because we know it, in pre-war days, the famous, it's Middle Road, the whole length of Middle Road, they had these ten cents stores, and there they sell, everything is ten cents, and all the beautiful things from Japan.

Sarah The ten cents stores.

Mrs. Siraj He was friends with us from pre-war days, from '36, '37. When the war started, he disappeared. So we didn't know what happened, we thought he might have been taken as a prisoner of war. Because a lot of these Japanese shops were suddenly closed, and all of them disappeared, so we thought all have been taken as prisoner of war, so we just kept quiet. Of course, we later heard that Middle Road was full of tunnels underneath, from shop to shop. They pulled the wool over our eyes, you know. We never knew. They were such courteous people. It seemed as though they never stopped their bowing. Such lovely chaps they were before the war. They brainwashed them, perhaps, to make them cruel, the soldiers. Really lovely, though, before the war. Before the war, we didn't know.

8

Sarah Tony, do you think we should just decide to be rich? I mean, make a conscious decision to be rich?

Tony Yah, man, why not?

Sarah No, seriously.

Tony Slow progression, what. Working towards a goal. I'm very in favour of being rich. It's not a bone of contention.

Sarah Do you think it's shallow of me?

Tony Security, what. Not shallow. But just don't go overboard, lah. I want to ask you something. Do they pay you per old person? Each old-person interview so many dollars? No, right? Salary, right? That's the problem. Where's the incentive for excellence? What is your motivation to go the extra mile? After all, if history is unlimited, but your salary is limited, why not switch to telemarketing? The final frontier. Free and easy. Happy-go-lucky.

9

Sarah [*voiceover*] Session number 8230. Mrs. Mohamed Siraj. Reel 18.

Sarah How are you today, Mrs. Siraj?

Mrs. Siraj I'm all right, you know, thanks be to God, I always say. We soldier on, ah? Soldier on! Come, take some tea.

Sarah If you don't mind, Mrs. Siraj, today I'd like to talk about your late husband…

Mrs. Siraj Yes. Yes. He was such a good man. A very good man, you know?

Sarah Now, you got married during the war?

Mrs. Siraj Nineteen forty-four we got married. It was done in the big house. Because it was Japanese time, we had to cut everything down, because people cannot move around, cannot what, and still we had at the house and everything was done, so all the food people eat in the house.

It was very beautiful. The shelter at the back was still there, but inside all…My mother is very good, very artistic, she had it all done well…This time everybody sat on the downstairs, like tea, you know—table and chairs. But of course upstairs we had the ceremony, the huge house, so upstairs people sit on the floor, as usual, lah, with the *pelamin* and all that.

And then people came downstairs and had the food. That time we still managed. Even Japanese time, that time, if you had the money, somehow you still managed to get. But now these days, people can call how many thousands of people, but those days, Japanese time, you cannot, so you had to cut down. And people also, that time, Japanese time, many people don't come out. They're scared. We managed to get the food. We managed the meat, the chicken—it came from Malaysia.

Sarah You managed to get meat and chicken during the Occupation? For how many people?

Mrs. Siraj We had about five hundred people. Food for five hundred. And that is cut down, you know. Usually it's one thousand, two thousand. My *nikah* was on the fourth of June. Three weeks after that, we had all this ceremony, the *bersanding*. Nineteen forty-four. But still people came.

10

Sarah [*voiceover*] And how did you realise the war had started?

Mrs. Siraj [*voiceover*] From the bomb, the first bomb dropped. I tell you, it shattered us. We never suspected. Shattered.

We made for Telok Kurau in our big Packard, the family huddled all together in three cars, a convoy fleeing bombs for safer parts of town. Instead we drove into a battle; all around, you heard the shots. Australian troops were on one side. The Japanese were shooting them. We had to hide, got down and hid inside the drain while overhead they fired their guns. I was sixteen. And when they fled, or when they died, the guns fell quiet and we came out. The Japanese had won the field. It was a rout.

They didn't kill us, though they took our Packard car and drove away with all our things, our tins and jars of food, our clothes and all. At least we were alive. And so we settled in to face the war, we five girls and our brother, Mak, an uncle, and the cook, the black and white *amah*s, and the assistant cook. The servants carried on with us. Where would they go? They ate with us. They ate the same as us, you know. We couldn't turn them out, they'd been with us so long. And so despite the war and all, we carried on.

It shattered us, that first bomb.

11

Sarah An eerie whistling noise that terrifies is first, then followed by a drunken roar that seems to curse the earth it bursts apart. The song of bombs.

"And when they dropped those early bombs, it shattered us." For though their outward forms weren't cracked, a hideous internal crumble happened in the way they saw the world, exploding all the views they had before and ramming home the lesson that the British might was not as mighty as they might have hoped. Despite the protestations of their Churchill that this isle could never fall, it fell, and falling, took the smiles from all their faces, buried them without a trace, and fixed on four-year masks of tension in their place.

On my bookshelf, bought and not yet read: *White Teeth* by Zadie Smith; *Foreign Bodies* by Hwee Hwee Tan; *The God of Small Things* by Arundhati Roy. For what it's worth.

12

Mrs. Siraj Al-Fatihah:

> In the name of Allah, the Compassionate, the Merciful.
> Praise be to Allah, Lord of the Worlds,
> The Compassionate, the Merciful.
> Owner of the Day of Judgement,
> Thee alone we worship, Thee alone we ask for help.
> Show us the straight path,
> The path of those whom Thou hast favoured;
> Not of those who earn Thine anger nor of those who go astray.

A bomb did land on us in one of those air raids. It blew apart the wall in front, destroyed the gates, and cracked the terrace that our shelter was beneath. The house's walls themselves it cracked like boxer's teeth knocked out by uppercuts, until such gaps appeared that one could enter through the holes, and as we feared that people unimpeded might begin to steal our things, we had to build internal gates to seal our compound's space. We spent the war within those halls. And all around us, mockingly, the ruined walls.

13

Sarah [*voiceover*]   Session number 8230. Reel 21.

Sarah   What happened when Singapore fell?

Mrs. Siraj   You see, at the start of the war, you had to be quick. Think fast. The Japanese are coming, no, they're here! What do you do? You've got to find, amidst the fear, a plan, some action, something useful. Can't just freeze, you've got to think, to force the mind to work, to seize a moment in the chaos for a bold manoeuvre. Peril's everywhere, the Japs are on the move, with bayonets fixed they're laughing on Serangoon Road, *hor hor hor hor!* My brother acted, quickly sent two lorry loads of ship's provisions back to us, which, stored away, made sure we did not starve, and we can talk today.

Sarah [*voiceover*]   Two lorry loads? How much was that?

Mrs. Siraj   We filled a room as big as this, this HDB, this five-room flat. A room this big was stocked with tea and butter, sugar, salt, flour, great sacks of rice, and tinned sardines, tinned meats and vegetables, all sorts of things in tins.

Sarah [*voiceover*]   Things that had been waiting to be sent to ships now sunk? Supplies for sailors now in camps or drowned, their bunkbeds under water, action stations dull, their mess now neat beneath the harbour's murk?

Mrs. Siraj   I must confess those thoughts did not enter our minds. We packed it, floor to ceiling, stockpiled high with goods, then locked the door. It wasn't long before they came to search our place, but we'd prepared: we hid our jewels without a trace all wrapped and sealed inside an iron pot we dropped into a hole, concealed by building a stand on top and propping some old giant jar above, as though the jar had sat domestically for years, with no great secret buried two feet down. We hid some cash.

   Some jewelry stayed out as alibis, just flash and tinsel, nothing good, enough for fiction's sake, just things for taking, if the Japs were there to take. They wanted crystal, actually, and silverware, and when my sister's husband tried to stop them there, before they pilfered from the great collected gleam of leaded glass and English sterling, without screams or fuss they simply slapped his face. With that his pride gave way to fear, and he gave in to them. He'd tried, perhaps, to make them think that that was what we prized so that they'd not suspect our trove of food. Their eyes were closed, by the grace of God: they walked right by the store. They opened every room, but did not try that door.

14

Sarah   The other day, after my interview with Mrs. Siraj, instead of going back to the office, I went for a job interview. There's a small company that does cool-hunting, trend-spotting in Southeast Asian markets for Japanese apparel and electronics industries. It was interesting.

Mr. Ogawa   If you ask me, personally, as a today's Japanese, I think it's very important to examine seriously the wartime period. It is a great pity, but Japanese government is very reluctant to have any discussion on this matter. In fact, I have met some persons from Japan Foundation who say they are wishing to conduct some research on this wartime period in Asian countries, but they say the Japan Foundation office become pressured by Japanese Embassy to stop this project. So even if individually within different department they are wishing to make some study, they cannot, because Japan Foreign Ministry is very opposed to this. It is a great pity.

15

Sarah [*voiceover*]   So you lived the whole war on that food?

Mrs. Siraj   No, no, I mean if it was just us or what, we can, but we give to people, whoever ask, we give. Cannot refuse.
    It all came down to food, and who had food to share, and so we shared our things until the room was bare and mocking, still a secret, empty now, the hoard dispersed to hordes of worse-off folk than us, the store exhausted twelve months in. But for that year, we gave to poor and rich of every sort.

Sarah [*voiceover*]   You probably saved their lives.

Mrs. Siraj   I doubt we saved their lives. We didn't think dramatically like that. It was just the thing to do—to help and not to bat an eyelid doing so. Before the war, we'd done the same, and when war came, we stayed as we'd begun.

16

Sarah   The theme of food is central here. We must conclude that any Occupation tale that won't allude to food is flawed, unsound, a story starved of truth and fat with lies. The Occupation's sound is tooth incising empty space, a tongue that tastes the void, the absent paunch, the too-clean plate, the gut annoyed by sullen gastric juices coating nothingness. And further in, the swollen calves, the swift caress of life deficient in a thing or two. It's lack that we're about, and lack paints life in white and black. No tones of grey. No brighter hues, just One or Zero: Food/No Food. The binary blues.

17

Mrs. Siraj [*voiceover*]   You see, before the war, those days there were young people who used to read the atrocities done by British in India. Here also a number of people interested in India, mostly young people, in 1939 started this Indian Youth League at 118 Race Course Road. The house, Mr. Ratnam he had given, and in the first election, you find me as secretary. That time I was not known as Siraj; I was known as Raja Ram.

The freedom fighters were started not because of the Japanese. It was already in the mind of the Indians, they were uprising against the British government.

18

Sarah   Some people, you feel they have people on their side, you know? Mrs. Siraj has people on her side. I was listening to her late husband's tapes; he had people on his side. But Tony and I, who's on our side?

Sarah [*voiceover*]   Reel 22.

Sarah   So what was life like in the Occupation for you? Day to day.

Mrs. Siraj   We didn't go out. Whole time we were inside the house.

Sarah   You never left the house? The whole three years?

Mrs. Siraj   Until I got married, I never left the house. Cooped up. Because the Japanese were wicked, they would take you away, you had to run and hide.

Sarah   So what did you do every day?

Mrs. Siraj   Well, we're having someone come to the house, for our studies, to carry on teaching us, English, maths, everything. I can't remember what his name was. Mr. Pillai? And then there was an *ustaz* who would come and teach the religion, Qur'an, and all that. Otherwise we'll forget everything and we don't know who we are or where we are.

Sarah   Who she was, and where she was. Some forty months she spent within the house's walls. Her mother, pre-war prim, now wartime grim, had called a halt to journeys. Out of bounds, the streets, the town, for fear of…fears unspoken, thoughts a mother found too horrible, and frankly now, after Rwanda and Yugoslavia, it still seems wise to coop up pretty daughters, hide them all from eyes and hands and worse. So cursed, this band of girls interned were even banned from peering out of windows now. They yearned to look, as look they did at boxers years before. But now no boxers trained, and danger lurked outdoors.

Sarah So what did you do that whole time?

Mrs. Siraj We would play cards, gin rummy, and that other game, snakes and ladders. That *dam,* what is it, checkers? And of course chess. And mahjong.

Sarah You played mahjong?

Mrs. Siraj Of course, I love it! *Pong! Pong!* Like that! After all we're inside the house whole time, what we're going to do?

Sarah So you had no contact with the outside world?

Mrs. Siraj My brother, brother-in-law?…they're all coming and going, though you've got to be careful Japanese time. So they will come back and tell-tell what happened, what stories.

Sarah So you did get to hear of how the Japanese were treating the Chinese, for instance?

Mrs. Siraj Of course. We've got a lot of Chinese friends, from those days. My mother had a lot of Chinese friends, especially those *bibiks,* the Straits-born. Everybody knew about them taking the Chinese away. It went round. And they would take the women. All the women had to run and hide. The Chinese they would line them up and shoot. Make them dig the hole.

   One of our friends, the only son. The only son and five daughters. One of our very good friends—they come in and out, *mari, makan, minum.* Peranakan. It happened to him. Poor thing, he's the only son. And he was one of them taken away. Never came back, of course.

Sarah How did you meet your husband if you didn't go out?

Mrs. Siraj Like this, like this. See. We were staying in the big house facing Serangoon Road, and our small door by the side was Burma Road. Behind us is this big, huge house, and that belongs to Mr. Karmakah. This Mr. Karmakah is an architect. He bought the land and he built, and behind—he was clever—he had rooms which he let out to families.

   And my future husband was with them from the beginning. He was giving tuition to the children. He stays with them, he has his meals-all with them, but in return for teaching all the children.

21

Haji M. Siraj [*voiceover*] Finding this situation, the Japanese got hold of us, took us away to find out how they could make use of us. I was made editor of *Azad Hind,* a daily Hindustani paper, which was very popular among the POWs from India, and the second paper was *New Light, New India,* and so on. All of these were printed as and when required. After that, Netaji Subash Chandra Bose came over in the submarine from Germany and took over the Indian Independence movement. He straightaway organized two divisions of the Indian National Army.

22

Mrs. Siraj So he used to walk up and down. And then, Japanese time, he used to come back from work. He works in the newspaper office. He was collared, you know the Japanese went around and collared people—how many of them!—and he was one of those collared. He was kept three months in the prison, you know they tortured them and all that. Then in the end they told him, You run this Indian paper, because he knows Hindi and this.

Sarah Did you like him?

Mrs. Siraj We-all always used to see him, and he was young, good looking. The only thing is he had bow legs. We all used to discuss, we used to talk, after all we are girls, we're not allowed out, we're not allowed to look, but we used to see, even the boxers so far away. You ask my sister. We used to talk. "My God, Young Frisco, he's so handsome." He's a Filipino, he's fair, handsome. And Young Gordon: Gordon is mixed Eurasian-Indian, he stays Lavender Street, we know.

Now, my uncle always used to watch him go up and down the street. My uncle is the sort of a person who will always criticise people and say this, that, and all that. But when he saw him walking, he would always say, "Now that is a really good man. So respectful, so hard working." And we got a shock. My uncle never talk about people like that.

23

Sarah On recent weekends I've been occupied by sums. I calculate my fiscal state, which has become a little parlous lately. Money flows from me and ends up who-knows-where, a fact that normally I shrug at, soldier on, and try to save a bit again, until I'm broke once more, at definite and regular recurring intervals of time. But now the newest pinch has pinched me hard, and climbing out to solvency will not be quite so quick. Money is always in the past for me. It's not future paper. It's eager portraits of founders of nations. It's the promise of something tomorrow, but it always wants to be yesterday. Do I envy her her monied youth? Is a "yes" good enough?

How many spent the war in mansions with cracked walls? How many had assistant cooks after the fall? How many had a hidden storage room of food? It's obvious that certain comments would be rude—and pointless too. The lady had a silver spoon at birth, it's true, and probably it was this boon that kept her hale while others died. I think she knows. And after sixty years I would not dare impose my knee-jerk, angry envy of the rich on her. She's kind. She prays to God. Her luck was good. She's here.

24

Sarah [*voiceover*]   Session number 8230. Reel 25.

Mrs. Siraj   But in this house we had the cook and the assistant cook. The assistant cook, he's the rascal. He's the one who goes in and out of the house. So one of these days he brought a note. He said, That chap over there in that house asked me to give you. And so we were quietly writing, exchanging notes-notes-notes, and he's the chap who'll go and give-bring, this assistant cook. All these notes were going back and forth. This fella, lah, he will *bodoh-bodoh,* go out, and then in the evening or so when he comes back, he will give the note. And nobody knows, not even the cook also don't know. And my sisters all-that also don't know. It's between him, me. We would just write quietly.

And he would write what time he's going to work, of course I knew what time he's going to work, at that time the car picked him, take him to the newspaper, and brings him back. So I would always go there to look at him.

25

Sarah   In March I drove up Upper Changi Road to see the Changi Chapel and Museum, where memories are manifold and artifacts abound, displayed in handsome cases, well preserved, a mute array that eloquently speaks of hunger, sickness, death in heat and light. The chapel's there, reproduced, wreaths affixed throughout, from embassies and ministers. Twice, tears came to my eyes. The guestbook, sinister, contained an insult from a Chinese from K.L.: "This museum is disgusting. It ignores the millions of Asians who suffered under the Japanese Occupation."

His name and address were appended. I don't know why, but I started to cry, and the girl at the counter quickly turned the page of the book so that a fresh leaf was displayed. But it stayed with me, and two weeks later I e-mailed Mr. Wong and asked him why he'd said that. Not in my official capacity, but as Sarah. As a Sarah who had put aside my city mask and daily chores to let the pain of sixty years ago impinge on me. He wrote back, civil, expansive, calm:

> Changi contained thousands of Indian soldiers from Britain's colonial armies. Their traces are nowhere to be seen. Their words, their sketches, their names. Where are their replica places of worship? Where are their heartwarming stories? Nowhere. Yet if you look at the exhibits carefully, you will see a diagram of the camp. It shows the European block, with 40 cells. And two Asiatic blocks, each with 260 cells. Maybe I'm wrong. Maybe I'm misinterpreting things. 520 cells for Asians, and 40 cells for Europeans. Yet their camp life is never seen. Life outside the camp in Singapore, they allude to what the locals went through. Yet in the camp, those Indians starved and bled and died too. Shouldn't we remember them? Or do only white people count, and Chinese?

26

Sarah History and me, secretly, we don't get along. It's the Forever Endeavour. There's no point. Why bother making sure that all the dots are joined together 'til the picture looks complete? It's not. It never is. The secret's plotting where the dots *should* fall, according to your preconceived design, telegraphed and tapped out by Spectacles Boy in HQ, then asking only what will make those dots align, so history runs through, straight and clean, a handsome form where completeness is moot, ambivalence the norm, and truthfulness is optional—though still allowed, judiciously—if truth will do the nation proud.

I was talking to Tony about this.

27

Tony You know, ah, the Japanese still don't get it, you know. They don't understand exactly what it is. The concept of their evil. At the Changi Chapel, ah, some Japanese fucker, you know what kind of note he wrote or not? "We hope we will never do such mistakes again." Hello, it's not a mistake. You write "shit" instead of "ship"—that is a mistake. You invade and murder and torture—that is an evil act. Crime. Sin. Mistake, fuck you, mistake, it seems.

They have never apologised. That time Hashimoto want to apologise as Prime Minister, his own party force him to cannot. So he apologise in his personal capacity. Not as Japanese government. What's that, man? Fucking bullshit. I don't care how many individual Japanese feel sorry. You feel so sorry, you force your government to say sorry. You force your emperor to ask my forgiveness. And you pay compensation for the murder and the rape. You don't simply write, "We will never make such mistakes again."

28

Mr. Ogawa In Malaysia recently, there was a film of the time during Japanese period, a wartime film. The producer of the film request me to take a part in it, as *kempeitai* commander. I am not actor but the producer is a friend of mine, so he say, Ogawa-*san*, I need some Japanese person, please, you are very good-looking face. I say I will try. But after this, I receive information that Japanese government has banned all the Japanese people from participating in this film. So I have to say to my producer, I am very sorry, but I regret that it is very difficult for me to continue. But I think he understand. But is a pity.

You know, I was filled with a great sadness when I had opportunity to visit Singapore Changi Museum. At the chapel, they have a place you can leave notecard for your expression of feeling. I wrote that I hope we never make such mistake again. I feel this very deeply. It is great feeling of shame.

29

Mrs. Siraj Quietly I used to go to the window to look at him, because we're not even allowed to stand at the window, my mother's like that. So far so good, donno how one day my mother found out. And then my stomach ache, so I went to the bathroom, and I was sitting down, she came in and beat me. My mother is very strict.

Dr. Lakshmi has a clinic in front of us, New World there, she and her husband had a clinic, and she would always say, "I feel sorry for those girls, they're just like the princess in the tower. They're not allowed even to stand at the window, they're not allowed to go out, I feel sorry for them."

But notes were going in and out. And also we'd use the telephone if my mother was not around. But we had to be very careful. We had a signal. *Ring-ring,* put down. But eventually my mother got wise. She's quite intelligent.

She's so strict. And she gets in her moods. Sometimes at night she'll want to fry something. Now upstairs, in her parlour, she's got a little-little stove for her if she wants to fry something at night or what, she'll do it herself. Then next to it, of course, for ventilation, there's a window. Lucky she didn't notice that is where I'd put the *tangga,* gone up to the roof. And he also would go up to the roof that side. And I would wave. And he would wave. Nothing. Wave only. One day I got stuck. My mother went to fry donno what, *keropok* or what, I could smell it. My sister also was making face at me, warning, Don't come, she's there. So I had to stay up there, lah. Waving. Lucky she didn't call me.

30

Sarah Her occupation: loving, being loved, across the roofs and scribbled scraps, minutes whispered, hours lost in girlish dreams of kind embraces, gentle looks, her days of whimsy and confinement, courier cooks, and rooms of food, and this and that and all that. I want to shout at her, Where is the horror? I want to say to her, Why aren't you making me feel sad? I want to hear how you suffered. Your tales of woe. And yet your occupation is this: loving and being loved, loving and being loved.

31

Sarah [*voiceover*] Reel 26.

Mrs. Siraj My future husband went to see one of our leaders, Dr. Munshi, and another man, they were the leaders of the Muslim community. Earlier they were trying to match him. He had converted already. He said, I'm ready to get married, will you go and speak for me? Of course Dr. Munshi was happy, he thought, Donno what or donno who's the girl.

Haji M. Siraj [*voiceover*] I was born 15th March 1914 at Chandwar, district Jaunpur, U.P., India.

Mrs. Siraj No, he said, I want to marry so-and-so's daughter. And Dr. Munshi got scared. He said, How dare you, I dare not! You know, they're very rich people, very well known and all that…and you know what the mother is like? I dare not go. I'm afraid to go.

Haji M. Siraj [*voiceover*] My father being in Singapore, I had to come back with my mother and thus I started my school at Anglo-Chinese School.

Mrs. Siraj Then he said, No, you try. So he said, If you dowan, I'll go myself.
    He said, Wait, hold on, I'll think of something. Then after some time, Dr. Munshi—he was very friendly with us, he used to come and talk—Dr. Munshi say to my mother, Look, you've got three daughters, why don't you get them married, this and that, and she would say, It's not I don't want, but when the time comes, they get married, lah, we all say *jodoh* you know, so he kept quiet.

Haji M. Siraj [*voiceover*] Senior Cambridge I remember I wrote two articles: "Mahatma Ghandi and Jesus Christ," a poem. And the other was my visit to the holy city of Benares.

Mrs. Siraj And one day Dr. Munshi went. Dr. Munshi, brave. Broached the subject. Then first of course, my mother and my brother were angry and all that, said all sorts of things and all that. So Dr. Munshi told them, he said, I know the man, he's a very good man. What to do, he's a convert, but he's a good man. Nobody has said any bad things about him. You go and find out.

Haji M. Siraj [*voiceover*] I went to Benares Hindu University to study medicine. But again the problem came with my father. He actually did not want me to carry on, but to get married in India and settle, by which they get a large sum of dowry and land and property.

Mrs. Siraj He was a very good man, quiet, good, and very respectful. That's the thing that hit all of us, even my brother. My uncle said, *Apa ini orang, budak budak pun dia ambik tangan mau cium.*

Haji M. Siraj [*voiceover*] But I did not like it, so with what little money I had saved, from the university hostel I took all my books, came to Calcutta and from Calcutta, deck passenger, I came to Singapore.

Mrs. Siraj But Dr. Munshi was good, he pestered, he was this-thing. He said, I guarantee. He said, You don't want to take my word? I guarantee, I know the man.

Haji M. Siraj [*voiceover*] So few days I was just brooding. And suddenly someone said, Hey, why don't you teach? Come and teach my son. So he took me to his house. This was Mr. T. Karmakah. He paid me seventeen dollars a month. Those days, small sums were very big sums.

Mrs. Siraj It took few months. As we always said, God willing. If God wants it done, it'll get done. Dr. Munshi told my mother, He already got a house, he rented. In Upper Serangoon Road. Near Koven Road. Nice bungalow on the stilts, it's got three bedrooms, then going down the kitchen, servant's quarters, very nice.

So Dr. Munshi told my mother he's already got the place, he's already got an *amah* in the house, and he's got a car. He said, What else you want?

32

Sarah What else do you want, really? The five Cs, maybe, recast for the here and now: contentment, compassion, charity, clarity, and calm. I'm not sure I have the stamina for the spiritual race. Perhaps the winning is in the running.

Things don't add up, necessarily. Facts don't make a life. Consider the raw data of mine: my parents, who married young, were too young to remember the Occupation. My grandparents refuse to talk about it. But is that why I became an oral-history collector? No. But will it be skewed that way if they were to interview me? Yes.

Do I love Tony? Yes, but not for the right reasons, and even the wrong reasons aren't even the usual wrong reasons, the right wrong reasons. I love him for the *wrong* wrong reasons, but how will that look in the report?

Let's face it. The canon's set, and everything outside of it we should forget. It's footnotes, codicils, appendices, all swept to ends of pages, afterthoughts, their lessons kept from easily disquieted minds. The people need some certainties to underpin the lives they lead, their nine-to-fives, their eight-to-sixes, their twenty-four-sevens. Reassurance heaven, that's the State historian gig. It's rock and roll, baby. Check my pass: ACCESS ALL AREAS.

The trend-spotters called. They offered me the job. Cool-hunter. Two-six a month, fifteen-month package. Can you be cool on two-six? Can you be cool at thirty-four? And if you're not cool at thirty-four on two-six, how do you hunt cool on two-six at thirty-four? Questions for our times.

Session number 8230: session ends.

33

Mrs. Siraj You know, that day I went to the wedding. These old friends, they were talking, and they said they remember him, they never forget what a good man he is. Everybody knows this, how he will bow and bow, even to children he will bow. Even the girl's family who used to live in front of us, they were saying, You cannot get another good man like that. I say, Yes, that's why he can rest in his grave.

And his grave also, the man who looks after, the last time we went, he came to tell me, he said, Auntie auntie, *banyak orang tanya tau, ini siapa punya kubur, tau. Saya bilang, nama ada situ, tengok,* lah. He said, No, they said, *Kita selalu datang tengok, kubur macam ada cahaya,* meaning it shines. The grave shines. There are some people who come and visit their relatives there, and even those who walk, and always they ask the man there. And he says, *Nama ada situ, tengok,* lah. Haji Mohamed Siraj. It shines. I said, Yah, because the man under there is a good man. Life must go on. Life must go on.

> In the name of Allah, the Compassionate, the Merciful.
> By those who drag forth to destruction,
> By the meteors rushing,
> By the lone stars floating,
> By the angels hastening,
> And those who govern the event,
> On the day when the first trump resoundeth
> And the second followeth it,
> On that day hearts beat painfully
> While our eyes are downcast
> Now they are saying: Shall we really be restored to our first state
> Even after we are crumbled bones?
> Then say: Then that would be a vain proceeding.
> Surely it will need but one shout,
> And lo! they will be awakened…

So when he was coming back from work he used to come. He was friendly with my brother, but he was more friendly with my brother-in-law. So he will come, knock the door. Why? Give *paan*…the betel. So whoever knocks the door he will give. And always, it was wartime, we cannot have bright lights, so we used to have dim, we put the cloth around. Then one day, I went to open the door—you see how God, God's this-thing—I opened the door, took the *paan.* My hand touched his hand, just like that, and then he went off. And it was from that, donno how, it's God's this-thing.

I was seventeen, eighteen when I opened the door. Just gave the *paan,* nothing, no talk, nothing. Just our fingers touched, like that. What else you want to know? What else you want to know?

George Yepes. *La Pistola y El Corazón*
(The Pistól and The Heart). 2000.
Oil on canvas. Photograph by John White.

from *The Real Life Test*

The transgender inmate Irene—*née* John Adams—landed on my psych caseload like a sack of dirty clothing no one else had time to launder. Driving to the prison for another intake interview, I remembered with a shiver Irene's unwavering dark-eyed stare. I felt sure I would get nothing more from her. The muscle-bound prison guard who stopped me at D gate told me "John" had asked to go to the weekly AA meeting and that I would find "him" in the chapel. The guard had a rough, beery-red face. I wondered if he attended AA meetings himself.

I walked as slowly as I could to the chapel, holding my breath against the pervasive stink of old cigarettes, body odor, and industrial coffee. Prison funk. The night before, I had drunk too much wine, and now every slamming gate and jangling key rang directly through my brain. Two skull-capped inmates walked by, one clutching an old basketball, and I involuntarily loosened my sweater. I am small breasted and angular and rarely elicit more than passing attention, but I felt unusually fragile that morning. I watched the two pass through the gate to the edge of the yard, and the basketball court soon echoed with the thump of the ball and the shouts of the men.

No one turned around when I slipped into the chapel. It was a small meeting: nine or ten men sipping their coffee and rattling their knees. Boo James was telling his story, which had something to do with a horse he had let die the year he wrangled in Colorado. I would have bet that he'd never left Washington State, that the whole story had been garnered from movies and other cons, but his tears and regret seemed real enough, and one or two of the other men passed a hand over their eyes at each turn of the tale. *I come out to the stable that morning, and Blue Bonnet was just a lyin' on her side pantin' like, and her water was gone dry.* Listening to the tense, pliant note in his voice, I was sure Boo had killed something while drinking—if not a horse, then a wife or a child in a car accident—or perhaps he had set fire to an entire office building with a lit cigarette, a crime that had never been discovered. Boo finished with a flourish and mimicked throwing down the reins.

He sat down in the first row of benches, and the man next to him, whose tattoos made him look as if he wore a long-sleeved green shirt, patted Boo carefully on the shoulder and offered his coffee. Boo took a sip. Instantly, he was composed again, his prison "mask" sliding over his face.

The twelve-step meetings at Twin Streams were always well attended, and there was an infinite variety to attend. There was AA and NA and Smokers' Anon and Cocaine Anon and Al-Anon and Gamblers Anon. I wouldn't have been surprised to come across Molesters Anon or a twelve-step sexual-assault program. At any given time, someone at the Streams was announcing his name and the fact that he was powerless before something higher. You asked forgiveness of everyone and everything, and then you forgave yourself for being weak and human. I would often come across inmates who used the terminology like weapons: "owning" their anger, "mounting" the steps.

Another inmate, Jim the Can, rose and took the podium. His hair had the stiff, greasy look of pomade combined with dirt, and his left eye wandered over the sharp bridge of his red nose, but he was an eloquent speaker. He held his audience so tightly that when an alarm sounded down the tier, no one turned around.

I was alone all my life. I was alone with my bro who raised me, and I was alone with my wife. The night she had my son, I was watching a football game at home with five six-packs around me. Yeah, by then I was too much of a drunk to even go to a bar. Yeah, by then I was just drinking at home, and fuck, I'm grateful for that—never killed no one with my car! But Angela hadda spend the food money on my beer. I made her do that even when she was carrying the kid. She lived on beans during that time and the boy don't digest food too good and cries half the night even though he's four. But I couldn't help myself. It was me and my booze. My only friend. No, I didn't know nothing but enough beer to make it through the afternoon. When I went into the gas station, I didn't wanna hurt nobody. I just wanted enough to buy liquor for the week.

The men nodded their heads and smiled sadly. One day they would all be released and again find alcohol readily available; usually, they started guzzling the hour they left the grounds. It was hard to tell how much credit their sobriety deserved.

Watching Boo and Jim the Can hold their audience captive made me want to forget Irene and return to the sanctuary of my office. I sat on a back pew and concentrated on steadying my breathing, a trick I had learned in my earliest days as a prison psychologist. Despite the years I'd been inside, the inmates sometimes had an effect on me, a lingering feeling of disdain followed by an impatience whose cause I could not quite identify. I think now that my impatience was driven by jealousy. I was not an alcoholic or a gambler or a drug addict. I was not transgender or abused. I could not go up to any podium and announce myself. There was no group that would freely offer me help and support and compassion. I felt lonely at the meetings I observed. I felt cast aside because whatever it was that drove me, it was not something I could explain to others like me. I felt cheated that I had made it through my life without a circle of people applauding my progress. Why should Jim the Can be applauded for the utter mess he had made of his life? Why should such a sad-sack loser receive a second chance at getting it right?

I glanced around until my gaze alighted upon Irene sitting in a corner pew. Flexing a lean, muscled arm, she was holding a waxed cup of coffee without drinking it. The dim light sculpted her face. There was nothing feminine in her features, but the compelling curve of her cheekbones and jawline suggested a beauty that defied gender.

When Jim the Can sat down again, Irene did not look up and murmur with the rest of them. Her strange, dark eyes were still. Sure that at any moment she would rise, I could not move from the pew, and for the first time in years, my deep breathing did not calm me. But Bennie Bickle rose quickly as Jim the Can sat. He was the coordinator of many of the meetings, a former Hell's Angel and trucker, a righteous con who had been jailed since the early eighties, out only long enough to father, with a Cherokee woman, a little girl whose name, he told me with eager pride, was Small Heart.

"I see new faces here," he said. "I see some wise people who want to deal, and we want to help you deal. There are people in the world who won't see what a brave step you're taking by being in this room. But we see, bro. We understand."

The only new face was Irene's. She seemed barely conscious of Bennie's hoarse voice being directed toward her. I willed her to get up, and after a moment or two she did. The group of men turned toward her like trees caught in a sudden wind. According to custom, she would say her name, and I was curious which name—John? Irene?—she would use. I should have known she'd ignore the customs.

"I'm not an alcoholic," she said softly.

The confusion in the room was palpable. The feeling spread from man to man as if someone had said the word *denial*. They leaned back, steadied by a familiar expectation of hubris.

"My parents drank," she said. "I think they drank because they liked the lines a little blurred. I mean, isn't it true that drinking makes things seem more possible?"

The question lingered in the air for a moment before it dissolved. The corrections officer sitting in on the meeting craned his neck. He was young and new, and he sat very straight in his chair and fiddled with his walkie-talkie. He gave Irene a narrow look.

"Alcohol makes you dreamy. It makes everything seem less important."

The men began to nod again as if she was approaching the right location, the turn in the road that would make them understand her direction.

"I don't know if that's a bad thing," Irene continued.

I could feel my hangover against my temples, pounding and reshaping into something larger and more difficult to ignore.

"What else do you have in here but dreams? Tell me. What is it that gets you through the nights in lockdown when all you hear is some punk getting beaten down the block and your cellie snoring like nothing bothers him? Isn't it dreaming about your woman that gets you through? It's all a dream. She's gone. She's riding the back of another bike. She isn't waiting for you. Maybe it never happened at all. Maybe outside is the dream." The men stopped nodding and looked to Bennie Bickle for direction. He flattened his palms. AA had no rules for sharing. There was no violation he could cite to stop this particular transaction.

"The last time I drank was the night she left me." Irene's voice was slow and heavy, as if she carried the weight of all the men's disappointments. "Later I was with Charlotte, at the river, with sand in my mouth. But before that, Irene left me. The real Irene."

The CO began to shift on the bench. His beeper went off a moment later, and without taking his eyes from Irene, he raised the device to his face and pressed the button, rendering it silent.

I stood involuntarily and made my way to the back of the chapel, leaning against the steel doors. I thought about the shapelessness of lives. You might, as a therapist, listen to one story after another about decadence and love and abuse and self-disgust, but the stories will not lead to conclusions. There is only the desire for narrative.

"We had a lot of alcohol that night. We drank a six-pack and then a bottle of rum—dark rum, the Jamaican kind. The river was shadowy. Some people were scared of the river at night. Some people were scared of the bridge, afraid they would lose their footing or jump—jump because it seemed so easy to swim the Irish Bayou, but it wasn't." Irene pulled her thick, damp hair out of the cord holding it back and let it fall around her face. She was like a female animal in that den of men. The way she arched her back emphasized her small breasts, and the denim shirt she wore began to darken against her shoulders. Even her voice changed to a sweeter rhythm. I felt myself sway slightly with her words, as though she was leading a pulpit. I wanted to enter the river with her and let my sins wash away—to be born again in the murky, snake-infested waters of the Louisiana coast.

"After we drank," she continued, "I was in love with the rum and the bridge, and I walked along the edge as sure footed as I'd ever been." She raised her arms and put her feet together as if the center of the room was a tightrope, her small hips shifting from side to side. "It was going to storm, and the storms on the river were big. I'd forgotten I wasn't alone. Irene was with me. We had to go back right away, or we'd be caught out there naked and liquorless for the rest of the night."

The men behaved as one unit, keening with understanding. Irene would be caught driving drunk. She would be naked. She would be taken to a jail cell, or she would beat up the lover with her, or they would find a gun. Here all her troubles would begin.

She waved her hands like a preacher on the mount, and from a great distance I heard the buzzer down the tier that meant it was time for the count. The CO rose up from the bench and sat down again as if he could not bear to miss the end of the story.

"So, drunk as we were, we found the car keys and started the ignition. The Irish bridge is ten miles long. Ten miles I pretended to be alone with the rain coming and the winds getting stronger and the tailgate of the truck flying up and down as if the end were coming—not of the rain but the world itself. And it was, it was. The bridge smelled of old rainstorms that had come and gone but left themselves on the sand, and I could smell the souls that had jumped into the river and sailed empty up the lagoon."

By now I had closed my eyes and tried to smell the river with her. The chapel was so quiet that I could scarcely hear the men breathe. Only Tiny with his asthma could be heard: hushed little gasps coming from his sad and narrow chest.

"I jumped from the truck the minute I got to the house, where the road turned. I left it running. I knew what had happened. I knew. I let her leave me. I don't know why. It was like her skin was my skin and I got in the door and my clothes dripped and all the lights were on. *Where is she,* I said, *where is she. Gone,* they said, *gone, gone.* All her things neat and in their places. She had walked away in the night, in the storm, over the ten-mile bridge, and if I hadn't been full of rum and sex I may have seen her go—I might have stopped her—"

The noise down the tier began to gather and swell. It was a wave of names that moved along through each tier, traveling from B block to D, alighting on F, and landing at C. The count. The men jumped from their places, their eyes hardening from alcohol survivor to con in seconds. Irene walked off the podium gracefully, as if she meant to end at this point. I walked up from the back of the chapel, and she smiled at me as if she was waking from a dream.

"We have a second intake," I said. The words felt foolish in my mouth, but she nodded.

"Guess I'll meet you back *home,*" she said. She held her arms out to the CO standing beside her. Since she was in protective custody and had not yet been released into the mainline population, her hands were slipped into cuffs and carefully attached to the bored young guard. He walked from the room with unconscious precision, as if he carried a burden more precious than he imagined.

"You are the first person," Irene said when she had settled in her cell again, "to truly remind me of Charlotte Val." She stopped as if such a phrase was self-explanatory. She had resumed our conversation as if no time had passed since our last. It was somehow charming: it made me feel remembered, chosen, as if I had remained on her mind.

I sat on the cement stool outside her holding cell. Irene had compared me to the woman she allegedly had murdered.

"That was quite a share," I said a little dryly, "for someone who isn't an alcoholic. If you aren't, why were you in there?"

Irene ducked her head. "Something to do."

"Are you practicing for Jerry Springer?"

She let out the deep chuckle I would come to treasure for its rarity. "I guess I wanted to talk."

"You want to talk, but not in group?"

"No, not in that group." She flexed the muscles of her arm. "Hope I don't lose all my strength in here."

"That isn't your biggest problem," I said.

She nodded.

"You said you aren't the real Irene. Who is the real Irene?"

"I'd best start with Charlotte Val," Irene said. She had also ended with her, but I let her go on. I was embarrassingly curious how Charlotte Val and I were connected.

"She lived on the river. They were real swamp trash, her family. Guess you wouldn't ever have crabbed? Well, the way to crab is to bait a wire basket with fish, drop it into the river, and pull it up full. Charlotte's family were life-long crabbers. Full surname: Valerie. She saw *Now, Voyager,* that movie with Bette Davis. It was the name of some character, Charlotte Val, so that's what she was called."

"Vale," I corrected. I forgot for a moment we were discussing a dead woman. I was cavalier after my years working inside, but the fate of Charlotte came back to me with a shudder.

Irene laughed. "Well, that was Charlotte to get it a little mixed up. Had some Creole in her, even if you couldn't see it. They had a little stand by the Irish bridge and sold crabs by the dozen. Poor white trash. Broke as a man without change for the bus. Sometimes you'd look out on the river and see Charlotte's brothers knee deep in traps. They all looked Creole, opposite of her: dark and thin-boned and exactly alike. Sometimes a girl would go out with one, and then another, and back and forth like they were just one person. Even their girlfriends couldn't tell the difference between them, I think." Irene extended a hand and put it up to the webbed wire and brushed my palm. The warmth ran through me. "Charlotte started to crab with them when she was about fifteen. I'd see her out there in waders. There's nothing sexier than a girl in waders, 'specially the kind that ride up over the hips like suspenders. Bathing suit top and waders. That's all. I'd go out by the weeds and help her pull her waders on. She told me how she liked the smell of rubber, the feel of it against her bare legs. She had a squeaky sort of voice and the kind of skin that had lines from the sun from when she was a kid. And her eyes were the purest blue. I was always hard by the time she adjusted the straps, hard just looking at her."

Irene never took her eyes off me. I felt her words linger, waiting for me to snap on them like crabs on the fish bait.

"She let me kiss her before she pulled on her boots, so she could wrap her ankles around mine like a tongue. That girl had breasts so knobby looking, I couldn't believe how soft they were when I touched them."

I realized I had been listening with my eyes closed. I opened them. It was cold in the block. They turned off the heat at 4 P.M. I had been there for an hour at least.

"By the time she was seventeen, the family went bust again. No crabs for one year. All the boys drifted off somewhere: one drove a truck, I remember. One drank himself in, and one worked for the law. Ran into that last one a long time later."

"And Charlotte Val?"

"Charlotte. Well, I wasn't the only one to help with her waders."

"I see."

"That was way after we found the diamonds."

"You found diamonds?"

"It happens. Things fall from boats. I once got the shock of my life when I pulled up a doll in a trap—thought it was a baby. Anyway, we were alone that day. There was a homecoming that afternoon, and all her brothers were on the football team. She opened up a trap and whistled for me. I knew it was real before she did. It was a bracelet, but too big somehow for a bracelet and too small for a necklace. We thought it was a rosary."

"An odd thing to find."

"Well, a lot of rich Catholics along the bayou had family heirlooms like that. Some of them dated back to the Civil War. People been known to dig them up—buried, you know, so the Yankees wouldn't find them. Course the families who weren't rich anymore couldn't sell them whole like that, and someone had begun to take this one apart. Couple of the stones were gone, and the chain was pried. We tested them on some glass and they cut, and later Charlotte took off her clothes and rolled in the diamonds."

I imagined a blonde woman naked on a shimmering bed, bleeding from her good fortune. I shook the thought away.

"But if that family found diamonds, why were they still so poor?"

"They didn't find them, *Charlotte* found them. We found them. There was a purse too. That's an important part. It was beaded and mangled yellow from the water, but there was almost a thousand dollars in the purse. In tens and fives, an awful lot of money then. Some folks didn't make a thousand dollars all year! I said someone is missing that money and that rosary pretty bad, and she said yes, someone was most likely praying for its return, and we laughed, thinking about it. The purse was probably just mad money for some rich woman riding one of the river cruises, and she probably wouldn't miss it much. That's what we decided anyway.

"We hitched to the city and bought drinks in every bar. There are a lot of bars in New Orleans. We bought rounds for everyone. We drank hurricanes and whiskey sours and threw the glasses out the window and watched them explode. We went to a dress shop and I picked her a black-velvet dress and stockings so fine that her legs were too rough for them, catching them a little. Some tiptoe heels with three little straps over the ankles. She walked in them like she had always owned shoes like that, like she didn't trudge around in rubber boots most of the time. She bought some rhinestone pins for her hair and looked like a lady-in-waiting for a princess, demure. She looked brand new in her black-velvet dress. It went down the back of her knees, covering all the scabby places, and dipped low over her shoulders so you could see the bones of her neck. You could cry because you wanted to touch those bones so bad. She was sheer muscle everywhere else. The only soft part of her was her breasts and her skin, like silk over the bone."

"And then?" I asked. Almost feeling Charlotte's dress on my own body, I perched on the very edge of the stool, close enough to smell Irene's musky, particular scent.

"Then she went to the best hotel in the Quarter and got a room. I had to wait for her. She looked like she belonged in that hotel and I didn't. I snuck in after she got the key. She didn't have trouble checking in alone like that, a young girl. I think she made the desk jockey believe she wanted him to knock on the door later. But it was me that knocked. And when she opened the door, I wouldn't let her talk. I took off her dress little by little, so slowly she whispered for me to hurry or bunch it above her waist, but I wouldn't. I undid the back and all the buttons. I still remember all those buttons: dozens of tiny hooks and buttons. She wasn't wearing any underwear—she never wore any—and every time I undid a button, I found another place on her body that was hers and then mine: a mole, a freckle, a little red bump on her spine. I ran my mouth down her spine, and she tasted a little salty, like the river. Finally, I slid off the last bit of black velvet from her feet, and we landed on that too big bed in that expensive hotel where they left a bottle of chilled champagne on the dresser. Spanish champagne."

Irene stopped and squared her wide shoulders.

"You had sex. Then what happened?"

Suddenly she looked angry, her strange eyes narrowing to slits. "No." Drawing back, she rolled up a bit of paper and put it in the corner of her mouth as if trying to calm herself. "Funny thing how paper is almost as good as a smoke sometimes. Thing is, it's just the reflex you crave. I can see you're trying to quit smoking."

"I *have* quit smoking."

"You still have that hungry look. Like a fat Pekinese watching a bag of potato chips."

I couldn't help laughing. "Why, thank you. I don't think I've ever been compared to a Pekinese before. So you got on the bed with that girl after undressing her and you didn't have intercourse? Why? Birth control?"

"Other reasons."

"What sort of reasons?"

Irene looked as if she was weighing how much to reveal. "She was displeased with me, you might say."

"What did you do to cause her displeasure?"

"I used the wrong name at the right time."

"I see. That would do it, I suppose."

"No, you don't see. How can I say this? Even with those fine things off and her body all long angles and silk…she wasn't the one I wished she was. She knew it and I knew it, and there wasn't much more to say beyond that. I'll never forget the way she looked at me. Like I was the last rung, and the ladder went nowhere—that's how she looked at me. Someone looks at you like that, they burn into your memory forever."

I nodded. "What happened then?"

"It was early, so we curled up and went to sleep, and later I found we'd spent every penny. Except for those diamonds. That was how Charlotte Val was: she didn't care a hoot that we'd spent a year's pay on one good time in the Quarter. She laughed about it, just laughed. She even left that velvet dress on the hotel floor, said she'd never have reason to wear it again."

"What happened to the diamonds?"

"We were still drunk when we got back to the Irish Bayou. Got a ride with a sad-looking woman with a baby bundled up. Charlotte handed one of the diamonds to her. I wouldn't let her give away any more, even when she said that they'd be bad luck, that the owner had drowned. But I don't think that was why she wanted to give them away."

"Why then?"

"She didn't think she could live up to those diamonds. She'd have to be the girl who found a fortune. That made her afraid. Took her feet off the ground."

"But she could have given them to her family—you said they went broke, they were so poor."

"They were. She didn't like any of them much, though. She knew her brothers would fight, and her daddy would drink up the money. She always wanted to bury everything special about her." Irene stood up and paced a moment. "It was because she wouldn't grab on to chance. She avoided her future. Her fate." Irene put her palm up to the webbing again. One of her fingertips grazed mine.

I did not ask what she meant. "Do you feel angry remembering Charlotte? Do you feel Charlotte Val rejected you?"

"She didn't reject me."

Just then Little Steve walked by, shackled and probably on his way to the Hole. He was known for his loud voice and bad knees. This time he got shanked for winning big at the tier's poker table, possibly cheating. He was OK, though. As he sauntered by, he waved: a tiny tip of his fingers that said, They got me, but I got my dignity.

"Did she say anything upsetting?" I asked. "Did she tell you you weren't a man?"

"But I'm not a man," Irene said easily. "Didn't take Charlotte Val to tell me that." I felt oddly disappointed in her response. She pulled a cigarette out of a pack from her shirt pocket and left it unlit, never taking her eyes from mine. The shirt was loose, and I could make out the dark area around her nipple.

"Did she feel you were the wrong gender?"

Irene contemplated my question with lowered eyes. "She knew I *wasn't* a woman. Even getting the right parts won't do that. She knew I just felt like I was…myself."

"Did you…did you ever feel sexually attracted to men?"

This time she smiled her crooked smile and smoothed back her hair. "I don't look at it that way," she said. "I'm attracted to some *people,* but not to other *people.*"

"I see." Something told me not to press further.

"What do you think the difference is?" she asked. "Between boy and girl—parts aside, I mean?"

"I believe gender is a continuum—"

"No, I mean: who cares? Why does everyone care so much?"

"If you feel this way, then why is it important for you to have a sex change? You said in your first intake that you want me to approve your sex change, for me to sign off on your real life test." All trannies need to live two years in the opposite gender, then find two therapists who agree that a change is necessary for mental health. This was politically tricky in prisons, and I hadn't signed off on too many of them. I sensed Irene knew this.

There was an odd expression on Irene's face, as if she was forcing herself to hide something from me, the way a mother will hide her fear from a child. "Charlotte told me I would never change." She rubbed her arms as if she had turned cold. "That's what she said." Irene's pale face turned fully toward me, like a flower opening all its petals. "It was the only thing she could say that would have hurt me."

"Why did it hurt?"

"Because she knew I wanted to change. I wanted to be someone who could change."

A small, nagging reason to kill a woman: if the man wanted only to be in that carelessly feminine form. "You can change," I said. "Everyone can change."

Irene shrugged. "I don't guess that's always true."

A few gates slammed. I had been in the block too long, and I hated fumbling for my own set of keys and codes so that I could get outside again. "We can continue this tomorrow," I said. I rose and picked up my tape recorder, then I switched it off and turned back to her.

"One more thing. What name did you call out with Charlotte Val?"

"My own name," Irene said, surprised. "Irene," she said, and she gathered her fingers gracefully into her palm and opened them again, as if her hands were birds released into the darkening light.

Wayne Alaniz Healy. *Pre-game Warm Up.*
2001. Acrylic on canvas.
Photograph by Peggy Tennison.

A Bar Mitzvah Boy

On a Sunday morning two weeks before Easter, there I was, Joey Santiago, in the kitchen cooking my favorite food: bacon. Ten strips of the crackling pig, equally spaced and lined up majestically in a black iron skillet. Three for my sister, three for my brother, and four—yeah, that's right, four—for me because *I* had to endure dancing around the hot, oily grease pops.

It was only a few minutes before the sugary, hickory-smoked smell wafted out of the kitchen and down the hallway, drawing my siblings out of their respective rooms. They soon appeared, rubbing their eyes, scratching their bellies.

"Oh. Good. Bacon."

Wesley's deadpan expression hardly hid the excitement he felt at the prospect of a crunchy bacon sandwich made with two untoasted pieces of spongy white bread.

"OK. So where's Mom?" asked Lu, sensing that something was not quite right in our world.

Although mildly annoyed—probably because she woke up that way— our older sister was in no way going to pass on the bacon offering. True, she could be a bitch, but we really had little choice but to look up to her. After all, she could go on for hours discussing the finer points of the guitar-playing skills of the various axemen of the Rolling Stones, from Brian Jones to Keith Richards to Mick Taylor. And she shared liberally the groupie stories she knew about the Stones: the apocryphal, the documented, and the wildly imagined. I'd been particularly awed by the alleged Mounds-bar incident, though I'll admit I really hadn't a clue as to what it all meant. You see, there was this reverential aura around my sister when she related a story, and that is probably what most impressed me. Still, I wondered, *Why all the fuss over a rock star eating a candy bar?*

Wesley didn't care much about any of that. It was 1974, and he was still secretly going through his David Cassidy phase. He felt no great desire to share this infatuation with his older sibs. Early in life, he had developed a facility for putting on a calm demeanor, one that almost always succeeded in unnerving Lu because the blank stillness framing his face convinced her that he was holding back on something, that he wasn't letting go of some crucial bit of dirt, dish, or data, which it was her right—as the *panganay,* the eldest sibling—to know about.

Strategically positioned right there in the middle of the Santiago family pecking order, I'd determined that my older sister and younger brother had an intangible, mystical *something* about them. While Lu tended to be too ready and willing to bask in her verbal glory, little Wesley was quietly content to work his wonderfully restrained mojo. Lu enjoyed nothing more than holding court, dazzling an audience with her witticisms or diatribes, then reveling in the impact the words had on her listeners. Wesley steered a gentler course, cutting a swath for himself that was way too self-assured for someone his age. Thinking about this stuff was often a bother to me, but I felt like I had the chops to sort it out. On this Sunday morning, however, I had more mundane matters on my mind: our upcoming, first-ever trip to the Philippines; the cute Jewish girl in my advanced-English class; and my ongoing project, which was to survive the seventh grade with all of my faculties intact.

"All right, it's obvious that our mother is off attending another conference," Lu said. She wanted to take charge. "And what, lo, is left in the pantry for sustenance? Let me guess: bacon, yes, there *will* be plenty of that, and—"

"Tuna," Wes and I chimed in, almost in harmony.

"That's right, my brothers: tuna fish. Solid white. Canned. Not exactly my idea of a rock-'n'-roll diet," Lu said.

Wes was, without a doubt, into the bacon thing, and he knew full well that I could slap together a tasty tuna-melt sandwich, but this limited-diet possibility he didn't like. His sphinx-like face tightened for an instant, betraying his anxiety. "But," he said slowly, "then who's gonna make the rice?"

"Wes, it's OK, she's only gonna be gone for two weeks," I assured him. I hated to see a crack in the sphinx's countenance. "Don't worry, this bacon's *kosher.*"

Lu shot me a precise, poisoned-dart look. She rested a gentle hand on Wesley's shoulder. "How can you think of rice at a time like this? This is our chance to free ourselves, if only for a while, from the tyranny of rice and all other Filipino food! Can you tell me that you actually *like* the pig's blood stew? Or that awful shrimp paste?"

"I happen to like rice, Lu. So does Joey."

Ignoring him, Lu continued. "Remember that time, Wes, it was late at night, Mom wasn't home as usual, we had just finished watching *Rosemary's Baby* on Channel 7, and you went upstairs to the kitchen 'cause you were hungry. You opened the fridge and you found that huge tongue staring you in the face. You fainted, passed out cold."

Wesley, the boy-sphinx, was now doing his stone-faced best to make like nobody else in the world existed but him. When he stared like that, you'd swear he could see through walls. Lu and I had grown accustomed to his traveling to this zone.

"Right. Well, he's off. As I was saying, that tongue—the one that knocked our little Wesley out cold way back when, and the memory of which has apparently now sent him on a little mind-space travel jaunt—oh man, that tongue. It's the ultimate rock-'n'-roll symbol, the actual logo of the Rolling Stones! Joey, it was a vision, right there in our refrigerator, making its first appearance just around the time they released *Sticky Fingers,* or was it *Exile on Main Street?*"

I began to sense, with some trepidation, the excitement mounting in Lu. I was afraid that she'd begin rummaging through her closets for her favorite concert accessories: a big, floppy, purple hat and a green feather boa, which she'd wear like a scarf.

"What does this have to do with not eating Filipino food for a while? Or Wesley's concern about who's going to cook rice? Or, for that matter, the merits of kosher bacon?"

That did it. Snapped her right out of it. I was relieved that she didn't get a chance to launch into her theories on the mysterious death of Brian Jones.

"The bacon is *kosher?* For godsakes, Joey, we're Filipino. Remember? *No* part of a pig can be kosher."

"But you just said that it's a good time to free ourselves from rice and all that. What about kosher hot dogs?"

Although Lu was on her way to becoming a bona fide rock-'n'-roll groupie hippie-chick, she could still put on, when necessary, a wide-eyed, authoritative expression that meant "I am your older sister and I know what's right and what isn't."

I was not going to be deterred. "Mandy Goodman's having her bat mitzvah next weekend, and next month Bobby Cohen's having *his* bar mitzvah. They told me they were each gonna make a few thousand at their party. So I've been practicing 'cause I've been thinking about having a bar mitzvah myself. *Barukh atah…*"

"Joey, stop it." Lu looked at the kitchen clock on the wall next to the fridge. "In less than an hour, your ride is coming to take you to catechism class. Do you understand what I am telling you?"

"Yeah, so I was born Catholic."

"Jews have bar mitzvahs; Catholics have confirmations."

"Yeah, and where is that gonna lead us all?"

"You can't be serious about the money thing, Joey."

Just then, each of us turned toward Wesley, whom we expected to see still standing there, deeply engaged in his mind-space travel. But he'd left the room.

One's status as a seventh grader at Y.A. Tittle Middle School could rise or fall depending on the kind of sneakers one wore. I was obsessed with the new Puma Clydes, which had just hit the market that winter. Bobby Cohen was strictly an Adidas man, partial to the Superstar model, fashioned in white leather and trimmed with three, black-plastic stripes.

The kids who played three-on-three hoops at the schoolyard every afternoon were in two sharply delineated camps: the Walt "Clyde" Frazier side and the "Pistol" Pete Maravich group. Clyde, of course, was the silky point guard of the New York Knicks, the sartorially splendid protopimp, chauffeured around Gotham City in his silver Rolls Royce. He was the black urban prince of New York City B-ball. The media had nicknamed Frazier after real-life gangster Clyde Barrow, and Puma had named its shoe after Frazier. Clyde was my man.

If Clyde's playing style exemplified an icy-veined, cool control, Pistol Pete's mop-topped, floppy-socked appearance and willingness to shoot the ball from any and all angles of the court dazzled his fans. And of the many kids who idolized and tried to emulate Pete Maravich around the Tittle schoolyard, Bobby Cohen had best mastered the moves—bounce passes between the legs, wild, 360-degree drives to the basket—and the look, from the lank bangs covering his eyes down to his Adidas Superstar sneakers. Bobby and I would debate endlessly who the better ballplayer was: Clyde or Pistol Pete. We'd talk smack for days, arguing about which of our heroes flashed more style or wore better shoes. When we played one-on-one, I could usually take Bobby in a game-to-twenty. Bobby'd always be going nuts—trying crazy hot-dog moves that made our friends go *ooh* and *aah*—and lose simply because he could not consistently put the ball in the hole.

One day music practice had let out, and Wesley approached us just as I'd won my third straight game-to-twenty. Rarely the gracious loser, Bobby had but one recourse: attack the Puma Clydes.

"Who do you think you are, wearing those things today? You've been going on idiotically about how you weren't going to wear them so that they'd still look new when you went to the Philippines. Look at 'em. They look like clodhoppers on you."

"Hey, Wes, how was rehearsal? I know: you've come for a ride in Joey's new boats, right?"

This, of course, went right over Wesley's head. Wes wasn't looking too good just then. More than a week of no rice had left him rather pale and lacking in the strength to make it through daily three-hour band practices. The responsibility of playing first violin in the school's production of *Fiddler on the Roof* was also taking its toll. He wanted nothing more than to go home and stare at a wall for a while. But Bobby was relentless.

"You guys crack me up. You're the only Filipino family I know who wishes they were Jewish. This one with the fiddle, playing 'If I Were a Rich Man,' and that one with notions of having a bar mitzvah."

"What are you talking about?" I shot back. "Every year *you* tell me that your family celebrates Hanukkah and Christmas just so you can get more gifts."

"Yeah, right," countered Bobby. Then, throwing overhand, he pegged me in the chest with the basketball.

At that moment, two figures walking down a steep, narrow path coming out of the woods at the side of the ivy-covered brick school building caught Bobby's eye. I followed my friend's gaze. It was a cold, raw, early-March afternoon. Thick streams of breath were blowing out of the mouths of my classmates, both girls, as they puffed down the hill. It was Mandy Goodman, my advanced-English crush, with her arm around Tillie Tisdale's shoulder, kind of supporting her and helping her walk. Tillie was sniffling, and her cheeks were impossibly red.

Mandy cupped Tille's elbow and placed her mittened palm on her friend's back as she eased Tillie up the bus steps. Before boarding the bus herself, Mandy looked back at me and shouted, "Are you coming to my bat mitzvah on Saturday?!" As I was about to answer, the doors closed and I looked around for Bobby. He was over at the base of the path and was pumping his arms and fists in a giddy way, like a victorious athlete. Giggling and smelling his fingertips, Frankie Puetti came skipping down the path. When Puetti reached level ground, Bobby clapped him hard on the back, then grabbed Puetti's wrist and jerked it toward his own face, desperately trying to smell the fingers.

The following afternoon at the Tittle schoolyard, Bobby razzed me about the old, white high-top Chuck Taylors that I was wearing.

"So you're finally wising up, Santiago. Wouldn't want to wear the Pumas, might get soiled. And you're leaving soon for the Philippines. It's almost Passover, when we go on spring vacation."

"You mean it's almost Easter. We get a break for Holy Week. That's why we're going to the Philippines."

Ignoring me, Bobby said, "Are you ready to have your ass kicked in a game of one-on-one?"

"Let's just play twenty-one."

"Why are you such a pussy, Santiago?"

"Hey, Bobby, what happened yesterday between Puetti and Tillie?"

"Why don't you ask your girl—Mandy Goodman?" Bobby bared his fangs. "You know, that's why they chose *you* to go on that TV show with her. Remember that, last fall? *The Big Blue Marble*—that silly show about all people from all cultures and all races living together in one world. They chose Mandy Goodman 'cause she's the prettiest and smartest girl in school."

"What are you talking about, asshole?"

"*You* were probably thinking that they chose you on account of you're foreign and they wanted to give different people a chance. But that's not it.

Remember how you and Mandy had that limo pick you up to drive you to the city? It's 'cause they knew that you were such a fucking pussy. They chose you because they figured that you're the only one who wouldn't try to do anything."

"Try to do what?"

"Try to do anything. With Mandy."

For the first two days and nights that we were in the Philippines, Lu, Wes, and I were always together, dutifully going to another family reunion at another *tita*'s house every afternoon and evening. But once Lu discovered The Hobbit House, a blues club in Malate, Wes and I rarely saw her. She became obsessed with a twenty-one-year-old Filipino rocker whose stage name was Pepe Longstocking and who was the lead singer for a popular Manila band called Juan Tamad. Luckily for Lu, we had a cousin her age who wanted to emulate her in every way. This cousin, who had the misfortune of being nicknamed Ninny, wanted to talk like Lu, dress like Lu, walk like Lu, and smoke like Lu. For four consecutive nights, Ninny drove the two of them, in her pristinely conditioned orange Volkswagen Beetle, to the blues club to check out Pepe and Juan Tamad.

At The Hobbit House, Lu was in her element. Juan Tamad's specialty was playing Rolling Stones covers, and the Filipino regulars at the club were charmed by Lu. Sure, they'd seen scores of American seamen on leave from the naval base in Subic: rowdy boys on the prowl who were looking for another beer joint where they could leave their piss marks. But a pretty, loud, laughing American hippie girl who by all outward appearances seemed as Filipino as their own sisters? Now that was a rare sight in Manila. If she toned down the Western twang when she spoke, Lu could pass for a *tibak,* a student activist, from the University of the Philippines, and that endeared her to them all the more.

Lu enjoyed the attention. At the beginning of each set, there she was, the only person standing, poised in front of the stage and anticipating the moment when the rhythm guitarist would bang out the first two jangling chords of "Brown Sugar," the band's trademark opener. Lu's whole being lit up at that charged moment. She would do her dance twirl with arms aloft, fingers lithely carving the air, and look up, smiling and bright eyed, at front man Pepe, cheering him on without realizing that she was revving up the entire club.

Meanwhile, Wes and I had our own adventures in Manila. We tried to play pool in a beer joint near a *tita*'s house. This was our first little victory in Manila: not being thrown out of the place for being underage. For a couple of pre-adolescent boys, Wes and I were passable pool players. What we found truly challenging was shooting on a plywood billiard table with no felt top. During a game, I struck up a friendship with a couple of local kids who looked a little older than we were.

The more outgoing of the two said to me, "We have the same name almost. Mine is spelled with an *h: J-h-o-e-l.* But you just call me Jhoel."

"Do you want to drink some Coke?" I offered.

"We like Fanta."

Jhoel could see that I didn't understand, so he continued, "Orange drink, Fanta. It's like orange soft drink."

I was eager to have an authentic Philippine experience, so I walked over to the concession counter and dug out a crumpled five-peso bill for two orange sodas in tall, clear bottles. I kept an eye on my brother while I waited for the drinks.

Addressing Wesley, Jhoel asked, "Do you like basketball?"

"Joey's a better basketball player than me."

"We can bring you to a place to play. It's just there near the school. *Malapit lang.*"

"Me and Joey bought a new basketball from Jupiter drugstore. But it's made of rubber."

"OK *lang yan.* Your brother Joey's wearing nice shoes. It's made of suede," said Jhoel, smiling. Then he turned to his quiet friend and said, *"Pare, porma lang."* The quiet kid let out a cackling, cocky laugh.

Unperturbed by what might have been a joke at our expense, Wesley marched on. "Joey's favorite player is Walt Frazier. He used to be on the Knicks before he got traded, and he was the *baddest* player in New York."

The quiet kid laughed again, and Jhoel said, "If he's a bad player, why does your brother root for him?"

"No, he's bad, meaning good."

When I came back with the drinks, I wasn't too happy about Wesley's unusually talkative state.

"Joey, we're gonna play basketball this afternoon. We can use the new ball," Wes said to me.

"That's good, Wes, that's real good." I eyed Jhoel warily. "Yeah, we can play for a little while, but we have to go to our uncle's later."

We played two-on-two to twenty. Wesley hit his first five shots, all from no more than ten feet out, positively giddy with the thrill of running around on an unfamiliar court. The banana trees, the strangely yellow sky, the acrid smells seemed not to faze him one bit.

I felt tight while we played, and to make things worse, I couldn't find my footing. I kept slipping and skidding on the slick cement surface of the court, which had a drab green sheen to it. The odd sound of the basketball slapping the cement and then echoing threw me off balance. I had a welcome moment of lucidity when I was able to isolate and identify the different sounds that had been bouncing around in my head: the *boing* of the ball being dribbled, the squeaking of our sneakers, an annoying *click-clack.* I laughed to myself when I realized that the last sound came from Jhoel and the quiet kid's *tsinelas,* the rubber slippers that we called flip-flops.

With new energy, Jhoel and the quiet kid got back into the game, eventually taking the lead. I felt fairly confident, however, that Wes and I had an advantage—perhaps our shoes. I took a perfect pass from Wes and drove to the basket for a lay-up. After the ball swished through the net, Jhoel held the bright-orange ball, wanting to break our rhythm.

"*Pare,* why are you crazy about Walt Frazier?" Jhoel asked.

I couldn't tell if he was teasing or taunting me. "Because he's smooth on the court, a really slick player."

"Slick player—I think you are a slick player. *'Tang inang* Walt Frazier. Is he the brother of Joe Frazier? *Pare,* Sonny Jaworski. *Yan ang* player. Jaworksi, *pare.*" I thought that Jhoel must be kidding around, singing the praises of an obscure Polish basketball player. Or was he making that stuff up? I don't know why, but I looked down and noted to myself with pride that nary a scratch or a scuff had marred my new sneakers. I called out to Jhoel with some force, "C'mon, gimme the ball. Game's not over."

"*Ano ka, Atenista? Coño* kid."

Wesley reacted like a safety valve, saying, "Don't forget about our uncle's, Joey. Maybe we should go soon."

Jhoel threw the ball hard, right into my stomach, knocking the wind out of me, but I recovered and dribbled quickly toward the basket. As I leapt, I clearly saw that I had a good shot at the rim. But then he moved in, elbowing me sharply in the ribs, while the quiet kid came from the opposite side, driving his shoulder into my side, just below the waist, so that I went sprawling to the ground. Jhoel caught the ball when it squirted from my hands, and then he walked up to Wes and handed it to him. "Here, *pare,* you take your new rubber basketball. *Umuwi na kayo.* Go home." Wes took the ball with two hands, but refused to glance up at Jhoel.

A yellow-and-green taxicab pulled up near the wooden-gated entrance to the basketball court. Lu flung open the door and leaned out, calling to us, "Hey, you guys, we're late!" Maybe she had gotten a new hairdo, or it could've been her sunglasses, but for a second there, I didn't recognize my sister at all.

MARK PANEK

from *Gaijin Yokozuna:*
A Biography of Chad Rowan

Editor's Note

   In 1988, Chad Rowan was an easygoing, eighteen-year-old part-Hawaiian living in rural Waimānalo, on the island of Oʻahu. At six-feet-eight, he'd played basketball in high school but was not inclined toward sports involving more aggressive physical contact. His mother later recalled that, when he first went to Japan to try his luck at *sumo,* "I didn't think he'd last, because to me, I didn't know if he was tough enough." In addition to being disadvantaged by his gentle nature, his body type was also wrong for *sumo.* "In a sport where a lower center of gravity and well-developed lower body is prized," said sports writer Ferd Lewis, "Rowan was a six-foot-eight giraffe among five-foot-eleven rhinos."

 Like most American kids, Rowan grew up knowing almost nothing about the national sport of Japan. But after being asked twice, he reluctantly allowed himself to be recruited to a *sumo beya* in Tokyo owned and led by a retired wrestler with the honorific name Azumazeki Oyakata. During a stellar professional career lasting from 1964 to 1984, Azumazeki Oyakata had competed under the name Takamiyama. He was born on Maui as Jesse Kuhaulua, was also of Hawaiian ancestry, and was the first foreign-born wrestler to win a major *sumo* tournament. By the time Rowan entered Kuhaulua's *sumo beya,* another recruit from Hawaiʻi, Salevaʻa Atisanoe was wrestling in the upper, salaried ranks under the name Konishiki. In addition, two lower-ranked wrestlers from Hawaiʻi, John Feleunga and Taylor Wylie, were training in the *sumo beya* that had recruited Chad.

 Rowan's introduction to the strict, hierarchical world of *sumo* was not auspicious, as this excerpt from *Gaijin Yokozuna,* Mark Panek's biography, makes vivid. Kuhaulua worried that he'd made a mistake by recruiting Rowan. "I remember the first time he put on a belt and wrestled. He didn't look very good," Kuahulua said. "Smaller people—a lot smaller people—were just throwing him around in practice." From this shaky beginning, Rowan transformed both his body and his character, using great mental discipline and an unparalleled work ethic. He rose through the ranks at a phenomenal pace. Within three years, he was in the elite, salaried ranks himself. Two years later, wrestling under the name Akebono ("dawn" in Japanese), Rowan had reached the rank of *yokozuna:* the pinnacle of *sumo.* Rowan was the first foreign-born wrestler ever to attain this rank and was only the sixty-fourth *yokozuna* in the history of the ancient, tradition-bound sport, the written records for which date back to eighth-century Japan. In 2001, Rowan retired from *sumo* at the age of thirty-two.

I remember getting on that plane very clearly. I remember that I had one Walkman, one tape, letters, pictures, and one set of clothes. I remember sitting in the back of the plane. Two of us were sitting in three seats. I was kind of surprised at that. I mean, I kind of felt good because it was going to be a long flight, and it was better to be comfortable. I remember sitting down and starting to feel real sad. I brought out a letter from my cousin that I really looked up to when I was growing up. He was about ten years older than I was. He gave me a letter, some pictures, and some other stuff. In his letter he gave me a dollar bill. He wrote that this dollar was supposed to be used only as my last dollar in this world. I still have that dollar up until today. I started crying. But I also remember the other sumo *wrestler telling me to take a good look outside because it would be my last look for a long time.*

Chad Rowan, journal entry

Most flights leave Honolulu for Japan in the morning, just after the trades have picked up and before waves of heat begin to shimmer above the tarmac. In winter, the air is so clear you can see the green points of inland mountains and, sometimes, neighbor islands more than a hundred miles away. The ocean never fails to look like something out of a tourist brochure, a perfect emerald green that darkens into the deepest blue. Shortly after taking off on flights to Japan, you can sometimes see whales playing in the sea below.

The landing approach into Tokyo is quite different. Through the plane's window, the city is almost always drab and gray. Thousands of flat-topped buildings, all similar in appearance, are crammed together and stretch out for miles from the city center. In winter, the surrounding rice paddies, the golf courses, and even the garish banners of Tokyo Disneyland look as if color forgot them.

Chad Rowan was going to Tokyo to make it big. This wasn't like getting recruited to play for the University of Hawai'i; his sponsors had paid for his plane ticket to Japan, like a pro team recruiting a star player. He had an escort on the trip, John Feleunga, who was already training in the *sumo beya* that had recruited him. Chad was now a professional athlete who would be fighting for big money, like the guys he saw on the Japanese TV station back home. Fighting like Konishiki, who had also been recruited from Hawai'i and now rode in limousines and stayed in hotel suites when he visited home.

As Chad emerged from customs, he found his new boss, Azumazeki Oyakata, waiting for him and John. Azumazeki Oyakata was easy to spot: he towered above the staff of the television crew that was there to record the arrival of the latest foreigner to take up Japan's national sport. In fact, the three huge wrestlers from Hawai'i dwarfed everyone in the crowded airport. It felt to Chad as though a sea of black hair and a loud babble filled the terminal.

He followed Boss outside into a blast of cold air—shocking for someone from the tropics—and into a waiting car. As they drove to Azumazeki Beya, Boss's *sumo*-training facility, Chad's head spun with the rapid chatter inside the car and the strangeness of what he saw outside. Sprawling across an area roughly the size of his entire home island of Oʻahu, Tokyo contained forty times the population. Men in long, dark coats and women bundled against the cold stood at street corners waiting to cross intersections that seemed to look exactly alike. Vehicles hurtled by on the wrong side of the highway, and construction disrupted the traffic flow on nearly every street. Rising above the confusion, brightly colored broadcast towers flashed their red lights into the twilight. And everywhere were more cars, more buildings, and more people.

After an hour, the car exited the freeway, then took a series of turns, crossed a big river, and stopped on a quiet, narrow street. Chad followed Boss into one of the buildings and down a dimly lit hallway, past a larger-than-life portrait of Boss painted during his fighting days, when he was known as Takamiyama, standing strong and apparently wearing only a kind of elaborate apron. A shout from down the hall startled Chad: five or six people barking out some kind of military greeting. A few wrestlers who were busy preparing the evening meal dropped what they were doing when they saw Boss and then bowed to him. He ignored the greeting and introduced the newest recruit to their ranks. Then he led Chad and the reporters upstairs, where they took off their shoes and stepped up into a large room with straw-mat floors and no furniture except for a television in the far corner. Still in a daze, Chad stood next to his boss and faced the television crew's lights. In his raspy voice, Boss translated questions directed at his young prospect. Chad remembered what his father had told him the night before he left for Japan: be humble; never brag or act big headed. Chad answered every question by repeating that he had come to Japan to work hard, follow instructions, and try his best.

When the television crew left, Boss went upstairs to his third-floor apartment, leaving Chad in the big room with twelve young men who ranged in age from fifteen to twenty-one. They also ranged in size, from surprisingly scrawny kids to the imposing, four-hundred-pound Samoans from Hawaiʻi, Taylor Wylie and John. Chad looked from one to the next as the other young wrestlers stared at him, sizing up the newcomer like a battle-seasoned army platoon eyeing an unlikely recruit. Each had his hair tied into a single knot and folded over, looking like a *samurai* in the movies Chad had watched on television. Purple welts and bruises covered most of their faces. Many of them had their arms folded so that the fabric of their robes stretched tight enough to display bulging biceps. Chad understood the energy he was sensing from them: testosterone. These guys fought for a living, day after day. They were fighters, and as of yet, he was not.

Some of the younger Japanese boys began shouting at him using words he could not understand. He turned to John and said, "Excuse me, John-*san*, what they wen' say to me?"

"What I look like?" John glared at him. "Your fuckin' interpreter?"

The blast of cold wind at the airport had shocked Chad less than this response. He stood motionless. It made no sense to him. While trouble might have been expected from the Japanese, John had been through exactly what Chad was now dealing with. He could have made things easier for Chad with a few simple words: *They wen' tell you for lay out your* futon, or *They like know why you so tall.* Support from John did not have to last forever, Chad thought, but he had only been in the country a matter of hours; the lack of aloha awakened him to the fact that, despite the presence of other recruits from Hawai'i, he was largely on his own.

With no choice but to be silent, he continued to observe this complex web of relations based on age, experience, aggression, and strength. In the last and most important of these categories, it was immediately clear that Taylor Wylie was The Man. Only eighteen, the same age as Chad, Taylor had come to Japan the year before and now ran the *sumo beya* for the obvious reason that he could kick the ass of anybody in the room. Taylor ordered two of the boys to set out a *futon* for Chad in the corner of the room, and they did so immediately. They showed Chad where he was to lay out his *futon* in the evenings and where he was to store it in the mornings. Finally, they indicated his personal storage area, which was larger than he needed for the few possessions he had brought.

All of the boys shared the big room. They spoke freely with each other, laughing occasionally from one corner to another. But beyond Taylor's initial gesture of help, no one made any effort to welcome Chad, including the other boys from Hawai'i, who bantered fluently in Japanese. He lay on the cold, hard floor. This was not the *sumo* he had seen on television: Konishiki's limo, stardom, big money. As he drifted off to sleep, all he could think about was home, and what a huge mistake he had made by leaving.

The next morning, he awoke to the sound of movement in the room. It was still dark, much too early. He was so tired that he could have slept late into the afternoon. Besides, it couldn't possibly be time to get up—not in the dark. Then he realized that he was colder than he had ever been in the morning and that a strange, sweet smell permeated the room. A few of the other boys were folding up their *futon* in the darkness. The smell came from the oil in their topknots.

As Chad lifted himself off the straw-mat floor, he was surprised by a single word, spoken suddenly and sternly by all those awake: "*ZaiMASsss!*" He recognized the sound as the greeting the boys had shouted when Boss had entered the kitchen the day before. He turned to see a slight, pretty Japanese woman in the room. She looked to be around forty and was smartly dressed in pants, her hair ending just below her ears. The early hour didn't seem to bother her. She was Boss's wife and was introduced to Chad as Okamisan, a title reserved for the wife of an *oyakata*. She had come to invite Chad to their neat, well-appointed apartment on the floor above.

Once there, Chad found that Okamisan had prepared a welcome breakfast to ease his adjustment to the *sumo beya* and his being away from home. He realized then how powerfully he missed his own mother. She had been against his Japan adventure from the moment he broke the news to her. He understood why she was upset at him for leaving, and he hadn't wanted to oppose her. But he agreed with his father: he'd been taking care of his brothers his whole life, and now it was time for him to set off on his own. On the way to the airport the day he left for Japan, the family had all stopped to eat breakfast. Over a large helping of Portuguese sausage and eggs, Chad had decided he would make it big in Japan, and that he would do it for his parents and his brothers.

A day later and half a world away, he sat down to the same breakfast of eggs and sausages. He was touched by Okamisan's special treatment and happy to have something so familiar in the midst of the overwhelming changes in his life. She told him that Boss had faced the same challenges, having also come from Hawai'i to Japan during winter, and that the welcome breakfast from his own Okamisan remained one of his most cherished memories. So she had done the same for Taylor and John when they arrived, and now she was doing it for Chad. While her English was not very good, Chad recognized the sincerity of her hospitality—a contrast to the cold welcome he'd gotten from the boys who were downstairs training. His introduction to *sumo*'s physical challenges would begin the next day.

The following morning, while Taylor and John continued to sleep, Chad awoke with the first group of boys. He followed them down the stairs to the basement locker room. Squinting against the bright fluorescent lights, he could see his breath as all the young wrestlers started to disrobe in the cold air. Once naked, they helped one another unfold long, narrow, neatly bundled lengths of black canvas. Each wrestler in turn straddled a length, and someone else wrapped it around his waist five or six times, forming a thick, strong belt, and then tied it in back. Although he was unused to the coarse fabric, Chad was eager to fit in by wearing his own *mawashi*.

The group then walked up a flight of stairs and emerged in the *keikoba*, a cold, dimly lit room beneath the one they had slept in. The *keikoba*'s floor was hard clay, and even after one of the boys spread a thin layer of sand on it with a straw broom, it felt like cold concrete. A circle about fifteen feet in diameter had been cut into the clay, and two short, parallel white lines about two feet apart marked the center. The area seemed too small for so many large boys to train in; the room itself was only slightly wider than the circle. Chad could not imagine getting thrown and landing hard on his knees or hands or elbows or back, especially on such a frigid morning. He asked himself a question that he would ponder often in the following days: *What am I doing here?*

He brushed aside the question at that moment by following the routine of the other boys. They limbered up with *shiko,* standing in a row with their legs wide apart and bending at the knee, then lifting each leg high in the air and stomping the hard clay with full force, squatting once again and repeating the motion, stomping with one leg and then the other. He gamely shadowed their movements, as much to overcome the cold as to learn the technique: he could lift his long, tight legs perhaps only a third as high as everyone else did, but believed that he would gradually improve.

The boys' feet pounded against the packed clay over and over, perhaps more than a hundred times, and everyone was soon steaming with sweat. When they finished, two of the boys faced each other in the ring as the others did more *shiko* or rhythmically slapped with open hands a wooden pole that stood in one corner. The boys in the ring squatted for a few seconds and then charged each other. They fought quickly and passionately, each thrusting hands to his opponent's face, then gripping the other's *mawashi* until one finally twisted the other from the ring. Several of the boys watching immediately jumped into the circle, shouting and reaching for the winner as if to ask for the next fight. The winner chose an opponent, and a new fight began. The matches were short and the pace fast, the pause between them lasting only seconds.

These challenge fights went on for a while, occasionally interrupted as higher-ranked *rikishi* entered the *keikoba.* Each time one entered, everyone except the two in the ring stopped what he was doing, bowed, and shouted, *"ZaiMASsss!"* then resumed practice. As each senior *rikishi* arrived, he looked at Chad, said something in Japanese, and laughed. Everyone but Chad joined in the laughter. Soon, Boss entered to even more spirited shouts and sat on a cushion that had been arranged for him on a raised platform near the ring. The matches became noticeably more serious, and Boss silently communicated either praise or disapproval, occasionally offering advice or instruction with single-word commands. To more shouts, Taylor and then John at last entered, bowing stiffly to Boss before beginning *shiko.*

The sight of Taylor dressed only in a *mawashi* was shocking. He was not only the biggest man Chad had ever seen, but with each stomp on the hard clay, his upper torso trembled. His thick legs and arms, proportional in mass to the rest of his body, looked as hard as rock.

Chad's first opponent had the same block-like build as Taylor, but was about a hundred and fifty pounds lighter. He looked like a football lineman without a shirt or pads. Chad towered over him, and because of his height advantage, Chad thought it would be a mismatch: just push the other guy out of the ring and you win. In fact, as he looked around the room, he figured he could defeat almost anyone when it came to a pushing contest—except maybe Taylor.

But in his first match Chad learned that *sumo* involves more than pushing. First, his feet slipped easily on the hard, sand-covered ground, making it difficult to get traction for the charge. And second, he wasn't sure when he should charge. The *rikishi* he had watched seemed to charge without any signal. The fight would be aborted if one charged before the other was ready, and the *rikishi* at fault would bow and apologize to his opponent. If it happened more than once, Boss would glare at the offender.

As Chad crouched down, he took care not to commit a false start. But the very instant he touched his hands to the ground, he was blasted straight back into the wood-paneled wall behind him. Shouts from the other *rikishi* filled the room as they swarmed around the winner, hoping to take him on next. Chad's smaller opponent had come in low, thrust a shoulder into his chest, and bulled forward with his legs. The match was over before Chad knew what had happened.

Boss pointed to the newcomer's long legs and laughed, saying something in Japanese. Despite the loss, he ordered Chad back into the ring. "*Tsupari*," he said to Taylor. Taylor stopped his warm-up, walked into the ring, and demonstrated *tsupari:* a pushing motion consisting of repeated, open-handed thrusts. Early in his own career, Boss had relied on this technique to compensate for the weakness of his legs. This early in Chad's training, his only hope seemed to lie in keeping the other guy away from his body. He tried *tsupari* in a walk-through with Taylor, noticing again how solid the guy was beneath his layer of fat.

More determined after his loss and the subsequent ridicule—and armed with the new technique—Chad crouched down to fight again. He lunged forward and got his hands up quickly, aiming for his opponent's chest. But his target spun out of the way, and his momentum carried him, arms flailing, straight into a platform on the other side of the room. As before, the other boys surrounded the winner and shouted to be picked next. Chad stood aside to watch the remainder of the practice fights, most of them spirited, violent, and closely matched.

Once the practice bouts were over, the boys began an exercise that reminded Chad of the drills that were run with blocking sleds on the Kaiser High football field. In the *sumo* exercise, the larger wrestlers were like human blocking sleds and were impossible to move unless they allowed themselves to be. When Chad got the chance to charge into Taylor's massive chest, he found he had no effect. Boss smiled and said something in Japanese, and again everyone laughed. Chad endured the teasing and charged again, with the same result: Taylor could not be budged. As Chad pushed, Taylor kept shouting in Japanese and smacking him on the head. Finally, the big Samoan threw him to the ground as easily as he had thrown the smaller wrestlers. Not knowing how to roll, Chad hit the floor with all his weight. "*Mō ii,*" Boss said at last. *Enough.*

Training continued for several more hours, Chad working his body to exhaustion with the unfamiliar exercises. Near collapsing, Chad was suddenly overwhelmed by a smell that began wafting through the room. *Someone was cooking food.* He could not tell what kind of food it was, but he hadn't had anything to eat since just after six the night before, and the smell made his stomach rumble. Two of the younger boys had left the *keikoba* and were preparing the morning meal for everyone, a task Chad would be expected to assist with once he had learned the full routine of *keiko.* He did not yet know that, like everything else in the *sumo beya* and in *sumo* generally, the meal would be served according to rank, a custom that would force him to wait the longest. All he wanted to do at that moment—even more than go home or be able to speak Japanese—was to eat, and to eat as soon as possible.

At last, Taylor turned away from the ring and with labored breath mumbled, "*mashita,*" indicating that he was finished with practice bouts. But instead of heading downstairs to the locker room, everyone gathered around to watch him and John go through the blocking-sled drill against each other. Eating was still far away, and the cruel, tantalizing thought of food hurt Chad worse than Taylor's slaps to his head.

Finally, it was time to file downstairs: first John, then Taylor, and then everyone else. Draped in steam and promising a warm bath, the changing room was the scene of more humiliating treatment for Chad. Instead of a bar of soap, he was handed the sweaty lengths of canvas from the higher-ranked *rikishi* and ordered to follow one of the younger boys upstairs. They passed through the kitchen, where some boys were chopping vegetables, and up to the second floor. The boy opened a window and draped each *mawashi* over the sill; it looked like a long, black snake, stretching almost to the ground. The boy then ordered Chad to follow him back downstairs.

Instead of heading for the baths, they stopped in the kitchen, where Chad was given a head of cabbage and shown how to rip it into small pieces. He wondered when he would be allowed to shed his own uncomfortable canvas, clean up, and eat. It wasn't going to be a plate lunch like the kind he would have eaten in Hawai'i, but the sight of cooked rice and a huge, steaming pot of sliced fish and vegetables was pure torment nonetheless. Only a day ago, this stuff—this *chanko nabe*—would have looked horrible, but now he was almost ready to eat the clay from the *keikoba*'s floor.

Taylor and the others who had bathed walked through the kitchen and into an adjacent room. Two of the younger boys carried a pot out to this room and placed it at the head of a low table next to John. Each of the *riki-*

shi sat next to the one who had preceded his entrance, one place further from the pot. Chad was ordered to stand with one of the younger boys and attend to anyone who needed more water, more rice, and so forth. He watched everyone inhale the food and listened to them chatter, but could only imagine what they were talking about.

When everyone had finished eating, he and the other lowly ranked boy took the dishes to the kitchen, washed them, and put them away. Finally, the two of them were allowed to bathe. After helping each other untie their *mawashi,* they showered quickly, eating having become more important than relaxing in the bath. They returned to the empty dining room and devoured what was left. Chad's mother had warned him that he wouldn't like the food, but ravenous, he forced it down quickly. Cabbage, grayish dumplings made from some kind of fish, a salty broth—no one back home would believe that this was what *sumo* wrestlers ate.

The other boy finished first and left his dishes for Chad to clean. Only when his last chore was done would Chad be allowed to go upstairs, where everyone else was napping. His fatigue turned simple tasks like clearing the table, washing the dishes, and putting things away into huge projects. He dropped things easily, could not figure out where the bowls were stored, and worried about where to put the towel and rag when he was through. The *sumo beya* was run like the military, and his uncle had told him enough about military discipline for him to know that everything must be put in its place and that every surface must be clean enough to eat off of.

When at last Chad had finished, he trudged upstairs on aching legs, stepped over the sleeping boys, and stretched out his *futon* in a corner of the big room. Sleep would be welcome relief. But no sooner had he drifted off than he was awakened by one of the boys kicking him, barking something, and pointing to his own mat and blanket. Chad's quizzical, dazed look earned him another kick, which immediately brought him to his senses. *Who's this fucking punk,* he wondered. At first he could only stare, taking in what was happening. He realized he was being ordered around because of his low rank in the *sumo beya* hierarchy. Just like in practice, just like with cooking, just like with eating—just like with everything. So instead of reacting as he might have at home, he decided it was best to do as he was told. He arranged the other boy's *futon* and blanket, and with that, the incident was over.

In the late afternoon, Chad and the lowly ranked boy he was paired with did the laundry, then helped prepare the evening meal. They served dinner as they had the afternoon meal, though no one ate nearly as much this time. And as before, Chad was allowed to eat only when everyone else was finished and everything was clean.

He stared at the *chanko nabe* in front of him: a few pieces of colorless, wilting cabbage drifting in a gray broth along with bits of the same kind of fish they had eaten for lunch. Earlier in the day, he had been so hungry that it didn't matter what food had been set before him, but now it was an effort to even look at the stuff. Floating in that nasty broth, the fish looked like pieces of dead flesh in a puddle on the side of the road. He could not understand how Taylor had gotten so huge or, for that matter, how everyone in the *sumo beya* had avoided becoming weak and scrawny. He was sure that, at home, his family was eating something with brown gravy—or spaghetti dripping with cheese—something his mother had probably made that very night for his brothers. He cleaned up without eating much and headed back upstairs, still hungry.

Though everyone turned as the tall foreigner entered the room, the testosterone level had subsided considerably since the first time they had glared at him. The boys lounged in the corners of the room, and after a glance all returned indifferently to whatever they had been doing. Except for one: the guy who had kicked him earlier.

Again the boy ordered Chad to bend down and arrange his *futon* and blanket for him. Everyone looked up to watch the foreigner swallow hard and then do as he was told: obey a *rikishi* who was perfectly capable of arranging his *futon* himself and, unlike Chad, had been getting plenty of sleep and eating well. As Chad finished, his antagonist whacked him on the head with an open hand and barked something Chad could not understand, pointing to the *futon* as if to say it was not straight enough or was upside-down.

Unused to such treatment, the stress of being unable to communicate, and his lack of sleep, Chad was on the verge of snapping. He used all his willpower and self-control to suppress the natural urge to fight back when hit. Even in his state of exhaustion, he could have easily thrown the boy into the wall. Outside the *sumo* ring the guy was physically no match for Chad. But in *sumo*'s complex system of rank and deference, the boys' seniority must have carried some weight; otherwise, Chad reasoned, he would not have behaved this way. Reining in his anger once more, he made an effort to fix whatever he was being blamed for. His attempt was met with another blow to the head, harder than the last. Again the guy barked something at him; this time, however, the other wrestler adjusted the *futon* himself, creating no change that Chad could detect. With all eyes in the silent room upon him, Chad bowed. "*Sumimasen*," he said. *Excuse me.*

A while later, Taylor took Chad aside. "Brah, you trust everybody too much. These guys, they your *sempai*, but they going walk all over you if you no stand up fo' your rights." *Sempai* means senior, Taylor explained; *kohai* means junior. Both were determined by the amount of time served. Over and above that, however, was the seniority that could only be earned by fighting and winning in tournaments. This rank came with far greater privileges. "You have to move up the *banzuke*, the ranking list, by winning matches," Taylor said. When you got high enough on the *banzuke*, he explained, you became a *sekitori*—one of the guys they show wrestling on TV—and then everything is taken care of: big money, women any time you want, people taking you out all the time, your own boys serving you. Taylor talked about it almost wistfully, as if becoming a *sekitori* were like entering a kind of Promised Land. At one rank you are a king, and at the one below, you are a slave.

Taylor realized that, because of Chad's easy-going nature, the bottom of the *banzuke* was a particularly dangerous place for him. "Especially because you're a foreigner, a *gaijin*, you gotta make 'em respec' you." The *sempai-kohai* seniority system meant that Chad had to bow to kids younger than he was. But there was also something else. Chad remembered the wave of testosterone he had encountered when he walked into the room for the first time. "You gotta stand up for your rights," Taylor repeated. "And all the way at the top of the *banzuke*: that's where the *yokozuna* stay," Taylor went on. "Mean. Can kick everybody's ass. They bigger than the bosses. You ever see one of them, like Chiyonofuji, you better bow low. And if he tells you fo' do something, you run and you do 'em."

Taylor went back to watching his TV show, leaving Chad alone to figure out how to act, what to do, what to say in a language he couldn't speak, when to stand up for himself, and when to bow. But at least Taylor had helped him understand the *sempai-kohai* system a little better, and had helped him learn *tsupari* at that morning's practice so he'd be able to protect himself better in the ring. He would have liked to talk more with Taylor, but his *sempai* led him to believe the conversation was over. He lay down, exhausted in every possible way, and plugged in his Walkman.

Chad had brought just one tape, *Feelings in the Islands.* A mix of backyard local music, some of it in Hawaiian, the songs on the tape were often played when someone passed the 'ukulele around at parties in his uncle's carport. If he closed his eyes, the music took him home. But the moment he opened them, he knew he was separated from Hawai'i by more than an ocean. He wasn't going to be away for a month or six months or even a year; he had no idea when he would ever again cruise Kalaniana'ole Highway with his cousin Bud. A year? Two years? It was a prison sentence with no end in sight. *Tsupari. Shiko. ZaiMASsss! Kohai, sempai, sekitori.*

The words to one of the songs brought back a flood of powerful images: the look on his mother's face when he would bring her flowers from work, the cheers he could hear from her over everyone else at his basketball games, how hard she always worked to keep him and his brothers in line. And the way she'd reacted to his decision to come to Japan: with surprise and anger. She wouldn't talk to him all the way to the airport, but he knew she'd been upset because she loved him and didn't want to see him leave.

What am I doing here? Listen to the sempai. *Stand up for your rights. Which was it? And when?* As the music played, he looked around the room. Taylor and John were absorbed in a television program he had no hope of understanding, and two of the younger boys were giggling with one another. He looked at the wall, up at the ceiling, and back at the wall again. At last he began to cry.

The next morning, his body ached as he stood and put away his *futon*. It continued to ache as he followed the other boys downstairs. He could again see his breath in the changing room and in spite of his soreness was eager to begin practicing, if only to keep warm. The same boys who had dressed first the day before led the way up to the *keikoba*. Everyone did the same number of *shiko* to warm up, but this time Chad found it even harder to raise his legs as high as the other boys did. As practice continued, he noticed that the same boy stepped into the ring first. Boss walked in after the same duration, and the wrestlers entitled to wake up later than everyone else entered in the same order, according to their rank on the *banzuke*.

Unfortunately for Chad, his performance in the ring was also the same. His smaller opponent rose suddenly from below him, thrust a shoulder into his chest, and slammed him into the wall. Again Boss said, *"Tsupari,"* but this time he addressed his new recruit directly. Again Chad missed the slippery target, and again his *oyakata* laughed at him. Once more he took the laughter good naturedly, assuming Boss was trying to put him at ease. Still sore from the day before, he had even more trouble during the blocking-sled drill, barely managing to move Taylor and getting thrown to the rock-hard clay several more times.

Boss seemed to let the drill go on forever: the inexperienced recruit charging, his *sempai* yelling, resisting, smacking him on the head from time to time, throwing him to the ground. Each time, Chad got up, faced his target, slapped the front of his *mawashi* with both hands, charged, and was thrown down. After a few more charges, he could barely lift his heaving body off the ground. Taylor shouted and kicked him gently in the ribs until he was up on all fours, and then he pulled him up by the hair the rest of the way. Chad could barely lift his arm to wipe the sweat from his eyes, and when he did, his sand-covered hand made them tear. He gulped air and felt nauseated. Taylor was yelling at him, *"Saigo! Saigo! Hayaku!"* Breathing burned his throat and the insides of his nose. But once more he slapped the front of his *mawashi* with both hands, put his head down, and charged. When he again hit the ground, he was grateful to hear the raspy voice of Boss saying, *"Mō ii."*

The rest of practice went as it had the day before: fights, *shiko*, turns around the circle. But this time, Chad had nothing left except his will and wanted nothing more than to lie down and sleep. Unwilling to give up, however, he followed everyone down to the changing room. This time the boy who had helped him the day before ordered him to hang out the *mawashi* by himself. After that, he had to go to the kitchen, help prepare the meal, and attend to everyone's needs as they ate. He noticed that they were seated just as they had been the day before, with John right next to the pot and the youngest boy farthest away. It all fit Taylor's explanation of the *banzuke.*

After the meal, Chad completed his chores in a daze, shuffling across the floor and laboring up the stairs. He was so tired that he could have done without his *futon* altogether and slept right on the floor, but he lay out the mat and blanket as he was supposed to. He hit the pillow as heavily as he had the hard floor of the *keikoba,* and just as quickly, he heard a familiar voice again shout: *"Gaijin yaro!"* And then a sentence that included the word *futon.* Chad knew from the tone and context that he was again expected to put away his antagonist's *futon.* He didn't like the boy's tone, and he didn't like being called *gaijin,* which now carried the weight of the worst insult he could imagine.

As Chad painfully raised his body, the boy smacked him on the head and shouted, *"Hayaku! Hayaku!"* motioning with his hands that he wanted the work done quickly. Chad began folding the *futon,* but was again smacked to the floor. *"Gaijin yaro! Hayaku! Hayaku!"*

It crossed Chad's mind that one or two of the *tsupari* he had been learning would have sent this punk-*san,* whose name he didn't even know, across the room and into the wall. It would have been so easy. He felt ready to act on Taylor's advice to stand up for himself, but what could he do without going too far? He lowered his head, moved forward, and did as he was told, uttering a single word: *"Hai!"*

That evening, as Chad cleaned up after dinner, Taylor came into the kitchen. "Hurry up, Hawaiian. We go." Chad finished putting the dishes away and followed Taylor out into the cold. In a tiny bar across the river, they found warmth by drinking beer and reminiscing about home. They began with sports, going back and forth about which high school had the best football team, and which the best basketball team. The talk soon turned to food, and the two of them debated for nearly an hour about where to find the best chili rice, the best laulau, the best chicken-katsu plate. Then the talk turned to the fights they remembered having taken place during their high school days. Each shared exaggerated recollections of one fight or another, who started it and who never backed down. Where Taylor and Chad came from, backing down was worse than losing. It then occurred to Chad that he had been forced to do exactly that: back down to the boy who had kicked him, slapped his head, and ordered him around. Taylor's words kept coming back to him as the beer buzz thickened.

Under normal circumstances, someone at Taylor's rank—just below the *makushita* division and some six hundred places up the *banzuke*—would never socialize with someone of Chad's rank. But they had a natural bond based on common struggles and a common language. Foreigners across Tokyo gathered in groups, sometimes living in affluent *"gaijin* ghettos" for years without ever learning a word of Japanese. While Taylor and Chad

had no choice but to learn the language of Japan's national sport, they could get away from Azumazeki Beya and find refuge in a bar, where they could behave as they would have back home when they needed to let off steam: suck up beers, talk story, get good and drunk.

On the way back to the *sumo beya,* Chad saw a two-by-four in a pile of construction debris beside the road. Perhaps it was the beer, or all the talk about home, or a combination of the two that caused him to pull the wood from the pile. Back home, you don't forget if somebody looks at you the wrong way or gives you attitude. And if the guy kicks you or hits you in the face, you fight back. By nature, Chad had been less quick to react than most guys, more willing to avoid fights when possible—not by backing down, but by waiting for the other guy to throw the first punch. Because of Chad's size and his menacing glare, the first punch hardly ever came. But his antagonist in the *sumo beya* had thrown the first punch three times already. Three times!

Just before curfew, Taylor and Chad entered the big room to find everyone asleep. Chad walked straight to his sleeping tormentor and kicked him awake, shouting, "Eh, you like me put away your fuckin' *futon* now, you fucka?" He raised the two-by-four and held it like a baseball bat—or *samurai* sword. His head was bowed slightly so that the whites of his eyes could be seen beneath his upturned pupils.

Startled and breathing heavily, the smaller boy stood and faced him, suddenly wide awake. This time the *gaijin* stood firm: no bowing, no *sumimasen,* and no *hai!*

"Go, Hawaiian!" Taylor urged. "Stand up for your rights!"

"We go!" Chad challenged. He held the two-by-four steady, the veins on his hands popping with the force of his grip. He glared down at his *sempai.* The shouts of *Gaijin yaro!* came back to him. The laughter in the *keikoba* came back. *Hayaku! Hayaku!* came back. He focused all of his anger and frustration on the head of the boy. "Come on, we go!" Chad yelled again. *"Hayaku!"*

Seeing the *gaijin*'s strength and his resolve to use it, the boy backed down. Suppressing his anger, he bowed, straightened his own *futon,* and lay down.

MARCELINO FREIRE

Three Stories

SOMEBODY KILLED THE LIFEGUARD

We're happy. It's Sunday in Brazil's Rio de Janeiro. Children roll around in the sand. The beach spins. There are asses here from every corner of the planet. If some of them make it worse, others make it better—like the drumming section of a samba school, like blacks playing soccer. Nobody wants to know about the rain. I'm not going to be the rain. In such sweltering weather, Sunday is a perfect day for dozing off. Rio is one big smile. Hey, this is beginning to sound like a guidebook.

We're happy because our coastline spans more than 7,367 kilometers. The water is clear and warm all year round. With its sea of automobiles, even the city of São Paulo has an ocean. Everything flows toward Suarão, Sonho, Cibratel I, Embaré, Ilha Porchat. Some of these beaches aren't fit for swimming. Others have diversions like waterfalls that gush into the waves, slapping the white sand like tongues. I don't want to know. Nobody wants to know what happened yesterday. Yesterday already was.

Why don't we talk about *futevôlei* instead? It is played the same way as beach volleyball except you use your feet instead of your hands. A player can use his chest, his head, and any part of his legs. You've got to stay on top of the sand and not sink down into it. Don't let the wind lift your serve from behind. Now I'm talking about sailing. There's a nautical term for every direction you send the ball: sail, cut, angle, line. But when you're at the beach, the only thing you really need to know is how to swim. In the case of the boy yesterday, it was something different. What boy you ask? Yesterday during that confusion.

There are those who go to the beach only to eat or get a tan. For these types, here's a bit of advice:

1. only use tested dermatological products;
2. remember that sixty percent of solar radiation is transmitted through heat;
3. in local restaurants, don't forget to try *sopa leão veloso,* a famous stew made of fish heads and shrimp; or
4. try *arroz-de-cuxá* from São Luis do Maranhão.

John Valadez. *Revelations.*
1991. Pastel on paper.
Photograph by John White.

It's also important to remember that although Brazil has more than 192 lighthouses, they are rarely built because of the dangers of the sea. The dangers of the sea. As if the Dead Sea, like the others, had never died. As if sharks had never been able to attack. As if the shipwrecks had never sunk to the bottom. As if pirates had never done any smuggling. As if oil had never flowed through pipelines. As if whales had never fallen after breaching. As if the boy yesterday had not also been the boy today, more alive than the early-morning sun. As if he had never been hit by that damned bullet.

What can you do? At the beach, there are tons of things to do. Surfing, diving, hiking, camping, and even nude sunbathing. Once you've gone nude—think about it—it's like being reborn into the world. To expose everything the way an Indian would, without even a thong bikini. Pedra Grande is one of them, a beach that allows the complete manifestation of paradise. It is located in Trancoso, Bahia. There's also Pedras Altas in Santa Catarina. Tambaba in Paraíba. Naked as a cloud in the sky. I don't want to make it rain. I don't have that kind of power. I want this story to have some usefulness—to give the traveler a bit of advice. I want it to be about the different climates one can find in this country. I also want it to be about the moon's oceans, or the boy's body, stretched out there.

Let me talk about the weather a bit. It's not just the blazing sun that can hurt you, but also the sailboats and the jellyfish. If you get sunburned, apply vinegar or alcohol. Don't drink too much—and be careful. You can lose your mind. You can get irritable. The sea is a trap that surrounds you on all sides. Don't swim in rough or dark waters. Be aware of some high temperatures: 30 degrees Centigrade for Recife, 33 for Macapá. The boy didn't know how to escape. Yesterday, the boy must have been recognized. I hope.

It's 608 kilometers from Rio de Janeiro to Vitória if you drive directly up the Brazilian coast. You pass through Magé, Tanguá, Rio das Ostras, Macaé. There are dirt roads, there are mountain ranges, there are forgotten cities, tollbooths, and highway police. At this time of night, do you think there will be an official working diligently on this case? Hunched over a beach chair? Or beside the pool? I wonder if, from the mountains above, the ridiculous white statue of Christ the Redeemer has not witnessed this bloodshed.

Do you know where Rio Vermelho is? This extremely polluted beach in Rio de Janeiro is filled with migrants from Bahia. It's divided into three sections: Mariquita, Santana (from where they make offerings to Iemanjá every year), and Paciência. I know every song and every pothole in all of Brazil. My sturdy car confronts peace and loneliness. The fervor of the sun burns my forehead and cracks my sunglasses.

Yesterday, someone robbed a man of his life on the beach in Copacabana. There were no witnesses. No one arrested the thief. It was yesterday,

Sunday. What a shame! My fear is that this wave of violence will drive tourists away to Miami.

I'm not sure how many kilometers away Brazil is from becoming *that* fiscal paradise.

LET'S PRETEND NOTHING. HAPPENED.

This is a children's story, but it is a bit bloody. Don't be alarmed. Don't be afraid. Once upon a time hardly matters. You think that it's gonna be rosy. You're going to remember your childhood. Who has never killed a gecko when he was a kid? It's the same thing. Who has never broken the wings of a little bird? It's the same thing. This is a story for reading and drifting off to sleep. For reading and reading again. For doing nothing but reading and rereading. And if you'd rather listen to it, ask your father, your mother, or your grandmother to tell it to you. It's a story without pity. It's a kid's story, silly and banal. You've heard worse before. It's something you can read to your kids so that you don't feel so. Alone.

Let's call this the Good Country. Simple as a short story. Simple as a song. It's a pretty paradise filled with waterfalls and crowded beaches. The sky goes on forever. Something smells a little strange, but that's OK. It's not quite time for things to stink. We still have. Time.

When I warn you that there's something rotting—something bloody—in this kingdom, it's because I don't want to deceive you. It's not pretty when you get to the middle of the story and you come across a decaying corpse. Beaten with steel pipes and broken into bits, this boy's body is not even. Eleven years old.

This story is a fable of hope. Read it through to the end, but don't rush. It's a children's story because it's dreamlike. Grownups know what they're doing; they know what they're reading, what they're seeing, and what they want to be when they. Grow up.

Setting aside these infamous words, let's move right along with this tale, which takes place in the Good Country. To be more precise, it takes place in a city of children and teenagers. I'm not really used to making such a distinction between kids and teenagers because to me they're all just babies. Some believe they're all just devils. But what can you do about it? This is not the moral of my story. What I really want is for you, the reader, not to forget my exotic tale. In the Good Country, everything is exotic, depending, of course, on your. Perspective.

And please forgive me here if I haven't given you more than a rough sketch that will leave the words a bit lighter or the rhythm a little less smooth. I might even evoke some American paintings. How about a drawing of a scorched body—with the eyes blacked out? Or one with a gunshot right in the head—with the eyes blacked out? Abandoned like a rat—with the eyes blacked out. All black.

And the little boy was black, too, the same hue as the Good Country, where everything is black. The sky, the houses.

All the other little boys were like him. Like him, they survived by playing games. I repeat. Who has never broken the wings of a little bird? Who has never cut short the life of a gecko? Everything is a little black. In the face of death in the Good Country, we still learn to count. Little sheep.

THE SHOOTING LINE

—Good afternoon.
—*Afternoon.*
—Pardon me for bothering you, missus.
—*I don't want any.*
—Any what?
—*Chocolate. You want to sell me a chocolate bar, right?*
—No.
—*Chewing gum?*
—No, no.
—*Are you a Hare Krishna?*
—No. God is my savior.
—*Are you from the Church of the Latter-day Saints or something?*
—No, I'm not.
—*Are you from the Association—*
—Missus, please don't be so rude. Can I speak?
—*Of course you can. Pardon me.*
—This is a robbery.
—*Robbery?*
—Yes, but we need to sit down.
—*But what a place for a mugging: the bus…*
—Sit down quickly.
—*But—*
—Just cooperate.
—*Mister—*
—It's a shame to be unemployed.
—*Uh-huh…*
—It's a shame to be hungry.
—*Uh-huh…*
—It's a shame to not even have shoes on one's feet.
—*Uh-huh…*

—It's a shame to—

—*It's a shame to not let me speak. Please, don't be so rude. Can I speak now?*

—Of course you can. Pardon me.

—*What do I have to do with this?*

—Missus…

—*I'm on my way home from my pain-in-the-ass job, exhausted and completely fed up.*

—But—

—*The boss thinks he's a prince, the client thinks he's a prince, everybody's a prince.*

—But—

—*Minimum wage is a shitty way to make a living. Money—*

—Money, that's what I'm talking about. Give it here.

—*What?*

—A bus token, a food stamp, any kind of coupon.

—*No, I don't think so. This may be a robbery, but you cannot rob me.*

—I can't rob you?

—*No, you can't.*

—What do you mean I can't?

—*Don't you see? We're on the same bus. I'm in the same shitty situation as you.*

—Oh no!

—*Shiiiittttt.*

—You don't need to use dirty language.

—*No, this isn't normal.*

—What, missus?

—*A moral lesson from a thief.*

—Then pass your purse to me now.

—*My purse?*

—*My* purse. Do it, please.

—*Never.*

—I'm asking you politely.

—*Oh!*

—I'm asking you calmly.

—*Oh really?*

—I'm feeling pretty good.

—*Good? Look, even if you throw me out the window, you won't get my purse.*

—Uh-huh…

—*Not even over my dead body.*

—Oh really? I'm going to count to three—to three. You're going to give me the purse or I'm going to—

—*Going to what? Scream? Get angry? Start kicking?*
—One.
—*What are you going to do then?*
—Two.
—*Are you going to kill me?*
—Three.
—*All right then.*
—Whoa, what's that?
—*A gun. Haven't you ever seen one before?*
—Turn it away from me.
—*Turn yourself away.*
—You.
—*You.*
—You.
—*Let's agree on something. Are we or are we not both civilized?*
   [Silence.]
—*Polite?*
   [Silence.]
—*Human beings?*
—Yes.
—*Then stand up, and let's get off the bus.*
—Yes, let's go.

Translation by Claude Henry Potts

John Valadez. *Pool Party.*
1986. Oil on canvas.
Photograph by Peggy Tennison.

Jungle Planet

Even on cable TV, it was the animals she loved. She had a neat, black, remote control as small as a candy bar, and she could find all the numbers in the dark.

They reserved television for the long, stifling afternoons. She and Lola liked to watch on the sofa together, the old woman snoozing upright by her side. Her father didn't want the lights on in the house during the day; it was a waste of power. Any day now, the men from the electric company would come to cut the wires, and her beloved beasts would be gone. Neither could they make too much noise. So they would sit together in the semi-darkness of the *sala* until twilight stole across the room and the evening news blared over the neighbors' sets, slipping past the shuttered windows and the door with its three locks.

She knew what number on the TV screen the volume could be set to before her father noticed. Smiling and with hardly a word, she and Lola would watch the animals.

Sometimes the screen was blue, and the dark shadow of a finned and rotund creature slipped through invisible water. Sometimes a vista of lazy yellow greeted her eyes, a savannah far off in Africa, with a big cat standing to one side and swiveling its head, about to gaze at her with mild annoyance. One afternoon when Papa was asleep and Lola was snoring gently, the little girl turned the TV on to a hell of screaming men and rapid explosions. Her heart pumped wildly for a few crazy seconds before she could find the remote control and squeeze the right buttons. All at once, there was a swelling silence and nothing but green. The blurry image came into focus, and she saw that it was a forest leaf so clear and perfect that she could see the network of tiny veins along its spine. As she watched, a small drop of crystal-clear water formed at its tip and quietly fell, round as a pearl.

By twilight, her mother would return, smelling of heat and the train. She would be cross and sticky and not nice to kiss. Papa never cooked; it was Lola's duty to do so, though the vegetables slipped through her gnarled fingers and tumbled in the dust. The four of them would sit at the table and eat without talking. The food was apportioned according to a tacit plan: if there was pork or chicken, the parents had it; the grandmother insisted on her rice and *monggo* beans; and the little girl fished out and swallowed the *saluyot* the chicken was cooked with because she could not stand the taste of flesh. She remembered the days when her parents would paddle her for refusing food, for gently pushing slivers of meat off the edge of the table and subsisting on a few onions or leaves. You don't realize how many children out there cannot eat this way, they would say, the grandmother gathering her leavings.

They had given up and suppers were now uneventful. The meal over, her father would leave the table to put on his uniform and take the bicycle, which they kept in the living room during the day for fear of thieves. Her mother would collapse in the darkness of the bedroom. The child would take the dishes over to the sink and carefully whisk the rice grains and stray *monggo* beans off the table, collecting them in her palm to deposit in the trash. She and her grandmother would then do the dishes and fill the drums with the next day's water supply. Sometimes the water gave out before they were done, and a week might pass before they could wash again.

There was no school because three girls had died. One morning the old janitor had found Sandra from the third grade stiff and cold in one of the lavatory stalls. Two months later, it was Marijoy. The teachers called a meeting. *These squatters,* someone hissed, and the teachers clucked their tongues to express their horror. At the other end of the room, an assembly of ragtag women insisted it was the men who had come from out of town and camped on the nearby ridges to put down filling material and build row upon row of hollow block homes. Someone else opined that it had to be a person who knew the routine of the school well, possibly someone the pupils trusted, and there was silence after this. The same month, another girl was pulled black and fetid out of the crawl space beneath the floorboards of the grade IV room. The school did not close. The mothers simply forbade their children to go back.

The girl learned all this in bits and pieces from her grandmother. It explained the shuttered windows, the set of locks on the door. Sometimes they awakened in the night to the velvet swish of someone stealing past the window, the odor of his cigarette lacing the motionless air for hours. The old woman and child were not to admit anyone day or night, even if he pleaded and begged, even if a mob beat him to death right out on the stoop.

Now it was October, and it poured in sheets and curtains of silver. When it stormed, you could not see the smoke that perennially hung in the air. The ditches backed up, and bubbly brown water streamed into the houses. Lola said there were live electrical wires in the streets. She talked longingly of the days when you could get trash collected and fallen wires cleared just by calling the government up on the phone.

The child asked, What do you mean "phone"? Lola tried to describe the thunderous transcontinental cables of her girlhood and explain fiber optics, but her voice trailed off, overcome with futility.

Their neighborhood lay over a marsh. It was wet and poisonous in the monsoon season. The government had done a rotten job of draining it, her father said.

They were lucky for their street lay on a shelf of solid rock. The neighbors a few blocks down were not as fortunate. When it rained, the distant creek that had once been a river swelled and turned streets into a vast brown sea, sweeping silently past islands capped in sheets of tin.

One morning the rain stopped, and in the quiet, her father could not get to sleep. He stood motionless in the doorway and gazed bleary eyed at the poisonous yellow of the sky. The child had disobeyed her mother's orders and was out alone, but played desultorily in the concrete yard, pulling weeds from the pots of ferns and herbs, too timid to venture beyond the hollow block wall. She straightened up when she saw him, but did not go to him. His attention was caught by something beyond the break in the wall. She followed his glance and saw movement, something black and low-slung and possibly furry.

The animal appeared, squeezing through the gap: first snout, then shoulder and the rest of its fragile wet body. It was a dog about a year old, its fur in mud-encrusted points. A piece of hemp rope with a frayed end circled its neck. Someone had caught it, possibly with the intention of eating it. It made no sound, but regarded them with an expression she had never seen on the wild beasts on TV. It was as though it was waiting to be welcomed. She gazed at it, unaware that she was smiling. Her father called to her, and at his voice the dog whipped around, scrambling through the gap in the wall. The last image she had of it was its round young rump and the white flag of its tail.

"If we put some food out, he'll come back," her father said. He had started a distracted circuit of the tiny property, beginning with the break in the fence. He stopped now at the back wall. She was crouching down behind the succulent stemmed plants with fan-shaped leaves that, in the summer, her grandmother wasted precious water on. The child called them elephant plants.

She watched her father through the stalks and made growling sounds in the depths of her belly, trying to get as low as the ferns without touching the mud. Today she was a tiger. Some of the plants were in old tin cans and some in pots of clay. From the clay, black with moisture, sprang a green lacework of moss. It was so beautiful that her heart stopped for a second: tiny shrubs and spears—some of it low and branchy and spreading, like miniature savannah trees.

"Bea!" her father called to her, and she saw that it was raining again. The warm drops, saturated with filth, pelted her skin. She did not sizzle and dissolve into a lump of viscera as her mother had threatened she would, and so she laughed.

She would not go back into the house until he did. They stood together, gazing at the back wall, at strange dark roots that had pushed their way through the hollow blocks, seemingly overnight. Chunks of green-gray wall lay at their feet.

"This thing will come apart on us," he said. "I don't know. It could be the water. The earth behind it is so loose."

Cold spears fell singly about them. Five hundred people had died, he told her, on the ridge above theirs. She had heard the story many times, but it seemed forever fresh to her, perpetually fascinating. The families had built their homes on what they thought was solid rock, but the ground had been layered with loose material that soaked up the rains like a sponge. One morning it had all turned to muck, and the pavements had cracked and fallen inward, houses and trees and cars sliding down into the soup.

Five hundred people—mothers, fathers, and children in their starched school shirts—entombed within rock, he said.

But that had been a long time ago, and now engineers were rebuilding, carting tons of rubble and rock to even up the ground.

"Nowhere left to put the houses but over the bones," her father said, smiling.

She recognized his tone and sobered up, deciding not to tell him she had been a tiger just a few minutes ago. His tone would be hard and forced when he learned of the game. Oh, a tiger! You poor thing, we thought you were dead!

—I was hiding.

—Who else is with you?

—Just me.

—No bears?

—Nup.

—No elephants?

—Nup…

There were many bad things on television, but the animals were not among them. Even the names of the animal programs were beautiful, the child thought, like titles of poems you might find in the grade IV reader: *Pathfinder, Jungle Planet, Legacy*. She wished she could find out why some of the beasts had gone as silently as the dinosaurs had sixty-five million years ago, but there were never any programs on that. The animals darted through prairie grass and over granite crags as though they had been filmed just yesterday, but some of that footage, her parents said, was older than Lola. Her grandmother liked the background music; it was what she called a full orchestra. Orchestras had been out of style when she was a girl; instead there'd been disco, rock. Lola wished they could pump up the volume, but her son could not sleep if they did.

The next day, the rain did not resume, but the sun did not shine either. It waited tentatively behind heavy brooding clouds. The child figured that too much sun killed the skin and too much rain brought the earth out from under your feet, but a little of both was not so bad. The dog came back. She fed him scraps from the noonday meal, carefully collected in a bowl. He ate them with his tongue, his hind legs stiff, his eyes darting back and forth between her face and the food. He didn't look like he'd had much since the day before; maybe he had been ranging through the crumbling houses and tin-roof shacks for weeks. His searching nose left twin triangles of wet all over the stoop. As soon as he was done, he tore off for the break in the fence.

She was a patient child. Sitting on a slab of concrete, she feigned disinterest, whistling as if to herself, cooing as though to the black birds that darted across the sky. Resting her chin on her knees, she gazed at him as she might a younger brother until the dog crept out and sat down in the concrete yard, shivering a little because his fur was still wet. What would her father say, she wondered, if she asked to keep him?

The following day, the rain began anew and she sat tensely by the window, surveying the fence and the unending fall of silver in the front yard. Her father slept, but Lola was restless, glancing every now and then at the clock on top of the refrigerator. The child thought of her mother in her black windbreaker, holding the umbrella with the broken rib and leaving for work that morning; how she'd had to wield that umbrella to deflect the rain. The path she would take went over sidewalks where the water bubbled from busted pipes and sped diagonally into the street, becoming a rushing torrent or simply pooling there, dammed by pieces of trash. Her mother would be exhausted even before the first jeepney ride of the day was over; and then there would be the mind-numbing process of elbowing her way onto the train and claiming a space of her own.

The child liked the train on Sunday mornings, when there was room in the coach to sit down, liked the feeling of being queen of the city, loved going so fast the skyline turned into a plain of gray rock.

But if this rain would not stop, they would all go insane. The dog had somehow found his way back to the house and was now sheltered among the junk beneath the bedroom window. It was noon, but the day was black. Bundled beneath a ratty blanket, the child heard someone loudly rapping on the front door. Her father, who still could not sleep, shuffled out to answer it; she heard grown-up voices in a conversation that seemed to go on forever. Burrowing into the mattress, she surrendered herself to a darkness broken by pinpoints of color, color that she knew came from the pressure of both fists over her eyes. *I am asleep,* she thought, *I am supposed to be asleep.* But all the while, her ears were tuned to the slightest sound from the dog—and to the voices.

When she got up to fetch a drink of water, her father told her about the explosion. The train, a black and twisted hulk, had fallen to earth. The station, her mother's stop, was gone, pilings giving way in the rain. Cars, beings, gravel, chunks of concrete tearing, twisting, crashing down on the pavement below. Great smoking holes in the factory roofs. On TV, a woman told them brightly that damage was temporary and casualties would certainly be light. There was no video footage; footage abetted violence. This government was a clean and wholesome one. Citizens were to stay in their homes. Her mother would not be back for a while.

The grandmother howled for the old days when a simple call would tell them whether and when. But of course they had no phone.

Throughout the night, the adults in the house did not sleep. Her father sat at the table and did not put on his watchman's uniform. Neither did he take the bike out. Every couple of hours, the wind and rain died, leaving a hot, close silence and then resumed battering the tiny house. Toward dawn, the child heard someone rise and whistle softly into the darkness, heard the dog moving gratefully into the house, heard him shaking himself all over the living room. She never remembered the precise moment that she fell asleep; when the throbbing in her bladder awakened her at last, she was astonished to discover that it was past noon and the rain had stopped.

There was a soft sound of water slipping over rock, water flowing, flowing as gently as it must have done in those long precious moments at the dawn of time. The adults were motionless, her father slumped over the table, her grandmother a crumpled form on the sofa. Barefoot, she went to the door and out into a world crisp and new, cleansed by the rain. In the yard of cracked cement, the flowing water made little eddies around her ankles as she picked her measured way over twigs, little shelves of leaves and debris, clumps of grass straining at their moorings and long and graceful as drowned hair. The landscape of the tiny yard so strange now after the storm.

The wall was intact and still held the mountain back from their property, but a section of it some meters away had given way in a tumble of rock and cement, and a neighboring house and all its inhabitants had been crushed.

She was conscious of voices, agitated and a great distance off, but she paid them no heed, gazing up at the mountain in silence and awe. It was beautiful, naked somehow, free of restraint. She could see where soil had washed down the treeless slope, noted where the water—gone to lower ground—had pried boulders from the mountain. Everything, she thought, is in suspended animation; if she moved, dislodged one single pebble, the whole world would come rushing down.

And as she stood there, she saw what the rain and the mountain and the sharply etched morning had conspired to bring her: a bright object, half buried in the sludge, catching the rays of a sun no one had truly seen for weeks. It was a skull.

Rigid, she examined it from a distance of a few feet—the nasal triangle with its tissue-thin walls, the perfect row of teeth—and understood it had come a long way, from within the bowels of the ravaged mountain, down its slopes, borne and scrubbed and washed in the flood. She cocked her head, like a bird, her small face intent and troubled, but made no move to touch the thing, and at last turned around and walked, shivering, back to her own home, her bare feet leaving soft imprints in the mud.

Her grandmother, wrenched abruptly from a world of dreams, was horrified when the child turned on the television: *No news! No news!* she begged. But her father asked what it mattered. For now, the child could do as she pleased. He sat at the table and refused to look at his daughter, passing his fingers time and again over his tear-filled eyes.

The girl's eyes, focused on the TV, were round and blank for, like the three dead girls at school, she had gone, exited neatly and quietly, from the world of looming skies and frightened afternoons. Her mother crossed the threshold hurriedly, abstractedly, wrenching on her windbreaker, struggling to raise her broken umbrella against the rain. *If I could just keep her within sight,* the child thought. *If she would only stay within my sight.* Reflected in the gentle curve of her retina, a frond unfurled, intricate and green. The forest welcomed the child into its depths as she crept, sure-footed, over a carpet of decaying leaves. Not once did she blink. She was taking in everything, for if she missed one single branch, one brilliant flash of wing, the magic would be powerless, over. She was saving the animals. If only she could find them, count them, fix them forever in this void after the storm, all would be well.

Margaret García. *Janine at 39,*
Mother of Twins. 2000. Oil on canvas.
Photograph by John White.

from *One Night in Pohnpei*

CHAPTER ONE

The Jungle Bar, Kolonia, Pohnpei, Stella

It's tourist feet, two pairs in the same fancy new sandals, one on each side of the puddle under the gate. Little red toes and Band-Aids under the straps, man and woman. They push inside in their yellow coats, trying not to be noticed in their yellow coats, then whisper and nod before they totter out again, worried they might catch giardia off a dirty glass, I think. I look around and see who's still here: just Mike and the new Peace Corps getting started, and Gene, poor Gene off all alone at the private table, poor Gene hoping and waiting in the dark, and then only old Castro like every payday drooling and passed out half on the pool table and I think, *Dead tonight, going to be dead tonight. Maybe have a little fun with Mike and Gene and the new Peace Corps. Ruthie can handle things by herself.* I give Ruthie a look.

"Sure, go ahead," Ruthie says. "I'll just fire you again." She's got a little TV under the bar to watch the soaps she tapes during the day, and she aims her remote at me and fires me, turning off her soaps.

Just the stereo now, nice without it having to fight the TV. I put three VBs and one for myself on the tray, plus the shots of Crown for Mike and the new Peace Corps, then I nod for Ruthie to pour one more. She slides it over, eyes me while I drink it. *Here's to us and a good night, and to you, Ruthie my best friend, Ruthie.* I give the glass a spin along the bar, the glass spinning in a nice curve back to Ruthie, and it drops inside the gutter, wobbling there like a drunk and almost tipping over, vibrating as it rights itself and comes to rest in front of the sink. "First one," I say.

"How you get to the last one is what I want to hear, 'cause it's gonna be some trouble with you tonight."

"It's no trouble," I say.

Ruthie laughs and gives me a wink.

I take the tray and smiling I cruise along with the music through the bar, teasing Mike and Peace Corps as I pass them by with their drinks, those two making me laugh, sitting there in the same POHNPEI HEAVEN shirts and both of them with their hair chopped flat on the top. A black and white, older and younger version of the same person, mouths stuck open like a couple of fish. "Hey," Mike says. I head out under the trees and through the torchlight, humming with the music and taking my time over to Gene at the private table, Gene hidden in the dark but for the glow of his watch, watching me and his time pass from under the cone of a shaggy thatched roof. The wind is picking up, blowing the old smells out again, feeling like warm ribbons of the bar's sour old smells twisting away through the cooler air.

"So you called her?" he asks.

"Still sleeping maybe." I take his empty and put the full one down on the coaster, him still looking at his watch.

"You think she'll come?" he asks.

I give him a shrug. Poor horny old men, all the same, can't help wanting the young ones.

With two fingers he puts a five-dollar bill on the tray, leaving it folded like a tent. "Keep it, please," he says. He's so polite about it, but he's a science man, supposed to be above it all, now like a poor boy he's got to try for it on the sly with a night-crawling girl. He'd sit in the dark till morning and come back the next night if I told him to.

The wind catches the five dollars and it flies off the tray and over the gravel toward the bar, tumbling. Ruthie already sees it coming, big yellow skirt hiked up to her knees and bare legs dodging left then right to catch it. Scandalous. She squashes the money flat with her foot, her zori slapping so loud against her heel that even Castro's head jerks up, a second or so later.

"Sorry," Gene says. He's put on a nice white *barong*, pressed even, but he's tucked it in and buttoned it up so tight it makes his sunburned head look like a red balloon. Around the bar the wind is making music with the trees: trunks creaking, moaning, branches rubbing and leaves shaking— storm chimes before the coming rain. It feels good, the wind blowing my hair around.

"It gets wet out here," I say, "so you better come back inside. Come hang out with me and Mike and the new Peace Corps. Marihna might come later; I'll call again in a little while if you want."

"I don't know them," he says.

"You'll come in when you get wet, maybe sooner when you get scared of the dark." I give him a smile over my shoulder as I leave, lots to smile about as I carry the tray back through the wind-blown torchlight, thinking, *Going to be dead tonight, going to have some fun with them tonight,* and then I come out of the torchlight just as the night blooms full of lightning, smiling now in the lightning with the same smile I had for Gene, this time for Mike and the new Peace Corps.

CHAPTER TWO

Mike

Here comes Stella, smooth and steady with her tray like she's just floating on over, lean as a wasp and deadly as one too in those skin-tight jeans and a too-small tank top, smiling. Good fun, that's Stella, that's what I told him. Peace Corps said one week on the island and already he's bored as hell, but it ain't boredom. Probably going to cut and run. Stella puts the tray in the middle of the table and sits down. "Help yourself," she says. "I'm fired again."

"You don't even have a shot," I say. I hold mine up and one finger so Ruthie can see. She's quick for a big girl, Ruthie, always quick with a drink. And she ain't tight with the bottle either, pours her shots full over the line and no sneaking you the cheap stuff, like Varner does at his place. She'll even comp you one every now and then if you tip her right.

"You really get fired?" Doug asks.

Stella laughs. "What you think?" He don't know what to say, so he just smiles back at her, the both of them smiling, one of those times you get stuck smiling at somebody and have to wait it out.

Ruthie brings Stella's shot, the two of them sharing a look. My treat. We raise our glasses for a toast. "Here's to getting fired, if I could be so god-damn lucky," I say and toss mine back. At first I'm thinking it's the whiskey, a rumbling in my head that takes me a second or two to sort out, feeling stupid as I realize it's just thunder. Then I remember seeing the lightning. It's like I didn't see it at first, but *remembered* seeing it, like it took a few seconds for my brain to register it. This morning I swore to God I wasn't gonna drink, but after paving all day I thought I'd hit town for a couple quick ones, just to get out of camp so I wouldn't have to drink in front of the lieutenant, then when not even Lopez wanted to come along, I said I wasn't tied to nobody's clock, and I ran into Dem at the store and he said he was coming down—then this guy Doug shows up and he wants to have a little fun, probably before he cuts and runs, and right away we're having a good time laughing at each other in the same damn shirt and both of us sportin' one of goddamn George's famous buzz cuts to boot, so I said, Why not make a night of it? Now we got Stella.

Stella leans in at Doug, her finger running around the rim of her shot glass. "You're new," she says.

He's looking past her, at some big gray dog that's been creeping around and now's lying down beside the puddle at the gate, sniffing at it. "Yeah," he says.

Stella unfolds her arms, hula style, like a flower opening. "Welcome to Pohnpei," she says. "Have a good time and do whatever you want." She laughs, and finally he looks at her.

"Stella used to be a tour guide," I say.

"It's true," Stella says. "I was captain of the guides. But I kept losing tourists, so they fired me." She smiles again, that same smile she had when she came over, her mouth sparkling with gold teeth. Her hair is swept back by the wind, held there by the wind.

Doug looks at me.

"Hey Stella, why don't you take us on a tour?" I say. "The Kolonia Nightlife Special. Doug here says he's bored."

"Sure," Stella says. "If he's not scared that he might get lost."

Doug looks at me again.

It starts to pour, thick sheets of rain bombarding the roofs, the wind blowing rain and leaves across our table, the rain so loud it drowns out the stereo I didn't even notice, like the lightning, until I couldn't hear it anymore. The torches go out, wicks dying in a puff of smoke. "Let's have another shot," I say. That gray dog just lies there, pelted by the rain, looking at us. Knows better than to come inside the bar, but not enough sense to go crawl under something.

"Hey Gene, get out of the damn storm!" Stella yells, and some chunky old guy trots out of the dark, squinting and ducking from the rain. His shirt is plastered to his skin, one of those Filipino shirts just about as see-through as plastic wrap when it's wet, dark hairs all over his gut and his nipples showing through. He sits at the table next to us, smiling at us and flapping his shirt to get it dry. His face is sunburned, his skin pale, almost gray under the shirt. In his late forties or early fifties, I think, not so old as I thought, actually has kind of a baby face, soft looking. What the hell was he doing over there in the dark? "You leave a girl over there?" I ask.

He chuckles, shaking his head, staring down at his foamed-up beer. Then he jerks his head back up and looks at me, bug-eyed. He sips some foam, not taking his eyes off me. "So you're with the Civic Action Team?" he asks, and he starts flapping his shirt again. "I saw you working on the roads."

"Nah, that must have been some other brother you saw. I'm just on vacation, hanging here while the statute of limitations runs out on a little complication back in Reno." He looks at me like I'm not even messing with him, so I tell him, "Yeah, yeah, I'm with the CAT Team. EO2 Mike Flear, at least that's what my tags tell me." I hold out my hand, and he reaches over and shakes it, his hand cold and wet.

"What a place to be stationed," he says. "So did you get on some kind of list, or did they just send you here?"

"Hey, you're pretty funny." Only guy ever asked to be stationed here turned out to be a nut job and killed a couple people—but that was before my time, if I even believe it. Stella would know.

"Mike helped build the mental hospital too," Stella says.

"Really?" He leans over like he really wants to hear about it.

"Yeah, why? You building one back home and need some tips?" It really was some good times, the mental hospital, especially at the end with me and Lopez taking our sweet time putting in the bars and dragging out the days, all that shade out there and a nice breeze blowing through, just me and Lopez and a few beers stashed inside the water cooler for when the girls came by. Now it's this road job, out in the goddamn heat all day—like breathing pure hell when the tar is cooking. He just looks at me, smiling. "So you are…?"

"Gene Frisby," he says. Then it's quiet for a second when he doesn't say who he is, just smiles. He reaches over and shakes Doug's hand, holding it too long and smiling a little too much, I think. "And you must be the new Peace Corps volunteer," he says. "Stella told me." Must want us to think it's a secret, what he does, even if he's got no problem asking us.

"Yeah, Peace Corps," Doug says, "but—"

"Amazing," he says, and he leans back in his chair. "I think it's amazing what you people get to do, the opportunity."

Stella looks at Doug, but he's staring again at that gray dog, still lying in the rain by the gate. "You don't think it's so amazing," she says, "do you, Peace Corps?"

"Huh?" He don't want to talk about it. He just wants to have a good time and then he's going to cut and run. "Don't get me wrong," he says. "I only been here like a week, but—"

"Let's have another shot," I say. I see another burst of lightning, three bright flashes making diamonds out of the driving rain, and I start counting, *One one-thousand, two one-thousand…*

"Oh, so you're less than satisfied with the Corps?" Gene asks. I bet he's CIA; they keep bringing new CIA here.

Doug laughs. "Less than satisfied," he says. "I like that, like right now I'm trying to get less than sober." Ruthie turns up the stereo, so we hear it again. All of us glance up at the speakers, crackling because the wires are wet from the rain.

"Sit over here with us, Gene," Stella says, patting a chair. "Why you sitting over there?"

"I'm OK," he says.

The thunder comes, everybody quiet while it passes. Sixteen seconds to get here, five seconds per mile. "About three miles away," I say. "The lightning, I counted from the lightning."

"Storm's moving fast too," Gene says. "The last flash was nearly twice as far away." He looks thoughtfully out at the rain, like he wants us to think he's gathering more weather data to share with us. He's no CIA. Then he does that head-jerk thing again, with his bug eyes, this time looking at Doug. "So is your problem with the Corps exactly, or is it just being so far from home, second thoughts maybe, some apprehension about how your world view might be altered by dedicating a good part of your young life to living within a Micronesian society?"

Doug looks at him. "I don't know about that, man," he says. Then he looks down at the table and takes a big breath like he needs it to get out what he's got to say, and he looks up at us and he says, "Listen, this place is a trip, no doubt, like this mad jungle everywhere, and the mountains always up in the clouds, everything all green and spooky and shit in the mist, you know—and I'm cool with the people too," he says, looking at Stella, "way cool, but it's like, where's the beach? It's like these freakin' mangroves all the way around the island, all swampy, like you don't even see the ocean unless you climb up on a rock. Then they got me staying on this pig farm way out in Awak. Like I grew up in Oxnard, OK—but we didn't have an ox, you know, and every morning I'm totally like, whoa, what the freak is up with these pigs going wicked off their bean? It's this farmer dude on dawn patrol, bringing their morning slop, and they're all screaming bloody hell and stomping all over each other and shit—like you think you're waking up in Frankenstein's nightmare, you know what I mean? I mean, I'm in this training group, OK, and next month they're sending us to Yap, not like some town in Yap where you can at least get a cold beer or snatch an air-conditioned minute sometimes, but way-out-in-the-boonies-Yap, you know, the Yap-that-time-forgot-Yap. And we get there, man, and then we gotta help start a sponge farm."

Stella and I look at him, and when we see he isn't joking, we laugh.

He laughs too, a little late, staring again at that dog lying in the rain. "I swear before I left I was totally into it, thinking, yeah, cool, defer some of my student loans for just cruising the islands, then I get here and I go, *What the hell was I thinking?*" He takes a long swallow of his beer, done talking about it. But that ain't all of it. Best he just cuts and runs.

"Hey, I like sponges," Stella says. "Nothing wrong with sponges."

"Headaches," Gene says, "do you get headaches?"

"Huh?" Doug says. "Yeah, sometimes. Why?"

Gene picks up his beer and comes over and sits next to Doug, looking serious. "How about insomnia?" he asks. "Maybe some digestive problems, feelings of anxiety, boredom, sluggishness?"

"Yeah, I guess."

Gene nods, expertlike. "Culture shock," he says. "What you're dealing with is just a little culture shock. Obviously, you've been drawn back to town as a means of re-associating with a more Western environment, which might improve your outlook in the short term, except if you keep coming back, I think it could really hurt your ability to embrace a more traditional island lifestyle. And the drinking, the drinking might develop into a pattern of compulsive behavior if you're not careful." Fucker sits in a bar with beer foam on his lip, saying that shit. What he needs is a shot or two with us, a couple more than three, and that'll help get his head straight.

"I'd advise you to just give things a little time," he says. "Immerse yourself in the local culture, learn to open yourself to different ways of thinking, of seeing the world, and I'd bet that by the time you get settled into Yap, you'll find you've recovered all your previous enthusiasm." Then he sits back, looking like he just settled everything and he's ready to move on and fix somebody else's problems.

Doug sort of nods at him. "Right, culture shock," he says. Then he goes back to looking at that dog.

"Compulsive behavior," I say. "I'll drink to that. Let's have another shot."

"None for me, thanks," Gene says, his hand up like he's stopping traffic.

"Three then." I hold up my shot glass and four fingers so Ruthie can see and he can't. He's not sitting here and not drinking with us, saying that shit. Ruthie's already on it.

"Hey, Dem is coming down," I say. We're all damp from the blowing rain, so it looks like we're sweating.

"Who?" Stella asks.

"You know, Demmeter, that big bald guy, always talking crazy shit. Drags that weird kid of his around with him, tries to get him laid."

"Oh, Baldy. That crazy white-ass."

Gene goes bug-eyed again and looks at Stella. "Damn, I don't like that guy," he says, his nose twitching.

"Yeah, he's a character all right," I say. "But boy, he can drink." Dem will keep up. He'll keep up just like Stella. Bugs start bubbling up from the quickly flooding gravel, some of them crawling up and over the concrete into the bar.

"What's up with that dog?" Doug asks. "It just sits there, getting soaked, staring at me."

"Never seen that one," Stella says. She squashes a bug with her foot. "So Baldy's coming on my tour too, eh? Gonna be one of those nights."

"I really don't like that guy," Gene says. "I don't like that guy at all."

"Maybe you're just less than satisfied with him," Doug says.

Here comes Ruthie, damp skin shining for an instant in the lightning. "I got you a shot anyway," I tell Gene, and I start counting, *One one-thousand, two one-thousand…*

CHAPTER TEN

Stella

The wind is picking up again, a north wind free of the storm and howling in from across the dark and crashing sea and filtered through the mountains, smelling of the mountains and the sea, cool and strong and gusting. Gene is laughing at Baldy saying sorry, looking a little silly, a little drunk.

"This is all too much," Gene says. His face is glowing, a red beneath the red, something ugly in his eyes when he looks at Baldy, but he's gonna pull through, gonna stick around now for the tour, laughing because he's gonna stay even though part of him is scared and telling him he better leave, telling him he never should have come at all.

"Just wait till we get going, Gene," I say. "You'll see somebody when we get where we going." I raise my glass, poor Mike with his already up, and we drink to a good time on my tour. Sometimes when the wind is blowing, I like to think I can feel within it all that it has touched, as if I can feel its giant fluid body connecting me with where it's been and where it goes, one wind touching another until all of the earth is in and out of me.

"So where are we going?" Peace Corps asks.

I give him a smile.

"Cannibals," Gene says, harsh through the whiskey that took away his breath. He tries to laugh, but it sounds like coughing. "Why does everybody think I'm here looking for evidence of cannibals?" He laughs, an uneasy look on his face, his beer clanking on his teeth as he tries to drink it.

"Then what are you doing here?" Peace Corps asks. "What are you really looking for out there at Nan Madol?"

Gene stops laughing, looks at us with those eyes of his. He can't say yet what he came for, ashamed of it—hasn't had it in so long he thinks he's not meant to have it, like he's got to steal it and spend the rest of his life ashamed and defending his right to keep it. He can't say what he found either—those bones that he knows aren't so old—can't even think about it. But there's no shame in what he wants, what every man wants. Here comes Ruthie.

"I'm sure you'd find the exact nature of my work quite boring," Gene says. He wants Peace Corps to be his friend, sees in him another part of what he's wanted for a long time now, what he's never going to get. He leans in. "But in its broader scope it can be rather fascinating, for the layperson that is: delving into the origins of an ancient civilization shrouded in so much mystery. And I'd think such knowledge of how we are uncovering the past would be a valuable addition to what you're already doing as a Peace Corps volunteer. Maybe a field trip could be organized, and all of you could assist with the dig one day." He smiles, beaming, thinking of being big papa for a day to all the Peace Corps. The torches blow out in a gust of wind, too wet from the rain.

"Tell him why you're really here, why you came out here in the first place," Mike says.

"Yeah," Baldy says, "fess up, Frisby—no shame in being one of the boys."

"I hardly think—"

Ruthie sloshes Gene's near-empty, sets it back down, and nods for him to finish it. "It's the new law," she says. "Can't have two beers at the same time." Gene looks at her, then like a good boy he finishes his beer in one big swallow, some of it running out of the corner of his mouth.

"This round's on me," I say, and I give Ruthie my new twenty. "So Peace Corps, you throw in Ruthie's tip." He starts counting through his money, careful with it, but no chance he'll hang on to any of it. He gives Ruthie a five. Somebody far away is pounding *sakau*—two stones pounding one after the other—the sound of it ringing on the wind.

"Damn cheap torches," Ruthie says, looking over. "Stormproof, they said, before the rain washed the stickers off." She's got the tray to carry back, so I tell her I'll get the torches, and she tosses me her matches. "You're still fired," she says, giving me a wink as she heads back to the bar.

"What you need torches for anyway?" Mike asks.

"Gotta have torches," I say. "Can't be a jungle bar without torches." I walk out to the path. They think I can't hear them, their voices riding on the wind.

"It's the young one, isn't it?" Mike asks, his voice low. "Stella's cousin—Marihna, that's her name."

Gene stares at him. "Fine then," he says. "Let's just get this out of the way and all of you can have a good laugh, but that's the end of it and I don't want to hear anymore about it. Yes, I am interested in the young woman, Marihna, but—"

"Pretty damn young, all right. You big stud," Mike says. "What she see in you anyway? No offense, you know."

You pull the wick up, where the kerosene is fresh, and it lights fast. I light one with the other and then I stab the first one back in the mud.

Peace Corps laughs. "Ain't it like the Hippomatic Oath or something, like you're a doctor, right—an archaeologist is still a doctor—and you're not supposed to be diddling the natives, are you?"

I come back quiet, making Peace Corps jerk a little when I sit down next to him. "Eh, what you said? You think it's something dirty with us island girls, something less than with white girls?"

"No, no," Peace Corps says, "I didn't mean it like that. I was just—"

"Good," I say. "All you Peace Corps should date an island girl first so you don't think like that." I give him a wink. "So how about it: you wanna be my date tonight?"

"OK," Peace Corps says, smiling—scared but smiling.

"Last guy who dated Stella needed an IV," Mike says. "That pilot, right?"

"Fucked him dry," I say.

"Please," Gene says, and he closes his eyes like it's gonna stop his ears from hearing.

"What, Gene, tell me you don't like to fuck, make me laugh. You white-ass make no sense: come here and fuck like dogs but pretend it's something bad. I like to fuck—no shame in liking to fuck, eh, Peace Corps?" He looks down in the hole of his beer can, lost there.

"Hey," Baldy says, "I like to fuck."

"Good, then go fuck yourself," I say. His kid is snickering, everybody laughing. It makes Gene feel better, seeing me riding Baldy's ass.

"Goddamn you, Stella," Baldy says, toasting me and smiling with that nice smile of his. Then real fast—not even a second—he gives his a kid a look, but it's like a silver glint flashing in his eyes, his head not even turning, only his eyes flashing at him with that silver glint, and I can see within him something of the rotten things he did to put it there. His kid stops laughing.

"You know, there can be more to it: *fucking*," Gene says, slurring the word.

"Oh, like it's something special with you and that girl?" Baldy says, and he gives me a look to check how far I'll let him go. "Maybe you put on soft music or something," he says, "pretend it's something special? Or have you even hit it yet?"

"You know," Gene says, "I apologize for trying to inject a little civility into this conversation. And everybody's had their laugh now, so I'd appreciate it if you could resist expressing your fascination with my personal life. It's none of your business."

"Sorry, Chester," Baldy says, "didn't mean to blow the cover on your little schoolgirl panty raid."

Gene's eyes get big again. "Let's get this straight," he says. "I'm quite aware of the age difference—it's not unheard of, you know—and before any of you jump to conclusions, she is above legal age. Maybe, Mr. Demmeter, before you chastise me, you ought to take a good look at yourself, dragging your underage son out to a bar."

"Hey, he's eighteen," Baldy says. "Old enough to drink around here, probably older than that girl of yours. So did you hit it yet or not?" He looks at me again, sure I'm gonna say something, but I just look back at him. He's funny, Baldy, always making jokes and talking his crazy shit, good fun to have around when you're drinking, and he's got that nice smile too and those pretty eyes, so you think maybe he's just another drunk, good fun even if he can be an asshole. But when his eyes get that glint, I can see he's rotten inside. It happens to people sometimes. They just go rotten—one thing then another that they do until they turn into something rotten, like a sailor I know. Bloodied himself and made himself a rapist king, and most times you can look at them and not even know.

"Seventeen, Dad," Baldy's kid says. "I'm seventeen." Nobody looks at him.

"I heard if you spend the night out at Nan Madol, you might die," Peace Corps says. "People have died or they go crazy or something. It's supposed to be haunted." He's nervous about all this talk about sex, nervous he might actually be my date, wants to change the subject before I reach down and give his balls a squeeze. He looks at me.

"Anyway, I think the drinking age is twenty-one here," Baldy's kid says, holding up his beer like it's got the rules printed on it.

"Oh yeah, it's haunted," Baldy says, leaning in toward Peace Corps, that glint in his eyes flashing so fast that Peace Corps don't even see it. "The ancient Celts would have called Nan Madol a *thin place,* where the veil between this world and the next world is passable. Sometimes things get through."

"O Mother of Mercy," Gene says. "It's just stories—nothing to be frightened of out there except some very nasty insects."

"So you wouldn't be afraid if you went there at night?" Peace Corps asks.

Gene laughs, a fake laugh. "Hardly."

Peace Corps looks around at all of us. "This guy, the guy who took us out there, he told us that in the sixties there was a Peace Corps volunteer who spent the night at Nan Madol—on a dare. They found him the next day, dead from a heart attack. Twenty-seven years old and he was dead from a heart attack."

"If I had a dollar for every ridiculous tale I've heard about Nan Madol," Gene says, "floating balls of light, giant bones, and platinum coffins. Ghosts wandering about and dwarfs and giants from the depths of hell, coming up to prey upon whatever poor fool happens to be wandering about at night. Nonsense. In fact—"

"And I heard the same thing happened to some Japanese soldier who spent the night out there back in World War II," Peace Corps says, "except his hair turned white and he went crazy instead of died."

"Oh yeah," Baldy says, "and ask Frisby about Kubary and Berg—what he knows about them. He knows."

"Hey," Mike says, "that's the law firm my ex-wife sent after my ass." Nobody laughs, so he shrugs.

"No," Gene says, irritated. "They did some work at Nan Madol around the turn of the last century—amateurs really—and any diabolical significance attributed to their deaths is pure fabrication. Berg died from heat stroke and—"

"That's what you say," Baldy says. "But I'll bet you wouldn't go out there at night. Like right now, if we went right now." He looks at me. "What about you, Stella? What's your take on Nan Madol? I bet you know a thing or two."

I give Baldy a shrug, smiling. "People believe what they want about that place."

"But what do you believe?"

I laugh at him. "I believe you should be more afraid of what's living than what's dead."

Baldy's kid looks at me. I give him a smile.

"Look," Gene tells Baldy, "I have no intention of traipsing out to Nan Madol just so you can make childish ghost noises and try to make me believe they're coming from the twilight zone." Those bones have really gotten to him, but we're gonna fix that, set things right.

"Hey, it might be fun," Baldy says, and he looks around the table. "Let's grab some girls and some booze and go out there tonight and see what's up for ourselves—a dare, in the tradition of the United States Peace Corps."

"What girls you think wanna go out there?" I ask.

"Man, that's nuts," Mike says. "Like I used to know these dudes who'd go to this cemetery sometimes, just to party, and—"

"You know, lots of bad things happen out there," Baldy's kid says, "for whatever reasons you want to believe—but it's a bad place to go any way you look at it."

"Yeah," Peace Corps says, "but how do you know that shit? I mean, dude, how can you really know that shit?"

"My dad told me, and he knows fucking everything." He gives Baldy a look.

Baldy laughs. "I actually had his blood tested a few years back, no offense to his mother." He makes a sloppy sign of the cross, grinning at his kid with that glint in his eyes, then he claps his hands together. "So how about it? Just a couple hours out there, just to see."

"Fuck that, man," Peace Corps says. "I'm scared as hell of ghosts."

"Listen," I say, "if you boys want to go out to Nan Madol and look for your ghosts, that's OK—I can put that on the tour for later—but first we gotta go to Varner's place, have a beer up there and meet a couple friends." I give Gene a look, smiling. "Mike's gonna drive us," I say.

"Who's Varner?" Peace Corps asks.

A faint burst of lightning brightens the night sky, too far away for thunder. Baldy stares at the dark sky where it flashed. "I can prove the existence of ghosts right now," he says.

"Save it a couple beers," Mike says. "Right now we gotta kick this pig in high gear. It's Stella's tour, first stop Varner's place." He stands up straight as a general. "Doug, you go get us some beers for the road while I go take a piss and fire up the Beast." He shakes the last drop of his beer into his mouth as he goes, then tosses the empty in the trash on his way out the gate. We look at each other, standing slow. Peace Corps takes out his wallet, looks in it, gives us a weak smile before he gets his legs under him, and heads to the bar.

"OK, boys," I say, "leave Ruthie a nice tip and follow close so nobody gets lost." Ruthie's trying to wake up Castro, wants him out of the bar before he pisses on her pool table again. I give her a wave as I go, and she nods back with Castro's head, up and down with his eyes half open. That *sakau* stone rings louder on a gust of wind, an ancient rhythm pulsing on the wind, stone on stone, ringing what's been rung for so long it's into everything now, part of the hum of the island. I hold open the gate and smiling I point Gene and Baldy and his kid to Mike's big green truck.

Mike is walking bowlegged beside it with his dick out, chasing a toad and pissing on it. Toads everywhere, hopping. Baldy takes his dick out and starts pissing on one too, laughing. "Get it in its mouth!" he says. "In its mouth!" Crazy white-ass.

"My God," Gene says. He heads for the passenger door, going the long way around to avoid the pissing.

"Me and Mike up front," I say. "The rest of you sit in back." Gene and Baldy look at each other, Baldy pissing in a high arc at Gene. Poor Gene, cursing.

It's nice out in the dark. With the storm past, the moon looks like it's racing through the newly opened clouds, moonlight like new chrome on the wet banana leaves whipping in the wind, and the cool wind howls down from the mountains as though it were coming from the throat of the earth howling in awe of itself. So here's Gene, poor Gene dying inside his own sorry plan, and here's Peace Corps, poor Doug the Peace Corps, on his last night out, and Baldy, his last night too, and his boy, cursed to have his father's blood, and here's Mike, lost Mike gonna take us here and there along the way to Nan Madol, and I think, *Dead tonight, gonna be dead tonight,* and now we just need to gather a few more.

Ester Hernández. *Astrid Hadad
in San Francisco*. 1994. Pastel on paper.
Photograph by Peggy Tennison.

Lizard _____

If you press your lips to the tongue of a snake and show fear, the snake will swallow you up. If not, it will guide you to the entrance of another world. The snake is a reptile of transcendence.

Jim Morrison, in the movie The Doors

"Want to hear the one about the smoke woman?" he asks me.

"Sure, go ahead."

He's smoking a cigarette, watching the smoke seep out of his mouth, twist, coil, and drift off. "OK. One day a man's body turns up. The officer at the scene finds the place *littered* with cigarette butts. The place reeks of cigarette smoke—so strong it covers up the smell of decomposition."

"So…?" I look at him wide-eyed, urging him on.

"So how'd he die? That's a good question. The officer investigates different possibilities. First, he schedules an autopsy—which is more involved than the usual exam. In an autopsy, you actually cut into the body as well as examine it for clues. And then the officer discovers something very interesting."

"What's that?"

"In addition to being naked from the waist down, there was a large quantity of semen."

"That's because men ejaculate when they die," I say with a shiver.

He shakes his head. "That's if you're strangled. But there were no signs of strangulation on this guy. If you're strangled, your neck is all black and blue. None of that on him, though."

"So?"

"So the officer suspects there's a woman involved."

"He could have been masturbating, you know."

"No, he couldn't. Not with the semen spread around like it was, strange as it all seems."

He is so confident in his reply that I have to give in. He's always like that—no doubts about *anything*. Words seem to come so easily to him. No hesitating, no beating around the bush. Talking to him is like watching a movie or reading a novel. And then he suddenly becomes distant. How long has it been since he started coming to my room? How long since he spread himself so naturally over the far corner of my bed? It's all because of the *lizard*. I turn to look at my walls. They're white and bare, except for the looming *lizard*.

"What are you thinking about?" He's noticed I've turned my head away.

I take my eyes off the *lizard*. "Nothing."

Men are always asking women what they're thinking, but women don't think the way men do. Men think with their heads; women think with their bodies. It can't be explained. All I can feel are the traces of *lizard* on my body. That's why "Nothing" is the only answer I can come up with.

"Go on with the story," I tell him.

But he just offers me a weak smile and shakes his head. "Later."

He dresses and goes out, leaving me with a *lizard,* a dead man, and a large quantity of semen. I have no idea where he's going.

I first met him in the fall of 1995. It was cold for that time of year, and extremely windy. I remember reading about a street sign getting blown off a pole and hitting someone's head. I had a job teaching English to junior-high-school students at a cram school in Kangnam and was about to photocopy some handouts when he walked in.

"Are you still looking for teachers?" he asked.

The funny thing was that I'd seen him get out of the elevator and plod up to the door, but he still took me by surprise. Maybe it's because he didn't look like he had any reason to be at a cram school. What was it about him? He did, after all, have the cram-school outfit: a navy-blue shirt and black pants. So what was it that threw me off?

I guess you might say there was something otherworldly about him. There are people like this. People that you bump into on the street and that make you feel like you've bumped into a ghost. People you walk up to and prepare to pass right through. People who will turn into a heap of ash if you nudge them a little. You can see them in the subways, too. They look as if they've been sitting there for centuries, as if the subways will run forever, just for them. There are people like this. And he was one of them.

"What do you teach?"

"Korean."

He made it sound so foreign that I wondered if we even taught it at the school. *Korean…Korean…,* I repeated to myself on our way to the principal's office. And from that day on, he taught Korean.

Indian shamans dedicate their first sexual experiences to those who drive them mad.   Jim Morrison, in the movie *The Doors*

"You have to transform yourself," he mumbled to me the second time we went drinking. With that, he produced an object wrapped in white paper and placed it on the table. "A present."

I tore the wrapping off and flinched. A *lizard*. A black, metal *lizard*. It was so elaborate that, if I hadn't felt it, I'd have thought it was real.

"Hang it so it looks like it's crawling down your wall. You'll get a rise out of your friends the first time they see it."

I felt a bit uncomfortable about all this, but put the *lizard* in my handbag nonetheless. "Where'd you buy it?"

"In the tropics. *Lizards* are as common as ants down there. From the time you're a kid, you get used to *lizards* crawling over your belly and your legs. They're everywhere. There's even a *lizard*-worshiping tribe."

"Really?"

"Did you know that a *lizard*'s tail grows back if you cut it off? That's why *lizards* symbolize regeneration and rebirth. People in Europe in the Middle Ages prayed to the salamander. They thought it was a fire-breathing *lizard;* they believed it lived in fire. Chameleons are *lizards,* too. *Lizards* have no past. That's what makes them gods. For them there's nothing but the present, the eternal present."

I gave him a long, hard look. I couldn't figure him out. I didn't know where he'd gone to school, where he was from, or where he'd worked. I'd been out with him twice and still not a word about his past.

After we said goodbye, I went home and dutifully studied the walls of my room, which were bare except for a single coat hanger. My friends tell me it doesn't look like a girl's room. It makes me realize I've never bought anything to decorate it, not even a simple picture frame.

I hammered a nail into the wall opposite my bed and hung the *lizard* by the loop in its twisty tail. He was right: it really did look like it was crawling down the wall. And suddenly the wall was shivering all over.

I saw the *lizard* in my dreams that night. I knew it was supposed to be hanging motionless, but there it was, crawling down the wall, slow and sinuous, expanding and contracting. The strange thing was that none of this struck me as the least bit unusual. I actually grew impatient to see it moving so slowly. Bolting awake, I looked at the wall: the *lizard* was hanging there, just where it was supposed to be.

This world has no beginning and no end. To have lost a loved one in this world means that you are left with nothing.
                                          Jim Morrison, in the movie *The Doors*

Right around the third time he and I went out drinking, the *lizard* started coming to me. I came home that night and discovered that the boiler was off and my room was cold. So I jumped into bed. The alcohol I'd drunk was leaving an uncomfortable path as it traveled through my blood vessels. I turned off the lights and stared at the *lizard* hanging on my wall. I wondered if I should give it a name. Later, I decided. I couldn't come up with anything anyway, and I was drifting off to sleep.

The *lizard* is creeping down the wall. I can't move; I feel like I'm tied down. I can't make a sound. There's music: the slow, solemn beat of a drum, the rhythm familiar but unrecognizable. The beat is punctuated by a hiss. Is that what it sounds like when the *lizard*'s tongue flicks? I keep my eye on the *lizard*. It's the only thing I can do. The *lizard* creeps toward my bed. And then he's out of sight. Now I'm scared. Scared but excited. The hissing grows louder than the drumbeat. There—the *lizard*'s head—at the foot of my bed.

Suddenly I'm in a rain forest, but still in my bed. There's bright sunlight all around and birdsong and the beating of drums in the distance. The *lizard* mounts my leg. It's like an electric shock. And then a voice—my father's voice. I can barely hear it, and he's speaking very fast. I'm frightened; I've been bad. I don't know what I've done, but I beg his forgiveness. He's naked as he approaches my bed in the rain forest.

Meanwhile, the *lizard* has slithered up my thighs. I feel self-conscious with my father there. His face is red with anger. He's going to beat me, I know. I'm scared. The *lizard* stops. Out comes the tongue, and it starts licking my thighs. Feels like ice water running down, uncomfortably cold, but ticklish. Despite my efforts to control myself, the *lizard*'s tongue awakens sensations long dormant. Father comes closer, looking back and forth between me and the *lizard*. I can hear my mother laughing from afar. She tells him, *See, I told you. I told you she's got spunk.* Father doesn't respond.

The *lizard* reaches my vagina. I want to scream, but my father and mother are looking on. My father scolds me: *Dirty whore. This* lizard *is yours?* I want to defend myself, but the words won't come out. Pleasure overwhelms me.

It's all so strange. I have never been satisfied by a man. Either they're in too much of a hurry or they're totally awkward. I'm twenty-five, and I've slept with three men. The first one was just a boy. He'd kiss like he was trying to suck my tongue out, then tear my clothes off and penetrate me as fast as he could. I suppose I should feel grateful he took the time to kiss me. The second one would make a dash for the bathroom to wash himself the moment he'd ejaculated, as if I'd soiled him. Then he'd pass out for the night while the foreign substance was still wiggling inside me. The third one was just plain scared of sex. He'd go through with it, but obviously wanted to get it over as soon as possible. He kept asking if he came too soon, if his penis was too small, if I was really satisfied. It drove me to distraction. He never gave me an orgasm, but rather than disappoint him, I lied. *Oh yes, it was lovely—absolutely wonderful*, I'd say, and then he'd go to sleep. I don't think he believed me.

But this is different. A sharp wave of pleasure spreads through me. I can hardly stand it! I don't hear the drumbeat anymore. I can't see Mother or Father either. I now see the face of the man who gave me the *lizard*. He stands in the dark, a faint shadow, smiling.

And then I'm awake. The sun is coming out. I stare at the wall. The *lizard* is nowhere in sight. I shake my head violently, trying to clear my thoughts. I feel along my wall for the light switch and look at where the *lizard* should be hanging.

It is there, exactly where it's supposed to be.

I am a puppet; God seems to be pulling my strings.
Jim Morrison, in the movie The Doors

My father was a minister in a small church he had established himself. It was on the third floor of an apartment complex, maybe a thousand square feet or so. Mother was busy from sunup to sundown doing the things you would expect a minister's wife to do: staying in touch with the parishioners, cleaning the sanctuary, helping Father with his sermons, and keeping up with the housework. She was even busier on the days of early-morning and late-night prayer meetings. Father was always somber, Mother always obedient. I was always bored. We lived in a small room off the sanctuary; I felt like we were surrounded by hymns. Once in a great while, I'd hear Mother and Father having sex. Father's heavy breathing would wake me, and I would hear Mother moaning from somewhere inside the blankets. Her moans resembled the inarticulate recitations of the parishioners. I could never understand what she was saying. Sometimes she'd cry out, only to have Father scold her.

Once in a while, he beat her, too. The house was dirty, or she had misplaced the sermon. Mother took the beatings silently, the big wooden cross looming over Father's head.

A large sign hung at the entrance to the sanctuary: FAITH, HOPE, LOVE. But neither Mother nor Father seemed to have any hope for me—or faith or love, for that matter. I spent my days on the swing in the neighborhood playground or poking around the shops nearby. I hated church.

Years went by, but Father's church failed to grow. Then Mother disappeared. She left no word, just up and vanished. The parishioners talked about her whenever they could, their gossip revolving around Satan, snakes, and running away. At the time, I had a habit of drawing snakes in my diary. I'd write, *Mommy, I miss you,* and decorate the words with writhing reptiles. The adults whispered into my ears that a snake had wrapped itself around my mother. What a joke; I knew it was a lie.

Father eventually remarried and moved his church. His new wife was a churchgoer ten years his junior. I transferred to a university in Seoul, finally leaving home. I lied to Father when we spoke on the phone: *Yes, I go to church every day; the minister's sermons are great, really inspiring. I'm in the choir, too.* At school my major was mathematics. I spent four years struggling with differential and integral calculus. The innocent and straightforward world of mathematics appealed to me. The first midterm I took in differential and integral calculus asked me to "prove that 1 is larger than 0." I did it using epsilon and delta. I even produced a complex drawing of a flower as part of a calculus problem. That's how I spent my early twenties: hovering between 1 and 0.

I think I was jealous of my mother. I also wanted to run away from that church and its oppressive hymns. To a place where I wouldn't have a cross looking down on me all the time.

The first time I did it, I saw God.   Pamela, in the movie *The Doors*

The *lizard* entered me a few days after the dream. I think it was late in the afternoon. I dropped off to sleep while sitting in front of the TV with a cold beer and watching a Hollywood action flick.

The *lizard* darts down the wall. It doesn't scare me. I've seen it move before. The *lizard* approaches the bed. I remember that if you cut off a *lizard*'s tail, it starts to grow back right away. I'd like to talk to the *lizard*. It climbs on the bed. Mother is going somewhere. *I'm sorry, Mom.* I beg her forgiveness, not knowing what I've done wrong. Meanwhile, the *lizard* has climbed up on my foot and is coming closer. Its tongue is caressing my every curve. *Oh, please.* I can't move, I bite down on my lip, I cry out.

Suddenly, I'm younger. I'm lying down. I'm wearing a short skirt and a ribbon in my hair. The *lizard* presents me with a series of images. I'm a little girl, and I'm playing with myself as I gaze at the pictures of naked Adam and Eve. Excitement rushes over me. The scene changes. I'm in Sunday school, touching the penis of one of the boys in my class. I slowly lower his trousers, staring at his penis, wanting to put it in my mouth. Then it's suddenly bigger, and the boy is as tall as an adult. A lush forest of hair rings his penis, and I delight in running my fingers through it. I put his penis in my mouth and feel it harden. My mouth starts to hurt. His penis has turned into a block of wood, and I can barely get it out of my mouth. Then it becomes a neon cross. I kneel piously before this red, glistening cross. My saliva dribbles from it. I wonder who this man is. I raise my head and look into his face. I've never seen him before.

The images end and the *lizard* proceeds to crawl over my crotch, its tongue and tail teasing my inner thighs and vagina. I'm sweating all over. The *lizard* is coming closer and closer. My legs are wide open. The *lizard* is gazing at my sex. I'm ashamed—it's inspecting a part of me that I myself have never examined. It draws its tongue in and starts to enter me. I thought it would hurt, but it doesn't. I am wet enough, and this fact both shames and excites me. I can feel the *lizard* wiggling into me. My head feels like it's about to explode. When only its tail is visible, something inside me trembles violently. It could be the *lizard,* but I'm not sure.

What are you up to? Mother asks, suspicious. I pray she won't see the *lizard. Deeper,* I beg it. I urge it all the way inside me, but its tail is still showing. Mother hasn't seen it yet. Even with her looking on, my excitement slowly reaches a climax. The ice-cold *lizard* is making its way deeper inside me. I grimace and try to control myself. Mother looks on, dispassionate. *Mother. I hurt terribly.* She looks like she doesn't believe me.

Mother will want to take the *lizard* away from me, I know. I tense my muscles to keep the *lizard* in me, and it crawls deep inside, so deep its tail disappears. Mom won't see the *lizard* now. It's mine, all mine. I grin at my mother as the ice-cold *lizard* wiggles and turns inside me. Mother grins back, her grin growing wider and wider until the head of a snake appears at her mouth and slithers out. Mother bends over to help it emerge. She looks like she's vomiting. *Mommy,* I ask her, *where's the baby? It died, you know that. I mean, we killed it, don't you remember? Mommy, no. I didn't kill it. I never saw it.* The snake that crawled out of my mother has vanished. I wake up from my dream and look at the wall. The *lizard* is gone. I shut my eyes again, and the dream resumes. The *lizard* wiggles inside my belly again. My anus throbs with pain. *Please, no.* The *lizard* starts to crawl out my backside. I want to have a baby. *Mother. I'll have your baby for you, Mother.* I entreat her, but she leaves without listening. The *lizard* exits my body. I am overcome with pain and exhaustion. Slowly, I wake up, then look at the wall. The *lizard* is not there. It's still with me, asleep. The phone rings, clearing my head. Wrong number. I look again at the wall. The *lizard* is there, exactly where it's supposed to be.

Lizards have no past. That's what makes them gods. For them there's nothing but the present, the eternal present.   Kim Yŏngha, "Lizard"

Since the *lizard* first entered me, I have had sex with a few men. I looked up one of my old boyfriends I'd lost touch with a long time ago. But it was business as usual when I slept with him, which is to say that I felt nothing. During sex, I kept thinking about the *lizard.* "I wish your penis was colder," I told him afterwards. He sat up and said, "You weren't like this before." He had a solemn expression on his face.

That was the end of that; he never came back. Maybe I really had changed. I snorted. And what if I had? The man who gave me the *lizard* told me I had to transform myself. I remembered his words when I looked at the *lizard.* It was regularly appearing in my dreams. It would enter my anus and exit from my mouth, or enter through my vagina and exit through my eyes. Either way, the sensation was almost the same. The days following the dreams I was too exhausted to talk. I did feel oddly refreshed, though.

At the cram school, I'd occasionally see the man who had given me the *lizard.* He'd pass me with a knowing smile. I wondered sometimes if he was there in my dreams, watching. It felt like he could see right through me. Maybe that was why I felt myself blush whenever I spotted the nape of his neck. Why it was the nape of his neck, I can't say. But once I saw him in the cram-school cafeteria in the basement. He was all by himself, spooning hot soup and rice into his mouth. I stood at the door, my eyes fixed on his back. He ate silently, his head lowered, while I focused on the nape of his neck. There was a tenacity in those clenched neck muscles. The overall impression was one of lonesomeness. Something about that neck, I don't know what, reminded me of the *lizard*. I wanted to embrace him—just rush up to him, put my arms around him, and press my lips to the nape of his neck. I couldn't eat at the cafeteria that day.

I occasionally saw him after that. He came over to my place once a month or so. We listened to music, shared drinks. He didn't want to have sex, and I wasn't interested either. We'd sit together, talking quietly and refilling each other's drink. He told me he enjoyed traveling, so working at the cram school was an ideal situation: no relationships to commit to; the freedom to leave at any moment.

And here we are. I'm waiting for him to come back and finish the story about the smoke woman. Then again he may never come back. Maybe I'll have to finish the story myself. I imagine that he is back.

"Come on, finish the story."

He starts talking. "The detective discovers the dead man's diary at the scene."

I light a cigarette for him. Smoke seeps deep into my lungs.

"The diary tells of a most captivating woman. The victim wrote: 'Will I see her tonight? She overpowers my senses. I spend the whole day just waiting for this woman.' The detective does some investigating and learns that the man graduated from college but was unemployed and spent his days doing God-knows-what in his room. He was poor, friendless in Seoul. His few acquaintances said they never saw him with a woman. So who was she? A prostitute perhaps? He didn't exactly have the means to buy a woman."

"Didn't you say he'd been scheduled for an autopsy?" I ask.

He answers, "He was, and the finding was that the victim had a fatal heart attack. The detective resumes his search for evidence, but finds nothing he can connect to the woman in the diary. So he gets to thinking. He goes back to the scene, does another search, and a second diary turns up. This diary contains the following entry: 'My one pleasure is making creations out of smoke. Yesterday, I made a car and an alcoholic beverage. I drank my smoky drink and drove my sporty car. To keep the smoke inside my room and keep the air still, I shut the windows tight. Nonetheless, it lasts only a moment. I need a woman.' The detective closes the diary and concludes his report. Direct cause of death: heart attack. He rules out homicide and suicide. This was a case of death by natural causes."

"I understand now," I say. "The man created a woman out of smoke. He was caressed by her, and they had sex. His every sense was overwhelmed. But he's not allowed to touch her. If he does, she'll disappear."

He nods in agreement. "That's right. But the detective keeps that part of the story to himself. Who would believe him?"

"Cigarette smoke can be very comforting," I say, smoking a cigarette myself. I look up at the *lizard*. It looks bigger than usual today. I crawl into bed, craving sleep. He doesn't come near. I turn off the lights, and soon I'm asleep.

Later, I sense someone opening the window to my room and climbing in. I think it's him, but my head is heavy. I hear him taking his clothes off. We've never slept together, and yet he calmly climbs into my bed as if he were my husband. His hands move gently from my feet to my knees and thighs. His hands are cold. I feel goose bumps all over my body. He climbs on top of me. His cold, hard penis pushes inside me. I mustn't shout, and I mustn't touch him. If I do, he'll vanish. His penis moves slowly. Violent pleasure explodes inside me. I tremble with a satisfaction I've never felt with a man. A neon cross flashes in the distance. His thrusts are stronger now. "You must transform yourself," I remember him telling me. His words reverberate. *Ahhh,* I'm going away—go past the tropical sunshine, through the forest of crosses, and you'll arrive at the playground. I want to scream, but nothing comes out. My ears ring with the beating of tribal drums. It feels like his penis is coming out of my ears. My eardrums are about to explode.

Afterward, I'm languishing. He gets up and dresses, and then he's gone, like smoke. I open my eyes carefully and look at the wall. The *lizard* is gone. I don't bother turning the lights on to make sure. I just close my eyes again, and fall asleep. A most tranquil sleep. I never want to wake up.

Translation by Dafna Zur

Adan Hernández. *La Estrella que Cae*
(The Falling Star). 1991. Oil on canvas.
Photograph by Peggy Tennison.

Coming Home

The room in my mini-hotel on Le Van Huu Street was large, clean, and high ceilinged in the old French style. It had yellow walls, a ceiling fan, and heavy, black teak furniture ornately carved with dragons and *yin-yang* symbols. The armoire was huge, and the bed the largest in Ha Noi. On the wall near the bed, a set of laminated rules was posted in two columns, like the tablets of the Ten Commandments: one in Vietnamese, the other in what my friend Phan Thanh Hao once referred to as Vietglish. Rule number 7 read:

ANIMALS, WEAPONS, EXPLOSIONS, INFLAMMABLE MATERIALS, AND DISGUSTING BADLY SMELT THINGS ARE NOT ALLOWED IN THE ROOM.

The room had double doors that opened to a balcony overlooking the street. I went out and gazed down at the tops of purple-flowered bougainvillea, at the street pulsing with colors and light and motion fragmented through the lace canopies of the trees. Le Van Huu was lined with *pho* soup stalls where customers hunkered over steaming bowls; the crowded communal tables and low, blue plastic stools blocked the narrow sidewalks. Nearby, street barbers were clipping the heads of men perched on folding chairs, while next to them women were stacking bamboo cages stuffed with miserable chickens, their bead eyes darting frantically as if all the panicked motion their bodies were calling for had gone into them. The intersection swarmed with motor scooters, bicycles, and cyclos—their horns blaring like the sonar emissions of bats—swerving around each other in near collisions and forming a pattern glimpsed but not understood. When I finally understood it, I would belong here.

Some café people and *pho* vendors were staring up at me, and I smiled and nodded at them too enthusiastically.

I drank my coffee and looked down at the corner. It was crowded with cone-hatted women from the countryside, squatting behind heaps of vegetables and flowers that blazed in reds and yellows against the chipped and muddy pastels of the buildings. "Hello, hello," they called to me, and I waved to them, to the whole scene, suddenly feeling a kind of stupid happiness for simply being there. The people on the street busily going about their lives seemed to me a counter-parade to the invisible, unacknowledged procession of dead and damaged that I could not help seeing too: the outtakes from the movie I worked on, the explosions and inflammable material and disgusting badly smelt things that weren't allowed in the room. I stood on the balcony for a time, until I again became aware of someone else: a younger self who stared at me over the rim of a foxhole, surprised at the middle-aged man whom he'd become and who was somewhat at ease in the enemy capital.

There was a knock on the door. When I opened it, the novelist Ho Anh Thai strode in and began examining the room critically. I pointed to the blanket on the bed. It was imprinted with pictures of little angels and the repeated phrase I LOVE YOU/I LOVE YOU/I LOVE YOU: BE MY LITTLE ANGLE. I explained the error in spelling.

"Mister American Man," Thai said. Shaking his head when I pointed out rule 7 to him, he laughed and said, "Can you manage?"

"It's a restriction I have to live with." I looked at him. "How about you?"

He smiled sourly and said nothing. He was fiercely nonconformist and daring in his writing, and he cared only for writing. But he knew that to live in the room, he had to be aware of and abide by the rules—and he knew the rules were more complex and flexible than they seemed. Things could be done with them; they never had one use only. "Mister American Man," he said again.

We both grinned. On one of my previous trips to Ha Noi, he'd arranged for me to stay in a mini-hotel near the Lake of the Restored Sword. None of the staff spoke English, and I was the only Western guest. They would address me with "*Chao ong.* Hello, hello, Mister American Man." Thai had adopted the nickname since, addressing his e-mail messages to MAM.

"Middle-Aged Man," I said. "You know what else? I remembered this the last time I got a message from you: Military Age Male. I meant to tell you. It's what we used to call the Vietnamese we suspected could be Viet Cong."

"How fitting. You've become VC, yes?"

"I've been so accused."

"Yes. But now you're Mister Movie Star. Why have they called you back? I thought the film was finished."

"Apparently not. They want to rewrite parts of the script, reshoot some scenes."

After my work on the film had ended last August, I'd gone home, thinking that the filming was to be wrapped up in a few months. But now—in May—I'd gotten a request from the filmmakers asking me to return. There were some problems.

Thai laughed. "I'm glad we're getting a chance to see you, but I think some people will be pleased there's trouble." He named a man we both knew. "Instead of *Song of the Stork,* he calls the film *Song of Your Cock.*"

"Why the hostility?"

"Oh, some think the filmmakers are too ambitious. Others because it's something new, and it wasn't supposed to succeed. Others because they think the war is something the filmmakers don't have a right to touch."

"Bullshit; they're good kids." I began rummaging in my bag. "I have a few presents for you and your family. The DVD is for you. This is for your brother and sister-in-law and the kids."

"*Sunshine,*" he said, reading the title of the DVD. "What's this about?"

"I think you'll like it." I handed him a large teddy bear that had drawn stares in customs. "This is for your son."

He looked at the purse I'd brought his niece. "She'll like this," he said, ignoring the bear.

It was very Vietnamese. If you don't want to reply to something that is said, you don't; people will understand your reticence and not press you. So I didn't. I was somewhat worried about him though. I knew that Thai and his wife were separated, but that was all I knew.

In some ways, he was more open with me than with many of his Vietnamese friends. He could say things to me, a foreigner, that he'd feel uneasy bringing up with them. Not necessarily things about politics, but about other subjects difficult to discuss because of the complex web of social and familial relationships. Even so, he wrapped whatever was happening in his marital life tightly inside himself. Outwardly he seemed happy, at least as happy as writers get—and particularly happy with the family life he did have. I remembered how good it had felt visiting him at the house he shared with his brother and sister-in-law: everyone fit with one another so seamlessly, good-humoredly, lovingly. I remembered his niece taking my hand and holding it with an ease that seemed to express the same security the whole family readily extended to a stranger who had been accepted by any one of its members. It was a lovely enfolding, but, as with everything else in Viet Nam, it was more than that.

When Thai had come to visit me at my rural home in the States, he couldn't understand how people would want to live in houses so far apart. Thai, the fiercely independent writer who knew how to stretch the rules, knew also that, without being fibered to some defining knot of family, he could be set adrift like a wandering spirit, a restless ghost of the sort most Vietnamese, secured in their skein of relationships, feared becoming. This is not an unusual attitude anywhere, though in Viet Nam it was one reinforced almost to hysteria among the generation that had preceded Thai's: those Military Age Males and Females who had come back from the battlefield hungry for normalcy and continuity—to have a family, to have a child, to surround themselves with evidence that a future was possible, to affirm that they had defeated death. You married whom you could. You married someone you were attracted to, who was socially suitable, who could give you a child, who was available. Who was alive. Love was something else. Love was something you found later, maybe—not something you waited for. If you did find it after you'd created your place in the world, you took it, you enjoyed it, you romanticized it—and you kept it separate from the reality and stability of your family. There was *tinh*—passion, emotionalism, spontaneity, love; and there was *nghia*—duty, adherence to social norms. *Tinh* and *nghia* were not in opposition: you accepted both. *Yin* lived with *yang*. You shared the cold flesh of the dead whenever you shared the warm flesh of a new lover. You entered the relationship with the mutual understanding that opportunities for earthly joy should not be passed over lightly—and that such love could be as short as a burst of machine-gun fire or the blast of a bomb. It was thus best kept compartmentalized, not to be trusted unless bound somehow—by blood or economic or social necessity—to strict necessity, which could also kill it. Nothing was ever only one thing. Everything contained its opposite. You did what you had to so that the center would hold. You created whatever center you could create, and clung to it.

When Thai once related a story to me about a girl he had known, I found myself considering what the story said about him. The girl had been one of the children he'd been evacuated with when he was a kid, taken from Ha Noi to a small, supposedly safe village in the countryside during the American bombing. When the girl's parents had come to see her, they were killed by an American plane that bombed the village. Afterwards, the girl had disappeared; no one could find her. Years later, Thai ran into her in Ha Noi. He found that she had been adopted by—or had simply attached herself to—a mentally impaired veteran who had wandered into the village. The man had found her after the bombing and had taken her to Ha Noi. With him, she created a family that mimicked the one she'd lost. The title of the film we were working on, *Song of the Stork*, came from the fable of the stork who is snared by a farmer. The stork tells him to be sure to cook her in clean water. If you knew you were going to be killed and cooked, you tried to turn the bad karma into something good. You tried to make sure that at least the water was clean.

I thought about the way Thai's telling the adopted girl's story reflected his own condition, his need for a center. I thought about the way the film's title became clear to me only after I understood the significance of the stork fable to someone like him. It was this shift in perspective that allowed me to connect with him, just the way reading the Vietnamese stories he and fellow writer Le Minh Khue had sent me over the last ten years had enabled me to see Khue's face as if it were emerging from the jungle where she hid as I flew overhead, hunting her with a machine gun. In that light-bathed moment when I met her, I realized how she would have seen me during the war, and all at once I found I could mourn whatever had been subtracted in me that would have once allowed me to kill her.

I want to make you see, Joseph Conrad wrote in one of his prefaces. Those of us who wrote about the war could add, should add, *so that it should be harder to kill. I want to make you me, and me you, so that killing would be suicide.* To compel that kind of seeing was the task we'd been given. I could be me and not me; not me and yet me. I could not be Thai or Khue; or I could. I could not be the girl in Thai's story; or I could, if I were able to find what threaded me to her—if I could see, if only a little, through the eyes given to me by such a blessing.

"So tell me more about the film," Thai said.

OUTTAKE

Even though she is only six, Lanh knows—from the way the country suddenly opens and changes when the train takes them over the Long Bien Bridge and out of Ha Noi—that her eyes have changed the way they see. Before this, she fit into a flow of people and space that seemed fluid but was really fixed, held as the river was by two banks. Her eyes would, could wander only so far before her vision was stopped and held by buildings leaning into each other as if they were tired. The sky itself, whenever she tipped her head back to stare at it, was banked by two jagged rows of tiled roofs. Every morning at the same time, she would watch the twin Ngo brothers wash themselves on the iron balcony across the street. On the balcony was a large tin cistern from which they would ladle water over their heads and chests. Carrying her plastic knapsack on her back and wearing her red scarf and red shorts, Lanh walked to school down a street lined with bougainvillea trees. She said good morning to Auntie Lam, who sold shoelaces, and sometimes bananas and lychees, on the corner. Everything and everyone were known and named. She was younger sister and daughter, and there were older sister and uncles and aunts and fathers, and each was as fastened to a name and a house and a particular combination of shapes, colors, tastes, and smells. Each had a particular quality of filtering, sparkling dust to her. Early in the morning, she would pass Hoan Kiem Lake, the old men and women doing *tai chi* by the shore and moving as if they were under the waves, and the lovers sitting on the benches. She would look not at Tortoise Pagoda but for Tortoise itself—the divine tortoise that, her father told her, had taken back the magical sword of Emperor Le Loi after he had used it to drive out the Chinese invaders. She would stare and stare, learning how to slide her sight under the sparkle that played on the water and looked like glittering scales of armor, until she could make out its dark, giant form gliding just beneath the surface of the lake. Slowly its scaly head would break the surface, draped with moss and floating scraps of trash, its cold eyes staring at her. *Good morning, Grandfather,* she would say, and Tortoise would blink at her, the transparent carapaces of its lids slightly magnifying its liquid gaze.

When the first bombs fell, she huddled in a shelter with others. The ground pitched and shuddered, and the shudder moved into her skin and didn't stop. Dust puffed from the walls and ceilings with each blast. A network of fissures appeared on the wall, illuminated by the flickering kerosene lamp. People held each other as if they thought their flesh more stable than the dissolving concrete. In the aftermath, some adults became enormous, as big as gods. Others became children, frolicking or whining in the ruins. Lanh saw patients tending doctors in a collapsed hospital. One day, she saw her teacher weep like a child and wet his pants, while the custodian became Emperor Tran Hung Dao defeating the Mongols, protecting his subjects, telling them where to sit and how to move and act. Things fell apart.

"You must go, my darling," her mother whispered to her. "But who will say good morning to the tortoise?" she demanded. Her mother and father glanced at each other, and then her father smiled grimly. "Maybe he'll decide to restore the sword to us," he said. "It seems like it would be a good time." He squatted down, gripped her shoulders with his large, callused hands. "Lanh," he said, "it's time you grew up. You have to take care of yourself. We'll come and visit just as soon as we can."

On the train leaving the city, she sees, for the first time, expanses of rice fields, and all she has seen and heard over the last few days comes together into a knot she feels opening behind her forehead and unraveling into the air. *The world can be this, or it can be that.* The revelation frightens her more than the sudden scream of the airplane, the whistle and explosion of the falling bombs—normal and expected now. The train screeches to a stop, and she is told to run off, with the other children, into a rice field. She stretches out on a dike and looks back at the city. As she watches, the city turns into a field of gigantic roses and then disappears.

The space and light around the village confuse and disorient her. She stands outside the house of her new parents and sees nothing but the green of the rice fields, a single areca tree, the river, its water yellow with floating pollen, and the black jagged line of mountains like dragon's teeth biting the sky. The thatched roof of the house is covered with drying sugar-cane leaves, and her mat is in a room hung with fruit and corn ears, thick with the salty smell of *nuoc mam* stored in cool earthen jars. She soon refers to Cao and Duc as Mother and Father, Kim as Elder Sister, and Thang, until he goes south for war, as Elder Brother. In the morning, Cao smiles at her with lacquered teeth as she wraps her hair in a bun and gives her a hot glass of sugared soybean milk.

Lanh and the other children from Ha Noi can go into any of the houses, and the aunts and uncles will smile at them and give them sugar cane or, if it is mealtime, a plate of whatever they were eating, often in bigger portions. Instead of sharing a cramped, dark, smelly toilet with families in her housing unit, she now goes to the fields and squats, feeling the breeze across her backside. The world has reformed, and she knows now that it can, that more than one shape is possible. And it no longer disturbs her.

She goes to classes in a pagoda built around a sloping brick courtyard. Teacher Chinh is a kindly man, a Hanoian like them, he tells the evacuee children as he points to his heart with tobacco-stained fingers. One day, Lanh recites the opening lines of *Kim Van Kieu* to him. She doesn't understand them, but her father taught them to her, and at night, on her mat, she will often repeat them, the poem becoming as much of a companion as Tortoise was:

> A hundred years—in this life span on Earth
> How apt to clash, talent and destiny!
> Human fortunes change even as nature shifts—
> The sea now rolls where mulberry fields grew.
> One watches things that make one sick at heart.
> This is the law: no gain without a loss,
> And Heaven hurts fair women for sheer spite.

Teacher Chinh listens to her and then turns away, and she sees two tears fall from his black eyes, glisten on his cheek. It makes her nearly cry herself, from happiness and pride.

Then Mad Tinh appears. Her friend Thai, one of the other Ha Noi children, is at the train station when he arrives. Later Thai tells her that the train had stopped and then left, and in its wake was Tinh, standing with heels together and hands pressed to the seams of his ragged, filthy trousers. Thai had not seen him get off the train. It was as if he and the train had arrived on parallel tracks. Shod in dirt, he was dressed in the rags and tatters of a soldier's uniform, and backward on his head was a battered pith helmet with a faded red star.

Tinh walks into the village and stands for a long time in front of the house of a woman named Hai Mat, whose husband, Cuong, like most of the husbands, has joined the war. Two lines of drool fall from the corners of his mouth. Hai Mat comes out, sighs, and talks quietly to him. Then he goes to another house, stands and stares, and another, and another. Some of the villagers come out to look at him, but no one says anything. A woman presses a bowl of rice, sardines, and *nuoc mam* into his hand, and he puts the bowl on the ground and laps the food like a dog. The children laugh, and their parents let them, saying nothing to Tinh. When he comes to Lanh's house, she is squatting outside, playing with a beetle tied to a string and flying in circles around her head. Tinh's shadow falls on her. She looks up into eyes that are black wells. They seem to be drawing her in, pulling apart the seams of the day one by one. She screams and runs inside her house. Holding the door ajar, she sees Tinh squat and poke at the beetle, then pick it up and eat it. *"Buzz, buzz,"* he says. He pulls off his rags and rolls naked in the dust, then sits, patting the dust on his body as if he were bathing. Lanh screams and screams.

Mother Cao picks her up and holds her. "It's all right, little one. What we send to the war sometimes comes back to us."

He was, some of the village children whisper to her later, a famous fighter. But his soul has been cut from his body and now wanders, lost. If he stays here, where his umbilical cord is buried, the villagers say, perhaps his body will find him.

Mad Tinh becomes part of the village, the landscape. People feed him, and sometimes he wanders off for days, but he always returns. Lanh can't accept him, can't weave him into her new vision. He is the bomb falling on the street or the bridge: he tears the world apart again. Whenever she sees him, she cries or screams, then runs away as fast as she can.

At harvest time, the fields become a patchwork of green and gold, and she learns how to walk in a line with the women and other girls and, bending down, to grab two clusters of rice stalk with one hand and, with the other, cut them swiftly with the scythe, leaving short, jagged stubble. The cool mud oozes up between her toes, releases a rich, pungent odor. She is coming back from the fields one day—to her delight, Cao had put her on the back of a water buffalo—when she sees Ha Noi Mother and Father standing in front of the house, Father wearing a uniform and leaning on a wooden crutch. One of the legs of his trousers has been pinned up, and her eyes frantically search the ground below for what would complete him. For a moment she stops, confused, shapes forming, shattering, reforming in her mind.

But only for a moment, and then she runs to Ha Noi Mother and Father, crying. Their arms embrace her. Behind her, the other Ha Noi children stand silently, their eyes shining with envy and joy. "Lanh, come bathe with us," Thai calls out suddenly, his voice strained.

"Go bathe with the others, Daughter," Cao says. "Wash the mud off, then come home, and we'll all eat."

Her mother kisses her all over her face, even her eyelids. "Go ahead, Lanh. We'll help Mrs. Cao."

Her heart singing, she runs off, oblivious to the glum faces of the Ha Noi children. They and the village children had gradually coalesced—formed groups and alliances that had nothing to do with where one or the other came from—but the appearance of the parents from the city suddenly splits them into their original groups. While the village children laugh and sing, the Hanoians remain silent. Lanh suddenly feels she belongs to neither group. When they strip off their clothing and jump into the river, she is aware, for the first time, of her nakedness and hides herself behind a curtain of reeds. An image comes to mind: Tinh bathing in dust outside her house. She shudders.

At that moment, a huge noise booms all around her, shaking the reeds, slapping hot air against her back and head. The children freeze, their silence like a trough in the wave of noise. They have all heard it before. Now it has followed them here. A second later, she sees something she hasn't seen since the day she left Ha Noi: a silver jet streaking across the sky and then swooping down towards the village.

The pilot has no more targets. He's expended his load on the Red River Bridge, as he'd done last week, seeing, in his sights, the patchwork repairs jerry-rigged since his last visit. *We bomb it, and they build it back,* he thinks. Coming back time and again to this stretch of river, leaving behind friends who disappear in a flash, erased. He's had the vision of the arched back of a huge black turtle breaking the waves: he returns over and over, endlessly blowing up an endlessly regenerating beast. But there is comfort in routine; it is better than death. His world has narrowed to this, just as his vision narrows to his gunsight.

But this time the SAMs had been worse. He had to dive and dodge frantically, and one missile streaked by so close he could read the numbers on its fusilage. *Escape and evade.* Then he realized he had been separated from his wing man and the rest of the squadron. In such circumstances, the plan was to wheel north and west and then circle around, coming up over the heavier coastal defenses from behind. He is doing this when he realizes he still has a bomb on his right wing. He scans the ground for a Target of Opportunity. For a few seconds, he is burning gas, hauling ass, seeing nothing but paddies, a green-and-gold patchwork. Then a village appears. Good enough. He dives in close, sights, releases, feeling, as always, the bomb leaving not the plane but his own body: a giddy rush, a sudden lightness. As he heads home, the explosion blooms like a rose.

The children scream and run back to the village.

One bomb has fallen on one house. Dripping wet, the children stand silently as the adults form a bucket brigade from the well and paddies and throw water on the house. The sugar-cane leaves on the roof send a thick, sweet smell into the air. An earthen jar filled with fish sauce suddenly explodes. The splattered contents look like blood. The wet bodies of the children dry in the heat of the flames.

It isn't until much later, after the structure is nothing but ashes and they are sifting for the bones of Cao and Duc and the visitors from Ha Noi, that Teacher Chinh looks over at the crowd of children. Lanh is gone. He asks them if they have seen her. They look at each other as if waking from a dream.

Lanh is in a tunnel that presses in on all sides and only allows her to go in one direction. It is a gray tunnel, soft as ash, but an ash that will not yield or dissolve. Instead it turns rubbery and stubborn when she touches it. At the end of the tunnel, she steps out into the light, and the railroad station is in front of her. This is where she had disembarked when she'd come from Ha Noi, and it is where her parents must have arrived. It isn't much of a station, just a shelter of woven palm fronds and some jars of water standing on the hard-packed earth. If she can return to the tunnel, it will take her back not in space but in time. In reverse, the black bombs will tumble upwards, into the bellies of the planes. When Lanh thinks of the bombs, she sees them as infants, sucked backward into the birth canal, where they curl and stay.

She feels a hand on her shoulder, and when she looks up, she isn't surprised to see Mad Tinh. The hand is hard and scarred, the yellow nails long and pointed. He doesn't frighten her. Surrounded by scabs and crust, his eyes—the eyes she has always been afraid to look into—mirror her own pain. As soon as she looks into them, she becomes aware of that pain and begins to howl. Mad Tinh pats her shoulder and then embraces her, holding her against him, rocking. She breathes in the smell of stale sweat and blood, the odors of a living body, and finds them comforting. He takes off his shirt and puts it on her. It is ragged and comes down to her ankles. His bare chest is streaked with filth and crisscrossed with the raised welts and puckered craters of old scars. A train pulls up: it is the weekly train to Ha Noi. The conductor looks at Tinh and the girl, then nods and helps them up. Mad Tinh sometimes rides back and forth. The crews know him and his past and give him free passage. He sets Lanh next to him on the hard wooden bench.

During the ride, one of the crew finds some black trousers and a singlet for Lanh. Tinh gets back his shirt and nods gravely, like a father. But when they reach Ha Noi, he seems bewildered. Lanh takes his hand and leads him through the streets near the railroad station. It is dark, and no one is out except the beggars and the railroad prostitutes. Lanh stops before two girls standing in front of an alley and holds out her hand. Mad Tinh watches and imitates her. The girls laugh and tell them to go away. They don't move. The two girls look at them, and one shudders. "That you daddy, Younger Sister? Maybe mine look like that now too." She presses a few *dong* into Lanh's hand. "Get the hell out of here now, Younger Sister," the other says.

"Home," Lanh says, shaking her head.

"Home," Mad Tinh says.

"You're both nuts," the first girl says uneasily. "Leave 'em. Let's get the hell out of here." She looks around nervously. The people's militia have recently been sweeping the area near the station, picking up civilians for the labor corvées.

The other girl shakes her head. "What about Uncle Trung's place?" she says.

"I don't have fucking time."

"Fucking time is all we got. Stay here, you want."

Trung, a beggar both girls used as a shill, was found dead on the street the day before. He had picked up an undetonated American CBU that remembered its function as soon as it was in his sack. Thuy leads Lanh and Tinh back over the tracks and through rows of ramshackle tin sheds, a maze of twisted metal, bamboo frames splintered like broken fingers, and jagged pieces of smashed concrete, all of it set haphazardly into what looks like a sea of black ash. In the shadows of a narrow alley, against a ruined brick wall, a piece of tin is propped up by bamboo poles. Jute sacking is piled on the ground beneath the tin.

Thuy points. "Home," she says.

Lanh nods. She takes Tinh's hand and leads him to it, then makes him sit on the sacking. She sits next to him and stares out at the junk heap in the alley.

Thuy shakes her head and leaves.

Lanh takes some of the jute sacking and drapes it over the sides of the small lean-to. She makes Tinh lie down and covers him with more sacking. While he sleeps, she goes out and begs for more money. Stealing a little bowl from a *pho* restaurant near the station, she does what she has seen the Buddhist monks do: she holds it in front of her on sidewalks, by several cafés. People put *dong* in, and sometimes rice and a little fish. That night, when the air-raid sirens go off and the tracers begin flying up at the American bombers and illuminating the night, Mad Tinh begins trembling and crying silently, tears and drool running down his face. Using the sleeves of her new blouse, Lanh wipes his eyes and nose and mouth, and holding him to her under the noise of the bombs, she begins to tell him about a giant tortoise that lives in the lake. She knows now that what she saw when a little child were just floating bits of garbage and debris tangled into a suggestive shape by duckweed. But it doesn't matter. All that matters is keeping the flimsy walls she has built around the two of them from falling down.

from *Hawaiian Son:*
The Life and Music of Eddie Kamae

Author's Note

Since founding his legendary band, the Sons of Hawai'i, more than forty years ago, Eddie Kamae has been a leading voice in Hawai'i's cultural renaissance. The following chapters are excerpted from a new biography published in fall 2004 by 'Ai Pōhaku Press in Honolulu. Tracing his career as both musician and filmmaker, *Hawaiian Son* is a Polynesian odyssey measured by the numerous teachers Kamae has met along the way: dancers, storytellers, healers, and elders who have guided him in his quest to find the sources of a rich musical tradition and thus to find himself.—J.D.H.

Have You Heard of the Tutu Man?

Eddie had been hearing reports of an old songwriter, a Tutu Man, who lived out near Waipi'o Valley, or had once lived there, on the northern side of the Big Island of Hawai'i, past the end of the county road. That's where Sam Kamae, Eddie's father, had grown up. Maybe that would be a trip worth taking. As of 1970 Eddie had been hearing stories and rumors about this fellow for quite some time, like folktales heard around a dinner table late at night with the lights turned low. Waipi'o was known for its waterfall, Hi'ilawe, which provided the title for Gabby Pahinui's first slack-key hit. Some musicians in Honolulu thought the Tutu Man was the original composer of that song, one of dozens he'd written. Others said, No, it was the long-dead father, though the son had been a legendary fiddler in his day. Others said, Well, whoever wrote that song, they're probably dead now, but if we sing it, they won't be forgotten.

Eddie went to his teacher and fellow composer, Mary Kawena Pukui, then the foremost authority on Hawaiian language and traditional lore.

"Kawena," he said, "I wonder if you have heard of Tutu Man Li'a."

Her eyes opened wide, as if taken by surprise. "You mean Sam?"

"I think so. Yes. Is he the one who wrote songs?"

She nodded, smiling. "I know him. Sam Li'a Kalainaina. He's a very fine poet too, one of the best."

"I heard he lives in Waipi'o."

"Pretty close by."

"You think he's someone I should meet?"

"Someday I hope you can meet him…" Her eyes held him as she went on. "Yes. I think the time has come for you to meet Sam Li'a. And I can tell you where he lives."

"Should I get in touch with him first?"

She shook her head. "He will be there, and he will be glad to see you. And I will tell you how to find another man too. Both of them have spent their lives on the Big Island—long, long lives. They know things you can only find there. But Sam…he is the one. He is like no one else. He is the last."

Eddie watched her warm eyes fill with moisture and the brightness that comes when joy and grief are intermixed.

"The last what?" he said.

"This man writes in the old way, Eddie. No one knows how many songs, or where they all are. He never cared about recording. He writes in Hawaiian, and he gives it away, with his aloha. In our time, there is no one else like him."

The intensity in Kawena's eyes told him this was more than information. This came as a message, a kind of directive.

Where the Songwriter Lives

A week later, Eddie and his wife, Myrna, were heading north from Hilo, following the Hāmākua coast. A two-lane road hugs the shoreline, crossing countless streams that lace the rain-watered slopes of Mauna Kea. For several miles a muddy cane truck slowed them down, then swung off onto a plantation trail, rumbling inland.

They passed through Honoka'a, the main town out that way, a plantation town where porches tilted under darkly rusted sheets of metal roofing. From there the round-the-island belt road bore left toward Waimea, Parker Ranch, and the leeward side, but Eddie continued north along the coastline, passing the village of Kapulena, where a two-wheel track climbed away to the left, toward the tract of land where his father had been born eighty years earlier. As they passed the turnoff, he told Myrna how he'd gone out there once before, in search of the site, and how he'd met a Chinese woman who said she had known his father.

"I have a picture of him in uniform, she told me, and that made me stop and think. You sure it's my father, I said? He was never in the service." Then the Chinese woman showed Eddie the picture, and it was of a smiling, handsome Hawaiian youngster in the uniform they used to require all the boys to wear at Lahainaluna School, on Maui, right after the turn of the century.

Two more miles and they came to Kukuihaele, the last community before the coast road ended. Eddie slowed down and rechecked Kawena's directions. A grocery store would be on the right, she'd said, and across from the store would be the social hall, and next to the social hall he would see Sam's house. You won't have any trouble finding it, she'd said. And she was right. It was a wooden cottage raised off the ground for ventilation, with a long roof sloping out over the porch.

Eddie parked his jeep and walked across the grass. As he neared the steps, he saw an old man sitting in a straight-backed chair. Through tinted spectacles, he was watching Eddie approach. His face was lean and brown, capped with thick white hair. A white crescent moustache shaped his mouth. The glasses gave him a scholarly look. He wore a white shirt and a necktie and a black suit with the coat buttoned, as if on his way to church or a wedding.

Eddie said, "Sam Li'a."

The old man nodded.

"My name is Eddie Kamae."

"I know," he said in Hawaiian. "I've been expecting you."

Eddie felt his scalp tingle. He had not called ahead or sent a message.

"I didn't know how he knew," Eddie says now, looking back, "but he was waiting for me that day, in his best suit. He was very erect and dignified, and he had a notepad in his lap. Eighty-nine years old and he was working on a song. Right then I felt like I had met this man before. His house was familiar to me. It could have been my father's house. I felt like I had known Sam all my life. And I know now that he felt the same thing about me, though he didn't say it at the time. Later on he would say, 'You remind me of me when I was a younger man.'"

Sam invited Eddie and Myrna to sit with him on the porch, and they began to talk, first about Kawena, who had looked up Sam back in the days when she herself was still roaming around "out there" in search of songs and stories.

Eddie had brought along an old songbook published in Hawaiian soon after Sam was born. *Ka Buke o Na Leo Mele Hawaii* (A Book of Hawaiian Songs) was bound in worn leather, its pages dappled brown with age. The first Hawaiian songbook to be published in the islands, it was a rare collection of early lyrics, but with no musical notation. One song in particular had been on Eddie's mind. *Ka Buke* called it "Waimanalo." While he liked the words, he had almost given up finding anyone who might remember its melody. But on the day they met, Sam Li'a remembered. He recognized the composer's name, "Figgs," a whimsical pseudonym sometimes used by King Kalākaua. Sam knew these lyrics by an alternate title, "Na Ke Aloha," a romantic ballad composed by the king in the late nineteenth century. Sam's long memory gave the song new life.

Eddie thanked him and said this was why he had come to visit, to meet a fellow musician who could help him learn more about the music, the history of the songs, and also how they were played and composed in Sam's day.

The old man thought about this, then said, "You got a car?"

"I got a jeep."

"Good. Let's go for a ride."

Sam took off his coat, put on his hat—a porkpie with a narrow brim—and grabbed his cane. They drove the last mile of the coast road and parked where the pavement ends, on a high bluff with an observation railing. Overhead the sky was blue, but offshore a rainsquall spilled from gray overhang. A cool, wet wind blew in off the water. They stood in the wind and gazed down into a broad valley. Sheer, verdant cliffs made it a tropical amphitheater. Below them, square taro ponds glistened among palms and groves of wild banana. Leaning on his cane, Sam gestured with his free arm as if offering them all this and said in a graveled, commanding voice, "Waipi'o."

The word means "curving water." Through the bottomland, a stream curved toward the beach and a narrow, surf-rimmed bay. Across the valley, a furrowed headland met the sea with blunt finality. Up the farther cliff, a climbing zigzag line marked a trail to the next valley, one you could only reach by horse or by boat and now uninhabited. With his arm flung outward, Sam reverently spoke its name. "Over that way...Waimanu."

In Eddie's jeep they descended, plunging down a rutted track. As cliffs rose around them, the wind dropped off and the air grew still and sultry. The valley floor was laced with little tributary streams that crossed the muddy road. After they had forded a few of these, Sam told Eddie to pull over in front of what looked to be an abandoned farmhouse, set back from the road. A wild tangle of vines and greenery had begun to repossess it.

They got out of the jeep and looked around. Under a rainforest canopy that blocked the sun, some fragments of lava-rock fencing lined the roadside. Off to the south, at the far end of a secondary canyon, twin-ribboned falls dropped a hundred yards down a shadowy cliff face.

"Hi'ilawe," Sam said.

Then he said the name of the place where they were standing.

"Nāpō'opo'o."

His low, grainy voice made each of these names sound like a kind of incantation.

Pointing toward an open space in the grove behind them, Sam said it was where he was born, back in 1881, when this was still a village and hundreds of Hawaiian families still lived in the valley, farming and fishing. There had been a schoolhouse here, he said, and a store and a church and poi factory. Now all that remained in Nāpō'opo'o was Mock Chew's empty house. Hardly anyone lives in Waipi'o now, he said, not since the great tsunami of 1946, when thirty feet of water poured inland for two miles, burying fields and trees and houses and graveyards. Sam remembered that day. He was in his sixties then. He pointed to the top of an ironwood tree to show them how high the water had risen, and Eddie could feel the ghost of that flood still alive and floating through the valley air. Nowadays the farmers who work the taro live up above, Sam said, in Kukuihaele or in Honoka'a, and come down the road in the morning and go back home at night, heading for higher ground.

They drove toward the falls to get a closer look and to hear the rush of spilling water, then turned and moved farther back into the valley. They drove past the rows of taro, where broad leaves gleamed in their shallow ponds, lo'i, some of them laid out centuries ago, Sam said, along with irrigation systems that were still in use.

When heavy growth finally stopped them, they looped back toward the beach, where they spread out a picnic lunch Eddie and Myrna had brought along. Right behind the beach, Sam said, there had been the site of an important temple, erected hundreds of years back by Waipi'o's legendary chief, Umi-a-li-loa, in the days when this valley was a community of many thousands and one of the most influential regions in all of Hawai'i. Great chiefs had their houses here, near the beach, he said, and there was a wrestling court where they practiced their combat skills, a sacred house where the bones of the chiefly ancestors were stored, and a temple with stone walls thirty feet high. When Sam was a boy, some of those walls still stood. Then he spoke the name of the site that will always be a sacred place.

"Paka'alana."

The way the Hawaiian islands are laid out, there is nothing north of Waipi'o until you reach the Gulf of Alaska. Swells roll in uninterrupted, cracking over one by one in the blue water of the bay. After lunch, the three sat and listened to the waves and felt the gathered energy of this old habitat, supremely tropical and almost empty now, yet still filled with the spirits of the lives come and gone.

When they climbed back into the jeep, Sam was in a good mood. He loved his valley and all the layers of it. The time they'd spent together was as meaningful for him as it had been for Eddie and Myrna. Sam wanted to commemorate the occasion and so proposed that they make a song. Eddie would do the music, and Sam would write the lyrics. It would give Eddie a reason to return. More important—as Eddie realized when he heard the old man's verses later—this little pilgrimage had been Sam's first lesson: to know his music, you must first learn about his valley.

On Eddie's next visit, Sam would show him a song made of twelve short verses, each one naming a stop on their journey or one of the places they'd seen: the lookout point, the stretch of shoreline, the rush of distant water pouring down a canyon wall, the dark sea in front of Paka'alana, the long-gone temple of the royal ones.

"Let the refrain be told," the last verse says, "The mind has seen Waipi'o."

It was the kind of song Eddie had written with Kawena. But this was different. This time he felt he was somehow *inside* the music in a new way. Sam's place was also an ancestral place for Eddie, the home region of his father, his grandfather, his great-grandfather too, and who knew how much further back it went.

Two Fathers

By the time I met Sam, his hands were so gnarled and knobby he couldn't play anymore. But he loved to talk about playing, and he could still laugh about the good times he'd had. He played everything: guitar, 'ukulele, piano, organ. Later in life he played organ at the church in Honoka'a. He conducted the choir there too. Of all these instruments, his favorite was the fiddle. The first time he heard one, he just fell in love with the sound, the same way I fell in love with the 'ukulele.

He was about eight years old, and a band of roaming musicians came to Nāpō'opo'o, the way they used to do, riding down into the valley on horseback, going from place to place to serenade the country folks. There would be a uke, one or two guitars, with a fiddle usually playing lead. This was the 1880s, before the steel guitar. When the steel came in about twenty years later, it would take over that high-melody role from the fiddle. But in Sam's day there were still some great fiddle players in Hawai'i.

So one of these serenading bands played outside Sam's house. When they started to ride away, he begged his father to ask them to stay and play a few more songs. The next day he went out into the forest and cut some bamboo and made himself a kind of fiddle so that he could start playing. When I asked him what he used for strings, he told me number ten thread, with mango wax.

He got his first real fiddle about four years later, when he was visiting his brother-in-law and saw one on the bed. He picked it up and started playing. The brother-in-law heard him and came into the bedroom and listened for a while and said, "That's beautiful. You keep that violin. It belongs to you."

Sam played that instrument his whole life. He played it way past the time when you would have heard a fiddle in any kind of Hawaiian band in Honolulu. On the day I met Sam, he still had it. He showed it to me, and I thought about the 'ukulele my older brother found on the bus and brought home for me to play. I was about the same age when that happened. I know what an effect it can have on you.

That was just one more thing connecting us. The more we talked, the more I understood why I felt so close to this kind man who had welcomed me into his life and treated me like his own son. It really clicked into place when he told me his family had sent him over to Maui to attend Lahainaluna School in the 1890s. That's where my father went, just a few years later, coming from this same area of the Big Island. They grew up in towns just two miles apart, with only about nine years between them. And they were both named Sam!

As young guys going to school on Maui, they both learned printing on the big press there at the school. After that, they followed different paths. My father went on to try his luck in Honolulu and left his childhood home behind. Sam came back to the Big Island and never left. When I saw all that, I knew why I saw him as my spiritual father. I loved them both. But in different ways. Sam's whole life was in touch with the spirit of the place my father came from. All his music came from there too: the same kind of music my father heard when he was growing up and loved so much and always wanted me to play.

One summer Sam came home from Maui and got a job typesetting with the old Hawai'i Herald *in Hilo. He was eighteen. He was supposed to go back that fall, but the interisland steamer got delayed for two weeks with engine trouble, so he missed the start of school. He kept working, and he never went back to Maui. He stayed with the* Herald *for four years. He might have stayed longer because he liked the work, but he got word that his eighty-year-old father was sick. So Sam walked home to see his father. It took him three or four days. It was about fifty miles up the coast, along the muddy plantation road. After that, he never went back to Hilo.*

He stayed in the valley, taking care of his father, and pretty soon he had written his first song. He wrote it to help out a friend, which is how Sam wrote all his songs. For a certain person or to mark some special time. Just the way his father wrote "Hiilawe" about the beauty of the waterfall, but also about two lovers who meet there secretly. At the time he wrote it, there would be references inside the song to tell everyone in the valley who they were.

Joe Perez was Sam's schoolmate from Lahainaluna who also came back to Waipi'o, where his father farmed taro. Joe was getting married, so he fixed up his old family house, repainted it, brought in some new furniture. He did such a good job that his relatives got jealous, especially one brother-in-law. They accused Joe of having a house too fancy for the common man, and this hurt Joe's feelings. He asked Sam to help him out by writing a song of welcome. So Sam did. He put a band together with three other fellows, and they played it outside Joe's house at the wedding on Christmas day. It praises Joe Perez and the beautiful valley they all shared. Some of the folks who were there could tell from the lyrics that they too were in the song. So it brought them all together, and the band had to play several encores.

Sam called it "Heha Waipio" (Drowsy Waipio). He gave the song to Joe as a wedding present. A few years later, one of Joe's sisters who lived in Honolulu showed it to Henry Berger, the famous bandmaster from Germany who had taught Queen Lili'uokalani, and Sam's first song was performed by the Royal Hawaiian Band. Since then, other bands have recorded it—the only song by Sam that ever got recorded in his lifetime.

He wrote "Heha Waipio" in 1904, when he was twenty-two. In those years he worked at a lot of different jobs: farming, driving wagons for Parker Ranch, muleskinning for one of the big sugar plantations. I have seen pictures of Sam from that time: a big husky guy, his moustache bushy and black, his hair thick, and his eyes strong, but soft too. I have heard he had a reputation as a ladies' man, and they say he had a taste for the home-brew we call 'ōkolehao. At least he enjoyed it as much as anyone else in Waipi'o. It was just part of the world he knew. Everybody worked hard in the taro or the sugar fields, then they got together to play music and talk story and have a good time. They say once you start drinking 'ōkolehao, you better have a comfortable place to sit, because that's where you will stay. Later on, your head might say, "It's time to go." But your legs will be saying, "We're not going anywhere."

They brewed it from the root of the ti plant, which had to be washed first, then sliced, then cooked for a few hours in an earth oven, the imu, then mashed up soft, to get it ready for the still.

I heard one story about Sam that I made into a song of my own, called "Okolehao." On his way home from the fields, Sam would sometimes stop to visit a guy who brewed his own at the back end of the valley. One day, Sam stayed so long at this guy's house and drank so much that they had to tie him to his horse and point the horse toward home.

I heard another story from my friend Herb Kane, the artist. His father and grandfather both lived in Waipi'o and knew Sam in the old days and told him about the time Sam was riding home late one night, feeling no pain, and coming down that steep road at such a gallop his horse just went right over the side and rolled down the cliff. The next morning, people saw the horse at the bottom of the cliff, and it looked like something terrible had happened to Sam, but they couldn't find his body. They looked all over, feeling so sad they were starting to weep with grief. Then they saw Sam come walking down the pali road. Just before his horse went over, he had fallen off. He'd passed out up there and slept all night, and now he was wondering, did anybody see his horse?

Whatever Sam did in those days, he always had a band of traveling sere-naders like the ones he'd heard when he was a boy. I met a man in Honolulu, David Makaoi, who was in his late eighties, a retired high-school principal who lived in Nu'uanu, and he remembered roaming around in one of these bands when he was fifteen. One day Sam told him to grab his 'ukulele and join in. Sam was the leader. Someone else played banjo, and there was a gui-tar. David told me how they would meet on their horses in late afternoon. In those days Sam was always riding a white horse. That was his trademark. He would sit on his white horse and hit a G note on his fiddle. When they were all tuned up, Sam would shout, "Let's go!" and away they went.

In towns up on top they would play outside the plantation manager's house and the schoolteacher's house, then ride down into the valley and play outside the farmhouses, taking turns singing. One time I was curious about the way Sam handled his band, and I asked him, "How did you approach your boys and playing the music?" and Sam told me, "Let each and every one of them share their mana'o—their intention and feeling—the way they want to play their song, and share the way they want to strum along with you. I let *'em do that," he said, "and all I tell 'em is play it simple, play it sweet, don't forget the rhythm, and don't forget the melody line…"*

People would always pay them a little something or invite them to share some poi or some pig, whatever they had. David Makaoi remembered getting back to his own house at dawn, when Sam would count out the money they made and split it four ways. When I talked with David seventy years later, he was still impressed with this.

"I was so much younger than all the other guys—only fifteen then—and I only knew one song I could take the lead on, but Sam said everybody gets the same."

That's the kind of world it was back then—everybody shares—the world my mother remembered when I was growing up. I saw it with her, the way she called out to everyone she passed. I saw it with Sam Li'a too.

Words and Earth

In the months that followed their first meeting, Eddie and Sam Li'a became more than good friends. Sam eventually demystified their first encounter. One day he looked at Eddie with a sly smile and said, "I knew you were coming to visit me."

"No," said Eddie. "I didn't tell anybody I was coming out here."

"I knew."

"How did you know?"

"Tutu Kawena wrote me from Honolulu. So then I knew you would visit me one day."

"You tell me this now? After a year?"

"Yes."

"But you had your suit on, your necktie. And you didn't know what day I would come."

"I knew, Eddie. People tend to wait for the right person to come along. I been waiting for a long, long time."

If Eddie had found a spiritual father, Sam had also recognized in him someone he'd been looking for and hoping to meet. It took another musician to appreciate all that Sam knew and what was still in his head. His fingers were too stiff to play it anymore; but Eddie could play it for him.

They spent many hours together on Sam's front porch in Kukuihaele or in his sitting room, among his song sheets and books and instruments. Eddie always brought along a tape recorder, and Sam would talk, sometimes in English, sometimes in Hawaiian, laughing, singing, chanting, his voice dusted with age, yet still rich with resonance and feeling. Sam's voice was itself like a rare recording preserved from a long-gone era, linking the 1880s to the 1970s, a pure channel for the spirit of a place and an earlier time.

In Sam's mind it all turned together and no one piece of it could be separated from the whole: the past, the present, the lives lived, the words, the music, the ancestral valley. He'd composed songs about every aspect of

Waipiʻo, and every song came with a story. One afternoon he told Eddie about the song he'd written for Prince Kūhiō, nephew of King Kalākaua.

Sam had lived so long he remembered the days when Hawaiʻi was still a monarchy. When the king died in San Francisco, in 1891, Sam was already ten years old. When the government, led by Kalākaua's sister, Queen Liliʻuokalani, was overthrown in 1893, he was twelve. News of such events took days and weeks, of course, to reach the valley people Sam lived among. The lives and politics of the royal family had always seemed far removed—until the day Prince Jonah Kūhiō Kalanianaʻole paid a visit, in the fall of 1918. No one could remember when a man of his rank had come into Waipiʻo, perhaps not since the time when the great chiefly families still occupied their thatched compounds along the beachfront.

As the delegate from the Territory of Hawaiʻi to the United States Congress, Kūhiō was touring the outer islands before heading off to the mainland. When his entourage made its slow way down the trail and finally reached the village, Sam happened to be in the social hall. He recalled that before he and his friends could stand up, the prince took a chair, eager to sit with them and talk story. He was down-to-earth, at ease among country people, and Sam liked that so much he wrote a song on the spot: "Elele No Hawaii Aloha I Wakinekona" (Hawaii's Delegate Is Going to Washington). Before the prince departed, Sam and his band played this song asking each island to contribute a lei made of its favorite flower, to honor this leader as he set out to represent his people.

There was also the story of a song Sam had written for his wife, a woman he still spoke of with deep affection, almost reverence. He didn't marry until he was thirty-three. She was only sixteen at the time, a local girl named Sarah Poepoe Kepela, and her father was not at all pleased to hear she was being courted by a man twice her age. But Sam was crazy about her. Defying the father's wishes, they eloped. In those days Sam traveled everywhere on his famous white horse, tipping his hat to anyone who passed. This time Sarah sat behind him, with her arms around his waist, as they rode together into the back end of the valley and up a winding trail to the ranch-country town of Waimea, where they were married by a judge, one of Sam's former Lahainaluna classmates.

"After that," he told Eddie, "my father-in-law couldn't do anything about it."

They made their home at Nāpoʻopoʻo, where Sarah bore him a daughter and a son. And they stayed together for almost forty years, until she passed away in 1951. By that time, Sam was seventy. For the rest of his life, he talked about her, and eventually he wrote a song about her, this one from the perspective of an old man thinking back upon his youth. The title, "Hina Hina Ku Kahakai" (My Flower by the Sea), refers to a delicate blossom still found along the beach at Waipiʻo. This flower, hinahina, also refers to Sarah, the wife he longs for. In the song, he has three legs—a way of saying he has to walk with a cane—but he can still savor their good times together and remember all the treasured places where they once made love.

During his ninety years, Sam had composed dozens and dozens of songs this way. He couldn't remember them all. But those he remembered, as well as those that would turn up later on, took Eddie somewhere he had not been before. Sam Li'a Kalainaina was not only a repository of songs in the style of an older era; he was a composer who wrote in Hawaiian and still *thought* in Hawaiian. When Eddie brought some of Sam's lyrics back to Honolulu to show Kawena, for translation, she looked at the page for a long time, then removed her glasses and looked at him.

"Nobody writes like this anymore," she said, "in the old poetic way. His choice of words is simple, but the flowery images are full of so much meaning. We are both lucky, Eddie. We have met the last of the true Hawaiian poets."

Sam's melody lines could be deceptive, sometimes echoing American folk tunes he might have heard as a young man. But there was more to his songs than melody, more to them than the word play with double and triple meanings. A new kind of knowledge began to move through Eddie, like a long, glowing beam of light, bringing into full clarity things he'd known in his bones to be true—things he'd known to be truly Hawaiian. Sam Li'a had led Eddie to the source: the essential dialogue between a place and its poet. Sam was a man whose mind was still in harmony with the valley of his birth. In one way or another, all his songs were tied to Waipi'o. This valley where he'd spent his life had nourished and inspired him. He in turn gave voice to the beauty and the mystery of the place in an ongoing dialogue, and each song was part of it, each song a poem made of words and earth.

In their days together, something passed from Sam to Eddie. It was much, much more than a collection of songs. The Hawaiian word is *mana*, which in its broadest sense means "power." Not the power to conquer or subdue by force, but the power of the spirit that wells from within. When mana passes from a teacher to a pupil, it is a power lodged in the very nature of a tradition or a practice—in this case, music. It gave Eddie a new place to stand, and rekindled his passion for the songs he loved to play.

The Palmist

The palmist closed up early because of the pains. He felt as if he was being roasted, slowly, from the inside out. By noon he could no longer focus on his customers' palms, their life and love lines having all failed to point to any significant future, merging instead with the rivers and streams of his memories.

Outside, the weather had turned. Dark clouds hung low, and the wind was heavy with moisture. He reached the bus stop's tiny shelter when it began to pour. He didn't have to wait long, however. The good old 38 Geary pulled up in a few minutes, and he felt mildly consoled, though sharp pains flared and blossomed from deep inside his bowels like tiny geysers and made each of his three steps up the bus laborious.

It was warm and humid on the crowded bus, and a fine mist covered all windows. The palmist sat on the front bench facing the aisle, the one reserved for the handicapped and the elderly. A fat woman who had rosy cheeks and who did not take the seat gave him a dirty look. It was true: his hair was still mostly black, and he appeared to be a few years short of senior citizenship. The palmist pretended not to notice her. Contemptuously, he leaned back against the worn and cracked vinyl and smiled to himself. He closed his eyes. A faint odor of turned earth reached his nostrils. He inhaled deeply and saw again a golden rice field, a beatific smile, a face long gone: his first kiss.

The rain pounded the roof as the bus rumbled toward the sea.

At the next stop, a teenager got on. Caught in the downpour without an umbrella, he was soaking wet, and his extra-large T-shirt, which said PLAY HARD…STAY HARD, clung to him. It occurred to the palmist that this was the face of someone who hadn't yet learned to be fearful of the weather. The teenager stood, towering above the palmist and blocking him from seeing the woman, who, from time to time, continued to glance disapprovingly at him.

So young, the palmist thought: the age of my youngest son, maybe, had he lived. The palmist tried to conjure up his son's face, but could not. It had been some years since the little boy drowned in the South China Sea, along with his two older sisters and their mother. The palmist had escaped

Leo Limón. *Wild Ride.*
1996. Pastel on paper.
Photograph by John White.

on a different boat, a smaller one that had left a day after his family's boat, and, as a result, reached America alone.

Alone, thought the palmist and sighed. *Alone.*

It was then that his gaze fell upon the teenager's hand and he saw something. He leaned forward and did what he had never done before on the 38 Geary. He spoke up loudly, excitedly.

"You," he said in his heavy accent. "I see wonderful life!"

The teenager looked down at the old man and arched his eyebrows.

"I'm a palmist. Maybe you give me your hand?" the palmist said.

The teenager did nothing. No one had ever asked to see his hand on the bus. The fat woman snickered. Oh, she'd seen it all on the 38 Geary. She wasn't surprised. "This my last reading: no money, free, gift for you," the palmist pressed on. "Give me your hand."

"You know," the teenager said, scratching his chin. He was nervous. "I don't know." He felt as if he'd been caught inside a moving greenhouse and that, with the passengers looking on, he had somehow turned into one of its most conspicuous plants.

"What—what you don't know?" asked the palmist. "Maybe I know. Maybe I answer."

"Dude," the teenager said, "I don't know if I believe in all that hocus-pocus stuff." And, though he didn't say it, he didn't know whether he wanted to be touched by the old man with wrinkled, bony hands and nauseating tobacco breath. To stall, the teenager said, "I have a question, though. Can you read your own future? Can you, like, tell when you're gonna die and stuff?" Then he thought about it and said, "Nah, forget it. Sorry, that was stupid."

The bus driver braked abruptly at the next stop, and all the people standing struggled to stay on their feet. But those near the front of the bus were also struggling to listen to the conversation. "No, no, not stupid," said the palmist. "Good question. Long ago, I asked same thing, you know. I read same story in many hands of my people: story that said something bad will happen. Disaster. But in my hand here, I read only good thing. This line here, see, say I have happy family, happy future. No problem. So I think: me, my family, no problem. Now I know better: all hands effect each other, all lines run into each other, tell a big story. When the war ended in my country, you know, it was so bad for everybody. And my family? Gone, gone under the sea. You know, reading palm not like reading map." He touched his chest. "You feel and see here in heart also, in guts here also, not just here in your head. It is—how d'you say—atuition?"

"Intuition," the teenager corrected him, stifling a giggle.

"Yes," nodded the palmist. "Intuition."

The teenager liked the sound of the old man's voice. Its timbre reminded him of the voice of his long-dead grandfather, who also came from another country, one whose name had changed several times as a result of wars.

"My stop not far away now," the palmist continued. "This your last chance. Free. No charge."

"Go on, kiddo," the fat woman said, nudging the boy with her elbow and smiling. She wanted to hear his future. "I've been listening. It's all right. He's for real, I can tell now."

That was what the boy needed. "OK," he said, then opened his right fist like a flower and presented it to the palmist. The old man's face burned with seriousness as he leaned down and traced the various lines and contours and fleshy knolls on the teenager's palm. He bent the boy's wrist this way and that, kneaded and poked the fingers and knuckles as if to measure the strength of his resolve. In his own language, he made mysterious calculations and mumbled a few singsong words to himself.

Finally, the palmist looked up and, in a solemn voice, spoke. "You will become artist. When twenty-five, twenty-six, you're going to change very much. If you don't choose right, oh, so many regrets. But don't be afraid. Never be afraid. Move forward. Always. You have help. These squares here, right here, see, they're spirits and mentors, they come protect, guide you. When you reach mountaintop, people everywhere will hear you, know you, see you. Your art, what you see, others will see. Oh, so much love. You number one someday."

Inspired, the palmist went on like this for some time. Despite his pains, which flared up intermittently, the old man went on to speak of the ordinary palms and sad faces he had read, the misfortunes he had seen coming and the wondrous opportunities squandered as a result of fear and distrust. Divorces, marriages, and deaths in families—of these, he had read too many. Broken vows, betrayals, and adulteries—too pedestrian to remember. Twice, however, he held hands that committed unspeakable evil, and each time, he was sick for a week. And once, he held the hand of a reincarnated saint. How many palms had he read since his arrival in America? "Oh, so many," he said, laughing, "too many. Thousands. Who care now? Not me."

When the palmist finished talking, the teenager retrieved his hand and looked at it. It seemed heavy and foreign. Most of what the palmist had said made no sense to him. Sure he loved reading a good book now and then—reading was like being inside a cartoon—but he loved cartoons even more. And even if he got good grades, he hated his stupid English classes, though it's true that he did write poetry—but only for himself. He also played the piano. A singer? Maybe a computer graphic artist? Maybe a movie star? He didn't know. Everything was still possible. Besides, turning twenty-five was so far away—almost a decade.

Before she got off the bus, the fat lady touched the teenager lightly on the shoulder. "Lots of luck, kiddo," she said and smiled a sad, wistful smile.

Nearing his stop, the palmist struggled to get up, wincing as he did. The teenager helped him and wanted to say something, but he did not. When the bus stopped, he flashed a smile instead and waved to the palmist, who, in turn, gave him a look that he would later interpret as that of impossible longing. Later he would also perceive the palmist as the first of many true seers in his life and realize that, in the cosmic sense of things, their encounter was inevitable. At that moment, however, all he saw was a small and sad-looking old man whose eyes seemed on the verge of tears as he quietly nodded before stepping off the bus and into the downpour.

The teenager lived near the end of the line, past the park. As usual, the bus was nearly empty on this stretch, and he moved to the bench the palmist had occupied. He could still feel the warmth of the vinyl and felt insulated by it somehow.

With nearly everyone gone, he grew bored. He turned to the befogged window behind him and drew a sailor standing on a sloop and holding a bottle. The ocean was full of dangerous waves. The boat, it seemed, was headed toward a girl who had large round breasts and danced in a hula skirt on a distant shore. He drew a few tall mountains and swaying palm trees behind her. He hesitated before mischievously giving her two, three more heads and eight or nine more arms than she needed to entice the drunken sailor to her island. And then he pulled back to look at what he had done: the scene made him chuckle to himself.

Through his drawing, the teenager saw a rushing world of men, women, and children under black, green, red, blue, polka-dotted umbrellas and plastic ponchos. He watched until the people and storefront windows streaked into green: pine trees, fern groves, placid lakes, and well-tended grass meadows. The park…beyond which was the sea.

The rain tapered off, and a few columns of sunlight pierced the gray clouds, setting the road aglow like a golden river. The boy couldn't wait to get off the bus and run or do something—soar above the clouds if he could. In the sky, jumbo jets and satellites gleamed. People were talking across borders, time zones, oceans, continents. People were flying to marvelous countries, to mysterious destinies.

With repeated circular movements of his hand, he wiped away sailor, boat, waves, and girl. Where the palmist's thumbnail had dug into the middle of his palm and made a crescent moon, he could still feel a tingling sensation. "A poet…not!" he said to himself and giggled. Then he shook his head and looked at his cool, wet palm before wiping it clean on his faded Levi's.

John Valadez. *Car Show*. 2001.
Oil on canvas. Collection of Dennis Hopper.
Photograph by Peggy Tennison.

Friends

By day, Kathmandu's tourist district, Thamel, hawks trinkets and curios. The Dutch, the Italians, the Germans, the Japanese, the French, the Americans, the Israelis—tourists all—come to the memorabilia shops to buy Buddhist mandalas, turquoise bracelets, Gurkha knives, bottled water, *pashmina* shawls, demon masks, rice-paper notebooks, chocolate bars, hiking boots, embroidered T-shirts that read I LOVE MOUNT EVEREST. A roll of Fuji film sells for three hundred here and twenty rupees less over there; each price is negotiable. All day, the streets bustle with bargaining: "Sixty." "Last price fifty." As evening falls, Thamel crowds travelers into its low-budget restaurants, and they become wide-eyed with wonder because serendipity has brought them together in—of all places—Kathmandu, Nepal. For less than two dollars each, they eat eggplant lasagna, garlic *naan*, schnitzel, swimming *rama*, stir-fries, buffalo dumplings, risotto, curry, and pizza while swapping adventure stories and worldviews. "My meditation teacher said flowers bloom even in the desert." "I found an awesome used bookstore selling Pico Iyer." "The first main thing I don't like of Nepal," some tourist declares in broken English, "is the dirty air." Indeed, the exhaust from the city's cars and buses is one of the largest cracks in this patched, foggy mirror image of Western dreams: a mirror quicksilvered with incredible mountain stories, some fantastic tales of Kew, and a Cat Stevens song about Kathmandu.

The traditional Nepalis who inhabit Thamel, however, cannot begin to identify the syncopated beat of Bob Marley competing with the wail of Joan Baez around the corner. Hoping to profit by the tourists nonetheless, most locals have rented out their houses to hotels, restaurants, and shops and moved their families to quieter neighborhoods. Proper Kathmandu shuns Thamel. Driving by on some rare occasion, the nation's who's-who murmur, "This is where we used to play ball as boys. It was just an empty field," and then exclaim, "There was a sweetmeat store—and look: there it is, still, beneath that INTERNATIONAL TRUNK CALL FAX PHOTOCOPY SERVICES sign. I wonder if it's still run by that pock-marked shopkeeper."

The sweetmeat store, as it so happens, has changed hands several times and now belongs to Kuber Sharma, a recent migrant from the south who takes the growth of concrete houses around his shop as a personal insult. "Why can't *I* have a house of my own?" he mutters to a picture of Laxmi, the Goddess of Wealth, as he heats the oil in which he fries, for one despondent hour every morning, the crisp, sugared sweetmeats that he sells for the rest of the day. Warding off flies, sipping weak tea, counting change for customers, Kuber Sharma curses his fate and his young wife, who makes expensive demands of him; but he does, at the end of each month, make enough to pay his rent and meet his living expenses.

Tenzing Namgyal, keeper of the art shop next door, doesn't believe in God because he is Tibetan, and the Buddha said there is no God. Tenzing is flexible, though, and will question his views when talking to a foreign woman. The prettier the foreign woman is, the more religious-minded Tenzing is inclined to become. "This is Avalokitesvara, future Buddha," he says serenely in his high-school English, spreading for her benefit a scrolled acrylic painting. "One-hundred-percent vegetable dye." He strokes the deity's pink navel. "For you, only two thousand. Where you from—Italian?"

Kamal Malla, a young computer programmer, strolls by Tenzing's store every evening on his way back from work. He is charmed by this part of Kathmandu, so different from his own staid, duty-bound corner of the city. When the sky darkens and halogen lights switch on, he hears old men and women greet each other as though a new day has begun. And indeed it seems to have. Rust-colored lights warm the air. Peddlers press close and whisper, "Hashish?" "Tiger balm?" "Change money?" Irate tourists brush past. "No, no, no." Flutes and saxophones riddle the night. Kamal stops to take in picturesque sights: a white man with a long, pierced nose. Fantastic! They stretch the imagination, the things he sees here. And so each day after work, he ambles along in the vicinity of—one block away from, one story down from, one door over from, one street up from—Thamel dwellers like Dilip Basnyat, the owner of La Vie Boheme Restaurant, who worries about his skinny cook. The cook makes a fine borscht soup but disappears for days, explaining when he returns that he has had to consult his village witchdoctor about an illness that won't go away: "I lose weight no matter how much I eat." Of course Kamal doesn't know Dilip Basnyat, and he's never been inside La Vie Boheme—such restaurants are for tourists—and yet the tensions of the neighborhood at night affect him. It's as if he becomes less familiar to himself, more volatile, changeable, edgy, like the waiter at Third World European Cuisine, Lal Bahadur Rai. The waiter keeps a lookout for single foreign men to ask them if they want a nice Nepali girl—hoping to marry his sister, at sixteen, to a kind and gentle foreigner, preferably a Britisher because they are civilized. In Thamel, Kamal awakens from his traditional life and becomes a little more modern; I can see this from the open, interested expression on his face as he passes by my small but centrally located convenience store.

On one of his evening walks last year, Kamal came across Rishikesh Pandey, a Nepali who had recently returned from the United States, where he had lived since childhood. Rishikesh actually saw Kamal first and recognized him by his candy-striped shirt, which Kamal wore almost every day. "It's you," Rishikesh said, extending his hand to get Kamal's attention.

Kamal had been inspecting a display of peach strudels and was startled. He turned and smiled slightly, unable to place the lean, lanky boy smiling down at him so familiarly. The boy spoke Nepali but wore tourist rags and was as pale as a foreigner.

Rishikesh was smiling. "Do you live around here?" he asked, leaning into Kamal as a man swept by hissing, "Hashish?"

"Yes, I remember," Kamal answered, brightening up. "Your Pentium—Toshiba, I think; yes, now I'm sure. Laptop." Then he stopped smiling. "I've been meaning to telephone you."

Rishikesh asked which way Kamal was heading, and the two of them walked together into the crowded center of Thamel, past my shop and towards a row of carpet vendors, halting every time a bicycle or battered taxi swerved too close. Kamal talked about the computer. "You need a new motherboard," he said, trying to remember all the details, and he mentioned a friend's shop, where prices were middling. "I'll put it into the computer if you like."

Rishikesh had already looked into buying a PowerBook and preferred, anyway, a more casual tone for their conversation because Kamal had struck him as nice when they'd met at the National Computer Center. He watched Kamal pull out a pack of Khukuri filters and light one without offering him any. This seemed very Nepali to Rishikesh, who studied other Nepalis in order to learn about himself. Despite Kamal's smart office clothes—so Western—the man looked utterly native: jet-black hair, ashen skin, elongated eyes, sharp nose, and the chiseled brown lips of a cast-iron Buddha. Rishikesh hoped he might share with Kamal his insights into their native land.

"There's a nice garden restaurant here," Rishikesh said, stopping in front of La Vie Boheme Restaurant. "Can I buy you a beer?"

Kamal hesitated, too polite to say no, but as soon as they took a table he worried about his sister, who would be cooking dinner for him at home. While Rishikesh ordered beer ("San Miguel, not Iceberg") and snacks ("Do you have chips? And that special borscht soup?"), Kamal wondered if he had time to call home and say he'd be late. But the waiter moved away and there was this boy Rishikesh, relaxed in a cane chair, his unkempt hair falling on his forehead and shading his wide, friendly eyes.

Without any prompting, Rishikesh began to talk about himself, explaining that it had been just a few months since he came to Nepal. "I wanted to find out who I really am," he said, his tone so frank that Kamal was intrigued. Apparently, he was staying with his uncle—"But I don't think family is as important as friends"—and he was a journalist working for the *Kathmandu Newsflash*. Kamal noted that he spoke Nepali like a child and used many English words.

The beer and chips came, then the soup, and they shared everything, Kamal slowly drawn into Rishikesh's curious musings. He seemed simple, like a boy who couldn't contain what he felt and had to blurt it out. "I don't know anything about my own country," Rishikesh admitted with embarrassment. Kamal noticed the flush in the boy's face, but didn't think much about it. He was enjoying this garden restaurant filled with tourists and, over the scratchy speakers, Billy Joel singing praises of a girl from uptown. A naked bulb cast deep-blue shadows on Rishikesh's sunken face. "I don't even know," Rishikesh continued—breaking out in English, which he spoke more naturally than Nepali—"the difference between Pandeys and Mallas."

The beer buzzed in Kamal's mind, and he decided to match Rishikesh's frankness with his own. He replied in English, "There is some differences in what festival your family is celebrating and my family," he said in an assuring tone. "Small-small differences. But all this is nothing about culture and religion. You have to be modern and not look back."

Rishikesh lifted his glass of beer and toasted this. When he put down the glass, he asked in English, "What language do you speak with your family?"

"Newari." Kamal shrugged, then laughed. "You are probably speaking English at home. Nepali is both not our mother tongue."

The two men eased into their chairs and spent the next hour chatting about Kathmandu in general terms, Rishikesh asking questions and Kamal outlining the city's various problems: poverty, pollution, and politics. He did not say anything that Rishikesh hadn't heard before—all Nepalis seemed obsessed with poverty, pollution, and politics—but Rishikesh enjoyed listening to him. There was something about the way Kamal talked—perhaps a soothing, familial tone—that made him feel less alone in this city.

Kamal savored the novelty of sitting in a restaurant he would never go to and talking to a half-American boy who spoke so guilelessly, like a child. La Vie Boheme Restaurant—he must remember the name. The music and the borscht soup, the exotic cane-and-cotton decor put him in a giddy, lighthearted mood.

Outside La Vie Boheme, Kamal lit up a cigarette.

Rishikesh asked for one, too. "It's a nice night," he said, still feeling chatty.

Kamal laughed. "Only at night Kathmandu is beautiful," he said, departing with a nod.

Alone in the cool, dark night, each man felt affirmed by the exchange.

R.P. Aryal, the editor-in-chief of the *Kathmandu Newsflash,* liked putting the Pandey boy down. "The Cultural Attaché of the Bangladesh Embassy," he would say, making the assignment sound important as he handed Rishikesh the attaché's calling card. "We need some pictures of floods." And like a peon, off the boy would go to fetch pictures wearing ugly German sandals. Radiant and sincere, Rishikesh seemed to invite, even facilitate, his own degradation. He didn't know about office hierarchy and never asked for taxi money, perks, or reimbursement for the fares of autorickshaws. He covered all his expenses with his meager three-thousand-rupee salary. R.P. figured that the boy's father was rich—one earned millions in America—and liked the thought that Rishikesh was bringing that wealth back to Nepal. Yes, R.P. enjoyed this thought immensely. To his friends who came by the office to drink tea and gossip away the afternoon, R.P. would say, "Green-card-holding, pure Nepali boy, that one." His friends would turn to look at Rishikesh, wearing loose-fitting, natural-fiber clothes and looking like a hippy. R.P. would add, "Says he wants to live in Nepal—who knows for how long." And R.P.'s friends would speculate.

Rishikesh knew none of this, but he felt isolated in the *Newsflash* office, where he was the youngest staff member. Though he admired R.P. because the man knew everyone, he didn't really like him; there was something sinister about the way R.P. looked at people, as if appraising their worth. Neither did he like the assistant editor, who didn't show Rishikesh any of the warmth he displayed to the rest of the staff, who—perhaps because of their limited English and his limited Nepali—kept their distance. Most days, Rishikesh sat alone at his desk and proofread his colleagues' articles. Their grammar was so strangled that he often had no choice but to rewrite whole paragraphs, sometimes whole articles. If he asked, he was also allowed to write his own articles, which made him feel that his life in Nepal had purpose. The other journalists noted, with bitterness, that Rishikesh Pandey's articles were grammatically correct but gratingly high-minded. The journalists knew much more about deforestation, homeless children, hydropower, sustainable development, and urbanization; they just didn't have good English.

Rishikesh blamed himself for each rebuff in his bid for friendship with his colleagues; perhaps, he thought, he didn't know how to behave, how to fit in, be like a real Nepali. At the end of each day, he went home feeling exhausted from his efforts—not that he regretted coming back to Nepal. Every day he saw so much and learned so much about his country. What was a green card after all? He was still a Nepali citizen. Yes, he was glad he had returned home—yes, why not call it home—but there was no denying that life in Nepal was, at times, a bit of a struggle.

About a week after their drinks in Thamel, Rishikesh walked into Kamal's office at the National Computer Center, realizing, as he passed through the dusty halls, that his crumpled orange shirt and baggy pants made him look like a tourist. He found Kamal at his desk, tinkering with electrical wires. Kamal stood up, pleased to see him, and immediately produced a wedding invitation—his sister was getting married—with Rishikesh's name written in English as RISIKES. Kamal asked, "Tea?" then rang a tinny bell on his desk, which summoned a peon to the door. Kamal ordered two cups, then said, "Here is your Toshiba," picking it out of a stack of keyboards, cables, and monitors at the side of his desk.

Rishikesh took the computer and listened to the other man's slightly formal description of what had happened to the motherboard. This wasn't what he'd come for. "Do you have a cigarette?" he asked when Kamal was finished. Kamal cocked his head, smiled, and pulled out a pack of Khukuri filters, and both men smoked.

The tea came, weak and watery. Kamal told the peon to offer a cup to Rishikesh first, then took his own cup and sipped it while he listened to Rishikesh complain about his work. "I get so tired," Rishikesh said, and his face suddenly seemed all bone and cartilage. "I write my own articles and edit everyone else's, but nobody ever says, 'Good job.' Nobody gives a shit."

Kamal was at first put off by this expletive, then pleased by its novelty. He watched the younger man—who must be, what, twenty-three at the most—and felt moved by his pout, his flighty gestures, his indignation at the complexity of life in Nepal. Kamal used the tone and bearing of an older brother, a role he immediately liked: "You don't know how mean Kathmandu's people can be."

"But why?" Rishikesh cried. "Why are they mean?"

"They are very devious, you do not know," Kamal said. "I have been here all my life, and I have seen all that they do to each other with their small-small minds."

"Small thoughts," Rishikesh sighed. Then realizing he'd gone on too long, he asked Kamal about his work. "Is it like that for you, too?"

Kamal glanced at the door. "It is all crap," he said with a rasp, surprising himself. He lowered his voice. "These government offices are all crap. These small-small people, I almost go crazy. Junior staffs like me they make to repair equipment. And senior staffs and bosses attend training programs and seminars abroad—all crap."

Sitting forward, Kamal continued, "In Pakistan, Madras, South India— so many countries, the software is major industry." The thought flustered him. "Is highly specialized labor, and in this parts of the world, it is cheaper for big-big companies to hire. We could do programming in Nepal, too, but the government is too unstable—who would like to invest money here? Every six months, a new government. If the government stable, we could start software industry. Software, it is challenging. But not this hardware repair and crap. I get so excited, even thinking…" Kamal checked himself, sat back, and smiled. It wasn't good to get worked up like this about such remote possibilities.

Rishikesh stood up. He had a newspaper errand to run and thanked Kamal for looking at his laptop.

"No need for thanks," Kamal insisted. Rishikesh was a friend now and didn't have to be so formal. Kamal reached over and took the boy's hand—a gesture Rishikesh found very Nepali. He reached for his wallet, but Kamal said vehemently, "No, no—no payment," and shooed him out of the room. This boy acted too American at times.

Alone again in his office, Kamal returned to his wires, but was distracted by ambitions simmering inside him. Four months before, he had applied to the master's program in computer science at the Asian Institute of Technology, located in Bangkok. It was March now: about time for their response.

All of this took place last spring, when my husband and I were selling clothes because tourists, it seemed, wore anything. Someone had designed clashing blue and red pants and the brightest, most tasteless patch skirts— but even these, tourists tried on, called "cool," and bought. Our store was full of these mad rags and also stocked with sweaters, shirts, caps, and socks, all made in Nepal. My husband and I had taken a loan, so we needed at least eight thousand a month to cover our interest, rent, and food. I had found two low-caste boys from our district—we're originally from Syangja, in the western hills—to be our tailors, and they sat in the back of the shop, stitching cotton patches on the clothes to make them look fashionable. Our store didn't do well, though, and sometimes it looked like we'd never be able to pay back our loan.

Dilip Basnyat, the owner of La Vie Boheme and a moneylender from our district, was the one who had loaned us the money. Each time we visited him, he advised us to display our products better. "I know a Kashmiri family migrated here, rented a space. Not even as big as yours. But they spent thousands on spotlights, on a showcase for their window. A year later," he would say, making an expansive gesture, "they're already building a house."

He didn't seem to realize we couldn't afford to buy things like spotlights.

"You don't need a good space," he would say with the certainty of the well-to-do, "if you know how to market your products."

Then he would explain why he couldn't lower our interest rate and dismiss us with a wave. On our way out, my husband and I would stop by the kitchen to talk to my cousin, the restaurant's head cook, who looked sicklier with each passing day. He had a terminal blood disease that Dilip Basnyat didn't know about. If my poor cousin were to die suddenly, La Vie Boheme would definitely suffer, I thought, because no one else in Kathmandu could make the borscht soup that the restaurant was renowned for.

In the days leading up to his sister's wedding, Kamal stopped coming to Thamel because there was too much to do at home. One day when he got back from work, he found his father and uncles and cousin brothers in the ground-floor rooms watching satellite TV and making plans for a bakery they wanted to open. Kamal's mother, aunts, and cousin sisters were in the second-floor bedrooms sorting cardamom, cinnamon, walnuts, coconuts, and rock sugar for the wedding banquet. Kamal went to the top floor, where he found his sister at the stove in the kitchen. She motioned for him to sit, then said, "Have tea," and went through the familiar, intimate gestures of brewing it. "You must be hungry," she said next and then turned her attention to the lentil patties she was frying for snacks.

Kamal studied her face: so serene, all smooth surface. She was a perfect girl in every way. Since high school, she had stayed at home, bringing him tea in the morning, making his bed, and ironing his clothes. At night she cooked the family dinner. Now a Poland-educated civil engineer had asked the family for her hand in marriage, and they had all urged her to accept. Was she happy with this decision? Impossible to tell. "Only a week left," Kamal remarked, looking at her closely and trying to decipher the meaning of the subtle shrug his words elicited.

His own ambition stirred like a cloud storm as he drank the tea and wondered what it would be like—if he got an acceptance letter—when he told his family that he was leaving Kathmandu and going to Bangkok. He hadn't even told them that he had applied. If he went, would his parents feel abandoned by their only son? Would his sister accuse him of failing them? She who had never failed in any of her duties as a girl—or woman.

Rishikesh attended the wedding, but he was uncomfortable seeing so many unfamiliar people who, unlike him, looked like they belonged there. Kamal attended to him in the gracious way of Nepali hosts: urging him to eat more, drink more, stay longer. "You've only just gotten here," Kamal told him. But that week, Rishikesh was preoccupied with a chain of events set off by a letter he'd gotten from his girlfriend in Boston. Reading her announcement that she needed her freedom, he had called Eliza and found out that she had gone back to the boyfriend she'd had before him. For several giddy days, Rishikesh had felt alone in this vast world. To allay his fears of being unwanted, he had slept with an American volunteer he had met while writing an article on the Peace Corps. Jessica was an opinionated thirty-year-old who felt that Nepali peasants would benefit from eliminating the country's upper classes, and Rishikesh realized, even as he crept out of her lodge at dawn, that he had made a mistake. When he told her so later, he fueled her class antagonism; she accused him of being a self-absorbed and indulgent man of privilege, the son of a millionaire (oh yes, she had heard what Nepalis paid for migration papers), and not even a real Nepali like the villagers of the hill district Khotang, where the Peace Corps had posted her. Miserably, Rishikesh realized that he didn't even know where Khotang was.

Back at the National Computer Center, Kamal flipped absent-mindedly through the *Kathmandu Newsflash* and wondered when the Asian Institute of Technology would send word of his acceptance.

A few weeks passed. My husband and I realized we'd make more money if we sold things people couldn't do without, so we fired the two tailors, shoved our stock of clothes to the back corner of the store, and set up a modest window display of plastic combs, Chinese soap, dandruff shampoo, sandalwood incense, playing cards, Nivea cold cream, mineral water, Colgate toothpaste, and Indian nail cutters. We added postcards, rice-paper calendars, and prayer wheels to our stock, and some Nice biscuits as well. "What shall I buy you, my little round love," my husband would say, embracing me at night, "with all the money we'll make?"

Now I'm not the kind of woman who needs jewelry, lipstick, clothes of the latest design. I'm educated, I work hard, and I'm full of confidence. But I live for tenderness. "Such talk," I'd say, curling into the heat of my husband's body.

He worried about fulfilling his duties as a caretaker. "I should get a peon posting," he'd say to me in the dark. "I should support both of us—not rely on your store to feed us."

"You'll get a job soon," I kept assuring him. "With your high-school degree, your charm, you'll work one day at a government office. Just you wait and see."

"What it takes is connections," my husband would say. "And those, we don't have."

Dhan Raj Kafle, the peon at the National Computer Center, was a wrinkled old man in eternally crusty clothes who seemed, at first glance, resigned to the menial tasks of making tea, running personal errands for his bosses, and delivering mail. But like any of us, he had needs, desires, and family demands to meet. He was on the lookout for better opportunities so that he could become a bit more secure in this world, eat just a little better. Who wasn't? And he hoped that one day he could afford an English-medium boarding school for his eldest son.

One late-spring day, Dhan Raj was delivering his mail as usual, shuffling from one office to another, when he noticed a letter for Kamal Malla Sir from a foreign country. He used his fourth-grade English to make out the word "Thailand" and reflected that it was irregular for a letter to go straight to Kamal Sir without going through his bosses. Dhan Raj was due for a raise. In order to demonstrate his loyalty to the supervisor, he took the letter to the man's desk and said, "This letter is from abroad," leaving it in the supervisor's hands. How was he to know that the supervisor begrudged others prospects that were better than his own?

Kamal finally tired of waiting in thrall for his dreams and telephoned Rishikesh to invite him out for beer. Not that he could afford it. His salary at the Computer Center was four thousand rupees a month, and one Iceberg beer was seventy rupees. But he felt defiant. He was college educated, capable, and just twenty-six. If nothing came of his application to the institute, he could resign from his job at the center and start a business—maybe a computer store—to support himself. And if worse came to worst, he'd do whatever was necessary: he'd even become a partner in his uncle's new bakery.

"The same place?" Rishikesh asked over the phone, and Kamal said, "Somewhere else. Somewhere I've never been. You decide."

Rishikesh suggested San Francisco Yeti Pizza Hut. Kamal didn't know where it was, and at half past six, he stopped by my store, asking for directions. He politely addressed me as an older sister and spoke in a low, modulated voice. I told him to head straight till he reached the Rum Doodle Bar, then take a left towards the Pilgrim's Book Store, if he knew where that was. He said yes. He was early, so he bought a pack of cigarettes, lit up slowly, and lingered outside my store, his serene, shapely features accented by the blue of a neon sign above the shop next door. It was a warm evening, and the crowds of tourists were thick, babbling, colorful, brimming with an otherworldly energy. I watched him walk slowly, with poise, into the clutter of foreign souls.

At the San Francisco Yeti Pizza Hut, Kamal found Rishikesh waiting at a table by the window, which overlooked tangled electrical lines. He ordered beer, and Rishikesh ordered Sprite, and they decided to share a spinach pizza. Kamal had never eaten pizza before. He asked about Rishikesh's work, but found the responses vague, evasive. So he talked about his sister's wedding. But Rishikesh seemed distracted. During a lull in the conversation, Rishikesh tilted his head and hummed along with the song that was playing over the restaurant's tape recorder: *Taking a ride—on a cosmic train.*

"Cat Stevens," Kamal said, remembering the singer's name.

"You know it?"

"I used to listen to it in India."

Rishikesh was surprised to find out that Kamal had gotten his bachelor's degree in computer science in Madras, South India. He had just assumed that Kamal had never left Nepal. He listened to the other man suddenly speak in an unfamiliar way. "Some of the college boys listen to wild, wild songs," Kamal said, thinking back to his youth. "Pink Floyd, Led Zeppelin, Uriah Heep. I never went wild, of a kind, but some of them did."

"Uriah Heep?" Rishikesh asked.

Kamal sat forward, lit a cigarette, and followed the lead of the memories that unfolded. "They went," he said, ignoring the pizza that the waiter put down, "those Indian boys, they went to the States and Britain and Australia to work after college. I also wanted to go, but my parents…They are getting old, and I am the only son. They need me. Some of the boys got doctorates even. I have one classmate went to a place called University of Pennsylvania."

"U Penn," Rishikesh said. "That's close to Boston, where my parents live. Maybe six hours' drive."

"He is a brilliant boy," Kamal said, getting agitated. He stubbed out his cigarette and said emphatically, "My parents are proud I am a computer engineer. It is a big thing for them. But if I have to spend my life at this kind of job, doing nothing, earning one, two thousand, I think, 'Why I studied? Why I worked so hard?'" He tried to smile, but couldn't, and continued bitterly, "I don't want to spend my life thinking twice before having a cup of coffee. Even ten rupees is a big thing when you work in the government." Then, composing himself, he laughed, but Rishikesh, listening closely, could tell that his mirth wasn't genuine. Kamal frowned again and said, "What kind of life is that?" Then he lowered his voice and revealed his secret: he had applied to AIT in Bangkok. "Very good university," he said. "Most of the graduates they go to work in Australia later. Australian companies even come to recruit them."

The Cat Stevens tape ended and was replaced by the screech of Nirvana.

"Australia," Rishikesh said, disappointed that Kamal seemed less Nepali than he'd thought. Then he added in a disagreeing tone, "Though Kathmandu's not that bad, if you think about it. Sometimes I think it's just our attitude, you know? If we could simplify our life, get back to basics…" He began to describe the yoga classes that he had recently begun to take and the amazing, expanding effect meditation had had on his consciousness. "It's like we need to find all the good parts of being Nepali," he said, cringing at the odd sound of his words. "Without that shit about the caste system and all, you know." He frowned, and his bony, angular features suddenly looked harsh. He continued, "It was the Brahmin pundits who reinterpreted Hinduism so that it would benefit them. They began the caste system and all. But things like yoga, like meditation—they're timeless."

Kamal couldn't quite follow Rishikesh. "But you are also speaking like a real Brahmin," he said, laughing uncomfortably.

"I was always sort of interested in my roots," Rishikesh answered solemnly. "In college I read the Upanishads and Vedas and practiced *ayurveda*. Now that I'm meditating, I'm beginning to find something I like—that's ours, truly ours." He noticed the quizzical expression on Kamal's face and suddenly let go of his argument. "Yeah, I guess I am speaking like a Brahmin. When will you hear from the school in Bangkok?"

Kamal shrugged. "You have to put all traditions and crap behind you," he said in a tone that he hoped sounded neutral. As a gesture of friendship, he offered Rishikesh a cigarette.

"None for me," Rishikesh said. "I'm cutting down; it isn't good for you."

"You talk like hippy American," Kamal responded, letting the smoke rid his mouth of the pungent taste of pizza.

Rishikesh noticed that there was an edge to the rest of their conversation. Every time he mentioned yoga or meditation, Kamal seemed to smile sardonically. Rishikesh countered by lecturing briefly, when they parted, that Nepal wasn't a bad place to live. "It's all in our minds," he said testily. "This city is what we make of it."

How would he know, Kamal mused as they took leave of each other; Rishikesh had only lived here a few months and could return to America whenever he wanted.

The next week, they met for lunch at Laughing Buddha Thai Restaurant. Rishikesh invited Kamal this time, after realizing that he shouldn't have judged his friend's desire to go to Bangkok. Why shouldn't he go? Rishikesh thought. We all need to see the world.

Kamal had regretted his comments about Rishikesh's hippy spirituality. Their friendship was too special to treat so thoughtlessly. After all, he had no one else to talk to this way. In all his other relationships, he acted out the roles defined for him by society. Rishikesh was free, like an American, and he loaned Kamal some of his freedom. The least Kamal could do was support him in his desire to be a different kind of Hindu, or whatever he wanted to be.

These warm impulses Thamel nurtured. Laughing Buddha Thai Restaurant was bright, lively, and distracting with its checkered linoleum floors, clashing tablecloths, and pulsating Hindi love songs. At the start, both friends listened respectfully, trying to make the other feel comfortable. When it came to each man's turn to talk, he willed himself to be open and trusting. Quickly enough, they settled into an easy, rambling conversation about everything that came to mind: family obligations, politics, childhood events, the software industry, journalism, the electricity shortage. As the afternoon progressed, Kamal raised his beer and Rishikesh his Pepsi, and they toasted their unknown futures. Afterward, they stopped by Kuber Sharma's shop, and each bought a sweetmeat; their mouths were thick with syrup when they said farewell.

It was then that their lives diverged. Kamal decided that as it was now May, he should send a fax to AIT's admissions officer, a Mrs. B. Sirichanda, whose signature was decorated with ornate curlicues. He received a reply—unsigned but from the admissions office—that they had given his seat to someone else because he had never responded. They wished him the best in furthering his education.

Stunned, he called up AIT. "I did not receive any admission letter!" he cried into the telephone, but the response on the other side was unwavering.

For days, Kamal walked about in a fog, doing no work and questioning everyone at the office about a letter from Thailand: had they seen it anywhere? The peon Dhan Raj Kafle, who had gotten his raise and harbored no particular resentment toward Kamal Sir, told him that he thought he'd seen such a letter on the supervisor's desk.

Kamal staggered at the thought. There were those Nepalis, he knew, who harmed others because they had to, competing for meager resources. Then there were those, like the supervisor, who harmed others purely because they wanted to; envy rotted their hearts, led them to hold down everyone who might rise above them.

Kamal saw his future slip away. Sleepless one dawn, he cursed his luck, his society, and his parents, whose traditional expectations had jinxed him, he was sure. And he railed against his sister, whose narrow, duty-bound world he was now trapped in. He was so wracked by fury that he didn't want to continue working at the center.

In the meanwhile, Rishikesh came to hate Nepal. This started the day the *Kathmandu Newsflash* received a letter to the editor objecting to Rishikesh's weekly articles about true-versus-false Hinduism. The letter was odd and cranky, but what upset Rishikesh the most was the haste with which R.P. insisted on printing it. Surely he could have waited a little, or not printed the letter at all. Most of the letters to the editor were faked by the staff anyway. Another letter criticizing Rishikesh's articles came in the next day's mail. The one after that was personal in tone. "We don't need a green-card holding boy to telling us our religion," a certain Manamohan Dhungel wrote in a laser-printed note. "Please you tell him that if he lives in Nepal all his life, only then he will unedrstand what it is Hinduism. Not this superfacial dharma-talk from America."

R.P. printed that letter, too, with apparent relish.

Rishikesh tried not to give any of this significance, but he couldn't ignore the way his colleagues turned around to watch him as he passed. It almost seemed like they hated him. What harm had he done them? Or perhaps he was being too sensitive…He tried to remind himself to constantly breathe from his stomach, but he soon tired of shielding himself from what seemed to be the hostility of those around him.

He called his parents in Boston and mentioned that he might come back.

Kamal noticed that Rishikesh's name had disappeared from the *Kathmandu Newsflash* masthead, but he was too busy helping set up his uncle's bakery—and too unhappy—to call. A week later, Rishikesh called the Computer Center and found out that Kamal had resigned. Rishikesh didn't have Kamal's home phone number; so, in a Nepali gesture, he dropped by the house he had gone to for the wedding and left word with Kamal's elderly parents that he was leaving the country.

The next week, the two men met at Third World European Cuisine, where the waiter Lal Bahadur Rai mistook Rishikesh, who arrived first, for a foreigner, because what kind of Nepali wears wrinkled orange pajamas like that? "You like to make pretty wife, sir?" Lal Bahadur asked. When Rishikesh responded in Nepali, *"Ma ta Nepali hun,"* the waiter reddened. Awkwardly, he asked if Rishikesh wanted something to drink. Luckily, another man then joined him—now *he* was clearly Nepali—and Lal Bahadur took their orders and went to hide in the kitchen.

For this last meeting, both friends were careful to remain respectful and be attentive to each other's plight. Each listened carefully to the other, praised his recent decisions, and assured him that the path he had chosen would lead in the right direction.

"You go to America," Kamal said in an assuring tone. "You take a job nicely and be free, and become a Hindu saint if you want. It is much better than wasting a rotten life here. You don't know," he smiled to soften his point, "how small-small people think here, how they destroy others to make themself feel good."

"And you," Rishikesh said, his voice full of conviction, "you should reapply to AIT next year. With your experience, your background, your promise, they'll accept you. Think this way: you're only delaying your plans by a year."

Kamal, who had spent all day among the muffins, cakes, apple pies, turnovers, and strudels at his uncle's bakery, appreciated this thought.

It was rare, both men realized, to find a friend like the other. They held hands warmly when they took leave. And in the following years, they sent each other a postcard, a letter, some newspaper clippings, then stopped corresponding eventually, but always took strength from the thought that the other was out there somewhere—a source of goodwill in this world.

Or maybe they remained fast friends. Rishikesh sent Kamal computer magazines with ads for technical schools, and Kamal applied to one, got a scholarship, and left Nepal. Or Kamal sent Rishikesh news of a United Nations position in Nepal, and Rishikesh applied, got the job, and returned. It doesn't matter because I made both men up; a woman sitting alone in a shop all day long needs stories. But this story is true to my desire. All day, I sit here and want Nepalis, like foreigners, to meet each other in wonder in Thamel—to forge the heart connections our society discourages. Why are we jealous and resentful, mistrustful of everyone? Why can we not become friends the way foreigners can: full of goodness and grace? This is what I want. What I have is something else: a life that is filled with debt and obligation, that is leading me towards treachery even though I know, I know it's wrong.

These days my life has become as random and senseless as my neighbor Tenzing Namgyal's views on God. My husband has given up hope of ever finding an office job. He drinks too much, speaks harshly at night, and doesn't help me out in the shop. Alone all day, I now sell books, magazines, and tapes—and yak cheese, playing cards, Johnson & Johnson sun-block cream, Everest toothpaste, Nescafé, crampons, mineral water, Sherpa soap, Kraft cheese, Pantene Pro-v shampoo, prayer beads, Saltines, and myrrh. But I still can't pay back our debts. Every week, I visit Dilip Basnyat, trying to postpone our loan payments, and afterwards I stop by the kitchen to see his cook, my cousin. My poor, skinny cousin—my father's sister's son—sometimes I wish he'd die soon. It will avenge me, his death; it will ruin La Vie Boheme and show Dilip Basnyat that not even he is safe from misfortune. How I wish my cousin would die.

Carlos Almaraz. *Sunset Crash.*
1982. Oil on canvas.
Photograph by John White.

Renata

Jordan Escovedo gunned the car up the road to the town where he'd been born. It was a hot, bright morning in May, though with the air-conditioning turned up to maximum he felt no discomfort. The vehicle was a Ford Telstar on loan from one of his provincial relatives. It was a lousy car, he fretted. Slick but cheap, the metal as vulnerable to the trauma of minor collisions as a tin can. He had driven better. But in the town of his destination, its teardrop lines were sufficient to enhance the macho mestizo image that had always flustered him and, in the latter part of his twenty-fourth year, now needled him incessantly.

His birthplace was called Renata. A haven for decrepit humanity, an outpost without a middle class, it lay lost in the middle of sugar-cane fields. Now that it was summer the heat blasted off a million rows of dull-green cane, off leaves that, glinting in the sun, were like long, sharp knives. The land, when stripped of its harvest, was a vast tract of impermeable rock. A ribbon of dusty highway linked Renata to Monroy in the north and Fortugaleza in the south. They were all alike, these cane towns: church, plaza, school, municipal hall, disintegrating storefronts, faded residences all hugging a short stretch of asphalt, the hovels of the poor dotting the road for a few hundred meters or so before giving way to the fields.

Tinted glass separated Jordan from the scenes on either side of him, and for a moment, sitting in the cool, isolated interior of the car, he almost convinced himself that he was still in the sheltered world he had left behind. He had a degree in legal management from Ateneo de Manila (though this distinction had been achieved after a series of indecisive shifts: in five years he'd been in premed, then into political science, before deciding that the road to a legal career and political prominence would begin in his ultimate selection). He hadn't known at his graduation that what seemed so turbulent was only a prelude to the real crisis. In the year that followed, he worked in a Makati firm amid the button-down yuppies, and it had taken all his strength to suppress the restlessness, the questions. In the end he'd had to leave.

Now he was unemployed, and searching. He still looked like a student, in faded jeans, a blue shirt with sleeves rolled up to the elbows, sneakers. It was an outfit of sterile simplicity. Yet it infused him, as he knew it did other young men of his sort, with a certain unattainable elegance. He could spot a fellow preppy anytime. He knew the upstarts, the pseudo-intellectuals as well. Dress up a stick and it remained a stick. Such people were of no consequence.

Shifting his gaze idly to the passing detail, he saw that some of the fields had been reduced to charred stubble. Vaguely human figures, swathed from head to toe to protect them, wandered through the sharp stalks. Jordan steeled himself, averting his eyes from the sun-blackened children who ran screaming after the Telstar. In a classroom, he had once leapt to his feet and spoken passionately about the squatter shacks that he passed while driving to school. He had been so angry then, his helpless rage nearly palpable. But that was before the awful white heat of the silent fields had engulfed him, had become his reality. He had been driving through the sea of cane for only a couple of hours, but already his doubts were threatening to claim him.

Jordan shifted to low gear, in deference to pedestrians and dogs, as he entered the town. Passenger tricycles blundered past, oblivious to the rules of traffic, tempting him to lay on the horn and plow into their midst. He controlled himself, lit a cigarette. Though he could easily have paid his way out of any sticky situation, he wished no unpleasantness. Inexorably drawn to the municipal building, he eased his car into the tiny parking lot. Arms folded, he stood for some time against the hood, planning his next move. He had no desire as yet to locate, in the middle of the fields, his grandparents' house, which was where he planned to pitch camp. The town was too alien; there was too much to see and (though he had a hard time admitting it) it caught his fancy. He was beginning to enjoy the speculative stares of the passersby. He was quite conspicuous: a mestizo with a slick car. The vehicle was well known; it was commonly recognized as Escovedo property. The family, his family, had ruled in this town for over a hundred years, supported by cheap *sacada* labor and undisplaced by war or the caprices of politics.

He lit another cigarette, drummed his fingers on the car's hood. The vehicle had been repainted twice, each time after a minor collision. Its original white was now an elegant ivory. Best enjoy the car, he thought, before it went back into circulation, passed back and forth among the younger male members of the Escovedo tribe, who regularly tore around town at night to the screech of tires and the thump of rock music. Jordan knew that the young men were whispered about in the houses of the town, their European features giving them matinee-idol status. He wondered how long it would be before his own name would be property of all Renata.

Jordan's eyes followed a couple of brown-clad women as they tottered across the street to the church. The church. It was a weathered structure, built in the middle of the nineteenth century. Blocks of limestone, furry with moss and punctuated with the outlines of petrified bivalves from a long-forgotten sea, formed the walls. Season after season, the patient, pious congregation, their faces a uniform terra cotta from the relentless sun, had worshipped here.

But the church's air of weary dedication was disturbed by the statue on the roof: a crude painted horseman in green hose and doublet and a conquistador's helmet. Santiago, the patron saint of Spain, faithfully adopted by the good citizens of Renata. The saint reared back upon a rampaging steed. One arm was raised, the hand gripping a long sword of real metal. Poised to cleave the skull of the stone Moro cringing beneath the horse's hooves, the sword caught the sun's rays like a blade of sugar cane.

The Moro was painted brown. He wore a loincloth of red. A stone vest lay stiffly across the painted torso. A band of orange was tied about his head. Jordan seemed to remember from a history class that orange was the color of the old Malay nobility. The Moro lay in the summer heat, pained eyes starting from the stone face, mouth a red O of terror, an arm raised to ward off the sword that was inexorably descending to split the Muslim's skull.

"That's an interesting statue. Where did the parish get it?" Jordan asked the town mayor at last. It was a week after his arrival. He had gotten into the routine of dropping by for a private audience with Mayor Feliciano; that is, if the latter happened to be in his office. A rotund fellow in a designer sports shirt and slacks, the mayor was always ready with a cup of native chocolate for Jordan's visits, and would order his clerks to put away their knitting and their makeup kits every afternoon lest the Atenista, his wife's nephew, drop by.

Now the mayor looked pleased at the question. "Donations," he replied. "The bulk of which came from your very own people, *hijo*. Very dramatic, is it not? It has done a lot of good for our town. Something for the tourists to talk about. In the Sinulog season the Kodakmen in the park are always busy, taking pictures with the church as background."

"Tourists…in Renata?" Jordan could not quite believe it. The town was the same dusty, oppressive municipality he had known as a little boy, the same place his mother had escaped for a more exciting future in Manila, and ultimately the States. It seemed impossible for anyone, apart from himself, to go out of the way for a visit.

"For the Fiesta," the mayor beamed. "We put up a little show every year, since my election. I mean, why not? Monroy has its Mardi Gras, and Fortugaleza the Buglasan. No reason why Renata shouldn't have anything to be proud of. So I organized the first Sinulog five years ago. I swear it gets better, more colorful each year."

The mayor sipped his chocolate, gave an old man's belch, and waved away his secretary, who had appeared with a sheaf of papers for him to peruse. "We used to have the Sinulog—or *moro-moro* if you prefer—every year when I was a boy. Not as festive as now, of course. Small groups of performers roaming from front yard to front yard. *Sacadas,* mostly. They never asked for much, and anyway we were glad to help. But Father Alberto, that feeble old priest—sorry, *hijo,* I know he's a relative of ours—persuaded old Mayor Martinez to put a moratorium on it twenty years ago. Said, of all things, that it was bad for the citizenry. We never had bleaker fiestas, not since the war! Fifteen years. Fortunately, he retired a few months before my election. Now he gives me dagger looks on the street."

"I remember…," Jordan said absently.

He was six years old. Conscious of neither place nor season. A party of weary, sun-browned men, half in G-strings, the other half in makeshift doublet and hose, entered the front yard of his *tita*'s home by the plaza. Stammering, he plucked in vain at the forest of indifferent grown-up legs: there were strangers on the lawn, armed with long, wavy-edged swords. Nobody heeded him. Gradually he became aware of an expectant hush settling over the well-heeled mestizo crowd lounging about the terrace.

And then the beat of the drums.

The drums. The drums.

Taking up positions, the men began to battle. Half-naked brown bodies, glistening with sweat, flashed in the sun. The ritual was riveting. The players circled each other, feet and arms weaving in perfect synchronization, physical control matching that of the world's most accomplished dancers. Jordan's blood pulsed to the rhythm. The drumbeats reached a crescendo, faded, and surged again to heighten the drama, as one by one the panting Christians were felled, the remaining contingent inexorably beaten back to the far corner of the lawn until at last only the carp pond and the grotto with its stone dwarves in obeisance were behind them and further retreat was impossible.

At that moment the iron gates flew open.

The horse was huge, white, the first Jordan had ever seen. To a terrifying crash of the drums, it barreled into the front yard. The rider wore a swirling cloak of green, and long brown curls straying from the back of his conquistador helmet snapped and leapt in the gust of his passing. He galloped twice around the lawn, narrowly missing the terrace with its massed spectators, his sword held aloft. And as if by magic, the beleaguered Christians were revitalized. They rushed screaming from their positions by the grotto, or hefted their broken bodies from where they lay sprawled on the grass, to renew their assault. The drumbeats swelled to a crashing finale as crusader blades flashed in the air and descended in glittering arcs, as lances were jabbed again and again into quivering Moro bodies.

A long, drawn-out sigh echoed through the crowd. This was the catharsis the fine citizens of Renata had awaited for twelve long months. The
Christians stood triumphant over the corpses of their Muslim foes as the
horse cantered daintily through the litter of the front yard, the rider's spine
straight, his sword at last sheathed. Hoofbeats faded on the wind as man
and mount disappeared down the street.

The drums stilled themselves.

As quickly as it had formed against the wire fence and up the neighbors'
fruit trees, the crowd dispersed, leaving the usual somnolent relatives at the
mahjong table or on the low balustrade. Jordan, his eyes wide, his mouth
agape with the power of the experience, made a slow, dreamy circuit of the
lawn, pausing by the carp pond where the horse's hooves had splashed
water, weeds, and gasping fish onto the flagstones, by the bachelor's buttons where a fresh pile of dung was ensconced. In wonderment he touched
the broken Bermuda lawn. Bits of tinsel and exploded plastic bags of red
paint punctuated the greenness. A red sash lay abandoned in the grass.
Picking it up, he felt a surge of satisfaction.

The ritual slaughter had done its work once more. The paladin of the
heavens had descended to rout the enemy, and now the Moros were again
subdued.

Painstakingly, Jordan gathered up the offensive plastic bags of fake
blood, and as he toddled over to the lamppost he saw his uncle hand something to an old, old man in loincloth and vest, who remained as the rest of
the performers shambled down the street. The old man, grey haired and
sunken chested, turned away with great dignity. Jordan's uncle, coming up
the walk, replaced his wallet in his pocket and smiled amusedly down at
the boy.

"How much?" his aunt, at the gate, inquired. "Ten," said his uncle. "The
thieves."

A couple of months after Jordan's visit to the mayor, a delegation appeared
on the doorstep of Jordan's grandparents' house. In the wash of light from
the upstairs bedroom, he saw an odd collection of individuals: twenty or so
nervous high-school boys and four or five very old men. Too many to fit in
the living room, so he did not invite them in. Instead he stood in the semi-
darkness of the yard, listening to a softly spoken appeal.

The Fiesta would be celebrated in a month, with the Sinulog and the
moro-moro dances that the incumbent mayor had revived. This year was to
see the most lavish production by far, with the town divided by school or
barangay, each unit competitively producing its own version of the *moro-
moro,* a play depicting a decisive battle between Christians and Moros.
There were twenty groups in all. When the prize money was mentioned,
Jordan let out a whistle of disbelief. It seemed a disproportionately large
sum, and suddenly he realized how serious the men were.

"We want you to help train our team," one of them said.

Jordan was flabbergasted. His immediate reaction was a flat refusal.

The men persisted. They had been speaking to Mayor Feliciano and had learned that Jordan seemed uncommonly interested in the statue atop the church and the festival that accompanied it. He was young, well educated, a figure in authority the high-school adolescents could relate to. He wasn't particularly busy, was he? They'd noticed that he stayed mostly at home, in the company of his books or his laptop, or drove around visiting his uncles or their friends in government, badgering them about their politics. He, ahem, didn't seem to hold a job and appeared to have a little more time than most on his hands...

"I'm...I'm...," he began, but could not think of a plausible excuse. He had relinquished his role as a Makati yuppie for this silent, sun-baked town, hoping to find something that somehow he had missed out on: influence? a lover? transcendent friendship? Whatever it was, he had not found it yet, and if he stayed within the narrow range of his current social contacts, it would continue to elude him.

"All right," he said at last. "I'll help you." He had never worked among what his activist acquaintances called the *masa*. Yes, he'd had surges of enthusiasm, had wallowed through earthquake-devastated streets distributing relief goods ("Happiest moment of my life," he'd told his girlfriend), had tried to join the Jesuit Volunteers of the Philippines but failed the first psychological tests.

And so he bound himself to train fifteen young boys whose language he had already forgotten.

As the youths filed out of the yard, the coordinator, whose name was Payoyo, said in an undertone: "There's a young man named Juancho Salavarria. He's a hard case. That's where you can help. He is your first cousin and boasts of you all the time. He says you are a Manila Boy with lots of women."

Jordan flinched.

"You might be the one person he respects," Payoyo said.

The contest seemed trivial at first, but to Jordan's surprise he saw the *barangay* captains urging on their men with intense fervor. Movements and dance steps were dragged from the musty cupboards of human memory and set to life once more. Feet thumped and bent arms and wooden swords arched through the warm night air as the dance grew upon itself. For the next three weeks Jordan dragged himself to the evening rehearsals, held in the halls of the Immaculate Conception Academy, the only place where there was sufficient space for his team to rehearse. The dancers were boys fifteen and sixteen years of age. Sweat from their bodies permeated the air with a vinegar stench. The muscles of their arms turned to rope with each stylized slash of their swords, and as they leapt and dodged, beads of sweat flew from their crew cuts. They had volunteered for the roles because it meant exemption from PE class for a couple of months. They went through the traditional routines with a mindless glee. Jordan could scarcely distinguish the Christians from the Moros. But the old man who was their trainer, who had been performing the dance since childhood, was infinitely patient. His name was Labitag, and he had promised to secure the white horse that Juancho Salavarria was to ride.

"You should have seen him when he was younger," Payoyo commented one evening while Jordan stood helplessly watching the practice. Payoyo was in his early thirties and had a degree from one of the lesser Cebu schools, yet could not keep a certain deferential note out of his voice. Twice he had unwittingly addressed Jordan as "Sir."

"Labitag had a big white horse," Payoyo went on. "He played Senyor Santiago year after year, front lawn after front lawn, until the priest and the old mayor put a stop to the *moro-moro*. He paused, seeing that Jordan seemed unusually perturbed, and waited until the younger man had lit a fresh cigarette. "You are…how old? Twenty-two? Twenty-four? Ah, you wouldn't have remembered. What a misfortune. By the way, your Tito Miguel was a great fan of the *moro-moro*. He used to have Labitag and his men over to perform every year."

They stood in silence, watching the shrunken old man correcting a move, and Jordan, wreathed in smoke, heard hoofbeats fading up a street, saw the final glint of a sword disappearing into its sheath. In another twenty years Labitag would be forgotten…

But not the dance. Never the dance. Turning his head a fraction, Jordan saw his cousin Juancho slouched defiantly against the metal bars of the basketball goal. In his hand he held a sword. It was only a prop, fashioned of wood and carefully sprayed with silver paint. But Jordan had seen Juancho sweep it through the air with the reckless abandon of one in a perpetual rage against the world. One night it had nearly broken the jaw of Marcelo Bongcawil, his faithful retainer. Jordan had glimpsed Juancho's desperate pleasure. The boy would drive his motorcycle at hair-raising speed down the midnight highways, mowing down unfortunate creatures frozen in the beam of his headlight.

Juancho stood, menacing in his quiescence, absently twisting the sword this way and that so the smooth blade caught the light. Labitag would be forgotten, Jordan thought, but in Juancho, "Senyor" Santiago lived on.

Juancho dwelt in an atmosphere of quaint European affluence, attended by tiny, brown-uniformed maids who addressed him as Señorito. There was tension in that house, Payoyo confided once. The father was a womanizer. Many nights Juancho had driven him home from some fiesta in the neighboring towns, the man too drunk to see straight. And then the boy had been forced to lie to his beautiful, prematurely aged mother as she stood wordless in the two o'clock darkness of the *sala*. His father he obeyed, but his mother he venerated, and it was eating him up from the inside.

Despite the coordinator's optimism, Jordan had foreseen some hostility from the boy. But not this smoldering, contemptuous resistance. Juancho made it a point to show up an hour or so late, arriving atop his motorcycle, a rattly, hand-me-down Clipper. His speech was guttural, unschooled; his shirt (white, with a crest, the uniform of the Immaculate Conception Academy where at age sixteen he was still a high-school freshman) hung limp and sweat-saturated in the heat. He was invariably surrounded by a squad of retainers: screeching youths (the lumpen proletariat, Jordan thought), reeking of sweat and the elusive, alien odor of marijuana. Not farmers, not field hands, Jordan realized one day. These were the sons of the riffraff of the town. Jordan felt their silent scrutiny, their amusement assaulting him the moment he stepped out of the borrowed Telstar in his spotless clothing.

Marcelo Bongcawil developed the cruelest tactic of all. He would watch mockingly as Jordan attempted to pantomime a move, relishing Labitag's incomprehension and Payoyo's pathetic attempts to copy Jordan's Ateneo accent. And then, as Jordan's thin voice rose against their indifference, Bongcawil would glance eagerly at Juancho for approval.

In time, Payoyo took over, Jordan flushing as the older man marshaled his charges in the condescending tones of a teacher supervising a high-school parade. Jordan had been reduced to an expensive decoration. At night, peeling the sodden clothes from his pale, thin body, he shrank from himself. Mestizo, true, but alien to any the boys had ever known. He didn't do drugs or indulge in women. True, he had a weakness for female company, but he required his girls smart, a far cry from the servile bimbos who clung to the back of Juancho's bike. His college degree, his alma mater, his excellent English—once his keenest weapons against the world—were unwieldy in this primeval town. Once he heard the boys discussing him— the Atenista—in contrast to Juancho's academic shortcomings, and the boy had growled in *binisaya:* "Why should I go to school? No one gets rich by going to school. Look at him, the *abogago*. See how bony his ass is? Probably beats off every night. Comes on his law books."

Did they think that he was deaf, that he was too stupid to comprehend those few elemental words? He had been born in this town. Juancho's words cut him like a silvery blade.

On the twenty-fifth of July, Santiago's feast day, Jordan awoke disoriented. Once more, he had fallen into tortured sleep atop the covers without changing his briefs and undershirt. It was not the early heat that had awakened him, though. Not the discomfort of oily face and unwashed clothing. Something else.

He heard it again.

The beating of the drums.

The sound came from somewhere up the street, its source lost in the shimmering mirage that covered the asphalt. He groaned, painfully aware that the parade and contest were scheduled for that day and he had to be out of the house by nine o'clock.

He had pulled through after all. The boys had learned the dance. Everything was in good working order. Everything, that is, except Juancho.

The night before, the youth had skipped the dress rehearsal, missing out on last-minute changes and sowing panic among the boys. What could be the matter, Jordan thought. Had he been off somewhere, among a stand of banana trees, trying to cadge some experience from a willing local girl? Furious, Jordan jack-rabbited through the somnolent traffic, pulling up in front of Juancho's house. A small crowd had gathered: Jordan's young charges, some clad in reasonable facsimiles of medieval Spanish armor, others in *moro-moro* get-up, tattoos painted on their skins. The costumes were incongruous, but they were not his idea in the first place.

"Juancho won't come out," Payoyo said, interrupting Jordan's critical appraisal. "He threw a tantrum when we tried to coax him into his costume."

Impatiently Jordan brushed the nervous youths away. He was now in the determined mindset that had carried him through final exams, term papers, quarrels with his girlfriend—the various crises of his life.

"Are you all right?" Payoyo asked with some surprise. He'd never seen Jordan so cold and businesslike.

"I've had enough of this," he said. "I'm going in after Juancho."

The front door was unlatched, and as Jordan stepped into the dim living room he was aware of polished surfaces, of blinds drawn to shut out the world. There was a spent atmosphere in the room, as though it had borne witness to a tremendous unleashing of emotions just hours before.

Juancho was slumped on the couch. His countenance was chalky, defenseless. There were dark smudges under his eyes.

"Get up," Jordan told him.

The boy raised a beleaguered face. "I can't go," he said in the vernacular. "Find someone else to take my place."

Impelled by the last vestiges of obedience, Juancho had put on the rudiments of his costume: the ill-fitting green suede pants, the sequined jacket that from a distance resembled chain mail. Jordan reached for the green cloak that lay abandoned on a chair and tossed it roughly to him.

"I cannot go!" Juancho croaked. "I am waiting for my pappy to return. I can't leave the house until I know he's here."

"Where is your mother?" Jordan demanded.

"She's gone, don't you understand?" Juancho's voice almost broke. "I drove her to my uncle's house in Fortugaleza at four o'clock this morning. I don't know if she'll be back…"

This last sentence was murmured mostly to himself as his eyelids drooped.

"I can't go." There was a whining note in his voice now. "I have to sleep…I've been driving all night. I went to Andoy's beerhouse at eleven o'clock to fetch my pappy, but he wouldn't come home, and so when I got back, my mother insisted we go after him. I didn't know…I didn't realize she'd slipped the ice pick into her handbag. They had a terrible fight. That *woman*…that *puta* from Almagro, was there too—"

Juancho broke off. His eyes, brown and vulnerable, searched Jordan's face, and suddenly Jordan realized that this was the moment he'd been waiting for: his own sudden moral ascendancy.

"Put on your goddamned costume," he ordered. "And get your ass outside. I don't give a shit what you do, but you are *not* going to screw up what *I* put together. Understand?"

Juancho glared at him. No contempt now. Just pure rage.

"*Get off that couch!*" Jordan's voice was so loud and shrill that it brought the other boys on the run. He grabbed Juancho by the arm and hauled him up. The boy was squat and stronger but did not resist.

"*You think you've got a problem?!*" Jordan screeched, and this time he did not bother with the vernacular. "Well, we all have problems. Now, you can be a wimp and stay groaning on your butt. Or you can be the Mr. Macho you try so hard to be, and get your ass over to the parade grounds. *Get out that door!*"

Adrenaline fired his muscles and he gave the boy a shove that sent him stumbling helplessly toward the terrace. Jordan flung the cape and helmet after Juancho. The youths who were watching were suddenly silent.

Then it happened. One of the boys let out a sharp bray of laughter. Juancho's head snapped up. He looked for the source of the noise, just in time to see Marcelo Bongcawil turn away involuntarily, as though to escape. But it was too late. Titters racked the other young men.

Juancho stared with hatred into each of the brown faces, lingering longest over his faithful retainers: the ones who rushed over immediately to right his motorcycle when he careened in a drunken stupor, the ones who taunted his rivals from Calle Castro with the most ferocity, the ones who hung about eagerly at drinking sessions, waiting for him to pick up the tab. And at last his eyes met Bongcawil's. The latter shifted uneasily, his broad face sporting an expression of stupidity. Juancho's face twisted with disgust. "You are dead," he said.

Jordan had regained his grip on the youth's upper arm. Juancho swiveled around to face him, and what Jordan saw unnerved him completely. The luminous eyes had darkened; sweat beaded the adolescent moustache. They stood in tableau: the older one in slacks and tie, fragile features pinched; the younger in the costume of medieval Spain, sword ready in his left hand, and his dark face—more Basque than Castillian really—filled with resentment. Then Juancho flung Jordan off, eliciting a gasp from the spectators. He pointed to Bongcawil, who seemed to shrink a full twelve inches in contrition.

"You are dead," he repeated.

And I should have listened then, Jordan berated himself that night. But the threat was lost in the confusion of getting the boys assembled, of misplaced swords, of sequins awry. A nervousness infused the youths. They danced through the streets to the fractured rhythm of a hundred drums, going through the pantomime of aggression with more verve than normal. It was obvious now who would win the street-parade award. The nineteen other teams paled in comparison. But Jordan felt no triumph. He tried to convince himself that the boys were merely fired by the excitement of finally performing before a real audience. But he knew it was Juancho's silent rage that aroused them. All throughout the day the scent of blood hung in the air.

Clouds gathered in the noon sky, and the heat grew oppressive. It was apparent that the good weather would not hold; the rainy season was too advanced. That afternoon an expectant crowd gathered in Rizal Park, the spot of manicured greenness beside the church. The drums let loose an incessant pounding as team after team performed, as Moros and Christians threw themselves at each other. And after each catharsis, as the sweating Christians raised their swords triumphantly over quivering brown bodies and the drums swelled in crescendo, the skies darkened even more and Jordan felt an unrelieved ache, debilitating and almost sexual, suffuse his body.

His team performed at four o'clock. They were nervous as rabbits, and the wooden swords and spears dealt real blows that contused flesh and sent up gasps of pure pain. The familiar drama unfolded: the Moros winning, the Christians dragging their broken bodies over the grass. Drums beat a bloodthirsty tattoo. Jordan could see Juancho now, steering Labitag's horse from out the ranks of the other performers. His face was livid, agonized. Locks from the long, brown wig strayed from beneath the conquistador helmet and snapped in the wind. He struck his mount again and again with the flat of his sword. The animal's hind legs gave out. Nearly collapsing, it righted itself as Juancho yanked the reins. Green foam flew from its mouth. Its eyes were terrified. The spectators cried out in alarm as the horse, whipped to a frenzy beyond Juancho's control, charged into the crowd. It changed course just as its hooves rose to pommel Mayor Feliciano's face, veering off into the little knoll of performers frozen on the grass. Closer and closer the horse came. Jordan leapt to his feet, crying out as it plowed into the young boys.

Juancho's steed reared up once, twice, its rider holding his sword aloft, throwing his tear-wet face to the heavens, and letting loose an orgiastic cry that hardly seemed human. Two of the Moros were trapped beneath the plunging hooves. One scrambled desperately to his feet and ran shrieking over the grass, leaving his comrade—Marcelo Bongcawil—screaming for mercy. One arm came up to ward off the horse's assault. Hooves shattered the painted chest, cutting the boy off in mid-cry. A freshet of red issued from his mouth.

Jordan stumbled over to where Marcelo lay inert. Hoofbeats faded into the periphery of his consciousness. Kneeling, he peeled off his navy jacket and wrapped it around the boy, shuddering at the great lacerated wound in the chest that the rain could never cleanse. All around them was a flurry of activity: technicians rushing to save the sound system, umbrellas blossoming over visiting dignitaries. Spectators and performers dashed to the church for refuge, saving morbid curiosity for later. A few of the boys, grotesque in the tattered remnants of their costumes, crowded around Jordan as he lifted up their fallen companion.

The rain had blurred the familiar outline of the park. Everything was a uniform gray. Jordan's soul cried out for a haven; the boys were leading him to the church, but no, he could not go there, he could never go there now. Labitag came up and touched his arm and through the silvery curtain addressed him. Jordan answered. He did not know what language he used, but Labitag seemed to understand. And in the end Jordan rolled Marcelo, navy jacket and all, into Labitag's arms and walked away. The rain swallowed him up immediately and continued to fall for an hour, two hours, until in the evening it slackened to a quiet drizzle that ringed the fields like a benediction, evidenced only by the gentle nod of the young cane leaves.

Marcelo Bongcawil lay for the better part of the night on the formica table at the De Jesus Maternity Clinic, attended by bugs and frightened relatives. The doctor was dead drunk from days of revelry, and the nearest hospital was in the city, two hours away by Telstar. But no one could find the Atenista, and Bongcawil's people refused—would not presume—to go knocking on the brightly lit houses by the plaza, where the out-of-town cars were strung bumper to bumper beside the street.

Jordan materialized at last among the toppled limestone blocks that, nearly a century ago, had formed the posterior wall of the church. It was almost dawn, but despite the hour and the events of the previous day the thumping disco music from the *bayles* all over town had not relented. The people of Renata lived for the occasional splash of color in their lives: a scandal in the ranks of the elite, the feast day of a saint.

The young man was a sight. His clothes were soaked, and earth from the fields obscured his shoes and the hems of his trousers. His lank hair was plastered to his forehead. The boys who found him kept a respectful distance, and it was Father Alberto who approached him at last. Jordan recognized the old priest, the man who had been responsible for the moratorium on the Sinulog for fifteen years. Jordan bowed his head in shame, one hand tentatively rising to check if the polished crucifix on its length of black cord, a relic from his college days, was hidden beneath his shirt.

"I'm sorry," he said when he saw the priest's shoes before him.

"Where were you?" said Father Alberto.

"Walking."

There was silence. Jordan tried to smoke. His trembling fingers could hold neither cigarettes nor matches. He lost two of the latter among the mossy stones underfoot before Father Alberto held out his own lighter. The young man inhaled deeply, body relaxing at the small pleasure.

"A teacher I once had said Santiago began as a legend," Father Alberto said. He scanned Jordan's face for a reaction. There was none. "The Moros had overrun most of Spain, and some means had to be found to frighten them, to scare them into believing that a heavenly being accompanied the Spaniards into battle, making them invincible." His voice was remote and formal, as though these were words he had rehearsed for years. "And so the man on the white steed was born. He may have been a real person, like El Cid of later days; I have read of a crypt where his bones were said to reside. But most likely he was pure fiction. Centuries-old, anonymous ashes have a way of attaining a life of their own, given time. Eventually, he was identified with the apostle Saint James: Santiago, the patron saint of Spain. Most likely the collective hopes of people oppressed made him a reality." The priest's words faltered, and his voice grew hoarse. "Oh, undoubtedly so."

Jordan could not speak, and when two minutes of awkward silence had elapsed, Father Alberto told him Marcelo Bongcawil was dead.

"And Juancho?" Jordan said dully.

"I feel for that boy," said Father Alberto. "I am an Escovedo too, you know. Through this event he'll come to comprehend just how much influence his family possesses. He's only sixteen. But at some point in our lives we all have to gain a little wisdom. The tragedy isn't in the lesson, but in the manner that it's learned." Father Alberto gave him a lopsided smile, more of a wince. "Come now, let's not be naive. You want to be a lawyer, and I am a priest. The case is already decided, and we both know the outcome." He sighed. "Go to the Bongcawils. Don't worry; they won't assault you. They never could. Commiserate with them. It's the best that we all can do."

Marcelo Bongcawil was buried the next day among anonymous mounds topped by disintegrating crosses, the diggers ripping through the *cadena de amor* that ran riot over the cemetery earth. The Bongcawils had rejected the money offered by the Salavarria-Escovedos for burial and indemnity. Jordan stayed away from their home until the required nine days of prayer were over, despising himself for his cowardice. Marcelo was lowered into the earth in a coffin hastily hewn out of a single log; his brother had gotten the measurements wrong, and the lid balanced precariously atop his *petate*-wrapped body as six of his relatives bore him to the cemetery, faded kerchiefs tied about their faces to ward off the odor of decay. The women followed, four of them, each carrying a garish blossom of orange and yellow crepe paper. From a distance Jordan watched.

The Bongcawil house was one of the last of the nipa huts that dotted the road out of Renata, before the silvery-green fields claimed the landscape. Jordan parked the Telstar in the shade of a solitary acacia and crossed the road, attended by giggling children and clouds of fresh dust. Marcelo's mother stood in the window. She was a wrinkled, brown woman, red-eyed from her loss, her face devoid of expression. With a swift, harsh command she ordered her nephews to the sleeping room, where they lingered with curious eyes just beyond the curtain. By the time Jordan stood at the foot of the bamboo staircase, she was alone. Softly, his gaze on his shoes, he called, "*Maayo*," the polite word of greeting that for more than half his life had been banished to the nether regions of his consciousness, along with the other phrases of *binisaya*. He thought he heard a grunt of assent and willed himself to ascend the staircase, suppressing the turmoil in his chest.

The hut still smelled faintly of burnt candles and of the more permanent odors of ammonia and animal feces. The woman's face was rigid. As he smiled tentatively and began murmuring tortured words of condolence, her features gave a momentary quiver and a sound—half-hiss, half-sob—escaped her lips.

"He tried to be good," she said to no one in particular. "But it was that wretched *barkada* of his…"

Juancho had never set foot in this hut, preferring to holler from the roadside, a summons Marcelo had always answered. The Escovedos, the woman thought. A red miasma of pain swamped her. The Escovedos. And now one of them was in her very home. Remote and untouchable in his pale slacks and shirt while all she could do was stare at him, wondering at the perversity that had brought him to her hut, waiting for him to leave.

"I must be going," Jordan said finally, when no more words would come. "I'm driving to the city first thing tomorrow—might find a seat on the eleven o'clock flight to Cebu."

He reached into his pocket for the envelope containing the *limos*. His fingers searched frantically: he had forgotten the money in the car. If he took one step, just one step out of the hut, he could never muster the strength to return. Averting his gaze, he took his wallet and pulled out all the bills it contained. He did not even know how much he held out to the woman. He could not touch her; he killed the impulse to take her palm and press the bills into it. Laughter and shouts from the children outside filled the silence between them.

At last he laid the bills as tenderly as he could on the rough table, pausing for a moment to look out the window at the silver fields that, watered with rain and the sweat and blood of the *sacadas,* were fertile anew.

"It's a beautiful town," he murmured absently.

The woman's eyes tracked him as he crossed the road, his steps long and contemplative. It was her first encounter with an Escovedo, and it was something she knew she could never forget. He unlocked the Telstar and got into the driver's seat, shutting the door gently. Sealed in, he was but an anonymous shadow behind the tinted glass. He started the engine. She watched, with wooden countenance, as the last of Jordan Escovedo disappeared down the dusty highway, an ivory boy in an ivory car.

About the Contributors

Carlos Almaraz was born in Mexico City in 1941 and grew up in Chicago and Los Angeles. He studied at the University of California at Los Angeles and the New School of Social Research in New York, then earned a master's degree in fine arts from Otis Art Institute, Los Angeles, in 1974. He founded several arts organizations in Los Angeles and for three years worked for César Chávez and the United Farm Workers Union in central California creating murals, banners, and other works. He was a founding member of the Chicano art collective Los Four, who were among the first Chicano artists to exhibit in mainstream museums and galleries, paving the way for others. Though he died of AIDS in 1989, he remains a major influence on younger Latino artists, and his work continues to be widely exhibited in solo and group shows throughout the world.

Bay Anapol is a former Wallace Stegner fellow whose work has appeared in the *Michigan Quarterly Review, Story Magazine,* and *The Pushcart Prize 2001.* She lives in Santa Fe, New Mexico, where she is finishing her first novel, *The Real Life Test.*

Robert Barclay lives in Kāneʻohe, Oʻahu, with his wife, Stacy, and their baby daughter, Ava Kimie. His first novel, *Melal: A Novel of the Pacific* was short-listed for the 2002 Kiriyama Prize.

David Borofka has received such awards as the *Missouri Review's* editors' prize and *Carolina Quarterly's* Charles B. Wood award for distinguished writing; his collection, *Hints of His Mortality,* won the 1996 Iowa short-fiction award. His novel, *The Island,* was published in 1997 by MacMurray & Beck.

David Botello grew up in East Los Angeles and Lincoln Heights and now lives in El Sereno, just north of East Los Angeles. *Alone and Together Under the Freeway,* reproduced in this issue, is the seventh in his series of paintings inspired by Hollenbeck Park, one of the oldest in Los Angeles.

Eddie Chuculate is a Creek and Cherokee Indian from Muskogee, Oklahoma. He graduated from the Institute of American Indian Arts in Santa Fe and received a Wallace Stegner fellowship in creative writing from Stanford University. He has published stories in *Weber Studies, Many Mountains Moving,* and the *Iowa Review.* He lives in Albuquerque and is working on a collection of stories.

Marcelino Freire was born in 1967 in the northeastern Brazilian state of Pernambuco. He has published several books of short stories: *eMe* (1991), *AcRústico* (1995), *eraOdito* (1998), *Angu de sangue* (2000), and *BaléRalé* (2003). He recently compiled *Cem menores contos brasileiros do século,* a microanthology of the twentieth century's shortest (fifty letters or less) Brazilian stories. His fiction in this issue is from *Angu de sangue* and *Geração 90: manuscritos de computador* (2001).

Bruce Fulton teaches Korean literature and literary translation at the University of British Columbia. He edited the Korean section of *The Columbia Companion to Modern East Asian Literature* (2003) and is co-translator of *A Ready-Made Life: Early Masters of Korean Fiction* (1998), *Land of Exile: Contemporary Korean Fiction* (1992), and *Words of Farewell* (1989). He was recently named general editor of the University of Hawai'i Press's new Modern Korean Fiction series.

Eric Gamalinda is a poet and fiction writer who teaches at New York University and Columbia University. His most recent novel, *My Sad Republic* (2000), was awarded the Philippine Centennial prize for fiction. He has two books of poetry, *Zero Gravity* (1999) and *Lyrics from a Dead Language* (1990).

Margaret García studied at California State University at Northridge, Los Angeles City College, and the University of Southern California, where she received her master's degree in fine arts in 1992. Her work has been exhibited in group shows throughout Southern California as well as in Texas and Mexico. She has also taught and lectured extensively.

Wayne Alaniz Healy was raised in East Los Angeles and first painted murals there in 1972. Today, Healy's East Los Streetscapers public-art studio produces murals, multimedia work, sculpture, and works in tile. *Pre-game Warm Up,* reproduced in this issue, depicts the posturing of high-school football players before the big game. The rivalry between East Los Angeles's Garfield and Roosevelt High Schools dates back to 1925, and their games can draw as many as 25,000 fans.

Adan Hernández has been a painter since 1980. In 1991, his work caught the attention of film director Taylor Hackford *(La Bamba, The Devil's Advocate),* who commissioned him to create more than thirty original paintings, drawings, and a mural. His work has been exhibited widely in museums in the U.S. and Mexico. *La Estrella que Cae* (The Falling Star), reproduced in this issue, was inspired by *Aguila que Cae* (Eagle That Falls), a sculpture of Cuatemoc, last ruler of the Aztecs.

Ester Hernández is a graduate of the University of California at Berkeley. In the seventies, she became involved with Las Mujeres Muralistas, the first all-women mural collective in the U.S. She has had numerous solo and group shows nationally and internationally. Her work is included in the permanent collections of such places as the Smithsonian's National Museum of American Art, the San Francisco Museum of Modern Art, the Mexican museums in San Francisco and Chicago, and the Frida Kahlo Studio Museum in Mexico City. She teaches at Creativity Explored, a visual art center in San Francisco for developmentally disabled adults.

James D. Houston lives in Santa Cruz, California. His most recent novels include *The Last Paradise,* winner of a 1999 American Book Award, and *Snow Mountain Passage,* named one of the year's best books by the *Los Angeles Times* and the *Washington Post.* The excerpt in this issue is from *Hawaiian Son: The Life and Music of Eddie Kamae* (2004).

Wayne Karlin has written six novels and a memoir and has coedited the anthologies *Free Fire Zone: Fiction by Vietnam Veterans; The Other Side of Heaven: Postwar Fiction by Vietnamese and American Writers;* and *Love After War: Contemporary Fiction from Viet Nam.* He edited, with Ho Anh Thai, an anthology of contemporary American fiction published in Viet Nam. He has received the Paterson Fiction Prize and two fellowships from the National Endowment for the Arts.

Kim Yŏngha was born in 1968 in Seoul. He is the author of four novels and three collections of short stories. In addition to writing fiction, he has produced essays and film reviews and is at work on a screenplay. He also hosts a daily radio show devoted to books and authors. "Lizard" (Tomabaem) was first published in his collection *Hoch'ul.*

Andrew Lam was born in Viet Nam and now lives in San Francisco, where he works as an editor for Pacific News Service. He is also a commentator on National Public Radio's *All Things Considered* and is working on his first collection of short stories.

Leo Limón was born in East Los Angeles, where he continues to reside. His paintings and drawings are exhibited in local galleries and are in the collections of national museums. His works have also toured in group exhibits internationally and are featured in several publications, most recently *Chicano Art for Our Millennium* (2004). In *Wild Ride,* reproduced in this issue, Xilonen, the Mexica Corn Princess, the Spirit of Life, rides sensually on a pencil, the transporter of knowledge, to offer sustenance and love to humanity and community; Tezcatlipoca, Smoking Mirror, the Spirit of the Night, descends to deliver his mystical games throughout dark space.

Mark Panek lives in Hilo with his wife, Noriko, whom he met in Japan while researching the life of Chad Rowan. The University of Hawai'i Press will publish *Gaijin Yokozuna: A Biography of Chad Rowan* in 2005.

Claude Henry Potts is the Latin American and Iberian studies librarian at Arizona State University and has traveled in Mexico, Spain, and Brazil. He wishes to acknowledge Eunice Park and Luiz Mendes for their assistance in translating the stories by Marcelino Freire in this issue of *Mānoa.*

Leigh Saffold is the recipient of the 2003–2004 Grace K.J. Abernethy fellowship in publishing, awarded by *Mānoa.*

Lakambini A. Sitoy was the 2003 David T.K. Wong fellow at the University of East Anglia in Great Britain. A journalist by profession, she has won numerous prizes in the Philippines for her fiction, including the Manila Critics Circle National

Book Award and several Palanca awards. The story "Renata," in this issue, is from *Mens Rea and Other Stories* (1997).

Huzir Sulaiman is one of Malaysia's leading dramatists. Currently residing in Singapore, he is the joint artistic director of Checkpoint Theatre.

Arthur Sze is the author of eight books of poetry. *Quipu*, a new collection of poems, will be published by Copper Canyon Press in 2005. His other books include *The Redshifting Web: Poems 1970–1998* (1998). He is the 2004–2005 Elizabeth Kirkpatrick Doenges Visiting Artist at Mary Baldwin College in Virginia and teaches at the Institute of American Indian Arts in Santa Fe.

Lysley Tenorio has published stories in the *Atlantic Monthly, Ploughshares,* the *Chicago Tribune,* and *Best New American Voices 2001*. A former Wallace Stegner fellow, he is an assistant professor in the MFA program at St. Mary's College of California.

Manjushree Thapa is the author of *The Tutor of History* (2001) and *Mustang Bhot in Fragments* (1992). Her latest novel, *Forget Kathmandu,* is forthcoming. She coedited *Mānoa*'s volume *Secret Places: New Writing from Nepal*.

John Valadez is a native and resident of Los Angeles. In 1976 he earned a baccalaureate in fine arts from California State University at Long Beach. In 1980, he was included in the group exhibition *Espina,* held at LACE Gallery in Los Angeles, and in 1991 he completed a mural for the General Services Administration in El Paso, Texas. From 1996 to 1998, he worked on a major mural commission for the federal courthouse in Santa Ana, California. A year and a half later, he completed *The Broadway Mural,* a photorealist oil painting eight feet high and sixty feet long that depicts life on one of downtown Los Angeles's busiest and grittiest streets. He has had numerous solo exhibitions in Los Angeles, San Francisco, and New York.

Patssi Valdez began her artistic career in the 1970s as a Garfield High School student in East Los Angeles and after graduating became the only female member of the seminal, four-member Chicano art group Asco. In January 2001, her solo museum exhibition *Patssi Valdez: A Precarious Comfort* opened at the Mexican Museum in San Francisco. Her awards include official artist of the fifth annual Latin Grammys (2004), New York's Business Committee for the Arts award (2003), a Flintridge fellowship (2001), and a Durfee artist fellowship.

Dionisio Velasco (Noel Shaw) is a writer and filmmaker in New York City. His one-act play, *Dust Memories,* was published in the anthology *Vestiges of War: The Philippine-American War and the Aftermath of an Imperial Dream*. The story in this issue of *Mānoa* is his first published work of short fiction.

John Whalen-Bridge is associate professor of English at the National University of Singapore, where he teaches courses in American literature and religious studies. He is currently completing *The Dharma Bum's Progress: Buddhism and Orientalism in the Work of Gary Snyder, Maxine Hong Kingston, and Charles Johnson,* a study of the artistic celebration of socially progressive forms of "Orientalism."

George Yepes was born in Tijuana and raised in East Los Angeles. His web site states that he was "formed by a hard street life of poverty, gang violence, and womanizing [and] rises above and beyond the Chicano genre by calling on classical master works from Velasquez to Titian for inspiration. Self-taught, with a refined renaissance bent, [and using] religious iconography to erotica, George Yepes brings a confidence and knowledge of his craft that calls to mind the great Mexican muralists. Imbued with a contemporary street sense, his paintings and murals combine the best of both worlds where bravado meets classical standards." In 1997, Mayor Richard Riordan named Yepes a "treasure of Los Angeles," and he has been called "the city's preeminent badass muralist" by the *Los Angeles New Times*. See www.georgeyepes.com.

Dafna Zur lives in Seoul, where she is conducting research and translating short fiction with the support of an International Communications Foundation translation scholarship.